Carla Cassidy is an award-winning, *New York Times* bestselling author who has written more than one hundred and twenty novels for Mills & Boon. In 1995, she won Best Silhouette Romance from *RT Book Reviews* for *Anything for Danny*. In 1998, she won a Career Achievement Award for Best Innovative Series from *RT Book Reviews*. Carla believes the only thing better than curling up with a good book to read is sitting down at the computer with a good story to write.

Jenna Kernan has penned over two dozen novels and has received two RITA® Award nominations. Jenna is every bit as adventurous as her heroines. Her hobbies include recreational gold prospecting, scuba diving and gem hunting. Jenna grew up in the Catskills and currently lives in the Hudson Valley in New York State with her husband. Follow Jenna on Twitter, @jennakernan, on Facebook or at www.jennakernan.com.

Also by Carla Cassidy

Also by Jenna Kernan

Discover more at millsandboon.co.uk

DESPERATE STRANGERS

CARLA CASSIDY

TRIBAL BLOOD

JENNA KERNAN

MILLS & BOON

First Published in Great Britain 2018
by Mills & Boon, an imprint of HarperCollins*Publishers*
1 London Bridge Street, London, SE1 9GF

Desperate Strangers © 2018 Carla Bracale
Tribal Blood © 2018 Jeannette H. Monaco

ISBN: 978-0-263-26567-5

39-0418

MIX
Paper from
responsible sources
FSC™ C007454

This book is produced from independently certified FSC™
paper to ensure responsible forest management.

For more information visit: www.harpercollins.co.uk/green

Printed and bound in Spain
by CPI, Barcelona

DESPERATE STRANGERS

CARLA CASSIDY

Chapter One

He wasn't a killer, but tonight he intended to become one. Nick Simon ran silently through the sultry July night. His heart beat faster than he imagined a meth head's pounded after one too many hits.

Not that he knew anything about drugs. In his thirty-three years he'd never even tried one. He'd always done the right thing. He paid his taxes on time, had never gotten a traffic ticket. He tried to be a good man, a thoughtful neighbor, and yet tonight he intended to murder a man he'd never met.

The flashlight, ski mask and gun in his pocket burned as if lit with the fires of hell. His thin latex gloves wrapped around his hands like alien skin.

At this time of night he hoped his victim was sound asleep. He hoped he didn't awaken to see Nick before he fired the gun. Nick didn't want to see that kind of terror in anyone's eyes. But if anyone deserved to be terrorized and killed, it was Brian McDowell.

Nick slowed his pace when he was less than a block away from Brian's home. He tried to control the beat of his heart by taking in slow, measured breaths and releasing them equally slowly. Sweat tickled down the center of his back and wept down the sides of his face.

The night air was thick…oppressive, but it was dangerous to go in frantic. Frantic made mistakes and the last thing Nick wanted was to wind up in prison. A dog barked in the distance and he jumped closer to a stand of bushes.

At just after midnight on a Sunday this neighborhood had been quiet. There had been no traffic to hide from as he'd made his way the three blocks from where he'd parked his car.

Get in, get it done and get out. He pulled the ski mask from his pocket. He had his instructions and if he accomplished this kill, another man would murder Steven Winthrop…the person who had destroyed Nick's life.

For just a moment a wild, unbridled grief stabbed through him. Debbie… Debbie. His dead wife's name screamed in his head as visions of the last time he'd seen her flashed in his brain. Bloody…broken and gasping her last breaths. He mentally shook himself and just that quickly the grief transformed into a dark rage so great it nearly took him to the edge of madness.

He yanked on the ski mask and then withdrew the gun from his pocket. Justice. It was what he and five other men were looking for. Justice that had been denied. The six of them had forged an unholy alliance to make sure justice was finally served.

With the sickness and rage of loss still burning in his soul and ringing in his ears, he walked faster toward Brian's house.

The instructions he'd received along with the gun had indicated that Brian had to die between the hours of midnight and one, and that his house wasn't air-conditioned so entry could be easily made through an open window.

When he reached the red-brick ranch house, he skirted around the side. If he was going to change his mind about this, now was the time.

It wasn't too late for him to run back to his car and drive home without the bloodstains of another human being on his hands. But Brian McDowell wasn't just any other man. He was a thief and a murderer. He'd beaten an old woman to death during a home invasion.

The cops had done their jobs. Brian had been arrested and charged with the murder when items belonging to Margaret Harrison had been found in his home. He'd been charged with the crimes and a year ago he'd stood trial. He'd been found not guilty when the evidence had mysteriously disappeared from the police department.

More important than anything Brian had done was the knowledge that if Nick killed Brian tonight, then somebody else would murder the man who had raped and killed Nick's wife.

With full conviction, Nick stepped around the side of the house and immediately saw the shattered glass of the sliding back door. A large red pottery planter lay smashed next to the door. What in the hell?

He approached closer, tension tightening his chest to the point of pain. He fumbled in his pocket for the flashlight. He clicked on the light and gasped.

Brian McDowell was just inside the door…on his back…with his throat slashed and what appeared to be a *V* carved into his forehead. The blood was bright red, obscene vivid splashes of death on the white T-shirt the man wore. The coppery scent of blood hung in the air, half choking Nick.

He stumbled backward, bile rising up in the back of his throat. He swallowed several times against it as he turned first to the left then to the right to make sure he was still all alone in the dark. With trembling fingers, he yanked off the ski mask.

Run. The internal command held a frantic urgency and he immediately complied. He turned, ran back around the house and headed down the sidewalk in the direction he had come. His brain reeled with questions.

How? Who was responsible? Granted, Brian Mc-Dowell was a creep who any number of people might want dead. But what were the odds that somebody would kill him on this particular night, during this particular hour?

Who had gotten to Brian just a short time before him?

He couldn't help the edge of relief that fluttered through him. The man was dead and Nick hadn't had to pull the trigger. He wasn't even sure he would have been able to shoot him. Still, he needed to tell somebody, but the men had all agreed there would be no phone calls between them, nothing that could be easily traced.

He'd see them in a week's time when they all attended a meeting of the Northland Survivors Club.

The place where they had all met a little over nine months ago.

Nick was two blocks from where he'd parked when a car without headlights came careering down the street. He froze and stared in horror as it crashed head-on into a large tree.

The car stopped running. The hiss of steam coming from the broken radiator was the only sound in the night. *Run*, that internal voice screamed. The last place he needed to be was down the street from a murder in the middle of the night with no reason to be there.

Run, that voice urged again. But he couldn't just walk away from the scene of the accident. Nobody had gotten out of the car yet, which meant somebody was probably hurt.

The airbag that had shot out with the crash depleted enough that one person was evident—a woman slumped over the steering wheel.

Even knowing he was putting himself in danger, there was no way Nick could just walk away. He yanked off his gloves and stuffed them into his pocket, and then hurried to the passenger door and pulled it open.

"Hello?" Her long dark hair hid her face. He knew better than to attempt to move her in any way.

Dear God, was she dead? He scooted onto the seat and picked up one of her lifeless hands. He quickly felt for a pulse. There…her pulse beat erratic and faint.

Crap, he didn't even have his cell phone to call for help and she needed medical attention as soon as possible. Noticing her purse on the seat between them, he quickly opened it and pulled out her cell phone.

He called 9-1-1, reported the address of the accident and that medical aid was needed. It was only after he disconnected from the call that a new panic set in.

If he hung around for help to arrive, then how was he going to explain his presence there? He'd done his duty, he'd made the call. Surely he could sneak off now.

He had one leg out of the car when she moaned. The pitiful mewling tugged at his heart and pulled him back into the car. "It's going to be all right," he said. "I've called for help."

She didn't move, nor did she moan again. Still he remained sitting next to her, bound to her by a whimper as he faced his own ruin.

He fumbled in her purse, withdrew her wallet and looked at her identification. Julie Peterson. She was thirty-one years old and lived less than a block away. An emergency contact listed her parents' phone number.

He stared at her driver's license picture for a long moment. Julie was a very attractive woman. He glanced at her left hand. No wedding ring. As the swirl of red and blue lights approached, a desperate plan formulated in his mind.

Although he wished her no ill-will, if she would just stay unconscious until they got her to the hospital, then Nick could establish an alibi. It was risky, but this whole night had been something out of a nightmare.

The next few minutes flew by as both a cop car and an ambulance arrived. The first order of business was getting the unconscious Julie Peterson out of the car and onto a stretcher.

Once the ambulance pulled away, Officer Tim Brown faced Nick. "You want to tell me what happened here tonight?" A tow truck pulled up where the ambulance had been.

The gun and ski mask in Nick's pocket once again burned with sickly guilt. "Uh… Julie and I had an argument. She got angry and jumped into the car. I got in the passenger seat and, before I knew it, we'd hit the tree."

"I'm surprised you aren't hurt since your airbag didn't deploy," Officer Brown replied. Nick's stomach muscles clenched. Did the man suspect something wasn't right? A vision of Brian McDowell, bloody and dead, exploded in Nick's brain.

"Was there any alcohol involved here tonight?"

"No, none." He hoped like hell Julie Peterson wasn't a drunk.

"And specifically what is your relationship to Ms. Peterson?"

"Fiancé. I'm her fiancé." The words blurted out of him without thought of consequence. He just wanted to be allowed to leave.

"Can I see some identification?"

"I'm sorry, I don't have any on me. I ran out of the house to stop her and didn't think to grab my wallet."

"Your name?" The officer took down Nick's name and address, and then patted him on the back. "The tow truck will take care of the car and I'll get you to the hospital. I'm sure you're worried sick about her."

The hospital? His web of lies coalesced to form an imaginary noose around his neck. When Julie Peterson regained consciousness, all his lies could potentially result in a real noose around his neck for the murder of Brian McDowell.

The ride to North Kansas City Hospital took only fifteen minutes and, during that time, Officer Brown talked about the hot weather and how the humid, intense heat made people snap.

"Crime is always up during a heat wave like this," he said. "Thank God the weathermen are predicting a few cooler days next week." He shot Nick a quick glance. "You're a bit overdressed for July."

Once again Nick's heartbeat raced to a sickly pace as his brain struggled to make a rational response. "I have to wear warm clothes whenever I go to Julie's place. I swear that woman keeps her thermostat at fifty degrees during the summer."

Officer Brown chuckled. "My wife and I fight over the thermostat in our house all the time."

They parked at the hospital and, to Nick's dismay, Officer Brown accompanied him inside the emergency waiting area. "Julie Peterson was just brought in by ambulance," Officer Brown told the woman at the receptionist desk. "Please let her doctor know I've got her fiancé here with me."

"I appreciate your help," Nick said to him as he sank down into one of the chairs.

"It's my job." The officer sat in the chair next to Nick's.

Nick had hoped to shake the man and get out of

there. Even though the cop had his name and address, he seriously doubted there would be any follow-up on the accident. But there would definitely be follow-up when Julie Peterson told everyone she didn't have a fiancé and she'd never seen Nick before in her life.

His stomach muscles twisted into a dozen painful knots as his mind displayed a horrifying picture of Brian McDowell. He'd scarcely had time to process that scene when the car crash had occurred.

And now he sat, next to a police officer, with a ski mask, gloves and a gun in his pocket that he'd intended to use for committing a murder. When Julie awakened and denied knowing him, would he be frisked?

The two men sat side-by-side for the next hour. Officer Brown made small talk and Nick could only hope he responded as a worried fiancé, but he couldn't stop thinking about the gun in his pocket and the fact that he was seated next to a cop.

Finally a tall, balding doctor walked into the waiting room and headed for Nick and Officer Brown. They both stood, although Nick was sure Tim Brown's heart wasn't beating as frantically, as desperately, as Nick's. His wrists turned icy, as if feeling the cold bite of handcuffs around them.

"How is she?" Nick asked after the doctor introduced himself as Dr. Mitch Carlson.

"The good news is her physical injuries are relatively minor considering the circumstances. She has some bumps and bruises and a mild concussion," Dr. Carlson replied.

"Can I ask her a few questions?" Officer Brown asked.

Dr. Carlson frowned. "Now I'll tell you the bad news. She doesn't remember anything about the accident."

Nick held his breath. Hopefully, Brown would leave with this news and he could get out of there within minutes. God, he needed to escape.

"In fact," Dr. Carlson continued, "the last memory she has is of her birthday party ten months ago. She can't remember anything that happened between then and now. She's been moved to a room for observation." He turned to look at Nick. "I told her that her fiancé was here and she's asking to see you."

"I'll come with you," Officer Brown said. "I'd just like to follow up with her."

Dr. Carlson nodded. "I'll take you both to her room."

Nick followed the doctor and the police officer down a hallway with a sense of overwhelming dread. Was her strange amnesia real? Within seconds he'd find out. He'd either walk out of there with his lies intact or he'd be called out. With no good reason to be on the street where the accident had occurred, he'd eventually be tied to a murder he hadn't committed.

JULIE PETERSON WAS AFRAID. She'd been afraid since she'd opened her eyes in the ambulance with no idea of what had happened to her or where she was.

She'd been told she'd been in a car accident. The nurse had explained to her that her car had hit a tree. But those facts weren't what scared her the most.

Why couldn't she remember the accident? More importantly, why was she missing ten months of memories? And since when did she have a fiancé?

Surely when she saw the man she was in love with, her memories would come tumbling back. Maybe, when her head quit pounding so fiercely, she'd remember everything.

She attempted to sit up as the doctor, a uniformed police officer and a tall stranger came into the room. "Julie, thank God you're all right." The very hot man clad in a pair of jeans and a black hoodie that clung to a pair of broad shoulders rushed to her side and picked up her hand.

This man, with his forest-green eyes and handsome, chiseled features was her fiancé? How had she gotten so lucky? And why, oh, why, didn't she remember anything about him?

"It's Nick, honey," he said. "You don't remember me?" Her anxiety must have shone on her face. "It's okay. Everything is going to be just fine." He released her hand and she immediately felt bereft.

"Ms. Peterson, I'm Officer Brown. Do you mind if I ask you a couple of questions?"

"No, I don't mind, but I doubt I'll be able to answer them," she said. She wished Nick would take her hand again. Even though she couldn't remember him, his hand around hers had brought her a small bit of comfort.

And she needed to be comforted at this moment. As the officer asked her questions about the accident, she tried as hard as she could to remember even the smallest detail about what had happened. But there was nothing.

"The last thing I remember is going to the Italian

Gardens for my birthday. My parents were there, along with my brothers and my sister. But since my birthday is in two months from now, I'm missing almost a full year of memories."

A hollow wind blew through her as she shifted her gaze from the police officer to the doctor. "Is this kind of thing normal?" she asked, although she knew it wasn't.

"Sometimes it occurs that after a traumatic event like a car accident, the patient has no memories of that particular event," Dr. Carlson replied. "It's the way the brain protects you from emotional pain and trauma. I haven't dealt with a patient who has the kind of amnesia we're talking about here. My advice would be to go home and surround yourself with familiar things and people. Don't stress yourself and hopefully those memories will return quickly."

Hopefully? The pounding in her head intensified. She glanced back at Nick. How could she have no memories of dating, of falling in love with him? What else had happened in the ten months she'd forgotten?

"I hope your recovery happens quickly," Officer Brown said. "And now, if you'll excuse me, I have to get back to work."

"If your memories don't come back on their own within the next six to eight weeks or so, then I'll refer you to a neurologist who might be able to help," Dr. Carlson said when Officer Brown had left the room. "I recommend no driving for the next week to ten days, and you take it easy. In the meantime, you're our guest for the rest of the night."

Once again she looked at Nick. "Will you stay here with me?"

"We can get you a pillow and a blanket," Dr. Carlson said to Nick.

"Of course I'll stay," Nick replied after a moment of hesitation.

"I'll send in a nurse," Dr. Carlson replied, and then he was gone, leaving her alone with a man, a virtual stranger, who she apparently loved but didn't remember.

"I hope you don't mind staying. I feel so alone right now," she said. It was such an inadequate statement. She was overwhelmed and terrified by her brain's malfunction. How had this happened? Why had it happened? She hadn't sustained any serious injuries that might explain it.

He sat on the beige recliner next to her bed. "You aren't alone."

"Aren't you warm in that sweatshirt?" It seemed an odd choice of clothing for a July night. She only knew it was July because the doctor had told her.

"Yes, I am." He got up from the chair. "I'll be right back." He disappeared into the adjoining bathroom.

This was so awkward. He knew everything about her...about them, and she knew nothing. Her fiancé. Had a wedding date already been chosen? What did he do for a living? Did they live together? Just thinking about what she didn't know hurt her head.

Nick stepped out of the bathroom, his sweatshirt a wad in his hands. The man had been a hunk in the hoodie. He was even more so in a white T-shirt stretched tight across his shoulders and chest.

He placed the black sweatshirt on another chair and then once again sat in the recliner. "Are you sure you can't remember anything about me?"

"Nothing. I'm so sorry, Nick. If we're engaged, then I'm sure I love you madly, but you're going to have to fill in a lot of blanks for me."

"I'll do the best I can."

"Thank God, you weren't hurt in the accident. My car…?"

"It was towed to Jerry's Ford. Tomorrow you'll need to call your insurance company to get things squared away."

"Was I still driving a blue Ford Focus?" What might have changed in the past year? Did she still live in the same house? Oh, God, had anyone she loved died?

He nodded. "That's right."

"I'm assuming I still work for my family's pawn shop, but what do you do?" It was far easier to focus on him than anything else at the moment. She couldn't think about anything else in her life right now. It was all so overwhelming.

"I'm a physical education teacher and football coach at JL Cook High School."

"That explains it," she murmured more to herself than to him. Broad shoulders, lean hips and a stomach that didn't appear to have an ounce of fat…the man appeared to have a great physique.

"Explains what?"

Heat warmed her cheeks. "Uh… You seem to be in

good health." Good grief, he was probably wondering now if she not only suffered from amnesia, but also if the accident had really addled her brain.

A nurse came into the room. "Here we are," she said with a bright smile. "One pillow and a blanket." She handed the items to Nick and then turned toward Julie. "Is there anything I can get for you?"

"My memories," Julie replied with a rueful smile. "Actually, I'm fine."

"You just ring your bell if you need anything at all."

"Thank you," Julie replied. "Tell me how we met," she asked Nick when the nurse had left the room. "Was it love at first sight?"

He changed position in the chair. "We met at the little coffee shop up the street from the pawn shop." His gaze didn't quite meet hers.

"The Coffee Bean," she said.

"That's right. I saw you and asked for your number and I was shocked and happy when you gave it to me. And that was the beginning."

"Does my family like you? I mean… I know how my dad and my brothers can be." Her older brothers had never liked anyone she'd dated. Why could she remember that and yet have no memories of her fiancé?

"I haven't met any of your family and we haven't told them about us. Uh… You wanted to keep it a secret until I put a ring on your finger."

"You haven't done that?" She looked down at her hand to confirm there was no engagement ring.

"Not yet." His gaze finally met hers. "We were shopping for a ring."

"Do we live together?"

"No. You didn't want to live together before the wedding. You know, you should probably try to get some rest. It's late and, needless to say, you've been through quite a trauma." He smiled for the first time and a wave of heat swept through her. He had a gorgeous smile.

"Yes, of course." She closed her eyes but sleep was the furthest thing from her mind. She still had so many questions.

The sound of the recliner chair going to a prone position let her know he was prepared to sleep. He'd probably been terrified when she'd been unconscious in the car.

She opened her eyes and gazed over to him. He'd unfolded the blanket and put the pillow behind his head. His eyes were closed but she knew he wasn't asleep.

"Nick?"

His eyes opened and he gazed at her. Oh, she could fall into those inviting green depths.

"Yeah?"

"Tell me about the accident. What exactly happened?" She needed to know at least this much before she could fall asleep.

He released a deep sigh. "We were at your place and we had a fight."

She raised the head of her bed. "A fight about what?"

"Something stupid. Something not worth fighting about," he replied. "You like your house cool...cold to me. I got irritated that I needed to wear a sweatshirt in July just to be comfortable at your place. You got angry and got into the car. I jumped in the passenger seat and, before I knew what was happening, you hit the tree."

"Where was I going?" she asked.

"I don't know. It doesn't matter now. All that matters is that you're okay." He closed his eyes again.

She lowered the head of her bed and once again shut her eyes. Maybe if she gave her brain a rest she'd wake up with all her memories restored.

Maybe when the sun came up in the morning she'd remember how very much she loved Nick and why. Despite the fact that she was safe and relatively unhurt, a dark fear whispered inside her.

Chapter Two

If there was prison time for lies told, throughout the long night Nick had earned a life sentence. Julie's amnesia had been both a blessing and a curse.

He now sat in the hospital cafeteria with a cup of coffee and the morning newspaper in front of him. He turned the pages slowly, a knot inside his chest as he searched for a story about a specific murder.

Had anyone seen him on the street before the accident? Had some late-night soul peeked out the window in time to see him running by? Would all of his lies come to light?

He couldn't get the vision of Brian out of his head. Who had murdered him? And what about the strange carving in his forehead? Did it mean anything or was it just a coincidence that it looked like a *V*?

He checked every single page, but there was no story in the paper about that particular murder. It was possible Brian's body hadn't even been found yet. He lived alone and Nick couldn't imagine the creep had too many friends.

But Nick couldn't be sure he was out of hot water

yet. He thought of the 1970's Son of Sam killer. David Berkowitz had terrorized New York by shooting eight people before a traffic ticket had led to his arrest.

And at the moment Nick's car was parked on a residential street where it didn't belong. No, Nick wouldn't breathe easier until Brian McDowell's killer was caught. Only then would he believe he was truly safe.

He shoved the paper aside and wrapped his hands around the foam cup of coffee. The murder wasn't his only problem. Julie Peterson. He'd intentionally taken advantage of her amnesia to save his own butt, but somehow he now felt responsible for her.

She'd made it clear when she'd awakened that morning that she was depending on him to get her through this difficult period. She'd almost begged him to promise to stay close to her until her memories returned.

He'd thought to get her home from the hospital and then disappear from her life. But how could he do that to her? How could he take away the one thing she believed was true when she was obviously struggling with her missing memories?

It didn't help that she had beautiful blue eyes that held more than a touch of vulnerability. It didn't help that her heart-shaped face and spill of dark hair fired up a heat inside him he found both unexpected and unwanted. What a damn mess he'd made of things.

Right now the doctor was supposed to be writing out her release orders. They would be taking a taxi home because his car was still parked on a street where it didn't belong. He had to figure out how in the hell he was going to get it and he needed to get it as soon as possible.

Julie had complained of a headache in the wee hours of the morning and they had given her something for pain. Nick wished somebody would give him something for the festering fear that tightened his chest to the point he could scarcely breathe.

He was terrified Julie would regain her memories and yet knew the only way to exit her life was for her to regain her memories. There was nothing worse than being an attempted murderer and having a conscience. He didn't even want to think about the possibility that she already had a boyfriend. That would be a complication he definitely didn't need.

It was a damned quagmire and right now he couldn't see his way out of it. The last thing he wanted to do was to hurt Julie, who had only been an innocent victim in all this.

He hadn't slept at all through the night. If it wasn't a nurse coming in to check Julie's vitals that kept sleep at bay, it was Julie softly calling his name to make sure he was still with her.

Checking his watch, he quickly downed the last of his coffee. He needed to get back to her room. She'd be anxiously waiting for him.

And she *was* waiting for him. Perched on the edge of the bed and dressed in the jeans and sleeveless blue blouse she'd been in when she'd crashed her car, she held papers in her hand and her IV had been removed.

She stood at the sight of him, her smile filled with

relief. "I'm free to go. I just have to wait for a nurse to bring in a wheelchair."

Once again he was struck by her beauty. Even with her beautiful blue eyes telegraphing a simmering panic, she was stunning. Her long, dark hair was slightly tousled. Her nose was straight and her lips were just full enough to tempt a man. If she didn't have a man in her life, he'd wonder why.

"Nick?"

She pulled him from his wayward thoughts.

"I need to use your cell phone to call for a taxi," he said.

"Of course." She dug in the purse next to her on the bed and withdrew the phone. "Want me to grab your hoodie?"

"No!" The word snapped out of him. He smiled quickly. "I'll get it. You just sit right there on the bed until your ride appears."

That was all he needed…for her to grab his sweatshirt and the gun and other items to fall out into the open.

He made the call for a taxi, his nerves once again tightening his gut.

"Here we are," a nurse named Nancy said as she pushed a wheelchair into the room. "First-class transportation for the patient."

"This really isn't necessary," Julie said.

"Hospital protocol," Nancy replied cheerfully. "No matter how you come in, you always go out in a wheelchair."

Within twenty minutes they were getting into a taxi

that would take them to her house. "I hope you can be patient with me," she said once they were under way. "I'm going to have a million questions for you." She grabbed his hand and held tight.

He tried not to remember the last time a woman had held his hand, but the memory exploded in his mind. Debbie…broken and stabbed on the marble entry floor of a vacant mansion…the odor of her blood rife in the air. Her eyes glazed as she fought to maintain consciousness. He'd fallen to her side despite the police officers attempting to keep him away.

That moment was etched deeply in his brain…the grief and the outrage, the disbelief and the overwhelming rage. He'd knelt beside her and had grasped her hand. "Debbie, who did this? Who did this to you, baby?" he'd cried.

"Winthrop." The name whispered from her just before she coughed up a mouthful of blood. Her fingers suddenly tightened around his. "Be happy," she'd said and then she was gone, forever stolen from him by an act of despicable inhumanity.

"…happy to be home." Julie's voice yanked him out of the nightmare of his past as the cab pulled to a halt in front of an attractive two-story house at the back end of a cul-de-sac.

She released his hand to get into her purse and pay the driver.

They both got out and the taxi pulled away.

Nick followed her to the front door, his chest tight with tension. Once they were inside, his lies would continue because he didn't know what else to do.

He couldn't very well confess to her the truth: that he'd used her and her accident because he'd been in the neighborhood to commit a murder and needed a fast alibi. His biggest concern now was getting his car off the residential street where it didn't belong.

She opened the front door and he followed her into an entry hall with a black-and-gray-tiled floor. She dropped her keys in a basket on a small table and then took a step into what he assumed was the living area. And gasped.

A white-brick fireplace graced one wall. A black-leather sofa sat between two glass-topped end tables. The glass coffee table held a centerpiece that show-cased red and bright yellow flowers. The furnishings were modern and tasteful, but the reason for her gasp was instantly evident.

The remnants of a floor lamp lay on the floor, the white-glass globe nothing more than glittering shards against the tiled floor. A large red candle also lay on the floor in front of the shattered glass of a painting on the wall.

She turned to look at Nick, her expression one of stunned surprise. "You said we fought…" Her voice trailed off.

He improvised. "We were both very angry. I broke the lamp and you threw the candle at the painting."

Somebody had fought in this room. Of course, he had no idea what had happened in her living room the night before. She was so vulnerable without her memories. Now he wondered if somehow Julie was in danger.

What or who had she been running from last night?

THE BROKEN LAMP and the shattered glass from the painting horrified her. She'd never been a fighter and rarely lost her temper. At least she remembered that about herself from a year ago. What had happened in the past ten months that had turned her into a woman who would throw a candle at a beautiful painting? Who apparently didn't have any control over her emotions?

Nick looked at the mess, grimaced and then gazed at her. "Let's get all this cleaned up." He set his hoodie down on one of the living room chairs.

She got a broom and dustpan from the utility room just off the kitchen and then returned to the living room where Nick had righted the floor lamp.

"This isn't who we are," he said as they worked on the cleanup. "We've both been under some stress and this was the first time something like this has ever happened between us."

His words made her feel somewhat better, but they did nothing to staunch a faint, simmering fear that had been inside her since she'd regained consciousness in the ambulance.

She knew instinctively the fear didn't come from being around Nick. Rather, strangely, he was a comfort, a solid anchor in a sea that had become alien.

They worked silently until all of the glass had been cleaned up. "I think I need to check out the whole house to orient myself," she said as she dumped the last of the glass into the trash bin.

"That sounds like a good idea," he replied. "I'll come with you."

She smiled gratefully. "I appreciate it."

Thankfully the downstairs was exactly as she remembered it to be. Her hand slid up the oak banister and with each step she wished Nick would just hold her for a moment and tell her everything was going to be all right.

She groaned faintly as she climbed upward.

"Are you okay?" he asked from behind her.

"I'm fine, just sore. I have to admit I feel like I was run over by a truck." Muscles she hadn't known she possessed now protested her movements.

"The doctor warned us that you would probably be sore for the next couple of days," he replied.

"I just hope everything up here is the same as I remember it," she said when they reached the landing. "I'd feel more centered if there aren't any more surprises."

"I hope so, too," he replied.

She breathed a quick sigh of relief as she walked straight down the hall and entered her bedroom. The coral-colored bedspread with turquoise throw pillows was achingly familiar. The knickknacks, the artwork on the wall, and the nightstands and dresser were just as she remembered them.

"You good?" he asked.

She turned and flashed him another smile. "So far, so good."

A quick glance in the other two bedrooms further assured her that at least here, in her house, nothing had changed. The room she used as her home office still had paperwork strewed across the top of the desk and the other bedroom was an attractive and clean guest room.

Even as relief winged through her, an overwhelming exhaustion struck her. Her body was sore and her brain was working too hard to remember something— anything—from the past year.

She stepped closer to Nick and wrapped her arms around his waist. She leaned into him. "Just hold me a minute, please." There was a moment of hesitation and then his arms surrounded her. Was the faint scent of his spicy cologne familiar? She wasn't sure, but it was definitely appealing.

"I'm scared, Nick," she whispered into the hollow of his throat. "I feel so lost right now. Could you stay here with me for a couple of days?"

Again, there was a small hesitation. "Of course," he replied. "But I'll need to go home and get some things." He dropped his arms to his sides and reluctantly she stepped away from him.

"I'm sorry to be a pain." She released a deep sigh. "I'm hoping my memories will return in the next day or so and then I won't be so anxious."

"It's fine. I'll just head to my house and pack up some clothes."

They walked back downstairs and it wasn't until they reached the living room again that she realized Nick didn't have his car.

"I'll need to drive you home," she said.

"No," he said sharply. He smiled then, as if aware his tone had been curt. "In case you forgot, your car is now in the shop, and besides, what you need to do is rest. It won't take me long to get to my place and get back here." He reached out and lightly touched her shoulder. "I don't want you to worry about anything. Maybe you should try to nap while I'm gone. I know you didn't get much sleep last night."

"I am exhausted," she admitted. She was definitely feeling the past night of too little sleep.

"Then get upstairs in that nice, comfortable bed and get some rest."

"You'll wake me when you get back?" she asked.

"I promise. I'll have to wake you because I don't have a key."

She looked at him in surprise. "I've never given you a key?"

"You told me you'd give me a key on the day we got married."

"Do I have a key to your house?" she asked.

"You did. I gave you one, but you lost it a couple of weeks ago. We hadn't gotten around to having another one made for you." He inched toward the front door. "Stop overthinking things and get some rest, Julie." With those words, he walked out the front door.

Immediately she felt bereft and vulnerable. For the next few minutes she wandered around the living room, touching familiar items in an effort to calm the anxiety and the crazy simmer of fear that coursed through her.

Surely these emotions were normal for somebody suffering from amnesia. Her mind wasn't her own right now. She was just grateful Nick had agreed to stay with her for the next few days. There had been comfort in

his arms. That must speak to the strength of their relationship…of their love for each other.

How she wished she could remember the excitement of dating him and the joy of falling in love with
him. She did remember being ready for love, wanting
to get married and start a family of her own. It didn't
seem fair that she remembered wanting these things
but had no memory of actually finding love with the
very hot physical education teacher.

She'd sensed his hesitation to touch her, to hold her,
and she understood it. He was in as awkward a position as she was. He knew she didn't remember him,
that he was basically a stranger to her. She was certain
he didn't know exactly how to treat her.

What he didn't understand was that she took it on
complete faith that he was her soul mate, otherwise she
wouldn't have been working on wedding plans with
him. She wouldn't be his fiancée without first knowing with utter certainty that he was the man she wanted
to spend the rest of her life with. Before her accident,
she'd obviously decided he was that man.

A clenched hand of anxiety continued to grip both
her heart and her brain. It had been there when she'd
realized she had no memories of so much time and it
hadn't eased up since.

If she thought it might help to beat her fists against
her skull, she'd do it. Hopefully, the doctor was right
and now that she was home her memory would return
quickly.

Sleep. She definitely needed to get some sleep and
to stop thinking so much. Deciding to stretch out on

the sofa instead of going all the way upstairs to her room, she was detoured by a flashing red light on the answering machine on one of the end tables.

Three new messages awaited her. She punched the play button.

"Hey, girly, where are you? You were supposed to open up shop this morning. Call me." It was as if she'd just heard her father's voice yesterday. Thank goodness he sounded strong and healthy.

"Where the hell are you?" The next voice spoke. "It's bad enough I usually have to cover Casey's shifts, but now you're going to be a flake, too?" The message had been left by her older brother, Max. Some things never changed and the irritation in his voice was as familiar to her as her own heartbeat.

She needed to call her family and tell them about her accident. Max should know her well enough to know she'd never shirk her responsibility at the pawn shop for no reason. She wasn't like their younger sister who often called in to get out of working. Or was she? She had no idea who she'd become over the past year.

"Don't tell."

She reeled back at the gravelly, unrecognizable voice that hissed over the machine. An icy chill instantly gripped her soul.

"You'd better not tell a soul or I promise I'll kill you."

The answering machine clicked off. Still, she remained unmoving, staring at the phone that had suddenly become an instrument of evil malevolence.

Was the call a joke? She instantly dismissed the idea.

She knew instinctively that nobody she knew would think that kind of thing funny.

Oh, God, what did she know? What had she forgotten that was so important somebody would threaten to kill her to keep it a secret? Who had made that call? The Caller ID read "Anonymous."

There was no way she was going to nap, not with that horrendous voice and threat ringing in her ears. Her legs trembled beneath her as she hurried to the front door and made sure it was locked. She then returned to the family room and sank down onto the sofa.

She needed Nick. Maybe he knew what this was all about. She hoped he hurried back because she'd never been so scared in her entire life.

Chapter Three

Nick ran out of the cul-de-sac, his brain on overload. All he wanted to do at the moment was move his car off the neighborhood street where he'd parked it last night. Had it only been last night? It felt like a lifetime ago.

His nerves were totally shot. It wasn't just a lack of sleep that had him on edge. It was a combination of murder and lies that ricocheted around in his brain, leaving him with a nauseating anxiety.

First things first, he told himself. *Get the car.* He slowed his pace to a brisk walk as he reached the street where he'd parked the night before.

Relief washed over him as he saw in the distance that the car was still where he'd left it. The relief was short-lived as he drew closer and saw a man in the front yard next to where he'd parked.

His stomach knotted and his mouth dried. He'd hoped to get his car and get out of there without anyone seeing him. Hopefully, when the body was found, the police wouldn't question people this far away from the scene. Would they?

The man was an older gentleman and he held a garden hose that spewed a small stream of water on a bed of red and purple petunias. "Good morning," he said cheerfully as Nick approached the car.

"It's a fine one," Nick replied, grateful his voice held nothing of his apprehension.

"It's going to be a hot one. Stay cool and have a good day," the old man said.

"You, too," Nick replied and quickly got into the car. He set the gun with the ski mask and the gloves all wrapped in his hoodie on the passenger seat, started the engine and pulled away from the curb.

Thank God there was no parking ticket under his wiper. And thank God none of the neighbors had gotten suspicious of a strange car parked on their street and had called the cops.

He headed for home, his heart thundering as he glanced at the hoodie. He wouldn't feel better until he got rid of the gun. Even though it couldn't be traced to Brian McDowell's murder, Nick had no idea what other crime it might be traced to.

He had been instructed to throw it into the bushes at the crime scene, but when he'd seen Brian's body, rational thought had fled his brain. Also the very last thing he wanted to do now was to toss it in a place where a kid might find it.

For the first time in twelve hours he felt relatively safe as he pulled into the driveway of his brick three-bedroom ranch house. He got out of the car with the hoodie in his arms, then unlocked the door and stepped inside.

The air smelled clean…like furniture polish and

bathroom cleanser. Although by no means a clean freak, he'd spent the day before cleaning the house in a frenzy to occupy his mind before heading out to murder a man.

He'd known the risks, that he might be arrested or killed himself. He'd supposed that if either of those things had happened, he'd at least be at peace that the police would find that he kept a clean house.

He sank down on his sofa and rubbed a hand across his forehead where a headache threatened. He hadn't had a chance to breathe since he'd stumbled onto Brian's dead body.

You could just stay right here, a small voice whispered. *Julie doesn't know your address. She doesn't even have your phone number.*

There was no question the thought was more than a bit appealing.

Then he thought about the hug he'd shared with her. Her slender body had felt so fragile in his arms. He'd felt not only the press of her breasts against him but also the rapid beat of her heart.

How frightening was it to wake up and lose almost a year of your life? How scary would it be to not have a single memory from that length of time? He couldn't imagine. But he'd love to go to sleep and wake up and magically lose the last three agonizing, lonely years of his life. He'd welcome the amnesia that would wipe away all memories of the brutal murder of the woman he'd loved.

Debbie. She'd been a go-getter. She'd gotten her real-estate license and had landed a job with an upscale real-estate company. She'd been dynamic and a hard worker and, within two years, she'd established herself as one of the top sellers in a four-state area. Nick had always said she could successfully sell the swamps in Florida.

Nick had loved her, but he'd grown to dislike her job, which kept her busy at all hours during the days and late evenings.

That job was what had taken her to an empty mansion to meet a potential buyer. That job was what had led to her murder. Nick shook his head to dispel his train of thoughts.

He couldn't go there. He couldn't think about her murder right now. He had bigger decisions to make at the moment. Should he just stay here or should he go back to Julie's and continue his pretense?

Debbie wouldn't want him to leave Julie hanging, especially given the fact that Nick had filled her head with a bunch of lies to save his own ass. By claiming her as his fiancée, Nick had given Julie an instant sense of false comfort.

He looked around, the very room where he sat evoking agonizing memories. He and Debbie had bought this house just before her murder. They had painted the master bedroom her favorite shade of light blue and had updated the kitchen. They had also planted a small redbud tree in the backyard. She hadn't lived long enough to see its first buds.

They had planned for children to fill the spare bedrooms. Dammit, they had planned a life together and some man—some animal—had taken her away from him.

He swallowed the familiar rage and got up from the sofa. He grabbed the hoodie with the gun, ski mask and gloves wrapped inside. He then went into his bedroom and opened the closet door.

On the top shelf were several folded blankets. He shoved the hoodie between them, knowing sooner or later he needed to get rid of that damned gun.

He picked up a duffel bag and placed it on his bed. He'd stay with Julie for a couple of days to help her navigate. Maybe during that time he could manipulate a fight and a breakup. That would be the best way for him to exit her life with no questions.

Still, when her memories returned, he'd have some explaining to do, but he'd face that when it happened. What concerned him more than a little bit was the scene in her living room. What had happened there in the minutes before she'd gotten into her car and hit that tree? It looked like she'd fought with somebody.

He had no idea if she was in danger or not, but that was another reason why, in good conscience, he couldn't walk away from her yet.

It took him only minutes to pack enough clothing and toiletries for a few days away. He then left his house and got back into his car.

He turned on the radio in an effort to clear his mind from all thoughts. He didn't want to think about how screwed up everything had become.

He was exhausted. He'd gotten little sleep in the nights leading up to Brian McDowell's murder. Now he feared that any sleep he did manage to get would be haunted by the vision of the bloodbath he'd seen.

Who had committed the crime? The question thundered in his head. If it hadn't been one of the other men in their murder pact, then who else knew about their plan to get justice that had been denied?

Tightening his hands on the steering wheel, he turned into the cul-de-sac and steeled himself to tell even more lies. He parked and grabbed the duffel, then walked up to the front door and knocked.

The lock clicked, the door opened and Julie launched herself into his arms as deep sobs exploded from her.

"Hey…what's happened?" It was obvious she hadn't regained her memory, otherwise she wouldn't be in his arms right now.

She shook her head, apparently unable to speak around her tears. He dropped his duffel and hesitantly put his arms around her. "Julie, talk to me. Tell me what's going on."

What he really needed her to do was to step away from him despite the fact he'd pulled her closer into his arms. Her trembling body against his felt far too warm as he became aware of the faint, attractive floral scent that emanated from her.

As if she read his mind, she took a step backward and instead grabbed his hand and held tight as he picked up his bag once again. She then led him into the living room. She dropped his hand and pointed to the telephone answering machine on the end table.

"What is it?" he asked. A new tension tightened his stomach. What now? As if this whole situation wasn't complicated enough.

Julie stared at him with wide, tear-filled eyes. "The

last message. You need to listen to it." She made no move to approach the phone, but instead stared at it as unmistakable fear leaped into her eyes.

With a sense of dread, Nick walked over to the machine and punched the appropriate button so he could hear the message. As the rasping voice filled the room, Julie sank down on the sofa and began to quietly cry again.

Fear replaced his sense of dread. The venom-filled voice hadn't issued just a warning…it sounded like a promise. What in the hell was going on? He'd escaped one murder scene only to walk into another potentially deadly mystery.

"You don't recognize the voice?" he asked. He hadn't even been able to tell if it was a man or a woman. It had obviously been computer distorted.

Once again she shook her head and wiped the tears from her cheeks with her fingertips. "I don't know the voice and I don't remember what I'm not supposed to tell. I was hoping you could tell me. Did I share with you anything that might explain the call?"

He sank down next to her, wondering what in the hell he'd gotten himself into. "No, I don't have a clue. You never mentioned anything to me about any kind of a dangerous secret."

"I'm in a nightmare," she said softly. "I'm in a damned nightmare and I can't wake up. I can't tell what I don't remember and how will the caller know I have amnesia?"

"We should call the police." As much as Nick didn't want any authorities involved with him, this sounded serious and he couldn't—he wouldn't—choose his own safety over hers. She didn't deserve that.

"No, I don't want to talk to the police," she surprised him by saying. She rubbed two fingers in the center of her forehead. "I'm not sure why, but my gut is telling me I don't want the police involved in this. Besides, what could they do? It was an anonymous call. It would be easy to write it off as some kind of a terrible prank. They aren't going to put manpower and effort into figuring it out and, without my memories, I can't help them at all."

She reached for his hand and her fingers clung around his tightly. Her blue eyes gazed at him with love…and need. "I'm just so grateful I have you, Nick. I don't know what I'd do right now without you."

He squeezed her hand. "I'm here and nobody is going to hurt you as long as I'm around."

An overwhelming sense of resignation swept through him. Damned. He had a feeling he was damned if he stayed with her and damned if he left.

JULIE BOLTED UP with a scream on her lips. Instead of releasing it, she gasped, her racing heart making it difficult for her to draw in a full breath. Her bedsheets were twisted around her thighs, as if attempting to keep her in the nightmare she now couldn't remember.

Morning light drifted through her thin, lacy bedroom curtains as her heartbeat slowly returned to normal. She drew in several deep breaths.

What had she dreamed? It had obviously been a nightmare. Otherwise she wouldn't have awakened with the taste of fear lingering in her mouth and a scream begging to be released.

Disappointment washed over her as no memories of the past ten months had come to her with sleep. But what she remembered vividly was the frightening phone call promising her death if she told what she knew.

What did she know? What secret was trapped in the darkness of her mind that was worth her death? Was she safe because she couldn't tell anyone? Would the caller leave her alone if she didn't spill whatever secret the caller thought she knew? Was that what she had dreamed about?

Nick. Just thinking his name caused a calming effect even though the night before had been a bit awkward. She'd just assumed he would stay in her room and sleep in her bed with her. Despite having no memories of him, she was fine with that. But he'd insisted he stay in her guest room.

She knew he was only thinking about her and she appreciated that, but it would have been nice to go to sleep last night with his big, strong arms around her. Maybe then she wouldn't have suffered from a nightmare.

She glanced over at the clock on the nightstand. It was a few minutes after seven. She'd called her father last night to tell him about her accident and her stolen memories. He'd immediately declared a family meeting at her place at eight thirty this morning.

It would be the first time her family met her fiancé. She hoped they weren't too hard on him, but the Peterson family was definitely loud and opinionated. And, as far as she could remember, they had never liked anyone she had dated, not that she had dated that often.

She got out of bed and went into the adjoining bathroom. Twenty minutes later she was showered and dressed. The scent of coffee met her as she headed down the stairs, letting her know Nick was already up.

She walked into the kitchen to find him seated at the table, a cup of fresh brew in front of him. "Good morning," he said with a smile.

"Good morning to you," she replied and beelined to the cabinet where the coffee cups were stored. He was a welcome sight, his buff body clad in a pair of jeans and a navy T-shirt that stretched across his broad shoulders.

Her heart fluttered a bit in her chest. There was no question that she was intensely physically drawn to him even without her memories. But what woman wouldn't be attracted to such a good-looking man?

"How are you feeling?" Nick asked as she joined him at the table.

"Pretty well, except for the memory thing. How did you sleep?"

"I slept fine." He took a sip of his coffee.

"Are you ready for the onslaught of my family?"

"I have to admit I'm a little nervous," he replied.

"Oh, Nick, it will be fine. I can't imagine a single reason why they won't like you. Besides, it's time to meet them. We've been dating a long time and talking about marriage."

He nodded and his gaze went to his coffee.

She took a sip of hers and continued to look at him over the rim of her cup. She still had a hard time believing this terrific guy was in love with her, but it must be so. Otherwise he wouldn't be here with her now.

"We have time for a quick breakfast before my family arrives. I'm sorry, I don't know what you like to eat."

He looked up and smiled once again. "I'm not much of a breakfast eater. I'm generally good with just a couple cups of coffee."

"Me, too." She was ridiculously pleased that they had even this relatively small thing in common. "There are so many things I don't know about you. Do you have a big family?"

His eyes darkened slightly. "No. It's just me. My parents were killed four years ago in a car accident and I didn't have any siblings."

"Oh, Nick, I'm so sorry."

The smile he offered her wasn't as big as the last one. "Thanks, but it was a long time ago."

It might have been a long time ago, but it looked like raw grief that had momentarily darkened his eyes.

"This is all so awkward," she said in an effort to change the subject. "You probably know everything there is to know about me and I don't know anything about you except for the really important things."

One of his dark brows quirked upward. "Important things?"

She nodded. "You must be a good man. You are kind and good and love me passionately. I wouldn't have dated you so long and agreed to marry you if you weren't that kind of person."

He frowned and shifted positions in the chair. "I'm

no saint, Julie. And while you can't remember me, don't try to make me into one."

She raised her chin and smiled at him. "Okay, but I stand by my feelings. I know who you are at your core, Nick. I wouldn't have settled for less."

He drained his coffee cup and jumped up. "Is there anything we need to do to prepare for your family?"

"Make a fresh pot of coffee," she replied. "Unless something drastic changed in the past year, my family chugs coffee like it's the fountain of youth."

"You sit tight, I'll make a fresh pot," he replied. "And while I'm doing that you can give me a quick refresher on your family members."

She took another sip from her cup, set it down and then leaned back in the chair. "I can only tell you what I remember about them from a year ago."

Grief and anger suddenly rose up in the back of her throat. Grief over the missing memories of the people she loved, and anger that her brain continued to betray her by not functioning right.

Nick poured the water into the coffee machine and then turned back to face her expectantly.

"George is my father and he runs the business and us with a heavy hand. Lynetta is my mother. She's loud and opinionated and as tough as Dad. Max is my oldest brother and he's just like my father...they both have a lot of bark, but not too much bite. Then there's Tony who is a year older than me. He's quiet and, like me, doesn't like confrontation. Finally, there's Casey. She's the baby of the family and is the apple of my parents' eyes."

She couldn't help the smile that curved her lips as she thought of her baby sister. "She's also spoiled and wild, a bit lazy and totally gorgeous."

"And all of you work at the pawn shop," Nick said.

She nodded. "That pawn shop isn't just our business, it's a family legacy of sorts. My grandfather started it, but it was Dad who built it into the largest pawn shop in Kansas City."

"Everyone has heard of Peterson Pawn, but I've never been inside the store."

"Once you meet my family I'll take you in with me and give you the grand tour." Once again a roll of emotions swept through her. What had changed at the store over the past ten months? What had happened in her family's life that she couldn't remember?

Had Max finally found somebody to date? What about her other siblings? Max and Tony hadn't even been dating anyone ten months before. Casey was the only one in the family who dated often, exchanging men as quickly as she changed her nail color. Had Julie gone to a wedding? Had she been Casey's maid of honor like the two of them had always promised each other?

She wanted to pull her brain out of her skull and shake it violently until it started working right again. What was the amnesia protecting her from? A car accident?

Don't tell. The two words thundered in her head, momentarily stealing her breath as an icy hand gripped her heart.

"Julie? Are you all right?" Nick gazed at her with a touch of concern.

"I'm fine." She forced a smile as she stood. "I'm just going to set out some cups and cream and sugar for when the family arrives."

"Can I help?"

"No, thanks. I've got it." She needed to do something to keep the simmering fear in her at bay. Not only was she afraid of the phone threat, now a new rivulet of anxiety swept through her as she prepared for her family to arrive.

She placed the cups on the countertop and then turned to face him once again. "How do you feel about little white lies?"

"What are you talking about?" He said the words slowly...a bit warily.

"I was just thinking that I'd like to tell my family we've been dating for well over a year. I don't want them to know I have no memories of you. That will just complicate things with them."

He leaned back in the chair and nodded. "If that makes you feel better, then I don't see why we can't tell that little white lie."

She sighed in relief. She loved her family, and her father and mother had raised them to be loyal to each other and to the pawn shop. She'd never made trouble. She'd worked long hours and done everything she could to be an obedient daughter.

She might not know what had gone on for the past ten months in her life, but one thing she knew for certain...if they made her choose between them and Nick, she wanted her man.

Chapter Four

"Who in the hell are you?" George Peterson was a tall man with broad shoulders and a slight paunch. As he glared at Nick, he raised his square chin as if in anticipation of a brawl.

He and his wife, Lynetta, had entered the house without so much as a knock and now stood just inside the kitchen.

"Dad, be nice," Julie said with what sounded like a nervous laugh. "Sit down and I'll get you both some coffee while we wait for everyone else."

George didn't move. Nick walked over to him and extended his hand. "I'm Nick Simon. It's nice to meet you."

George hesitated a moment and then shook hands. Nick couldn't help but notice the rolled-up morning paper in George's hand. When Nick had awakened earlier than Julie, the first thing he'd wanted to do was to check the morning news, but he hadn't been able to find the remote for the television.

"Sit down, George," Lynetta said as she took a seat at the table.

He moved to a chair next to his wife and placed the paper in the center. "I brought in your morning paper."

"To heck with the paper," Lynetta said. Her dark eyes lingered on Julie. "What I want to know is why you didn't call us immediately from the hospital last night after your wreck."

"Everything happened so fast," Julie replied as she poured coffee for her mother and father.

Once again Nick was struck by Julie's prettiness. Clad in a pink T-shirt and a pair of jeans that hugged her slender hips and long legs, there was no question that physically she stirred something in him. Her dark hair hung down just beneath her shoulders, looking shiny and soft.

It surprised him. She couldn't have been more different than the woman who had been his wife. Debbie had been blond and was always fighting with her weight, not that Nick had cared. Debbie had been short while Julie was tall and willowy.

Julie had just finished pouring coffee for her parents when Max and Tony came in. The two looked remarkably alike. They both had dark hair and eyes, but while Tony greeted him amicably, Max had a wealth of suspicion in his eyes.

Nick had just taken a seat at the table when Casey arrived. The long-haired, curvy young woman swept in and, with a dramatic wail, embraced Julie. "Daddy told us you hit a tree. You could have been killed." She released her sister. "What were you thinking?"

"I don't know," Julie confessed. "In fact, I don't have any memories of the past ten months."

"Before we get to that, let's talk about the white elephant in the room." Max looked pointedly at Nick. "This is supposed to be a family meeting."

"And soon he's going to be family. Everyone, this is Nick and he's my fiancé," Julie said.

Chaos broke out. Everyone talked at once until Lynetta raised her hands. "Everybody shut up," she yelled. Surprisingly everyone did. She looked at Julie. "And how is it that you have a fiancé we didn't know about?"

"Yeah, I can't believe you didn't even tell me," Casey added. "I thought we shared all of our secrets."

"I totally get why she kept it a secret," Tony said. "Every man Julie has ever dated, you all have chased off."

"Nick isn't going anywhere," Julie replied with a warm smile at him.

A sick guilt surged up inside him. Now there were more people to lie to and Julie gazed at him with such certainty, such open trust.

He was trying to be present for Julie, but it was becoming way more difficult than he'd anticipated. Besides, more than anything, he wanted to grab the newspaper from the center of the table and see if Brian McDowell's murder had made the news.

Her family members began to fire questions at him. Where did he work? How long had he held that job? Where did he live? What did he love about Julie? He answered them all as truthfully as he could.

"I'd like to know about your financial situation," George said. "One day Julie will own part of the business. That makes her quite a catch for somebody who has nothing."

"Dad! Enough," Julie finally said in protest.

"I want to know more about this memory loss thing," Max said. "Is it really true that you don't remember the last ten months?"

"It's true, but we're hoping that I'll get my memories back very soon," she replied.

"That's so weird," Casey said and gazed at her sister as if she were an alien from another planet.

"Weird or not, what I need to know is if you're okay to take your shift tomorrow," George said. "You're on the schedule to open and work until five."

"Please don't tell me I have to start covering your shifts. It's bad enough I have to cover for the baby half the time." Max shot a pointed glare at Casey.

Was Nick the only one who saw the dark hesitation that leaped into Julie's eyes as one of her hands rose to the base of her throat?

"What do you say, girly?" George persisted.

Julie's hand dropped to her side and she raised her chin. "As long as nothing has changed in the last year at the store, then I'll definitely be at work tomorrow."

Nick couldn't believe her family didn't think it a good idea for her to take a little time off given she'd been in a serious accident and had missing memories. But he kept his mouth shut. He didn't know enough about Julie or her family to form an opinion, although he wasn't especially eager to be friends with a man who called his daughter "girly."

George shoved back from the table and everyone

else rose as a unit. Lynetta gave Julie a quick hug and George cast Nick a dark stare. "The verdict is still out on you," he said.

Nick merely nodded in return and then they were all gone. "Why didn't you tell them you weren't really ready to return to work yet?" he asked.

"Was it that obvious?" she asked as she led him into the living room.

"Apparently only to me." He eased down opposite her on the sofa.

"It will be fine and it's not as if I have any real physical injuries. I've been working in the pawn shop since I was fourteen. I could do the work there in my sleep."

"You still should have told them you needed a few more days of recovery," Nick replied. "Remember the doctor said you needed time to rest."

She shrugged. "It will be okay." A worry line darted across her forehead. "I just realized again that I don't have my car."

"Don't worry, I'll take you and pick you up from work. That's probably for the best right now anyway." He didn't want to remind her of the strange and threatening phone call from the night before, but it was obvious that's exactly what he had done.

Her bright eyes changed to a midnight blue and she wrapped her arms around herself as if she'd just experienced a deep chill. "I can't lie. I don't mind you having my back right now until I remember what I'm not supposed to talk about."

"I've got your back." Meeting her family had been a particular kind of torment for him. It had been one thing to lie to Julie but quite another to lie to her entire family.

She rose suddenly. "I know it hasn't been that long since I got out of bed but, if you don't mind, I think I'll go upstairs and lie down for a little while. I have a bit of a headache starting."

He jumped up. "Is there anything I can do for you? Do you need anything?"

"No, but thank you for asking." She gave him a warm look that once again stirred a touch of desire that he didn't want and tried to ignore.

He watched as she went slowly up the stairs. When she disappeared from view he raced back into the kitchen. He grabbed the rolled-up newspaper and sat.

His heart pounded as he unfurled the paper and checked the front page. The usual headlines…sports, politics and advertising. Tension pressed tight in his chest as he turned to the second page. And there it was, at the bottom of the page: Northland Man Murdered.

Nick read the article that reported Brian McDowell's death. His body had been found by a friend. The news said that he had been killed by having his throat slashed, but mentioned nothing about the strange carving in Brian's forehead. Apparently law-enforcement officials were keeping that fact close to their chests.

Nick's heart nearly stopped as he continued to read. A witness had come forward to report that he'd seen a man dressed in black running away from McDowell's house. Police were asking anyone with information to come forward.

Had the witness seen him? Or had he seen the real

killer escaping from the scene? If it had been Nick who'd been seen, had it been before or after he'd torn off his ski mask? When had he taken off the ski mask? He couldn't remember right now with the dread that coursed through his veins.

As much as he hated it, this act as Julie's fiancé was the only thing that might save him from a murder charge. He slowly closed the paper. Right now it was in his best interest for Julie not to retrieve her missing memories. But, no matter how it worked out, there was still another victim in this mess.

If Julie regained her memories, it was possible she would turn him into the police, and her heart would probably be broken by the realization that there was no love, no engagement and no talks of marriage.

He was sorry as hell that he'd drawn her into all of this. In doing so he'd not only doomed himself, but her, as well.

"SINCE I SLEPT through lunch and you had to help your-self, I was thinking maybe I'd cook a couple of steaks on the grill and we could eat out on the deck this eve-ning," Julie said hours later when she was awake from her nap. She had gone upstairs and contacted her in-surance agent to get things moving on repairing her car, then had slept half the day away.

"Sounds good to me. Just tell me what I can do to help." Nick rose from the sofa.

"You can sit back down and relax. I've got this," Julie replied.

"Are you sure you feel up to it?"

She smiled at him. "It's amazing what a long nap can do. Besides, I want to make a good meal for my man." And she hoped at the end of the evening her fiancé would at least kiss her. She yearned for some kind of physical interaction with him.

"Could you turn on the television for me? I wasn't able to find the remote," he said.

"Oh, of course." She should have thought about it earlier. He'd been sitting on the sofa with nothing to do for most of the day while she'd taken her nap. "I'm so sorry you couldn't even turn it on while I slept."

She walked over to the coffee table where there was a hidden drawer in the center. She took out the remote, turned on the television and then handed it to him. She stood close enough to him she could smell the spicy scent of his cologne. "Feel free to put on whatever you want. I'll be in the kitchen if you need anything."

Within minutes she was working to prepare an early evening meal. As she worked, she thought of the dreams she'd had while she'd napped.

They had been flaming-hot visions of her and Nick making love. They had been erotic dreams and she didn't know if they were simple longing or memories.

All she knew for sure was that they had made her want Nick. She knew he was keeping his distance as a sign of respect for her and her missing memories, but that didn't stop her from wanting him.

Maybe tonight, she told herself as she scrubbed two big baking potatoes. She'd make him a good meal and then at bedtime she'd tell him she wanted him in her bed. She'd convince him that her missing memories weren't important. Whatever her brain had forgotten, she believed her heart remembered.

Thank goodness the cat was out of the bag where Nick and her parents were concerned. He'd handled them as well as anyone could. Although she had a feeling if her father caught her alone she'd be in for an in-depth interrogation about Nick.

She'd always had a feeling her parents would be just fine if she never married. That way she could devote all her time and attention to the pawn shop forever.

Maybe it was good for right now that she couldn't remember anything. How could her father interrogate her if she had no memories?

Within a half an hour the salad was made and in the fridge, the potatoes were baking in the oven, and the steaks had been marinated and awaited the grill.

She returned to the living room and sat next to Nick on the sofa. "I figure we'll eat in about an hour and I thought it might be nice to sit outside on the deck."

"Sounds good to me."

"What are you watching?"

He lowered the television volume. "Nothing really. I was just kind of surfing the channels for some local news, but all I'm finding is talk shows and game shows."

"Are you a news fanatic?" There were so many things she didn't remember about him.

"I wouldn't call myself a fanatic, but I like to know what's going on in the community. I want to make sure my kids at the high school don't get into any stupid trouble."

"Oh, Nick, I haven't even thought about the fact that you're a coach. Haven't football practices already begun?" She hadn't realized about how her neediness might be screwing with his life and work. Normally she wasn't so selfish.

"Actually, the practices start the last week of July, so I've still got two weeks of relatively free time left," he said.

"And hopefully before the practices begin I'll have all my memories back." She held his gaze for a long moment. "I can't wait to remember every single thing about you...about us."

"It will all eventually come to you. I peeked outside the window earlier to take a look at your deck. Do you need me to light the barbecue grill?"

"I can do it." She offered him another smile. He seemed so sober, so...distant at the moment. "I'm one of those women who doesn't mind playing with fire if a grilled steak is the end reward."

"Then, if you don't mind, I'm going to run upstairs and take a quick shower." He got up from the couch.

"Of course I don't mind. Despite everything that's happened, I'm sure you always considered this like a second home and I want you to continue to do so."

A touch of warmth lit his eyes. "I won't be long."

She nodded, her heart fluttering unexpectedly as she watched him walk up the stairs. Her racing heart was simply affirmation that she loved Nick and that she wanted him. And he must want her, too. He was here with her right now and he didn't appear to be going anywhere anytime soon.

She got up and started back to the kitchen. She'd only made it halfway there when a vision exploded in her brain. She was alone in the pawn shop with only the security lights on. Her knees weakened. *Danger!* The word exploded in her head as fear clenched her stomach into a hard knot. Her mouth dried and a cold sweat washed over her.

Reaching for the back of the chair to steady herself, the vision vanished as quickly as it had appeared, but left behind a terror that tightened up the back of her throat.

Just a strange vision? Or had it been a flash of memory? *Don't tell.* The words thundered in her head as she finally reached the kitchen and leaned with her back against the countertop.

Had something happened at the pawn shop with one of the customers? Certainly over the years she'd dealt with all kinds of people there. She drew several long, deep breaths until the last of the feeling faded away.

She grabbed a soapy sponge from the sink and carried it to the door that led out onto her deck, still trying to make sense of the vision her mind had momentarily presented to her.

At least this was a hopeful sign that more memories would come. Still, she had a feeling if she tried too hard to remember, then nothing would happen.

She began to clean off the round patio table with its bright red umbrella. The chairs held pads that were red and turquoise. The recliner nearby had the same patterned pad on it.

One thing she definitely remembered was how much

she loved her deck. It was a large space with steps that led to her heavily treed backyard. She was lucky that the property behind hers was a green space where nothing would ever be built and the forest-like area would remain.

More than once early in the mornings or at twilight she'd seen a herd of deer appear. Right now birds sang from the trees and her anxiety of moments earlier slowly ebbed away.

This had always been a place of peace for her after a stressful day at work, although she often didn't get a chance to enjoy it. She did remember how long hours at the shop ate into any free time.

She'd just cleaned off and set the table when Nick stepped out the back door. "Thank goodness it's cooled off a little bit," he said.

Oh, my, she didn't feel cooled off at all as she looked at him. His dark hair was damp and slightly tousled. The faint five-o'clock shadow he'd worn before his shower was now gone. He'd changed from his jeans into a pair of black shorts that displayed athletic, tanned legs. His short-sleeved, white-and-black shirt showed off his muscled biceps.

"Julie?" He raised a brow quizzically.

She realized she'd been staring at him. She only hoped her mouth hadn't been hanging open. "Sorry." Her cheeks flushed warmly. "Yes, it's nice it isn't as hot as it's been. There's a nice breeze blowing."

"It's beautiful out here." He walked over to the railing and looked out to the backyard. "I envy you all these woods. This is the best kind of scenery."

She picked up the long flame ignitor she'd carried out earlier. "I agree. You don't have trees in your yard?"

"Just one, a pretty little redbud tree." His jaw tightened and he grabbed the lighter out of her hand. "I'll light the grill for you."

He stalked over to the barbecue grill. As he lit the gas burner, his motions were stiff and unnatural.

"Nick, is something wrong?" she asked.

He jerked around to face her and, for just a brief moment, his expression was one of deep torment. The tense muscles in his face immediately relaxed into a smile. "Nothing is wrong," he replied. "Do you want to cook the steaks or do you want me to?"

"I'll do it. I noticed there was beer in the refrigerator. Why don't I bring you one and you can talk to me while the steaks grill?"

"I'll grab the beers," he replied.

She followed him into the house, wondering if she was losing her mind. Had she only imagined that look of anguish? Was her rattled brain tricking her? Unfortunately, she didn't have the answer.

Any concern she had slipped away as they sat at the table to enjoy the meal. The beer was cold and the steaks were grilled perfectly. The baked potatoes were also cooked to perfection and the conversation was light and easy.

"I think I had a memory a little while ago," she said.

"What did you remember?" He leaned forward in his chair, his gaze intent on her. He had the most intense green eyes.

She picked up her beer bottle and downed the last

swallow. "It was just a flash. I was walking into the kitchen and suddenly I was in the pawn shop." A chill danced up her spine. "And I was terrified."

He studied her features. "Did you have any idea of why you were so afraid?"

"No, it came and went too quickly. There weren't enough details." She released a sigh of frustration. "I wish I would have remembered, then maybe I would know what I'm not supposed to tell."

"What could be such a big secret at the pawn shop?"

She released a wry laugh. "Right now, your guess is as good as mine."

"I've never been in a pawn shop. What kind of people come in to do business with you?"

Evening was falling and the breeze had stopped blowing. The result was an oppressive heat and humidity. "Why don't we move inside and have a cup of coffee?" she suggested. "It's starting to feel a little close out here."

"Works for me," he replied.

For the next fifteen minutes they worked together to clear the dishes and clean the kitchen. Their previous conversation didn't resume again until they were both seated on the sofa with coffee cups in hand.

"You asked me about the people who come into the pawn shop. Some are really nice and I know they're just desperate for some quick cash to tide them over until their next payday or social security check comes in. These are the people we always hope pay their pawn on time so they won't lose their items."

She paused a moment to take a sip of her coffee and

then continued. "Other customers are just a little bit weird, bringing in bizarre items to pawn or sell. But some of the clientele are definitely a bit scary."

"Scary how?"

"I think we have a lot of drug addicts desperate for their next fix. They argue about how much their item is worth, some of them get really angry that we won't front them more money." She frowned, remembering how many times she'd been a bit half scared while working.

"Do you have security in the store?"

"The only security is a bulletproof glass and a good lock on the office area. But nobody really ever works alone. Dad always makes sure when Casey or I work, one of the men works with us." She looked at him curiously. "Didn't we ever talk about my work before?"

He shifted positions and reached for his cup from the coffee table. "Rarely. You always told me you wanted to leave your work at the store and just enjoy the time we spent together."

She nodded, knowing that about herself. "What about you? Tell me about your students and your ballplayers."

For the next two hours they talked. He entertained her with stories of working with high school students and it was obvious he loved what he did. In turn she told him about some of the more colorful characters who came into the shop.

Their shared laughter made her want him even more. He was the man she'd intended to marry, a man she'd dated for a considerable amount of time.

When had they last made love? The night before her car wreck? The week before? Didn't he want her? He hadn't even kissed her since the accident. Maybe she was like Sleeping Beauty and all she needed was a kiss from her prince to bring back all her memories.

Nick stifled a yawn with the back of his hand. "Sorry," he said with a sheepish grin.

"It's getting late and I've got a morning shift at the store tomorrow."

"I still think you should have told your family you needed a few more days of rest," he replied.

"I don't like to make waves." She leaned forward and placed her hand on his arm. "Nick, why don't you sleep with me tonight?"

His muscles tightened beneath her touch. "Julie, I'm just not comfortable with that kind of intimacy when you can't even remember anything about me." He rose from the sofa. "We'll have time for that when your memories return."

She also stood. She wanted to argue with him. She wanted him to know that it was okay with her. But he'd spoken his words with a finality that brooked no discussion.

"I just feel so…so disconnected from everything and everyone." She held his gaze for an intense moment, longing for his arms around her. "Could you just…just kiss me?" An embarrassed laugh escaped her. "God, I sound so pathetic right now."

His features softened as he reached out for her and pulled her into an embrace.

She pressed into him, loving the feel of his hard,

muscled chest against hers and the way his now familiar scent enveloped her.

"It's all going to be just fine," he murmured, his breath a warm caress against her forehead. "You're going to get your memories back and that will solve the mystery of the secret you know."

She raised her face and he lowered his lips to hers. It was obvious he meant it to be a quick, chaste kiss, but she would never be happy with that.

She raised her arms to his neck and opened her mouth, encouraging him to deepen the kiss. With a faint groan, he complied. His tongue swirled lazily with hers, igniting a flame in the very depths of her.

She wanted the kiss to last forever, but all too quickly he pulled away from her. Still, she was rewarded by a sweet desire that flowed from his eyes for just a moment. He did want her.

"Good night, Julie. I'll check the doors to make sure they're all locked. You can go ahead and get ready for bed."

She nodded, for a moment speechless by the flood of longing inside her. She headed for the stairs thinking she now had a new reason to want her memories back as soon as possible. When that happened, she knew Nick would take her to bed.

Chapter Five

Nick climbed the stairs fifteen minutes after Julie. How could she be so trusting as to want him in her bed when she couldn't remember anything about him?

And now that he'd kissed her, he wasn't sure how long he could stay strong against her obvious desire for him. It had been years since he'd had sex and there was no question that he was intensely drawn to Julie.

He'd love to have her in bed, with her dark hair splayed across the pillow and her body sleek and naked beneath his. It would just be a sexual release for him and nothing more. His love for his wife would always fill his heart to the point that there wouldn't be room for anyone else. His grief and rage over losing Debbie would always keep his heart firmly closed.

The problem was that his lies to Julie had been too good. She'd believed him hook, line and sinker. It was only natural that she'd want to kiss her fiancé. It was only natural she would want to make love to the man she intended to marry and spend the rest of her life with. How long could he put her off and not give in to his own crazy desire for her?

Thankfully, he didn't have to pass Julie's bedroom to get to his own. He used the bathroom across the hall from his room to brush his teeth and then returned to the room he'd been using while here.

It was a nice bedroom, decorated in shades of cool greens and white…the colors to soothe and calm. But as he climbed into bed, he had a feeling nothing could calm him tonight.

All day long his emotions had been all over the place. He'd awakened both anxious that she'd regained her memories with sleep and nervously wondering if Brian's murder would be reported. The anxiety had shifted to fear when he'd realized not only had it been in the newspaper but there had also been a witness who had seen somebody running away.

He'd held that emotion in check and had actually managed to relax while Julie was napping. The minute she'd walked down the stairs, a new tension had struck him…the nervous energy of a man pretending to be what he wasn't.

When he'd mentioned the redbud tree in his yard, he hadn't expected the rich, raw rage and the anguish of loss that had momentarily swept through him.

Now, as he tried to get to sleep, the final emotion of the day was desire. Kissing Julie had been a huge mistake. Her lips had been soft and warm and oh, so inviting. It would have been so easy to just let himself go to her room and have sex with her.

It wasn't just that mysterious sexual draw that enticed him. She had a wonderful sense of humor. She also had a softness of spirit, just a hint of vulnerability he suspected had been with her before the accident and the troubling phone call.

The phone call. Was it possible it had been nothing more than a wrong number? Some sort of a sick prank? The caller hadn't mentioned Julie by name. Still, he couldn't dismiss the signs of some sort of altercation in her living room. What was that about? So many questions with no answers.

And how soon might a police officer knock on this door after finding him not at his house after somehow connecting him to Brian's murder? Was it even possible something like that could happen?

Had he dropped DNA while he'd stood there panting and staring at Brian's body? Would Officer Brown have questions for the man who'd been wearing a hoodie in the middle of July just down the street from a murder scene?

With too many questions whirling around in his head, he finally fell into a troubled sleep. The nightmares began almost instantly.

He walked along a deserted highway and just ahead a neon sign flashed with the words Don't Tell. *The building looked like a motel and he desperately needed a motel. He'd been walking this highway at night for years and he just wanted to rest.*

When he reached the structure it was, indeed, the Don't Tell Motel. With a sigh of relief he entered the lobby. It was dark and dank, a layer of smoke swirling in the air. A man stood, his back to Nick, at the registration desk. "Got your room all ready for you, Coach," he said. "Room seven."

He turned around and it was Brian McDowell, his throat torn open and bleeding, the V *in his forehead oozing blood. Nick reeled backward in horror and ran outside.*

He raced to room seven and threw open the door. Debbie was on the floor next to the bed, broken and bloody. "No," he screamed in rage. Before he could reach Debbie, her features transformed into Julie's.

HE SNAPPED AWAKE, his body bathed in sweat and his heart thundering madly. He panted as if he'd been running for miles and it took a moment for him to orient himself.

He jumped out of the bed. Just a dream. No, a nightmare. He wiped his hand through his sweaty hair as his body began to cool off. He glanced at the clock on the nightstand: 5:30 a.m.

Normally he would be up around six. There was no point in trying to sleep again. Besides, if he did, he feared the nightmares might find him again.

He grabbed clean clothes from the closet and then silently crept into the bathroom across the hall. Hopefully, a quick shower wouldn't waken Julie.

Instead he took an unusually long shower, hoping to rinse the last of the nightmare from his mind. It had left him feeling unsettled and on edge.

Once he was dressed, he crept quietly down the stairs and into the kitchen where he got the coffee started.

Waiting for it to brew, he moved over to the window and stared outside. Dawn's light was just barely peeking over the horizon.

Julie's shift at the pawn shop started at nine and she wouldn't get off work until five. He knew what he needed to do during the long hours of the day.

He needed to touch base with Jason Cook and Matt Tanner, the other football coaches who worked with him at the high school. With practices starting in ten days, he needed to let them know he might not be participating in the sessions, at least initially, due to a personal crisis. Julie's continued amnesia had become his crisis the minute he'd told her the first lie.

Still, even if he didn't attend the practices, he could swing by his house and grab the DVDs of last year's games. He could then work on new plays that hopefully would keep the team winning games through the coming year.

He turned away from the window, poured a cup of coffee, then carried it to the table where he sat. It was ludicrous that he was thinking about football games when there were so many other, much bigger, issues going on right now.

Hell, for all he knew there might be a knock on the door at any time. A police officer could take him in for a lineup where a witness could positively identify him as the man seen running from Brian McDowell's on the night of the murder.

Or Julie's memories could suddenly return and she could call the police on him because he'd lied to her and she'd realized she didn't know him at all.

He both wanted and dreaded her regaining her memories. He wanted it for her, so she wouldn't feel so vulnerable and afraid living in her own skin. He dreaded it for him, not knowing what might happen when the truth finally came out.

Of course, he'd never tell anyone that he was at McDowell's house that night. Nobody would ever know he'd carried a gun, pulled on a ski mask and adorned gloves with the intention of murdering the man. That was a secret he would take to his very grave.

Another question whirling around in his mind... since somebody else had murdered Brian, did that mean nobody would kill the man who had raped and murdered his wife?

Nick tightened his hands around his coffee cup as the familiar raw rage swept through him. The survivors group he'd attended had talked about all the stages of grief.

He'd sat at those meetings every other week for months and had been unable to understand how anyone who had lost somebody to a violent crime ever moved past the stage of anger. He embraced the anger. He couldn't move into acceptance until he got his vengeance.

"Good morning." Julie walked into the kitchen clad in a short, lightweight, pink robe. Her hair was slightly tousled from sleep and a warm smile played on her lips.

Where Nick's stomach had clenched with his rage, it now tightened for an entirely different reason. Her scent eddied in the air, that light floral smell he found so wildly attractive.

"You're up early," he said, grateful his voice didn't betray any of the anger that had gripped him a moment before or of the swift desire her presence had stirred.

"So are you," she replied. She walked over to the coffeemaker and reached up in the cabinet to retrieve a cup. The action gave him a tantalizing view of her long, bare legs.

"Did you sleep well?" She poured her coffee and then sat in the chair opposite him.

"It was a toss-and-turn kind of night," he admitted.

Her smile faded. "I'm taking up too much of your time and energy. I'm sure you have other things to do besides babysitting me. I'll be fine here alone, if you want to go back to your house."

She wouldn't be fine. The slight tremble in her voice let him know the last thing she wanted right now was to be there all alone. "I'm right where I need to be," he replied. "However, if you don't mind, I'm going to bring over some football DVDs to study when you're at work."

"Of course I don't mind. Besides, I love football. Did I ever go to any of the high school games?"

He shook his head. "You were always scheduled to work at the shop on game nights."

She sighed. "And even if I had asked for the night off, Dad would have told me no and given me a big lecture about how the business was more important than anything else in life." She took a sip of her coffee and then continued. "I swear he'd be perfectly happy if I never got married or had children. That way, I'd never have any distractions from the shop."

"Did you ever think about doing something else?"

She frowned thoughtfully. "I always thought I'd like to be a nurse or even a nurse's aide and work in a doctor's office, but it wasn't in the cards for me."

"That's an admirable profession. You're still young, you could go to school and make that happen. Maybe your dad would initially be unhappy with you, but I'm sure he'd eventually get over it."

"Maybe," she replied, although her tone held no real conviction. "In any case, this morning you get your first exploration of the famous Peterson Pawn shop."

"I'm definitely looking forward to it." He liked it when he could make her smile. Her lovely face was meant for smiling. "Still, you would make a great nurse."

"You really think so?" Her smile widened and her cheeks flushed a pretty pink.

"Definitely. You have a calm, easy way about you that most patients would welcome." It was true. Despite everything that had happened to her, she had a softness that was appealing.

Her cheeks grew an even deeper dusty shade of pink. "Thank you. And now I'd better finish this coffee and head back upstairs to get ready for work."

At eight thirty they left the house. Julie had exchanged her robe for a pair of black slacks and a black T-shirt with Peterson Pawn in bold white letters across her chest. On her feet were black-and-white sandals that exposed her pink-painted toenails.

"Are there other employees besides the family members?" he asked as they left the cul-de-sac.

"A few, although Dad doesn't trust any of them and always thinks they're either stealing items or skimming money from the registers."

"Are they?"

"Not that I'm aware of. I keep the books and there's

nothing that would make me think anything improper is happening." She gave a dry laugh. "At least, that's the way I remember things."

"No more flashes of memory since yesterday?" He cast her a quick glance. The morning sunshine loved her features, casting them in a golden glow.

"None." She sighed. "I don't know why I'm so nervous about going back to work."

"Julie, you're missing a lot of memories. I'd expect you to be nervous about anything and everything," he replied. "And you did say that in that flash of memory you were in the pawn shop and you were afraid."

"I'm not even sure if that was a real memory or just some sort of strange anxiety about going back to work." She released another deep sigh.

Before he could stop himself he reached over and touched the back of her hand. "Everything is going to be okay, Julie."

He quickly drew his hand back. He shouldn't touch her. Her skin was so soft and warm, and he liked touching her way too much.

He had to stay focused on the truth of the situation. He'd told her everything would be okay and it would be as long as she didn't regain her memories and nobody killed her for "telling." Everything would be fine as long as no witness could positively identify him and he managed to forget the horrifying vision of McDowell's bloody dead body.

"Welcome to my world," Julie said as she unlocked the front door and led Nick inside the pawn shop. Directly to the left of the door stood a life-size suit of armor and on the right was a full-size skeleton holding a sign that read Shoplifters Will Be Prosecuted.

"Quite a welcoming committee," he replied with a laugh.

She relocked the door behind them. "I told you my father likes a little bizarre with the usual pawn items."

The faint simmer of fear was back inside her. Was it because she was missing her memories or due to something else? She couldn't know. She turned on the lights to further aid the sunshine that danced through the large front windows.

To the left were shelves of computers, monitors and televisions. To the right, musical equipment was on display for purchase. In between were the oversize items for sale. There were lawn mowers and leaf blowers, compressors and all kinds of tools.

Along the back wall stood glass jewelry display cases and the registers. Behind those was a glass-enclosed office and a back room where the customers weren't allowed.

"It's pretty much the way I always thought a pawn shop would look, just a lot bigger," Nick said.

"Wait…you haven't seen the other room yet." She tried to shove away the niggling sense of anxiety that had been with her since she'd dressed for work that morning.

She watched Nick's expression as she led him into the connecting room. Stunned surprise lit his features just before he released a pleasant rumble of laughter.

"This looks more like Ripley's Believe It or Not! than a pawn shop," he exclaimed.

She gazed around, seeking any changes that might have happened over the last ten months that she couldn't remember. The stuffed, five-legged calf was still there. As were the fat, seven-foot, resin genie seated on a pillow and an equally large, smiling penguin with a belly that opened and closed.

There was also the half dozen antique slot and pinball machines and the unusual artwork hanging on the walls.

Nick walked over to a plaster pink-and-white giraffe and then turned back to look at her. "Where does your father find these things?"

"He doesn't. They mostly find him. Once word got out that he was open to buying and selling almost anything, people started contacting him about unusual items. Come on and I'll show you the office." Her nerves slowly began to calm as she realized nothing much had changed in the shop.

The office was right next to an outer door in the back room, which held various items on shelving. "All the stuff up front is for sale and the things back here are being held for people to reclaim after they've pawned them," she explained. "We also own the building next door that we use to hold all of our pawned things."

"Quite a large operation." Nick looked at her for a long moment. "Are you feeling better about being here?"

"Somewhat better." She smiled. "I'm sure as the day goes on, the last of my nerves will completely disappear."

Still, even just saying those words, she jumped at the sound of the front door opening.

"Hello?" a familiar deep voice called out.

Julie instantly relaxed. "Joel."

She greeted the big, burly man with the slightly shaggy brown hair who would share the workload with her that day. "I'd like you to meet my fiancé," she said.

"Your daddy told me you got a touch of some crazy amnesia, but he didn't mention anything about you getting a fiancé." He smiled at Nick and offered his hand for a shake. "Hope you intend to take good care of this lady," he added after the two men had shaken hands.

"I do," Nick replied.

"She's one fine woman and deserves only the best," Joel replied with a warm smile at her.

"And I have the best," she said with conviction. "Nick, if you want to, you can head on out. It's almost time to open the front doors and I'll be fine here with Joel," she said.

"Walk me to the door?" he asked.

She smiled. "Of course."

"Nice meeting you, Nick," Joel said as they headed for the front door.

"Are you sure you're going to be okay?" Nick asked when they reached the door and the two of them stepped just outside.

"I'll be fine. Joel and I have always been great working buddies," she replied. She frowned. "Unless something happened between us that I don't remember. But everything seemed okay when he came in."

"I thought maybe I'd pick up a couple of chicken

breasts to grill tonight when you get home. I figured we should enjoy the slightly cooler temperatures and the deck while we can."

"Sounds perfect to me." Although most of that crazy simmering fear had eased, there was still a little bit left.

"You know, if you really aren't feeling up to this today, I'll take you right back home."

She shook her head, touched and pleased that he seemed to read all the nuances of her emotions. "I'll be fine...really."

"Then I'll be back here at five to pick you up." He leaned forward and kissed her forehead. "Have a good day, Julie, and call me if you need anything."

Before she could reply...before she could even process the gift of his warm lips against her skin, he turned and was gone.

"Should I go ahead and open the door for the day?" she called to Joel, who had taken a position behind the counter.

"I'm ready if you are."

She unlocked the door and her official day at work began. It was a busy morning with people coming in to shop or to pawn. Julie scarcely had any time to think about any lingering fear that might attempt to possess her.

Her missing memories didn't hinder her as the day went on. It was two o'clock and in the middle of a lull when a middle-aged woman came in. She walked hesitantly up to the counter, tightly clutching a worn purse in both hands.

"May I help you?" Julie asked.

"Uh… I don't know." The woman shoved a strand of her long brown hair behind one ear. "I've never done this before, but I guess I'd like to pawn a ring."

"May I see the ring?"

She placed her purse on the counter, opened it and withdrew a small envelope. Her fingers trembled as she shook out a small diamond ring.

Julie grabbed a jeweler's loop and looked at the ring carefully. It was only fourteen karat gold and the diamond was tiny, although had fairly good clarity. She looked back at the woman. "I can do a hundred dollars," she offered.

"That's all? It's my wedding ring and I promise I'll be back to get it, but I need a hundred and thirty dollars to pay for our electric bill. I spent too much on groceries and now I'm in a bind." She laughed, although it was a desperate sound. "But I'm sure you hear sob stories all the time."

Julie had definitely heard a lot of sob stories over the years, but something about this woman touched her heart. "I'll give you a hundred and forty dollars."

Tears suddenly misted the woman's eyes. "Oh… thank you. And this will be a secret, right. I mean nobody else will have to know that I've pawned it."

"Nobody will know unless you tell them," Julie replied. *Don't tell.* The words thundered in her head as she scanned Maggie Albright's driver's license. The two words resounded over and over again as she explained the terms and conditions of the pawn.

Had something happened here in the pawn shop that had prompted the threat to her? Why couldn't she remember? Had a customer somehow forced her to do something illegal? She couldn't imagine that being the case. She had always played by the rules but, without her memory, she couldn't fully dismiss such a scenario, either.

At three, Casey called to tell Julie she was running late and couldn't make it in to relieve her until six thirty or so. Julie called Nick so he would know to come later to pick her up.

"If that girl ever shows up on time for one of her shifts, I'll swallow my tongue," Joel said drily.

Julie laughed. "Nobody ever said Casey was dependable. Beautiful, yes. Fun, definitely. Her idea of responsibility is if she remembers to call in and let us know she's going to be late or not show up at all."

"I heard through the grapevine that your dad had a talk with her and told her it was time for her to grow up and pay her own bills."

She looked at Joel in surprise. "Now, that I haven't heard."

Joel released a small burst of laughter. "I'm not sure Casey believed him because she sure hasn't been too eager to pick up extra shifts."

"I doubt if the talk worried her much. She's always had my parents wrapped around her little finger," Julie replied.

She began to relax again as she and Joel talked shop and he regaled her with stories about his new puppy named Buster.

"Have you told me about Buster before?" she asked.

He smiled at her kindly. "Two weeks ago when I

first got the pooch. It's okay, Julie. I know you're missing some memories right now. I can't imagine what that's like."

"Unsettling and more than a little bit frightening. I'm just hoping before too long everything will come back to me. In fact, while nobody is in here, I'd like to go back into the office and read over the transactions from the last day I worked. Maybe that will help jog my memory."

"Knock yourself out," Joel replied. "It's really slow right now and, if I need you, I'll holler for you. Julie, if there was something I could do to help, you know I'd do it."

"Thanks, Joel." She gave him a grateful smile and then hurried into the office space and sat at the desk. According to the schedule posted on the wall, she'd worked the day before her car accident.

She pulled out the paperwork and pored over the transactions she'd been in charge of that day, trying to find something—anything—that would have to do with a deadly secret.

There had to be something to explain that terrible phone call she'd received and she needed to find out what it was sooner rather than later.

Chapter Six

"I went over all the transactions for the entire week before my accident and I didn't find anything suspicious," she told Nick when they were in his car and heading home.

"Then maybe whatever it is doesn't have anything to do with the pawn shop." He turned into the cul-de-sac.

"Maybe. But I had that faint sense of fear all day long while I was there, and I didn't have much of a life outside the pawn shop until you came along."

"But hasn't that fear been with you since you woke up in the hospital?" He parked the car and turned off the engine.

"I guess," she conceded. They got out of the car and walked to the front door. She didn't know how to explain to him that she had two different feelings of fear. One definitely came from her missing time with the amnesia. The other was more insidious…a sick anxiety that kept her on edge.

"Go straight to the deck and have a seat," he instructed her once they were inside. "I've got dinner covered."

"Are you sure?" she asked in surprise.

"Positive. Would you like a beer?"

"I think I have some white wine in the fridge. I'd love a glass of that," she replied.

"Done. Now go relax," he commanded.

"Yes, sir," she replied with a laugh. She stepped outside and was surprised to see the table already set. She sank down into one of the cushioned chairs and kicked off her sandals. It was after seven and she was exhausted.

"Here we go." Nick came out of the door with a glass of wine in one hand and two chicken breasts on a plate, seasoned and ready to go on the grill, in the other.

"Thanks." She took the glass from him and watched as he fired up the barbecue and then placed the chicken breasts on the rack.

Dark clouds had appeared in the sky over the course of the long day. "Is it supposed to rain?" she asked.

"There's a possibility of some storms in the area later this evening," he replied and sat across from her.

"The grass could definitely use the rain, but I absolutely hate thunder and lightning."

He grinned at her, a light, easy gesture that warmed her more than the sultry evening air could ever do. "So, you're a big 'fraidy cat and hide under the sheets when it storms?"

"Something like that. And over the past ten months, were there times when you hid under the sheets with me?"

"Once or twice." He jumped up from the chair and went to the grill to check on the chicken.

She took a sip of her wine and released a sigh. She missed the intimacy she and Nick must have had. She missed it even though she didn't remember it. And she desperately wanted to remember him. She needed to remember them.

She closed her eyes and instantly a vision filled her head. She was at the pawn shop and a man was yelling at her. His face was red with anger and he pounded a fist on the counter. She knew he was yelling at her because his mouth was moving, but she couldn't hear him.

The stranger's face melted and transformed into her brother Max's face. He was shouting at her, too. Angry. Her stomach clenched. An icy fist grabbed her throat. She couldn't breathe.

A hand fell on her shoulder and she jerked rigid with fear. Her eyes flipped open. Nick gazed at her with concern. "Are you all right?" he asked worriedly. "You disappeared there for a minute."

"A memory." She cleared her throat and swallowed against the thick fear that attempted to rise up. "At least, I think it was a memory."

"Want to talk about it?" He sat on the chair closest to her and took her hand in his.

She welcomed the warmth of his hand around hers as she told him where her mind had taken her. "We sometimes get customers who had lost their item due to non-payment and they often get very angry. As far as Max yelling at me…he yells at everyone, so that's nothing new." She frowned thoughtfully. "I don't know if any of it means something or if it all means nothing."

"I would imagine your memory is going to return in bits and pieces that might not make sense right now." He squeezed her hand. "Eventually it will all come back and everything will make sense." He stood and walked back to the barbecue where he turned the chicken breasts.

Dinner was pleasant and they lingered on the deck until lightning began to slash across the night sky and they had to move inside.

Nick insisted on doing the kitchen cleanup and she sat at the table while he worked. "So, how did you spend the day?" she asked.

"I immersed myself in football. I watched DVDs from last year's games and tried to identify the strengths and weaknesses of my players."

"Do you love what you do?" she asked curiously.

He turned from the sink. "I do."

"Did you want to be a professional football player?"

He shook his head. "No way. I always wanted to be a coach. I love the game and I love the kids."

"Did we talk about having children?" How she wished she could remember every conversation they'd ever had.

"Not really, although I assumed you wanted them."

"I do. I'd like to have at least a boy and a girl. What about you?"

"That works for me," he replied. He finished up with the dishes and joined her at the kitchen table.

"Now, do you work again tomorrow?" he asked.

"I'm on the schedule for early shifts for the next

four days," she replied. "And then I go to afternoon shifts for a few days."

"When is your day off?"

She frowned. "We rarely get days off."

"You're kidding. That isn't right. Everyone deserves a day off." He looked down at the table for a moment and then gazed back at her. "I don't want to make you angry, but don't you think it's maybe possible your family is taking advantage of you?"

She started to protest but instead nodded slowly in agreement. "I know they are. It's the way things have always been. I not only work long hours in the store, but I also keep track of the inventory, keep the financial records and do the taxes every year."

"Maybe it's time to change things up. Otherwise your obligations to them will choke any hope you have of being a wife and having children. You deserve more, Julie." He rose. "And now, I think it's time we both get a good night's sleep."

Within minutes she was upstairs in her room. Nick's words still echoed in her head as she changed into a short pink nightgown. Was it possible she'd mentioned to Max that she wanted a day off? Shorter hours? And had that been the memory she'd had of Max raging at her?

She believed she'd known for a long time that she wasn't particularly happy working long hours at the shop. Nick was right, she deserved more than a pawn shop in her life. She wanted a husband and children, and she wanted time to make those things happen.

She probably would have brought it up with her

brother before speaking to her father about it. She could see herself torn between the family business and time with Nick. Had she rocked the boat and asked for less responsibility?

With Nick in her life, she imagined her priorities might have changed. Maybe she'd wanted to go to one of his football games or to spend more than one night a week with him. Had she voiced her desire to stop working so much and gained Max's anger? Still, none of that answered what she might know that she wasn't supposed to tell.

She jumped as a rumble of thunder boomed. Terrific, she thought. Just what she needed on top of everything else. She'd been afraid of thunderstorms for as long as she could remember. Logically she knew they couldn't hurt her, but that logic went out the window when it thundered. She also knew she was a baby when it came to storms, but even that didn't help.

She was about to get into bed when she remembered her sandals beneath the table on the deck. They were one of her favorite pairs and they were part fabric. The rain would probably ruin them.

With a sigh of resignation she stepped out of her bedroom. The hallway was dark, as was Nick's room down the hall. He'd probably already fallen asleep.

Silently, and in the dark, she crept past his doorway and down the stairs. Despite her lack of certain memories, she knew her surroundings intimately. She walked through the living room and into the kitchen to get to the patio door.

She'd just reached it when lightning flashed, half

blinding her yet leaving her with enough sight to see somebody—some...thing—in the door window.

She froze. Terror gripped her. A roll of thunder shook the house and still she remained unmoving. Lightning once again flashed and this time she saw a face—a face with no eyes. What? Who?

Her brain went numb even as she stumbled backward from the horrific sight. Finally she managed to scream.

THE SCREAM PENETRATED Nick's sleep and bolted him upright in bed. Julie! He pulled on a pair of shorts and shot down the hallway to her room.

She screamed again and he realized she was someplace downstairs. He flipped on the hall light, his heart beating wildly as a surge of adrenaline had him taking the stairs two at a time.

He also turned on the living room light and then he saw her. She stood in a pink nightgown just inside the kitchen and her facial features were twisted in sheer terror.

"Julie! What is it?" He raced to her side, wondering what was happening. What was she doing down here? Had it been the thunder or the lightning that had her so upset? Had she suffered a nightmare? A frightening memory?

She raised a trembling hand and pointed to the back door. Nick turned and looked and jumped in surprise. What in the hell? A doll. It hung from the doorframe and might have stared inside if its eyes hadn't been gouged out.

He turned on the kitchen light. "It's okay, Julie. It's a doll. It can't hurt you." As she stumbled to the table and sank down in a chair, he opened the back door and grabbed the offending doll. It had been hung by a piece of thick string that easily gave way when he pulled on it.

It was monstrous. Along with the missing eyes, the hair had been pulled out and a small knife had been driven to its hilt into the soft skull. Across the bare belly the words *Don't Tell* had been written in a red marker.

"It's just a doll," he repeated.

Julie raised her eyes from the doll to him. Her face was deathly pale and her lips trembled. "Who is doing this?" Her dark blue eyes held a wealth of fear. "This is monstrous. This is…is so evil. Who…who would do such a thing to me?"

Nick grabbed a towel off the countertop and tossed it over the doll on the table. "I don't know, but I think it's time we call the police." The very last thing he wanted was any contact with the law, but he couldn't leave Julie at risk to save himself.

The danger the phone call had yielded had suddenly escalated with this gruesome find. Even worse, whoever had done this knew exactly where she lived, had actually been on her back deck.

"I'm just not sure what the police can do about any of this," she finally replied. A boom of thunder shook the house and increased the panic in her eyes.

"Julie, we still need to call them and make a record

of this. I'll go upstairs and grab my cell phone and be right back down."

"I'm coming with you." She jumped up from the chair like an uncoordinated colt, her knees buckling beneath her.

He grabbed her, afraid she might fall to the floor.

Instantly she wrapped her arms around his neck and began to weep. Her slender body trembled against his and he fully embraced her, knowing it was sheer terror that caused her tears. Certainly the doll had more than unsettled him. He wasn't sure whose heart beat faster, hers or his own. Who was doing this to her and why? And what might the next move be? How much danger was she really in?

He caressed her back and tried to ignore the press of her breasts against him and the dizzying scent of her that wrapped around him. "Come on, Julie. Let's go make that phone call."

She released her hold on him and he grabbed her hand. She held tight, radiating her fear in the iciness of her fingers as they headed up the stairs.

The storm was upon them with rain slashing at the windows and continuous lightning and thunder. She clung so close to his side it made their trek upstairs an awkward dance.

When they reached his room, she sat on the edge of the bed while he called the police. "They should be here in just a few minutes," he said, hanging up. "Let's go back downstairs to wait for them."

Before heading downstairs they went to her bedroom, where she grabbed a robe to pull on around her nightgown.

Back in the living room, she curled up into a corner of the sofa, her face still far too pale and her eyes silently screaming with her fear.

He wanted to take that emotion out of her eyes. He never wanted to hear her scream like she had again. But at this moment he couldn't even assure her that everything was going to be okay because he didn't know what might happen next.

"I saw some tea bags up in the cupboard. Do you want me to make you a cup of hot tea while we wait?" he asked.

She looked so cold with her arms wrapped tightly around her, as if the fear inside her had stolen every ounce of her body heat.

"That would be nice. There's a teakettle in the cabinet under the coffeemaker." Her voice was higher than usual and her lips trembled.

He had just put the water on to boil when a knock fell on the front door. As he walked through the living room to answer it, he hoped like hell all the cops in Kansas City law enforcement didn't have a sketch of him as a person of interest in the murder.

He opened the door and two officers flashed their badges and swept inside, their rain hats and suits dripping water on the floor. "Sorry," the taller of the two said. "It's a heck of a rainstorm out there."

"No problem," Nick replied. "Why don't I take your coats and hang them?" There was a three-hook coat hanger just inside the front door.

Introductions weren't officially made until their coats were off and they'd all stepped into the living room where Julie hadn't moved from her position on the sofa.

Officer Sean White and Officer Frank Roberts stood while Nick explained why they had been called out on a stormy night. As he told them about the phone call and then the doll, Officer Roberts's dark eyes gazed at him intently.

Paranoia immediately filled Nick. Did the officer know something about McDowell's murder? Was it suspicion that had the man staring at Nick so attentively?

A shrill whistle filled the air. Julie released a small scream and the two officers went for their guns. "It's the teakettle," Nick said hurriedly. "If you'll follow me into the kitchen, I'll show you the doll."

In the kitchen he quickly pulled the kettle off the burner, stopping its noisy hiss, and then took the towel off the doll.

"Now that's a nasty piece of work," Officer White said in obvious disgust.

"I hope you're going to take it away." Julie spoke from the doorway.

"And you don't have any idea what this is all about?" Officer White asked her.

Julie shook her head. "I…I had a car accident a couple of days ago and it's done something to some of my memories."

"You said the threatening phone call came from an anonymous number?" he continued.

She nodded.

"Probably a burner phone," Officer Roberts said. He turned his gaze back to Nick. "Can you think of anyone who might want to harm Ms. Peterson?"

Despite the coolness of the house, Nick felt warm... too warm. Why was the officer looking at him with such scrutiny?

"No, nobody," he replied.

"You're Coach Simon, aren't you?" Roberts suddenly asked. Nick nodded and the officer elaborated. "I knew I'd seen you before. My boy played for you a couple of years ago... Cody Roberts?"

Nick breathed a sigh of relief. "Sure, I remember Cody. He was a good tight end. Is he still at KU?"

"Yeah, but he's not playing football anymore. He's pretty focused on his classes. He wants to get a degree in criminology. Seems he wants to follow in his old man's footsteps." Roberts's broad chest puffed up.

"Enough about football and kids," Officer White said. "We need to get moving before the next wave of storms moves in."

Nick suddenly realized the thunder and lightning had abated and the rain had stopped. "There are more storms moving in?" Julie asked half breathlessly.

"The weather reports are for bands to continue to move in and out until dawn," Officer White replied. "We'll take the doll with us and attempt to pull off some fingerprints, but don't expect too much."

"This might be nothing more than scare tactics, but I'd say the best thing you can do is try to think of anyone who might have a beef with you." Roberts pulled on a pair of gloves, took a large plastic bag out of his back pocket and bagged the offending toy.

All of them walked to the front door.

Officer White took a card out of his pocket and offered it to Julie. "You call me if you think of anyone or if anything else happens. In the meantime, I'll open a file and if we get anything at all off the doll then I'll contact you."

"Thank you," she replied.

Within minutes the officers had pulled on their rain gear and left. Nick locked up after them and then turned to look at Julie. "Still want that cup of tea? I can reheat the water."

She stared at him, her eyes filled with fear and quiet despair. "I'm frightened and I've never been so cold in my life. I don't want hot tea. I want you. I want you to hold me through the night. I need you, Nick, and if you really love me, you'll sleep with me tonight."

Chapter Seven

Her hair smelled of peaches as stray strands tickled the side of his face. He had one arm around her and she fit perfectly against him, curled up at his side as he lay on his back.

He'd had no choice but to climb into her bed. It would have been odd for a fiancé not to hold the woman he professed to love through a dark and stormy night and after she'd had such a bad scare.

Thankfully, almost the minute they had gotten comfortable in the bed, she had fallen asleep. Sleep was the last thing on his mind. If her warm, curvy body next to his wasn't enough of a distraction, his racing thoughts kept sleep at bay.

What he wanted to stay focused on was the question of who was threatening Julie and not on the white-hot desire that pulsed in his veins.

Was it possible it was somebody in her family? None of them seemed the type to issue anonymous warnings. They were more up-front and in-your-face. Was it somebody who worked with her at the pawn shop?

Unfortunately he had the feeling that the police

would be little help in solving this mystery. They had much bigger crimes to solve—like the vicious murder of Brian McDowell. And crime certainly hadn't stopped with that murder.

His stomach clenched tight as he thought of how uncomfortable he'd been when Officer Roberts had eyed him so closely. Guilt had coalesced with paranoia and he'd been certain the night would end with him under arrest. How did real criminals live with that?

A faint flash of lightning lit the room, followed several moments later by a rumble of thunder. Thankfully, Julie didn't stir.

He didn't want her awake. Being next to her as she slept was difficult enough. He hadn't felt this kind of desire for a woman since Debbie. After her death, he'd believed he'd never want a woman again. But Julie definitely stirred that emotion inside him.

It wasn't just about feeling the softness of her skin next to his. It was far more than the heady scent of her. Her warm smile made him want her. Her laughter pulled him to her.

There had been so very little laughter in his life over the past three years. There had been very little life. He'd been dead inside since he'd buried his wife and Julie reminded him that there was still life and laughter and desire.

Not that it mattered. He wasn't in the market for a wife. And, in any case, he had damned any future relationship with Julie the minute he'd told his first lie to her. What he didn't understand was why this thought depressed him more than a little bit.

He must have dozed off because he suddenly jerked awake. Had the thunder awakened him? Perhaps. As he remained still, a bright flash lit the room and thunder boomed overhead.

Beside him, Julie moaned. "No." She punched at the sheet that covered them and thrashed around. "No. Go away." Her voice held a desperate appeal. "Go away!" She sat upright, her chest heaving and her eyes wild as lightning flashed again.

"Julie." He sat up beside her and reached over to turn on the bedside lamp. The pupils of her eyes were dilated, nearly usurping all their blue color. He said her name once again. She stared at him for a long moment and then released a startled gasp.

"I'm sorry. I'm so sorry. It was a nightmare." She drew her knees up to her chest as if attempting to disappear. "I didn't mean to wake you."

"Was it the storm?" he asked.

"No…it was the doll." She raised a hand to the bottom of her throat, a gesture he had come to recognize as a display of her anxiety. "I dreamed it was alive and it was trying to come into the house to kill me." She lowered her legs and turned toward him. "Nick, I'm so sorry I disturbed your sleep."

"Don't apologize for a bad dream," he replied. "We all have them at one time or another."

She rolled over so her upper body was on top of his bare chest. All his muscles tensed and he closed his eyes as a fiery desire coursed through him. She swept a hand across his skin and whispered a sigh against his neck.

He wanted to douse the flames she stirred inside him, but as she moved her hand lower on his abdomen, the flames only burned hotter.

"Nick," she said softly as her fingers toyed with the waistband of his boxers.

He opened his eyes and her lips were right next to his. Her eyes telegraphed need and want. With a groan, he pulled her closer against him as his lips captured hers.

Someplace in the back of his mind he knew this was wrong on so many levels. But that didn't stop him from rolling her over onto her back and continuing to kiss her. Rationality certainly didn't halt his hands that found her soft breasts and taut nipples.

He was going to make love to her. She'd believe she was making love with a man who loved her, who had committed his life to her. She wouldn't know yet that he was nothing more than a virtual stranger to her. Even with all that in his head, it wasn't enough to stop the moment.

Their tongues swirled together with a frantic hunger. She tasted of hot desire and he loved the taste of her as they continued the kiss.

He stroked his hands across her shoulders and down her arms. Her warm and silky skin was made for a man's caress. She moaned slightly against his mouth. The husky sound, so filled with her desire for him, heated the blood flowing through his veins.

He was half breathless and yet he didn't want to stop tasting her sweet lips. When thunder boomed overhead, she didn't flinch. It was as if she was completely lost in him. And that only turned him on more.

She finally stopped, only to sit up and shrug the spaghetti straps of her nightgown off her shoulders. The silky garment fell to her waist. The sight of her breasts in the flashing lightning coming through the window made him want to touch.

He covered her breasts with his hands, loving the feel of softness and the pebble hardness of her nipples. He moved his lips to cover where his hands had been.

"Oh, Nick," she whispered and placed her hands on the back of his head to encourage the intimacy.

As the storm raged outside, the rest of their clothes were abandoned. She was beautiful in her clothes, but she was breathtakingly beautiful naked.

She showed no shyness or hesitation. Rather, she was passionate and exciting. She had no idea this was the first time they had ever made love. She met him with the confidence of a long-time lover and a woman who was certain she was loved.

For every caress he gave her, she gave back to him until he had to take her completely. Anything less was impossible.

He hovered between her thighs. He gazed down at her. Her pupils were still wide, but he knew now it was from desire and not any fear.

"Take me, Nick," she said, her voice husky with desire. "I want you so badly."

"And I want you." He eased into her and was immediately lost in her heat. She met him thrust for thrust, moaning her pleasure as her fingers clutched at his back.

Too fast. Everything was happening too fast and he tried to slow down. He wanted her with him when he reached his peak. He wanted to make sure she was thoroughly pleasured before he allowed himself his own.

And then she was there, her body tensing as she moaned again and again. Small shudders swept through her and his release was upon him. Intense…wild, his climax rocketed through him.

He finally collapsed onto his elbows, keeping the bulk of his weight off her. She looked stunning with her dark hair splayed out on the pillow and her cheeks flushed with color.

She reached up, placed her hands on either side of his face and then rose just enough to meet her lips with his. He tasted her love in the softness of the kiss. A love she'd given to him without question, without any reservation.

"That was magic," she said when the kiss ended.

"Yeah, it was."

"Has it always been that good?"

"Always." He got up from the bed, grabbed his boxers from the floor and went down the hallway to the bathroom he'd been using. He didn't want to linger and give her an opportunity to say anything more about what they'd just shared. He didn't want to utter one more lie to her tonight.

He looked at his reflection in the mirror with disgust. This was the absolute worst thing he could have done to her. Hell, he hadn't even used a condom. He'd been so caught up in the haze of desire, he hadn't thought about protection.

When her memories came back to her, there would be no way to protect her from knowing he wasn't who he claimed to be. He'd taken advantage of her in so many ways and tonight in the worst way possible. He was a fraud pretending to be a fiancé for his own selfish purposes.

A boom of thunder sounded overhead.

Run, a little voice whispered in his head. *Get your things and get out of here now.*

"I can't," he said to the man in the mirror.

He was in way too deep now. Not only was he afraid for her, he'd also grown to care about her. He couldn't just run away like a coward, especially after what they'd just shared.

This whole ordeal had started because of his hatred, because of his rage toward another man. But now it was so much more complicated than that. At the moment that particular rage seemed distant and rather unimportant.

Pulling his boxers back on, he knew exactly what he was going to do now. He was going to return to her bed and hold her. He was going to continue to hold her until the thunder and lightning stopped because he knew she was afraid of those things.

He left the bathroom and went into the bedroom, where she was just getting back into bed. She smiled at him, but the smile was short-lived as thunder once again boomed.

"Let's cover up our heads," he said, hoping to keep things light between them despite what had just happened. Besides, the last thing he wanted was a recap of their love-making where she told him how very much she loved him.

"Sounds good to me," she replied.

Minutes later the light on the nightstand had been turned off and he was spooned around her back. Her body tensed slightly each time the storm made its presence known.

"I don't know why I'm such a baby," she said softly.

"Everyone has an irrational fear about something," he replied.

"What's yours?" she asked drowsily.

He couldn't tell her that his biggest fear at the moment was being arrested for murder. Or that his second biggest fear was what would happen when she regained her memories.

"Nick? Are you asleep?"

He didn't reply.

Within minutes her breathing became the slow and regular rhythm of sleep.

Sleep didn't come so easily to him.

He should be arrested. He should spend the rest of his life in a jail cell. His crimes against Julie would haunt him for the rest of his life. And tonight he'd committed the worst kind of felony against her by making love to her.

He needed to find out who was threatening her. He didn't want her to face whatever danger might be reaching out for her all alone. Once that mystery was solved, whether she had her memories back or not, he had to tell her the truth. He had to let her know that he wasn't her fiancé and he'd lied about everything.

He just couldn't figure out why his heart ached just a little even thinking about it.

JULIE WOKE ALONE in the bed with bright morning sunshine drifting through the curtains. She moved a hand to Nick's side of the bed and the warmth that lingered there let her know he'd gotten up only recently. The sheets still held the faint aroma of his cologne.

She closed her eyes and released a sigh of utter contentment. Making love with him had been wonderful. It had been everything she'd imagined it would be. He'd been so passionate and yet tender, and sleeping in his arms had felt like home.

She was almost sorry he was already out of bed. She wouldn't have minded a repeat performance. "You're going to have the rest of your life with him," she whispered to her pillow. The words warmed her. He was everything she wanted for herself. She just wished she could remember all the moments she'd spent with him before now.

Remember. The threatening phone call...the horrific doll... She so desperately needed to remember so she'd know where those threats were coming from. Who was responsible? She squeezed her eyes more tightly closed, trying to summon something—anything—from her not-so-distant past.

There was nothing there. It was like a big black hole that swirled and whirled inside her head but gave up nothing.

With a frustrated sigh, she got out of bed.

Pulling a short, cotton robe around her, she went

into the bathroom to brush her teeth and hair before joining her fiancé for morning coffee.

Her fiancé… Her heart thrilled.

Thank goodness he'd gotten over his reticence to make love to her and now they could truly enjoy the intimacy of a couple in love.

She wore a smile as she left the bedroom and headed down the stairs. She found Nick exactly where she expected him to be, at the kitchen table with a cup of coffee and the morning paper before him.

"Good morning." The words nearly sang out of her before she dropped a kiss on his forehead. She felt so much closer to him since last night.

"Somebody is in a good mood," he said.

She walked over to the counter and then turned to face him. "And why shouldn't I be? Fresh coffee is waiting for me, the storms have passed and I have the hottest fiancé in the world right here with me."

"And he's about to burst your bubble of happiness," he replied. "Grab your coffee and then I want to have a serious talk with you."

Her heart plummeted as she turned around to pour her coffee. Had last night's lovemaking made him suddenly decide he didn't love her anymore? Were her amnesia and the threats all too much for him to deal with? Was he about to break her heart? Oh, God, she hoped not.

She joined him at the table, her heart trembling with dread as she gazed into his dark-lashed green eyes.

"I've been thinking about the threats you've received and I think maybe you and I need to get more proactive."

A huge relief swept through her. At least he hadn't been thinking about leaving her. "Proactive how?"

"You need a security system and I'd like to get one installed here today while you're at work."

She sat back in the chair and looked at him in surprise.

"Julie, whoever is threatening you knows where you live. Somebody was on your deck last night. They could have easily gained entry into the house. We have to take this seriously."

"And you don't think the police will be able to get anything off the doll?" The icy chill from the night before threatened to overtake her once again. She wrapped her fingers around her coffee cup in an effort to get warm again.

"I think it's highly doubtful. I also want you to make a list of everyone who works at the pawn shop with you."

"I can do that, but what do you intend to do with the information?" She took a sip of coffee and eyed him over the rim of the cup.

"I'm going to play at being an amateur detective. At the very least, I can check out their social media and see if anything pops up that might give you a clue as to who is doing this and why."

"So, should I start calling you Sherlock?" She attempted to put a little levity into the situation to ward off the inner chill that threatened.

He flashed a grin. "As long as I get to be Sherlock

without the silly hat and the pipe." His smile faded. "Seriously, Julie, what do you say about getting the security system done today? I'll take care of all the details and will be here for it to be installed."

In an instant a hundred what-ifs went through her head. What if the person hadn't just stopped at the back door to hang a doll, but had broken the window and gotten into the house? With the rumbles of the storm overhead, she and Nick probably wouldn't have known that anyone was inside.

Somebody could have easily crept up the stairs and entered her bedroom. Who knew what could have happened.

"Yes, it's a good idea, and I'd like it done as soon as possible," she replied. She took another sip of her coffee, hoping the warm liquid could heat the cold places inside her their conversation had created. "I'll make that list for you right now."

She got up from the table and went to the built-in desk in the corner of the kitchen. She opened one of the drawers and pulled out a pad of paper and a pen. She then returned to the table and began to list the names of the employees of the pawn shop.

As she wrote down each name, she couldn't help but wonder... *Is this person terrorizing me? Is he or she wanting to harm me? What secret was worth all this?*

"Don't you have any friends? In all the time I've known you, you've never mentioned any personal friends." She looked up to see Nick eyeing her curiously.

She frowned thoughtfully. "I've never really had

time for friends. My mother and Casey are pretty much the only friends I've had. The three of us usually manage to go out about once a month or so for dinner and drinks. Why did you ask?"

"I just wondered if there was anyone else who needs to be written down on that list. Anyone you have interaction with who would know not only your phone number but also your address."

"Not that I can think of," she replied. "But since I can't remember the last ten months of my life, I guess it's possible there might be somebody."

She held his gaze for a long moment. "What I don't understand is, if I was in some kind of trouble before the accident, why didn't I talk to you about it?"

"Unfortunately, I can't answer that." He got up from the table and poured himself another cup of coffee.

Minutes later, after finishing the list of names Nick had requested, she was in the shower and preparing herself for another day at work. But her conversation with Nick lingered in her head.

She'd never really thought about all she'd sacrificed for the family business. There had been no friends in her life, no giggling girls at a slumber party, no best friend to tell all her secrets to. Casey had been a fun little sister, but a younger sibling wasn't the same as having a best friend.

There had been many sacrifices over the years. Running the family business had never been her dream, it had been her parents' dream for her. But she'd never really considered letting them down by choosing something else.

Nick was right. She was still young. She was only thirty-one. She could go back to school and fulfill her dreams for herself. As she rinsed her hair, she envisioned that future.

She and Nick would be married. She'd maybe get a job in a doctor's office where she could be home every evening with her husband. Eventually they'd have children and she would make sure that they got the childhood she'd never had.

Their children would have sleepovers and best friends and, other than chores, they wouldn't start working when they were eight or ten like she had. Instead their childhoods would be filled with laughter and they would have time to just be kids.

All she had to do to make that dream come true was to tell her parents she wanted out. Even thinking about that difficult conversation made her stomach twist and knot with anxiety.

Had she already told her parents she wanted to make some major changes in her life? Somehow she believed she hadn't told them yet. She didn't believe she would have told them until they'd known about Nick.

Until she had her memories back, she'd keep the status quo. She didn't need the drama that would take place in talking to her parents. She had more than enough drama in her life at the moment.

"WHILE YOU WERE in the shower, I contacted a security company who's coming out here at noon," Nick said when they were in the car and heading to the pawn shop.

"Just tell me what it costs and I'll write you a check."

"We'll worry about that later. The important thing is making sure nobody can breach the security of your home," he replied.

She stared at his profile, noting the strength in his jawline and the straightness of his nose. The familiar scent of his cologne wrapped around her. "I always feel safe when I'm with you."

He flashed her a quick glance. "That's nice, but eventually I'll have to go back to work and we'll be on different schedules. The security system will make me feel better about your safety when I'm not around."

Julie stared out the passenger window, dread rising inside her as she thought of Nick going back to work. Hopefully, by the time that happened, the mystery of the threats against her would be solved. And, hopefully, then the only thing on her mind would be planning a wedding.

"I'll be back here at five to pick you up," Nick said as he pulled up to the pawn shop front door.

"If I'm going to be later than that, I'll call you."

She got out of the car and waved as he pulled away.

The door of the shop was already unlocked. She entered to see her brother, Tony, wiping down the display counter with glass cleaner.

"I thought I was working with Casey today," she said.

"She woke up with a sore throat and called Dad, who then called me to come in to work." Tony smiled at her. "I don't mind so much since this gives us a good opportunity to catch up with each other."

"Sounds good to me," she replied. "Want some help?" She gestured to the rest of the dusty display case.

"Nah, I've got it. Just sit and relax while you have a chance."

She sat on one of the tall stools behind the counter and watched as he got back to work. There was only a year's difference in age between her and Tony and she'd always felt closest to him.

They were both alike in temperament. They were both non-confrontational and more introverted than their older brother and younger sister. They had understood each other and had felt most comfortable in each other's company.

"So, what's new in your life? Has anything happened that I don't remember?" she asked.

He finished up dusting and sat. "Absolutely nothing is new."

"Still no girlfriend?"

"Who has time? Your Nick has to be a real patient guy to have put up with your work schedule for so long," he replied.

They only had a few minutes to visit with each other before people began to come in.

Business was steady until just after noon and then once again she and Tony were alone in the shop.

"Why don't I go into the office and make a fresh pot of coffee?" she suggested.

"Sounds good, and while you do that I'll order us some lunch. How does Chinese sound?"

"Hmm, I'm up for some sweet and sour chicken," she replied. There were half a dozen places that delivered and a good Chinese place down the road was one of them. She slid off the stool and was about to head toward the office when he stopped her.

"Julie, you still really don't remember anything?" he asked.

"A few bits and pieces, but nothing that makes any sense."

"Then you don't remember the conversation we had the last time we worked together."

Julie shook her head. "What conversation did we have?"

Tony shrugged. "It doesn't matter."

"Tony, it must have been important since you asked. I'm not going to make the coffee until you tell me what we talked about."

He gave her a wry grin. "Holding coffee hostage is definitely an effective way to make me talk." His grin faded as he gazed at her soberly. "I told you I'd started taking some online college classes because I want out of here."

Surprise winged through her. "Have you told Mom and Dad?"

"No!" he said sharply. "I'm not ready to tell them yet. The only reason I told you was because you told me you wanted out of here, too."

"I do," she replied. "Although I haven't done anything to advance a move right now. But I know having Nick in my life has made me want a more normal schedule, and we both know I won't get that working here."

He nodded in agreement. "I just wanted to make sure if you did remember anything about our conversation that you didn't say anything to Mom and Dad."

"Don't worry, I'll keep your secret, Tony," she assured him.

Was this the secret she wasn't supposed to tell? Was it possible her brother had made the phone call and left the doll hanging on her door? No, it couldn't be possible. There was no way she'd believe it had been her brother. Tony wasn't that kind of man. Was he?

"I'll get the coffee going," she said as she consciously pushed thoughts of the threats she'd received away and Tony away.

She was headed for the office where the coffee machine was located when a vision leaped into her head.

SHE'D LEFT HER phone at work. It was midnight when she realized it. In her car and headed to the shop, she was irritated to be out this late. But she needed her phone since she wasn't working tomorrow...

She entered through the back door and walked into the office, lit only with the dim security lights. Her phone sat right where she'd left it in the middle of the desk. She pulled out the chair, sat and checked to see if any messages had come in that she needed to address.

As she tapped the button to enter her message box, the back door exploded inward. Instantly she jumped up, her heart pounding with terror. Was somebody breaking in to rob the place? On shaky legs, she moved to the office door and peered out—

THE VISION OR memory or whatever it was snapped shut in her mind. She found herself leaning weakly against the office door with the taste of fear lingering heavily in her mouth.

What had happened that night? Who had she seen come in the back door? Had the door been locked or unlocked? She raised her hands to the sides of her head and pressed tightly. Why couldn't she remember anything more?

Had the door been locked or had she left it unlocked when she'd gone into the office? It was an important question that went around and around in her head. If she'd locked the door, then it had been unlocked by a family member or an employee who had the key. If she'd left it unlocked, then any stranger off the street could have come inside.

Something bad had happened that night. She felt the rightness of her thought. It had been something so terrible that her brain was now trying to protect her by not allowing her to remember it. Had she been attacked? Dear God, had she been raped?

Don't tell. The words thundered through her brain and she squeezed her hands more tightly against the sides of her head. Was it possible somebody who worked here, somebody she had trusted, had attacked her and then threatened her not to tell?

Chapter Eight

"I'm sure something happened at the shop," Julie said as Nick drove her home after work. She shared with him the memory she'd had. "It was something bad. I think it was something terrible."

Nick glanced at her. She wore her anxiety in the tiny wrinkle across her forehead and in the way one of her hands moved against the bottom of her throat, as if she was having trouble swallowing.

"There is a bit of good news in all this," he said.

She eyed him in disbelief. "And what would that possibly be?"

"Whatever bad thing might have happened at the pawn shop, you survived it."

She appeared to visibly relax. "Thank you for reminding me of that."

"On another positive note, your new alarm system is installed. It covers all the windows on the lower level and all the doors."

"Then I'll feel perfectly safe when I have to be there all alone," she replied. He felt her gaze on him, warm and loving. "Although I feel safe whenever you're with me."

"But I can't be with you all the time." He tried to ignore the odd feeling of contentment that momentarily gripped him as he bathed in her obvious love for him. It wasn't real, this feeling of being...happy. It couldn't be real. He'd never expected to find happiness again.

It couldn't be real because he was a miserable bastard stuck in grief for his dead wife. It wasn't real because he'd been willing to do an unspeakable act to feed that grief. Finally, it wasn't real because everything he might feel for Julie or she might feel for him was based on a mountain of lies.

He consciously willed these thoughts away as he pulled into her driveway.

For the next twenty minutes he showed her how to work the alarm system.

"I set the code as 0615, but you can change it to whatever you want," he explained.

"Do those numbers mean something special to you?" she asked.

"No," he lied. "They're just random numbers that jumped into my head." But they weren't random numbers. It was actually the date his wife had been taken from him. It had been a beautiful June day that had ended his life as he'd known it.

He had consciously set those particular numbers to remind himself that he didn't belong there with Julie. He'd be reminded of that fact every time he entered Julie's house. This wasn't home and it never would be.

"Random numbers are good with me," she replied.

She plopped down on the sofa. "I don't know if you've thought about what we're doing for dinner, but I was thinking maybe we'd just order in a pizza."

"That sounds good to me," he replied. "What I didn't get a chance to do today is check out the people on the list you gave me. I'd like to do some internet sleuthing this evening if you don't mind me using the laptop in the kitchen."

At least that task would take his mind off the sweet scent of her, off the crazy desire to somehow make all of this real.

"What kind of pizza do you like?" she asked.

"Pepperoni is my favorite, but I'll eat almost anything with pizza sauce and crust."

"My first choice is pepperoni, too." She appeared utterly pleased that they had this in common. "I'm going upstairs to change my clothes and order the pizza. Feel free to use the computer. It's not password protected. I'll be back down in a few minutes."

He breathed a sigh of relief as she headed up the stairs. He wasn't sure why he felt so vulnerable around her this evening. He'd been acutely aware of her from the moment he'd picked her up after work.

Maybe it was because he now knew that beneath her Peterson Pawn shop T-shirt her breasts were soft and welcoming, and he wanted to touch her again. He wanted to make love to her again, and that irritated him. The first time it had happened had been a terrible mistake. If it happened again, he deserved the firing squad.

He walked into the kitchen and pulled the list she

had given him that morning out of his back pocket. He then sat at the built-in desk where a laptop awaited a touch of the power button.

There were seven names. Six men and one woman who worked at the pawn shop, along with the family members. If Julie believed something bad had happened in the shop, then all seven people were potential suspects in whatever Julie couldn't remember.

He was growing more and more ambivalent about her recovering her memories. He wanted her to remember what now had her in danger and yet he didn't want her to remember that she'd never known him before her accident. And that was wrong, so very wrong.

She needed to get her memories back so she would know their relationship wasn't real. She would hate him and throw him out of her life. It was possible she'd go to the police.

Maybe he deserved to be in jail. He'd had homicide in his heart on the night Brian McDowell had been murdered. Thinking about McDowell brought up thoughts of Debbie.

Before Nick could go completely down the rabbit hole, he typed in the first name on Julie's list.

Alexis Bellatore was twenty-seven years old and, according to her social media, she loved antiques, high heels and a man named Ben. She was a cute, slightly plump, woman with short, dark hair and big, dark eyes.

"If you sign into that account with my password, you'll be able to see all of her posts," Julie said from behind him.

He turned to see her in a light pink summer dress

that showcased her creamy shoulders and bare legs. A knot of simmering sparks leaped to life inside him.

She placed a hand on his shoulder and told him her password. "On this site, I'm friends with all the people on the list I gave you."

He typed in her password. "Thanks."

He hoped she would move. He wanted her to take her soft touch and sweet scent away from him. However, she remained.

In fact, she bent over and leaned closer. If he turned his head, she was close enough that he would be able to kiss her beautiful neck. And if that happened, there was no question in his mind she would encourage him to make love to her again.

He closed his eyes for a moment, filled with memories of how her silky skin had felt against his and how hot her mouth had tasted.

"Nick?"

Her laugh pulled him back from his lustful thoughts. He looked at the screen to realize he'd zoned out with his finger on the mouse and the screen now showed posts Alexis Bellatore had posted two years ago.

"Sorry, I zoned out for a minute," he said.

She laughed again, the sound as provocative as his previous thoughts. "I just wondered if you were some kind of an amazing speed reader and hadn't told me about that talent."

"Not hardly," he replied wryly. "I'm going to go through the last ten months of posts for each person and see if anything looks remotely suspicious."

"That's going to take a lot of time," she replied.

"I have plenty of time right now." In an effort to staunch the flames her nearness caused to burn inside him, he tried to conjure up thoughts of his wife.

What had Debbie smelled like? He frowned and stared at the computer screen, desperately trying to remember. He couldn't. All he could think about was the evocative floral scent of Julie.

Thankfully at that moment the doorbell rang. The pizza had arrived.

Minutes later they sat across from each other at the kitchen table.

"I'm not sure there's a better meal than warm pepperoni pizza and cold beer," she said and raised her napkin to wipe at a dab of errant sauce on her chin.

"Barbecue ribs and beer is a close second," he replied.

"I love all the foods that go with ribs…potato salad, baked beans and maybe some garlic Texas toast. Hmm." She half closed her eyes with pleasure.

It was the same kind of look she'd worn when he'd made love to her. Dammit, what was wrong with him? Why did his thoughts keep going there? All he wanted was to solve her mystery, make sure she wasn't in any more danger and then he'd go his own way. He'd return to his life of grief and bitterness, of anger and misery.

They ate for a few minutes in silence. He was reaching for his third piece of the pie when she sat back in her chair and eyed him curiously.

"What?" he asked.

"I didn't know you liked ribs and pepperoni pizza,

although I imagine I knew that before the accident. I was just wondering what else I've forgotten about you."

"You probably forgot that I squeeze the toothpaste tube in the middle," he replied lightly.

She grinned at him. "And I'm sure you remember that I do, too. What else?"

"There's that thing I do with my dirty socks."

"What thing?" she asked.

"Sometimes I forget to pick them up."

"Did I ever say anything about that?" Her eyes were a light denim blue that radiated pleasure.

"Oh, yeah. I believe more than once the word 'pig' popped into your vocabulary."

When her laughter stopped, he looked down at his slice of pizza and then returned his gaze to her. "I think you forgot that I've been married before."

Her eyes widened in shock. "I definitely forgot about that. How many times?"

"Just once." He picked up the slice of pizza from his plate.

"Did you get a divorce?"

He shook his head. Maybe, in talking about this, he'd remember the rage that had kept people at bay for the past three years. Maybe, if he went back to that horrendous day in his life, he'd remember why he wasn't good to anyone anymore.

"I'm a widower," he said. He dropped his pizza to the plate before him. "My wife Debbie was raped and murdered three years ago."

Julie's right hand moved to the base of her throat

and her eyes were soft blue depths he wanted to jump into. Instead, once again, he looked down at his plate.

"Oh, Nick. I'm so sorry," she said. Her hand immediately covered one of his. "How did something so terrible happen? Or maybe you don't want to talk about it."

For the first time since it had happened, he realized he did want to talk about it. "Debbie was a real go-getter and very ambitious. She worked in high-end real estate and loved what she did. One evening she went to show a mansion to a man named Steven Winthrop."

He picked up his beer and took a long swallow, waiting for the rage that usually consumed him. When it didn't come, he continued. "He raped her in that big, empty house. He raped her and then he stabbed her." Julie gasped and he went on. "When she didn't check in with her office, one of her colleagues drove over to the house. She found her and called the police and me. I got there at the same time the police arrived."

Julie's hand tightened around his. "You don't have to tell me any more, Nick. I don't want you going back to that horrible moment in your life."

He closed his eyes, already in that moment, and he waited for the jagged, piercing anger and grief that always found him when he allowed himself to think of Debbie's death. It didn't come.

Instead a deep sadness touched him. A sadness absent of the killing anger. Was this acceptance? Had he finally reached the final stage of grief? He didn't know when or how it had happened.

"It's okay," he finally said. "I don't mind talking about it."

"What happened? Did this Steven Winthrop go to prison?"

Nick shook his head. "Initially he was brought in for questioning, but there wasn't enough evidence to charge him. He got away with murder."

"And you're sure he was guilty?" she asked softly.

"Absolutely. When I got to Debbie, she was one breath away from death. I asked her who did that to her and she said Winthrop."

"But wasn't that enough to get him charged and convicted?" she asked.

Nick sighed. "Unfortunately none of the police officers heard her, and Steven's wife alibied him by saying he never went to the showing, and there was no physical evidence tying him to the scene."

For a moment Nick remembered the angry frustration that had coursed through him for months. "I begged the prosecutor to bring charges, to do something to get that man behind bars, but it didn't happen."

He squeezed Julie's hand and looked into her compassionate, caring, blue eyes. "It was a lifetime ago, Julie. I just needed to share it with you now so you know I'm carrying some baggage into this relationship."

He pulled his hand from hers, wondering what in the hell he was doing. He'd hoped that by talking about Debbie he'd distance himself from Julie, but now that he'd shared his pain with her, he felt closer to her than ever.

"I'm just sorry if you told me all this before that you had to repeat it all now," she said.

"And now we better finish up eating because I want to get back to the computer," he said. "I'm sorry I burdened you with all this."

"Nick, don't ever close off from me. I can handle your past. I can help you burden the pain."

This woman was killing him with her love. He got up from the table. "I'll keep that in mind," he replied, although that had been what he'd intended to do. He definitely felt the need to close off from her.

"I just want to get back to checking out the people on the internet before another day passes. I'm hoping I'll find something that might bring your memories back to you."

He needed that to happen and damn the consequences. He needed to have her gain back her memories before he made the huge mistake of falling in love with her.

Chapter Nine

"I should just stay here with you tonight," Julie said as she came down the stairs. Her mother had called her earlier in the day to make a date for Julie to join Casey and her for a girls' night out.

"I won't be here tonight," Nick replied. "Remember I told you I was meeting with the other coaches this evening."

She walked over and plopped down next to him on the sofa. "I'd still just rather stay at home." She drew in the scent of him, the combination of minty soap and spicy cologne that always stirred her senses and made her feel safe.

She'd been disappointed last night that he hadn't slept with her. When she'd gone up to bed he'd still been on the computer and when she'd awakened this morning she noticed he hadn't joined her in the night. She'd thought they'd moved past any awkwardness where that issue was concerned.

"You told me you always enjoy spending time with your mom and sister," he said.

"Normally, I do, but I have a feeling tonight I'll be

on the hot seat with Casey and Mom asking me far too many questions about you." She released a deep sigh, already anticipating the intense examination that would take place.

"Just go and have a little fun," he replied. "God knows you could use a little fun in your life right now."

"You're my fun."

He gazed at her soberly. "Enjoy your family while you have them, Julie. You never know when they'll be taken away from you."

Instantly she cursed herself for whining. Nick had not only lost his parents too soon, but he'd also lost his wife to a horrendous crime. "You're right," she replied.

She leaned forward and kissed him gently on the cheek. "And someday you and I will have children and we'll all be your family. Were you close to your parents?"

"Very close. As far as I'm concerned, I had the best parents in the world," he replied. "They encouraged and supported me in everything I did and, according to my grandmother, they spoiled me rotten."

A horn sounded from outside. She jumped up off the sofa. "Oh, I hate when Casey does that instead of coming to the front door. I'll be home by nine or so and then maybe you'll tell me some stories about your childhood."

He stood to walk her to the door. "I might be later than nine. I never know for sure how long these meetings are going to last. If you get home before me, just remember to set the alarm."

"Don't worry, I'll definitely remember the alarm."

The horn honked again. "Geez, she makes me crazy. I'll see you later," she said. She walked out the front door to see an unfamiliar car in her driveway. Apparently, Casey had gotten a new car during the time Julie couldn't remember. Julie was surprised she could afford it, especially if what Joel had told her was true and their father had cut her off financially.

Casey was in the driver's seat and Julie's mother was in the passenger seat. Julie opened the back door and slid inside, the smell of new car and rich leather greeting her.

"About time," Casey said as she threw the car into Reverse. "I had to honk twice."

"You didn't have to honk at all," Julie replied drily. "You could have just texted me that you were here or actually walked up to the front door and knocked."

Casey grinned at her in the rearview mirror. "Honking is way more fun."

"I'm just glad to have both my girls with me tonight," Lynetta said. "I've been so crazed trying to organize the house to get it ready to show, I could use a little fun and a few drinks."

"The house ready to show?" Julie looked at the back of her mother's head in confusion.

Lynetta turned around in her seat to look at Julie. "Oh, honey, I guess you don't remember with your amnesia thing. Two months ago your daddy and I decided to downsize. We've already put down a deposit on a nice apartment at North Hills Village."

"But isn't that a retirement place?" Julie asked.

"It is. Of course, we all know your father will never

retire. He'll probably drop dead in that pawn shop. But I'll definitely be retiring from cooking since all our meals will be prepared for us once we make the move." Lynetta turned back around.

Julie stared out the passenger window, her head filled with thoughts of this surprising news. "Where are we going now?" she finally asked.

"Brewsters," Casey replied.

Brewsters was a lively bar that served strong drinks, great burgers and other bar food. The three women had often gone there for a night of hanging out together.

"Casey, when did you get this car?" she asked.

"I've had it for a little over a week now," she replied.

A little over a week? How could she afford such an expensive car if their father had cut her off and she scarcely worked at the shop? He must have caved to his baby girl, Julie thought, not that it was any of her business. Casey had always been the thoroughly spoiled child of the family.

"A mysterious boyfriend is helping her pay for it," Lynetta said, answering Julie's question. "I swear I don't know what's up with you two girls when it comes to the men in your life. Why does everything have to be such a deep, dark secret?"

"Maybe over dinner we can get Casey to spill some secrets about her boyfriend," Julie replied. It would be great if the spotlight was off her and Nick and on Casey instead. "Besides, I did eventually introduce you to Nick."

She didn't want to talk about Nick or their relationship. Despite the fact she'd apparently been dating him for a long time, it all felt so new and so very special right now.

Thankfully, Lynetta continued to talk about the retirement village and all the amenities it offered until they pulled into Brewsters' parking lot. "I'm ready for a nice, refreshing gin and tonic," she said as they all got out of the car.

"And I'm ordering some of their mozzarella sticks with a big Margarita. What about you, Julie?" Casey asked.

"I'm definitely ordering a burger and maybe some fried mushrooms on the side," she replied. "I'm not sure I want any alcohol tonight."

Although Julie couldn't remember the last time she'd been in the bar, stepping inside, she felt instantly at home. The air smelled of onions and burgers and all things fried. The old rock-and-roll music played loud enough to hear but not loud enough to impede conversation.

Lynetta slid into one of the black-leather booths. Casey got in next to her and Julie sat across from them.

The menu was neatly printed on a large chalkboard behind the long, polished bar.

At least nothing on the menu had changed over the past ten months, Julie thought as the waitress approached their table. Minutes later they had all been served their drinks and had placed their food orders.

"So, how are things between you and Nick?" Casey asked.

"Couldn't be better," Julie replied. "Why don't you tell me more about this mysterious man you're dating?"

"Yes, I'd like to know more about him, too," Lynetta said. "Your father and I are worried about both of you with these secret boyfriends and fiancés popping up. You realize eventually you both will have a substantial inheritance and we don't want any man taking advantage of you."

"Ace isn't taking advantage of me, he's treating me right." Casey pointed to the purse on the booth seat next to her. "He bought this for me yesterday."

Julie recognized it as an expensive designer purse. "Pretty lavish. What does Ace do for a living?" she asked. Her sister had always had a penchant for bad boys.

"He's an entrepreneur," Casey replied.

"And what exactly does that mean?" Lynetta asked.

"It means he does a lot of stuff that I don't really understand, but it all makes him lots of money." Casey flipped a strand of her dark hair over her shoulder as if tossing Lynetta's concerns aside. "I don't understand his business stuff, but he's crazy about me and I'm crazy about him, and that's all that matters."

"How long have you been seeing him?" Julie took a sip of her soda and eyed her sister.

"About two months. It was love at first sight."

"Wasn't Granger love at first sight, too?" Julie asked drily. Granger was the last boyfriend she remembered Casey having. That "love at first sight" had lasted about two weeks.

"Granger is old, old news, and besides, that was just a silly crush," Casey replied. "Ace is the real deal," Casey said with certainty.

"And where did you meet this Ace?" Lynetta asked.

"At Freddy's," Casey replied.

Freddy's was a popular bar with a large dance floor that featured local bands. It was also known as a singles pickup joint.

"Do you have a picture of him in your phone?" Julie asked.

"Nah, I haven't taken any of him yet," Casey replied.

"You? The selfie queen?" Lynetta looked at her youngest daughter in disbelief.

Casey grinned. "Oh, I have lots of pictures of me. I just don't have any of him yet."

"So, when do we all get to meet him?" Julie asked.

"In time," Casey replied. "I'm not quite ready to share him yet. Besides, you took months before you let us meet Nick."

Julie definitely understood her sister's desire to keep her man all to herself. That must have been the way she'd felt about Nick in the months before her accident.

Before anyone could say anything else, their meals arrived and the conversation turned to Lynetta and George's move.

"I'm surprised Dad agreed to sell the house," Julie said. "He's got so much stuff in it, I can't imagine how you're going to fit it all into a smaller place."

The family home was a huge old Victorian with five bedrooms and enough "stuff" to fill several warehouses.

"We aren't. I told him he has to take his stuff and put it in the shop for sale or take it to the dump. I have to confess, he really didn't want to make this move, but I told him I was moving with or without him. We don't need all those bedrooms now that you kids are all grown and we definitely don't need a life-size statue of Elvis in our living room." Lynetta frowned. "I don't want second-hand junk in my personal space anymore. I want clean and new and efficient."

"You deserve the life you want," Julie replied with a warm smile at her mother. Lynetta had been a hard-working, hands-on kind of mom. She'd been strict but loving and had the patience of Job when it came to dealing with their father.

"Speaking of living the life you want, are you going to sell your house or is Nick selling his when you two get married?" Casey asked.

"To be honest, we haven't even discussed it," Julie replied. She hoped they'd decide to keep her place even though she had yet to see Nick's. In truth, she couldn't imagine Nick anywhere but in her home with her.

"I have to admit, I'm surprised you and Joel didn't wind up together."

Julie looked at her sister in surprise. "Me and Joel? Why on earth would you think there was anything romantic between us?"

"Before your amnesia, he was really into you," Casey replied.

"What do you mean? What are you talking about?" A faint roar sounded in Julie's ears. It was the roar of rich anger followed by a whimpering helplessness that she couldn't remember.

"About two months ago you talked to me and told me you thought Joel had a major crush on you. You really don't remember anything that happened before your accident?" Casey looked at her as if she were a bug under a microscope.

"Not much. A flash here and there, but so far I haven't been able to make much sense of them," Julie replied. "So, how did I feel about Joel having a crush on me?"

"A little creeped out," Casey replied. "At least, that's what you told me. I know he has lots of pictures of you up on his social media page, and that is definitely creepy."

Julie thought of the slightly overweight, easygoing Joel and a faint chill worked up her spine. Was it possible he was the one who had come through the pawn shop's back door on the night she'd forgotten her phone?

She had never been attracted to Joel on a romantic level, although she'd considered him a good friend and coworker. Had he somehow confronted her and professed his love for her that night and, when she wasn't interested in him, had he attacked her in some way?

She'd worked with him the day before and had sensed nothing off between them. He'd been his usual friendly and helpful self just like she remembered him from ten months ago.

But he'd also asked her a lot of questions about her amnesia during a lull in traffic at the shop. He'd asked what the doctors had told her about regaining her memories. Had she started to remember anything at all? Did she expect her memories to ever return?

Were they the normal questions that any person

might ask of somebody suffering from amnesia? Or were they the questions of an attacker assuring himself that he was still safe?

NICK LEFT JULIE'S place at just after seven, grateful that cloud cover would make the darkness of night arrive early. Since the time Julie had left the house, Nick had been consumed with thoughts of murder. And, thank God, on this night in particular, she'd had plans with her mother and sister, because he'd lied to her once again. He wasn't meeting with his fellow coaches. He was meeting with the men who'd planned not only Brian's murder, but the murders of five other people, as well.

The minute Julie had left the house he'd used the internet to check every local news source he could to see if there were any updates on the McDowell murder. He'd found nothing. He hated to be out of the loop on a matter that could touch his life in such a negative way.

He'd spent the rest of the evening pacing, contemplating what might come tonight when he met the others. The six of them had originally gotten to know each other at the Northland Survivor group meetings. However, since that time, four of the men had stopped going to the meetings. They didn't want a place where they were all connected should the police get close to them.

After the meeting, after complete darkness fell, they would all meet at the Oak Ridge Park. The space had once been a popular place for people to picnic and play baseball, but over the years better parks had been built. Now the trees and bushes, the grass and weeds, had encroached in an attempt to take back what had once been theirs.

The Northland Survivor meeting took place in the basement of a Methodist church, although it wasn't church sponsored.

At six fifty that evening, he pulled into the parking lot and steeled himself for sitting through the meeting. All he really wanted to do was to talk to the others about the fact that he had not been the one who had killed Brian McDowell. Somebody had committed that murder mere minutes before Nick had arrived.

As always, the meeting room smelled of strong, fresh coffee and deep, abiding grief. Janet McCall, the founder of the group, greeted him as he walked in.

Janet had been married for fifteen years when her husband had been brutally murdered as he'd left a downtown restaurant after a business meeting. When his body had been found, his wallet was empty and his cell phone was gone. He'd been killed for fifteen bucks and a phone.

According to Janet, her grief had nearly driven her to suicide.

Instead of taking a complete grief-stricken head-dive, she had started this group for people to talk and hopefully heal.

"How have you been, Nick?" Her brown eyes studied his features carefully.

"Not too bad," he replied.

"I can see a new lightness about you." She smiled at him warmly. "I'm glad. Now, get yourself a cup of coffee and don't forget to try one of my lemon bars."

"Will do," he replied. As he walked over to the refreshment table, he thought about what Janet had said about a new lightness in him. And that lightness had a name—Julie.

She had given him something indefinable, something that had brought him back from the brink of despair. With her, he'd found his laughter again. He was looking forward rather than backward. He didn't know what his future might hold, but for the first time since Debbie's murder, he actually believed he had a future.

If he wasn't arrested for a murder he hadn't committed.

He carried his coffee to sit in one of the folding chairs that formed a large circle. He nodded at several familiar people, including Troy Anderson. Three years ago, Troy's eight-year-old daughter had been kidnapped and killed. Troy was one of the six men who had come together in their need-for-vengeance pact.

Within minutes, people began to fill the seats. This group wasn't just about the collateral damage left behind by murder. It was also for anyone who had lost somebody in their life and was dealing with debilitating grief.

By the time Janet began to facilitate the meeting, there was only one unfamiliar face in the group. A heavyset woman with bleached-blond hair and heavy blue eyeliner sat next to Janet.

"Before we get started this evening, I'd like to introduce Jacqueline Kelly, who is with us for the first time." Janet placed a hand on the woman's thick shoulder. "Jacqueline, can you tell us what brought you here tonight?"

Huge tears welled up in her eyes as she looked around. "I'm here because my boyfriend was murdered and I don't know what I'm going to do without him." A huge sob choked out of her. "He helped take care of me and my kids, and he was murdered right in his own house. Somebody came in and slit Brian's throat." She began to weep in earnest.

Nick froze. His heart stopped and then beat so fast a whoosh of blood filled his head and momentarily deafened him. There was no question that she was talking about the man Nick had seen dead behind a shattered sliding-glass door. A man Nick had been prepared to murder.

As his hearing returned, he listened to Jacqueline's keening grief. God, he knew that grief so intimately. Yet, in the midst of his rage, he'd never considered that the people they'd intended to kill might have girlfriends or wives or daughters and sons. That they could have other family members and best friends who would deeply mourn their deaths.

The pact he'd made with the other men now felt more than a little bit evil. No matter who they murdered, it wouldn't bring Debbie or any of their loved ones back. He wasn't sure if he'd actually been able to pull the trigger to kill Brian McDowell or not. All he was certain of was his huge need to speak with the other men and maybe try to call a halt to their collective madness.

The rest of the meeting was a study in torture for

Nick. He tried not to look at Jacqueline and he also kept his gaze averted from Troy.

During the fifteen-minute break, he got another cup of coffee and one of Janet's lemon bars, and then returned to his seat. The program for tonight was being led by a psychologist who would speak about the power of forgiveness.

Nick only half listened to the plump professional, who had a dreadful, monotonic delivery and stood perfectly still as he spoke. Instead, Nick watched the big round clock on the wall, inching toward the time to end the meeting.

It was just after nine when the meeting adjourned.

Once again Nick was grateful for the cloud cover that made for an early nightfall. Talk of murder deserved to be in the darkness.

He clenched the steering wheel tight as he drove to the park, a large ball of tension rolling around in the pit of his stomach.

He was certain one of the other men had killed McDowell. Was it possible that somehow wires had gotten crossed? Adam Kincaid had taken the lead in the plan that had been hatched. He'd made sure the left hand didn't know what the right hand was doing. Had he somehow made a mistake?

It didn't matter now. Brian McDowell was dead. What did matter was that Nick intended to try to talk the other men into halting this madness…this lust for vengeance they had all fallen victim to.

Was justice really theirs to deliver? Who did they think they were to be the arbiters of death? He had to believe that somehow karma took care of things. He needed to believe that the guilty eventually paid a price, whether in this life or the next. But what he had planned with the five other men had been wrong.

Seeing Jacqueline had put a new spin on things for him. Or was it Julie's presence in his life that had calmed the beast inside him? He didn't know the answer, but he felt a huge shift had occurred inside him.

He pulled into the parking lot of the abandoned park and drove straight ahead, off the broken asphalt and across the old ball field toward a stand of trees.

He was the first one to arrive. He parked and then grabbed a flashlight from his glove compartment. He got out of the car and headed deeper into the woods.

Once he reached the designated meeting place, he eased down onto a fallen tree trunk to wait. A faint breeze whispered through the treetops and all around him the night insects clicked and whirred. Cicadas played their noisy rhythm as if telling him he didn't belong there.

And he didn't. He was ready to close this chapter of his life. Whatever his future might hold, he didn't want to carry the rage, the all-consuming grief and that bloodlust inside him anymore.

"Hey." Troy Anderson's deep voice pulled Nick out of his thoughts. "Intense meeting for you, huh. You okay?"

"Yeah, I'm better than I've been in years," Nick replied. There was no point in telling Troy about McDowell and Nick's change of heart before the other men arrived. He would just have to repeat himself.

"I guess tonight just proves it's a small world. Who would have thought McDowell's girlfriend would show up at the same meeting as you," Troy said.

"Yeah, who would have thought," Nick replied.

Before any further discussion could occur, Matt Tanner and Clay Rogers arrived.

Matt immediately walked over to Nick and patted him on the shoulder. "Thank you, man," he said, and Nick knew he was congratulating him on killing the person who had beaten Matt's mother to death and had gotten away with the crime. "I'm so glad that bastard is dead."

"Don't thank me yet," Nick replied.

Matt looked at him curiously, but at that moment Adam Kincaid and Jake Lamont stepped into the small clearing.

The unholy six men were together again.

Nick became aware that the woods had quieted. The insects had stopped clicking and the cicadas had stopped singing as if in disapproval of this covert meeting.

"We need to make this fast," Adam said. "You know we're all at risk when we're together."

"I didn't kill Brian McDowell," Nick said without preamble.

"What are you talking about?" Adam turned on a flashlight and directed it at Nick's face. "I sent you everything to kill him. You were the one I assigned to kill him, and I saw in the paper the report of his murder."

"Somebody got to him before me." Nick squinted against the brightness of Adam's flashlight beam and

told the men about the night he had gone to kill Mc-
Dowell. "If one of you didn't jump the gun, then somebody else is in on the game."

"Nobody else better be in on the game," Adam said.
"That puts us all at risk."

All the other men vehemently denied having told
anyone of the plan. "I want out," Nick said. "I think
all of us should just forget this whole idea and get on
with our lives."

"No way," Troy said, anger lacing his deep voice.
"You're just saying that because you saw Jacqueline
cry at the meeting. Just remember, if she'd had anything he'd wanted, he would have killed her to get it.
He beat Matt's mother to death. We did her a favor by
getting him out of her life. Besides, I want the man
who killed my daughter dead. I want him dead so he
can't prey on any other little girls."

"And I can't tell you how good it feels to know Brian
McDowell will never kill a vulnerable old woman
again," Matt said, his voice also rich with emotion.
"This is a good plan. We're taking out killers who we
all know would probably re-offend."

"Doesn't it bother you all that somebody got to Brian
on the exact night, at the exact time, I was supposed
to act?" Nick asked as he looked from man to man.

"McDowell was a creep. Creeps make enemies. It
was probably just a weird coincidence that somebody
got to him right before you did," Jake stated.

"I don't think so," Nick replied. "I don't know which
one of you is responsible, but one of you killed him."

When none of the others spoke, Nick released a deep

sigh. "I've said what I came here to say. I don't want this to go forward. I don't want to be a part of it and I definitely don't want one of you to kill Steven Winthrop. Nobody should have his blood on their hands. Let karma take care of him. In any case, he'll burn in hell for what he did." He'd said what he needed to say and there was nothing more that he could do.

"We're all in this together," Adam said sharply. "Anyone else have doubts about what we're doing?" He looked at each of the other men. "Anyone else want out?"

"We're all still in," Matt said firmly.

"Then I suggest we get out of here," Adam replied. "Wait for your instructions and keep your mouths shut."

"I'm out of here for good," Nick said. "My assignment is finished and there's no reason for me to meet here again. Don't worry, I will take this secret to the grave with me, but I'm in a place where all I want to do now is build my future."

Minutes later Nick was in his car and headed toward home. No, he corrected himself. He was headed toward Julie's place. It would never be his home.

He was ready to build a future, but how could Julie be a part of it? How long could he continue to live a lie? The longer they were together, the more difficult it would be when the truth finally came out.

A headache began to pound at his temples and a wave of soul-sickness, of utter exhaustion, overtook him. He had no idea who had killed Brian McDowell, but suspected one of the others was responsible. He'd been stark raving mad when he'd agreed to the vigilante plot in the first place.

That time in his life would always haunt him. The men who continued on the path of seeking justice would haunt him, as well. Even if they found the justice they sought, they would realize it was an empty reward.

He released a deep sigh and tried to empty his brain.

He was in love with Julie.

The sudden realization momentarily stole the breath from his lungs. Someway, since the night of the accident, Julie had become far more than a convenient alibi. She'd become the woman he wanted to spend the rest of his life with.

He'd be a fool to believe there was any hope for a future with her. He now had to figure out how to gain some emotional distance from her. He had to stop loving her.

More importantly, he had to make her stop loving him.

Chapter Ten

The minute Julie got home from dinner she sat at her desk and pulled up Joel's social media page. Looking in his picture section, she was surprised by all the photos she saw of herself.

Yet, as she looked at them carefully, memories began to blossom in her mind. She remembered three months ago when a customer had come in with a hat shaped like a snarling, long-toothed vampire. Her father had loved it and bought it. Julie had put it on, made a face, and Joel had taken a picture of her.

They had taken selfies together. He'd snapped a picture of her while she was dusting the jewelry display counter and another when she'd had her first bite of sushi for lunch.

Excitement and confusion filled her at the same time. She remembered in detail when each and every photograph had been taken, and that excited her. What confused her was why Casey would have thought the pictures were somehow creepy in any way.

They were just the kind of pictures coworkers... friends took of each other. They were ordinary photos. It wasn't like he had secretly taken pictures of her grocery shopping or getting out of her car in her driveway, as if he were stalking her.

But apparently she'd told Casey she'd thought Joel had a crush on her. She'd told her sister she'd been creeped out by it, and that's what had her confused.

She'd worked with Joel several days since her accident and hadn't gotten any strange vibes off him. Had he done something terrible to her that she just couldn't remember?

She started as she heard the front door open. The alarm system began its countdown to full siren, but halted when the code was punched in. Nick was home.

She jumped out of the chair, eager to see him, to find out how his meeting had gone and to talk to him about what Casey had said about Joel.

He walked into the living room at the same time she did. His shoulders cast forward slightly and he looked totally drained of energy.

"Nick, are you all right?" She grabbed him by the hand and led him to the sofa. "You look exhausted. Did something happen at your meeting?"

He pulled his hand from hers and sat back. "No, everything went fine. I'm just beyond exhausted tonight. How did your dinner go?"

"The same as they always go. It was fine." She studied his features. The lines of his face that she'd always found attractive were now deeper and his eyes were without their usual brightness. "Nick, go on to bed. You look absolutely sick with exhaustion."

"I think I'll do that." He pulled himself to his feet.

"You can sleep as late as you want in the morning," she said as she also rose from the sofa. "For the next few days, I'm working the evening shift."

He nodded, as if just too tired to speak. With a wave of his hand, he headed toward the stairs.

She watched him go, wishing he'd join her in her bed, but knowing he'd go to the guest room.

She'd wanted to talk to him about Joel. She'd wanted to tell him about Casey's new boyfriend and that her parents were moving, and she'd wanted to hear all about his meeting. But all that could wait until morning.

She returned to the kitchen where she turned off the computer.

It was late enough she was ready for a good night's sleep, as well. She climbed the stairs, a touch of worry and guilt rising inside her.

He'd said his meeting had gone fine, but she wasn't sure she believed it. What if the other coaches had given him a bad time about being so absent? Had he not told her that football practices had already begun and he wasn't attending them because he was too busy babysitting her?

The last thing she wanted to do was to cause him trouble where he worked. How much was she really interfering in his life? Or maybe she was just imagining things. Maybe he was simply a tired man and everything would be fine in the morning.

However, the next morning he was unusually quiet and withdrawn as they sat together at the table having coffee.

"Is something wrong, Nick? Have I done something wrong?"

"Not at all. Why do you ask?" His eyes were dark, guarded, as he gazed at her.

"You just seem rather distant," she replied.

"I've got a lot of things on my mind." He raised his cup to his lips and averted his gaze from hers.

"Is there anything I can help with?" She hated seeing him this way, without the sparkle in his eyes and the beautiful smile on his lips.

"No. I've just got some things I need to work through in my head. So, tell me about your dinner last night."

"We went to Brewsters," she began.

"I love their food. Several of us sometimes go in there to get a tenderloin sandwich after games."

"I've never tried their tenderloin. I'm all about their fried mushrooms," she replied, pleased to see him start to relax as his eyes began to sparkle.

"Nothing better than good, fried bar food. I'm glad you're a woman who doesn't eat rabbit food for every meal."

She laughed. "That's so not me. Sure, I watch my weight, but I also indulge my love of junk food whenever I can."

"Were there any surprises last night? Any flashes of memory?"

She shook her head. "The biggest surprise is that I didn't remember that my parents are in the process of moving into a senior living place. I didn't have any flashes of memory until I got back here."

He raised a brow. "What happened when you got back here?"

She explained to him what Casey had told her about Joel. "I remembered when all the pictures were taken as I looked at them. He does have a lot of pictures of me on his social media, but remembering when they were taken, they don't seem odd at all to me."

"And you didn't get any strange feelings about Joel?"

"None. But Casey said before the accident I was creeped out about him. I've worked with him a couple of times since the accident and I haven't felt creeped out at all." An edge of frustration leaped into her voice. "Dammit, I need my memories back right now."

"I know you're anxious to get them back." He paused to take a drink of his coffee. "I didn't get to Joel when I was checking social media for all the people who worked at the shop. He was one of the last names you wrote down." He drained his coffee cup and stood. "Let me check him out right now." He moved from the table to the hard-backed chair in front of the desk.

She got up and walked over to stand just behind him, enjoying the freshly showered scent of him that stirred a sweet, hot desire inside her. As he waited for the computer to boot up, she moved even closer to him and placed her hands on his shoulders.

She loved the play of his muscles beneath his T-shirt. She remembered how his warm, bare skin had felt against her when they'd made love.

She hungered to repeat the experience. Even though she didn't have her memories of him before, at least they were building new memories together every day.

He pulled up Joel's pages and leaned forward, displacing her hands from him. "You specifically remember when these were all taken?" he asked.

"Each and every one," she replied. "And I didn't feel anything odd or creepy when we took them. We were just goofing around at work."

He turned around in the chair and she stepped back from him. "And yet you told your sister he was creeping you out."

"That's what Casey told me."

They moved back to the kitchen table. "I worked with him and didn't feel a bit uncomfortable," she repeated, struggling to make sense of it all.

"When do you work with him again?"

"I think maybe tomorrow night," she replied. "But I think my dad is on the schedule that night, too."

Nick held her gaze intently. "Have you told your family about everything that's going on?"

"No. I haven't mentioned anything about the phone call or the doll. I haven't told them that somebody is after me for something I'm not supposed to tell."

"Why haven't you told them?"

She frowned thoughtfully. She knew the answer and she was slightly ashamed to say it out loud. "Right now the only person I completely trust in the whole wide world is you."

"Then you think one of your family members is responsible?" He looked at her with a touch of surprise.

"I don't know," she replied, the frustration back in her voice. "I certainly don't want to believe that, but right now I don't feel comfortable talking to any of them about this. There's a little voice in the back of my head that keeps whispering I should keep all this a secret where they are concerned."

"You need to remember, Julie."

"I know, but I feel like the harder I try, the less likely it is to happen." Anxiety tightened her chest. Her missing memories not only had her at risk, but she also thought some of the distance she felt from Nick was because of those missing memories.

"Nick, my lack of memories shouldn't play a role in our relationship," she said softly. "Even if I don't remember being in love with you, I'm falling in love with you all over again." She felt the warmth that leaped into her cheeks at this confession.

He scooted his chair away from the table and stood. "But it does make a difference to me. Every time I touch you, I feel like I'm taking advantage of you because you can't remember me."

"I love it when you touch me. Nick, the last thing you're doing is taking advantage of me. If anything, I'm taking advantage of you by wanting you here with me all the time. The last thing I want to do is interfere with your work."

"Speaking of work, I do have some phone calls and other business to attend to this morning. If you don't mind, I'll just head on up to my bedroom to get to it." He looked at some point just over the top of her head. "Just let me know if you need anything."

She watched him go, her heart thudding a dull rhythm. Was he tired of her? Tired of the drama that filled her life right now? She couldn't blame him if he was. He'd been a prisoner to her drama, trapped with her because somebody was after her and she couldn't remember why. Dammit, she was tired of it all.

She didn't remember loving him, but she had to do something to remind him of loving her. She just wasn't sure what to do to change the dynamics between them right now.

Somehow they had gotten all messed up since the night they had made love. She desperately needed to remember everything that remained in the shadows of her mind. She felt as if everything she held dear was slipping away from her.

Three days later nothing had changed. Nick continued to be distant and Julie continued to fear that the man of her dreams was about to walk out of her life.

They were a subdued pair as Nick drove her to work at four o'clock. The past three days had been difficult ones. Between meals, he'd kept himself holed up in his bedroom. During meals, their conversations were slightly strained.

She released a deep sigh as he pulled up at the pawn shop's back door. "I'll be back here at nine thirty to pick you up," he said, his gaze focused on the steering wheel.

She reached out and curled her fingers around his upper arm. "Nick," she said. His green eyes finally looked at her. "I don't know what's going on between us right now, but I don't like it. You're withdrawing from me and I don't know what to do about it. I miss you. I miss us."

His eyes darkened in hue. He reached out and

dragged a finger gently down her cheek. "I'm going through some things right now, Julie." He pulled his finger back as if her skin had burned him. "I just need a little space."

"Is it anything I can help with? I mean, whatever is happening, we're in this together, right?" She fought the impulse to tighten her fingers on him, the desire to keep him close to her forever.

He shook his head. "This is something I need to work through myself."

What issue could he have that he was working on? She wanted to ask him if they were in trouble. If his feelings for her had changed. But she was afraid of the answer so she didn't ask. "Okay, then… I'll see you later," she said and got out of his car.

As she opened the door to the pawn shop she wasn't sure what she feared most: the person who had left the doll for her or the possibility that Nick might leave her.

She'd never been a needy person before. But her life felt so wildly out of control right now and Nick was the only thing substantial she had to hang on to.

She was grateful that she was working with Max, even though he was irritated that he was taking over Casey's shift. Apparently, Casey had the flu. At least, that's what she'd told Max when she'd called him to tell him she couldn't work tonight.

Julie was glad to work with her older brother, who was superefficient and quick in dealing with customers. Casey usually flirted with all the men who came in and took forever to do a fairly simple pawn or sale. Julie also spent half her time working with Casey trying to get her out of the office where she'd sit and paint her fingernails or talk on her cell phone.

Still, it was a fairly difficult and busy night. Whenever the end of the month approached, more people came in to pawn items, desperate for a little money to get them by until their disability or pay check came in after the first of the month.

It was getting toward the end of the night when Ed Graham walked in. Julie stifled a groan. Ed was a frequent customer and usually threw a tizzy fit when they didn't offer him what he believed his "treasures" were worth. It was funny that she remembered him but couldn't remember the really important things in her life.

Max was busy ringing up a woman who was buying dozens of DVDs and Julie steeled herself as Ed stalked up to the counter.

"Ed." She greeted him with a pleasant smile that he didn't return.

"You've got to do me right this time," he said. "You've screwed me over and over again, but I need three hundred bucks until the third of the month." He dug into his pocket and withdrew a pocket watch. "This belonged to my daddy and his daddy before him." For a moment he held it tightly in his meaty fist and then laid it down on the countertop.

Julie grabbed a jeweler's loop and took a closer look at it. There was nothing special about the watch. It wasn't even fourteen karat gold.

"Ed, I can't give you anywhere close to three hundred dollars for this," she said.

"Dammit, Julie. It's an antique. It's got to be worth that." His broad face began to flush with anger and his nostrils flared. "So, how much can you give me?"

"No more than fifty," Julie replied.

"Fifty?" The word exploded out of him like a gunshot. "You've got to be out of your freaking mind." He grabbed the watch and shoved it back in his pants' pocket. "I knew you'd try to screw me again. You all are nothing but a pack of shysters. This will be the last time I'll ever come in here to do business."

As he stormed out the door, Max looked over at Julie and grinned. "He'll be back. He always comes back."

Julie knew Max was right. Ed Graham was one of their regulars and, if he stayed true to form, he'd be back tomorrow or the day after and take whatever they were willing to give him for the pocket watch.

It was just after nine when she and Max found themselves alone in the shop. "Since I wasn't even on the schedule to work tonight, can you close up so I can go ahead and get out of here?" he asked.

"No problem," she replied. Nick would arrive at nine thirty to pick her up and she certainly didn't anticipate a rush of customers at this time of night. It was rare that anyone came in after nine in the evening.

Minutes later Max was gone and Julie was by herself in the shop. And it didn't take her long to feel a little creeped out. She checked the clock. Ten after nine. To hell with it, she was closing up shop now.

Out of one of the cash registers' drawers, she grabbed the key she needed to lock up and then headed for the front door. She'd just locked the door when the lights went out.

She froze. What now? Did a fuse blow? It happened rarely, but it did happen. The only illumination now was from a nearby streetlight and that barely seeped into the shop.

There was a rush of air as a big shadow appeared out of the darkness. The shadow slammed into her. Her breath expelled out of her as she flew backward and to the floor. The back of her head banged against the wood and a moan escaped her.

Still, she scrabbled backward using her feet and elbows, her brain frozen with fear. Not a shadow… a person. And there was no question that he intended to hurt her.

She gasped for breath and finally released a scream as he grabbed her by the ankle and began to pull her toward him.

His grip was strong, so damned strong. Kicking and twisting, in the back of her mind she knew this wasn't a robbery attempt. In the faint light she saw him: a well-built man clad all in black and wearing a ski mask.

If he wanted to rob the store, he could have just waited fifteen minutes for her to leave. In horror she recognized he was after her. He'd been hiding someplace in the store and had waited to attack until she was all alone.

"What do you want?" she screamed as she fought to get away from him.

"I want to make sure you never tell what you know,"

he roared. He threw himself on top of her and wrapped his gloved hands around her throat.

Her scream was a mere gurgle as he tightened his hold on her. She tried to gasp for air, but there was none. He growled like a wild animal as he kept her pinned to the floor, his hands squeezing…squeezing… squeezing the very life out of her.

Her instinct was to grab his hands to try to pull them away from her throat as she weakened with every second. Instead she poked at his eyes in desperation as darkness began to seep around the edges of her consciousness.

One of her jabs finally hit its mark. He roared in pain and released his hold. She rolled away from him, gasping for air, and then staggered to her feet and ran.

"You bitch," he yelled.

The darkness was her friend now. She knew the inside of the pawn shop like the back of her hand. She moved silently among the shelves, working her way toward the office where she could either lock herself inside or escape out the back door.

Nick, where are you? How much time was left before he arrived? She stifled a scream as the man snarled again. He was like a panther hunting prey. A crash sounded, followed by another curse. Another crash… this one closer.

Suddenly he was there. She saw only the big, dark bulk of him, standing between her and the back door. She veered to the left and headed toward the second room.

She entered the room, her mind frantically trying

to think of a hiding place. The man was definitely too big and strong for her to try to fight. The only way she would survive this night was if she hid until Nick arrived.

Nick. Her heart cried his name. Wasn't it time for him to be there? God, it felt like a lifetime had passed since the lights in the shop had gone off.

Would the man find her behind the genie? She definitely didn't want to run into the bathroom. Even though it had a lock, she knew the man could get through the flimsy hollow wood door and then she'd be at a dead end with no escape possible.

She suddenly remembered the large penguin had a hidey-hole in its belly and that's where she went. She crouched down and slapped a hand over her mouth to silence the screams that begged to be released. Her heart beat so fast she felt dizzy.

"Julie."

The voice whispered so close by she imagined she could feel his fetid breath on her neck. Her heart stopped beating as she realized despite her frantic thinking she'd put herself in a space with no exit.

If he found her, she'd have nowhere to run.

Chapter Eleven

Nick parked outside the pawn shop's back door and got out of his car. He paused and drew a deep breath. He was exhausted. Trying to maintain emotional and physical distance from Julie was much more difficult than he'd imagined.

After Debbie died, he never thought he'd fall in love again, but now he couldn't figure out how to stop loving Julie. Was this his karma for even thinking about taking somebody else's life? That he would fall in love and see a future filled with happiness for himself but it would not be his to obtain?

He looked up at the moon, a thousand regrets sweeping through him. He felt as if he were a locomotive barreling down the tracks into a brick wall.

He released a deep sigh. The last thing he wanted to do was to stand outside in the dark and think of all the crazy twists and turns his life had taken since he'd made the pact with five other grieving men.

He opened the shop's back door and blinked at the darkness that greeted him. Every muscle tensed. What in the hell was going on?

"Julie?"

"Nick!" Fear laced her voice, which was oddly muffled and came from someplace to his right.

He took several steps in that direction and gasped as somebody shoved him from behind. He turned in time to see a man disappear out the back door.

"Hey!" Nick yelled after him at the same time his heart did a nosedive. Julie! What had the man done to her? Was she hurt someplace in the dark?

"Julie, where are you? Are you okay?" Dammit, without the lights he would have a hard time finding her.

"I'm here."

"Keep talking, honey, and I'll find you."

"Max left early and...and...the man must have hidden in the shop."

Her voice came from his right again and even though he wanted to run to her, he walked carefully through the darkness.

"He...he attacked me when I locked the front door." Her voice was louder now. "Is he gone?"

"He's gone. Honey, it's safe for you to come out now."

"Okay, I'm coming out." He heard her words right before she flew out of the darkness and into his arms.

"Thank God," she cried, her entire body trembling against him.

"What happened? Did he hurt you?" he asked.

She shook her head, unable to speak around her deep sobs.

"Come on, let's go outside." He wasn't comfortable standing in the dark shop. He didn't know where the man had gone when he'd run out of the shop. Or if he'd come back.

She clung to him as he moved them out of the shop and next to his car. He gazed around in all directions, tensing for any danger that might come out of the night. But he saw nobody.

Finally Julie's sobs eased enough that she could talk.

"He wanted to kill me," she said. She raised her head to look at him and in the depths of her eyes he saw her terror. "He...he said he'd make sure I never told what I know." A burst of hysterical laughter escaped her. "It must be one hell of a secret I've got in my stupid mind."

"We need to call the police." Nick grabbed his cell phone out of his pocket.

"And call my father," she said. "He needs to know what's going on."

Julie sat in the safety of his car while he made the calls and then he joined her there to wait for the others to arrive. He started the engine so the air conditioner would cool them down.

"He must have been hiding inside," she said. Her voice trembled and her face was shockingly pale in the light from the dash. "He waited until Max left. I locked the front door and the lights suddenly went out and then he attacked me." One of her hands rose to her throat. "He tried to strangle me but I managed to poke him in the eye and get away. I hide in that big penguin."

"I'm so sorry, Julie." He reached out and grabbed her hand. "I'm sorry you had to go through that." It was obvious now that they had underestimated the enemy.

The danger was real. It had come out of nowhere and had almost been deadly.

He squeezed her hand. "Thank God you got away." The back of his throat threatened to close up as he thought of what might have happened tonight.

Before he could say anything else, a police car pulled into the parking lot. The lights swirled blue and red colors that splashed across the back of the building.

They both got out of the car to greet the two officers who had responded to his call.

Nick placed his arm around Julie's shoulder as she explained what had happened.

The officers asked them both questions about the description of the person who had attacked her, but neither of them could say anything that helped. Nick hadn't even known the man wore a ski mask until Julie told the officers. Julie also told them about the phone call and the doll that had been left hanging in the doorway on her deck.

By that time George arrived. He jumped out of his car, a grim expression on his face. "What in the hell happened here?"

Julie briefly filled her father in on what had occurred in the shop.

However, the one thing she didn't tell George was about the man making it clear that he intended to kill her because of a secret she possessed.

With the aid of the officers' flashlights, George discovered the breaker in the office had been flipped, causing the electricity to shut off.

With the lights back on again, they all went inside

where George cursed at the loss of a large decorative vase that lay shattered on the floor and a television that had been knocked over and cracked.

"There had to be more than one person involved," Julie said. Her face was still void of her natural color. "Somebody had to be in the office to flip the breaker while the other person attacked me."

Nick's blood chilled. He hadn't considered that before. Having one person threatening her by phone and by leaving a horrible doll on her deck was one thing. Knowing there was more than one person involved was far more ominous.

He and Julie stayed in the office while Officer Jason Killion and Officer Mark Bradford checked out the place with George.

Nick and Julie waited in silence. The situation didn't warrant small talk and Julie appeared too shell-shocked to want any conversation.

She looked small and frail sitting in the chair in front of the desk. He hated it. He never wanted to see her as frightened as she was for the rest of her life.

Finally, George and the two officers joined Nick and Julie in the office. "There isn't much we can do at this point," Officer Killion said. "You told us he wore gloves, so there's no point in trying to fingerprint anything. And without any kind of description of the perp, we wouldn't know where to begin to find him."

"Call us if anything else occurs to you or if you remember something that would help us get the perpetrators," Officer Bradford said to Julie.

"Trust me, you'll be the first people I call," Julie replied.

Within minutes the officers were gone. "From now on, you aren't left alone in the store," George said to Julie.

"From now on, Julie is on vacation," Nick replied.

Julie gazed at him gratefully and George frowned in obvious irritation.

"Julie knows this place can't function without her, especially on such short notice," he said. "Tell him, girly. Tell him I need you here."

"I think I need some time off," Julie said softly. She didn't look at her father. "Dad, somebody tried to kill me tonight. I'm sorry, but until we figure out what's going on, I don't want to come in to work."

Nick watched as George's expression softened. "Okay, I'll figure things out here," he said. "Take all the time you need, honey."

"I'm taking her home right now," Nick said, knowing what she needed now more than anything was the sense of safety she would find at home behind locked doors.

George nodded. "Call me and let me know how you're doing," he said to Julie. "You know this was probably some sort of robbery attempt. Probably some druggie looking for a quick score of things he could fence."

"You need to install a camera in the second room so we can see from the office if anyone is in there at closing time," Julie replied.

"I'll get it done this week," George replied.

Minutes later Nick and Julie were headed home. "Thank you for telling my dad I was taking a bit of a vacation," she said. "I don't think I could face going back in there tomorrow night. I've never been so afraid in my entire life."

"I never want to see you that afraid again," Nick replied. Even thinking about what she'd experienced caused his heart to leap into his throat.

"I just wish I knew what was going on." She released a deep, tremulous sigh. "Maybe it's time I contact the doctor and get a referral to somebody who can help me retrieve my missing memories. Maybe I need to see a hypnotist and see if he or she can help me."

"I want you to do whatever it takes to get well." It was true. Nick wanted her to regain her memories because that might be the only thing that saved her from the people who wanted her dead.

It would be the death of his relationship with her but, more than anything, he wanted her safe. Eventually she'd forget about the man who had lied to her and she'd find a good man who would fulfill all her dreams.

A wave of dark depression descended upon him. It was the same feeling he'd had in the days and weeks after Debbie's murder before the rage had overtaken him.

He knew with certainty the self-destructive fury he'd felt at that time was gone forever, and yet it had been that anger that had brought Julie to him.

If he hadn't gone to Brian McDowell's house to kill him, then he wouldn't have been on the street when

Julie had wrecked her car. He wouldn't be with her now, already mourning the loss of her in his life.

"I need to take a shower," she said the minute they got inside. "I need to wash off the feel…the smell of him that I have on my skin."

"Is there anything I can do?" he asked. God, he wanted to do something—anything—to help her wipe away the memory of her attacker.

Her gaze held his and in the depths of her eyes he saw the shadowed darkness of trauma. "Just be here for me," she said.

"Julie, I'm here for you and only you," he replied.

She held his gaze for another long moment and then nodded and walked slowly up the stairs.

He watched her until she disappeared from sight. *Just be here for me.* Her words haunted him as he sank down on the sofa. Tonight had scared the hell out of him. While he'd been standing outside and ruminating about his life, Julie had been inside fighting for her very life.

What if he'd waited three minutes longer before entering the back door? What if he'd waited five more minutes? The odds were good the man would have eventually found Julie's hiding place. What if she hadn't been able to physically fight him off in the first place?

He'd lost love once to a violent, unspeakable act by another person. The last thing he wanted to do was to lose Julie to the same kind of death or any other kind of death.

He thought of the gun he'd hidden on the top shelf

of his closet. Maybe it was time he go to his house to retrieve it. Maybe it was time he started carrying it with him at all times to make sure nobody ever got close to Julie again.

Hell, he was no hero. Every decision he'd made lately had been particularly unheroic because it had been made to serve only him. He didn't care about himself anymore. He didn't care if the police somehow managed to link him to McDowell's death. He didn't give a damn if he spent time in jail. All he cared about was keeping Julie safe.

If he was caught with the gun on him, he had no idea what might happen. He had no idea if the gun had a history that would lead him straight to jail. That no longer mattered. The only thing that mattered was that he needed to protect Julie through this deadly threat.

He certainly couldn't rely on the police to do anything. They were as clueless as he and Julie were in this madness. His thoughts were interrupted as he heard her coming back down the stairs.

Despite the trauma she'd been through, she looked beautiful in a short, soft pink robe. She walked to the sofa and melted down onto the cushion next to him.

The scent of minty soap and spring flowers wafted from her as she snuggled against his side as if she belonged there. She believed she belonged there. He couldn't help but put his arm around her and hold her close.

It was amazing to him that she had accepted him so readily in her life. Without any memories of him, she had taken his word for it that they were engaged.

She'd just assumed she loved him and he loved her. Such trust humbled him.

"I always feel so safe in your arms," she said with a deep sigh.

"I want you to be safe always," he replied.

She raised her head to look at him and he saw her need there. She needed him and tonight he needed her. He had a feeling the end was quickly approaching and when it slammed into them he would not only crush her world, but he'd wind up back in that dark space of loneliness and pain once again.

Chapter Twelve

Julie awoke in Nick's arms. His naked body was spooned close to hers and his arm was flung around her. Dawn light barely crept into the window and the last thing she wanted to do was to think of moving from this place of feeling so blissfully loved.

Their lovemaking the night before had been wonderful, but with a touch of desperation. It had begun slow and gentle, then had quickly moved to fast and frantic. It was as if they'd both known there was no promise of tomorrow.

She frowned and closed her eyes once again as thoughts of those horrifying moments in the pawn shop with her potential killer raced through her mind.

Her ankle ached with the memory of his tight fist wrapped around it. Her throat threatened to close up as she remembered his hands squeezing her.

Who on earth wanted to kill her? And why? What could she possibly know that was worth her death? She couldn't imagine even possessing a secret that big—that important—to somebody else. She worked in a pawn shop, for crying out loud. She wasn't the type to get involved in anything illegal.

But apparently she did possess a secret that threatened somebody else. And that somebody wanted her silenced forever.

Damn, she'd forgotten her cell phone. Now she'd have to drive back to work to get it. The memory of that night began to replay in her mind again, this time with more vivid detail.

THE NIGHT AIR *had been hot as she'd driven to the shop. Her car air conditioner had barely started to cut through the heat when she arrived. Clouds had chased away the moonshine, making the night darker than usual.*

She hurried from her car to the back door and breathed a sigh of relief as she went into the shop's coolness. She flipped on the light in the office and spied her cell phone right where she'd left it, but just after she grabbed it, the back door flew open and she heard the sound of a man laughing.

The laughter stopped abruptly as she stepped out of the office and saw...

DAMMIT. THE MEMORY flew away and she released a sigh of frustration.

Nick's arm tightened around her. "Are you all right?" His sleep-deepened voice filled her with pleasant warmth.

"I'm okay. Go back to sleep. It's still early."

He stroked her arm for a moment and then she knew

he was asleep again. She was so lucky to have this man in her life. It was the last thought she had before she took her own advice and fell back to sleep.

She awakened to bright sunshine dancing through the curtains and she was alone in the bed. She rolled over on her back and stared up at the ceiling.

A wave of memories poured into her head…flashes of visions that filled some of the holes in her mind with missing information.

A lunch at a favorite Chinese restaurant with Casey…an argument with Max at work…and Tony telling her he wanted out of the family business.

The memories continued to assault her brain…her mother and father telling all the siblings that they were moving out of the family home…her shopping online for a coral-colored vase for her bedroom.

They were vignettes of a life, nothing earth-shattering, but they filled her with a huge relief. It was as if a dam had broken and assured her that sooner rather than later everything would come back to her.

What hadn't come back to her were any memories of Nick or anything having to do with why somebody might want her dead. Still, she was eager to share with him what had just happened. She wanted to tell him about the flood of memories that had suddenly come back to her.

She got out of bed and pulled on her robe, then working her fingers through her hair she headed down the stairs. As always, the scent of coffee greeted her and she found Nick at the kitchen table with a cup of the fresh brew in front of him.

Despite the fact that she'd made love to him the night before, a wild tingling swept through her body at the sight of him. He wore only a pair of jeans. His hair was slightly mussed and he gave her a sleepy smile as she entered the room.

"You look like you just rolled out of bed," she said and moved to the counter to pour herself a cup of coffee.

"I could say the same about you," he replied. They shared a smile and then she joined him at the table.

"Guess what?"

"What?"

How she loved that lazy smile of his. "I was just lying in bed and suddenly a ton of memories came back to me."

He sat straighter in his chair. "What kind of memories?"

"Just things I did over the past ten months…fairly boring, mundane things like having lunch out with my sister and Joel telling me about his new puppy. Unfortunately no memories of you or why somebody wants to kill me appeared. But at least it's a start, right?"

"Right," he replied.

"It seems like I didn't remember the very best and the very worst that happened in that missing time." She smiled at him again. "The best of course being our meeting and falling in love. The worst, whatever secret I supposedly know that's worth killing me for."

"And I hope you remember those things quickly," he replied.

She took a sip of her coffee and then frowned at him

thoughtfully. "You know, it's like a song title that's on the very tip of your tongue and the harder you try to remember it, the more elusive it becomes."

"What were you thinking about when the memories came back to you?"

"I was thinking about last night and how good we are together. We are good, aren't we?" She held her breath as she waited for him to answer. Just because she thought their love-making was magical didn't mean he felt the same way.

He released a small laugh. "Julie, we're better than good together."

"Why did you laugh?"

"Because you never fail to amaze me with your complete openness," he replied.

"Is that good or bad?" she asked.

"It's wonderfully refreshing and good."

She warmed beneath the smile he gave her. "You know what sounds good to me? Bacon and eggs. I know you aren't much of a breakfast eater, but I'm in the mood for some crispy bacon and a cheese omelet. What do you think?"

"I wouldn't turn up my nose at that. What can I do to help?"

"Absolutely nothing. Just sit there and look totally hot and handsome," she replied and then laughed. "Mr. Simon, I do believe I just saw a blush sweep across your face."

He grinned. "You make me blush when you say stuff like that. That's what I was talking about, you're just so open and up-front with your feelings."

"And that's one of the things you love about me, right?"

He laughed and then sobered. "Yeah, that's one of the things I love about you."

Her heart swelled with happiness and she got up from the table. "Just for that, I'm going to make you bacon and the best omelet you've ever had."

Julie got to work. She hoped if she kept herself busy all day she wouldn't think about the terror of the night before. By doing mundane chores maybe her mind would fill in the rest of the memories she lacked and so desperately needed.

Breakfast was pleasant and she imagined it was what it would always be like once she and Nick got married. She felt like she was already married to him. However, she also knew that the twenty-four-hour-a-day relationship they shared now wasn't reality.

Reality was them each going to their own jobs in the morning and then being together once again in the evening. But reality was also his face being the first one she saw in the morning and the last one she saw before she fell asleep in his arms.

She wanted to get back to a normal life, whatever that had been before her accident. She was sure Nick was also eager to get some normalcy back in his life, as well.

More than anything she wanted a ring on her finger from him. She wanted to talk to him about wedding venues and flowers and wedding cakes. She wanted to plan the ceremony that would make her Nick's bride.

It was just after two o'clock in the afternoon when her sister called.

"Mom and I want to take you out to dinner tonight," Casey said. "And don't give me any excuses. We aren't going to take no for an answer. After what you went through last night, we want—we need—a girls' night out."

Julie didn't want to go. What she wanted was to spend the evening watching movies or whatever with Nick. She wanted to snuggle up against him on the sofa, where she felt safe and loved, and watch a silly movie that made them laugh.

"Casey, I really don't—"

"I said we won't take no for an answer." Casey cut in. "Julie, we need to see you and assure ourselves you're really okay. From what Daddy told us, you had a terrible experience last night. It will just be for a little while. I promise we'll get you home early."

Julie looked over at Nick, who was watching one of his football tapes on the television. "Do you mind if I go out to dinner this evening with my mom and sister?"

"Are you sure you feel up to it?" he asked. She nodded and he continued. "Then while you're gone I'll head over to my place to grab a few more things."

"Okay," Julie said back into the phone. "Just tell me what time and I'll be ready."

With plans made for Casey to pick her up at six, Julie went upstairs to do a little cleaning while Nick continued to watch the tapes and make notes on a notepad.

Before Julie knew it the day was gone and it was

time to shower and get dressed for the night out. She didn't feel like going, but she knew her mother probably wanted to see for herself that Julie was fine after the ordeal she'd gone through last night.

Physically she was fine, but the thought of leaving the house caused more than a little bit of surprising anxiety to ripple through her, which was specifically why she was forcing herself to go. She didn't want to wind up agoraphobic, afraid to leave this safe space of her home for fear danger would come to her. She should be perfectly fine with her mother and sister.

At five to six she came downstairs and moved to the front door to watch for Casey. Nick joined her at the door. "That red dress looks gorgeous on you. You look way too nice to be going out without me," he said.

"I could say the same about you," she countered. Tucked into his white shorts was a short-sleeved, button-up, hunter-green shirt that popped the green color of his eyes.

"When am I going to get to see your house?" she asked. "I know I've been there before, but since I don't have any memories of it, I'd like to see it again." She wanted to see the space he called home. You could tell a lot about people by the things they surrounded themselves with.

"We can go tomorrow if you want," he replied.

A honk sounded from the driveway. She rolled her eyes. "I'm sure she sees me standing right here but she has a horn fetish."

He grinned at her. "I can think of worse fetishes to have."

She laughed. "Now, how about you give me a good-bye kiss that curls my toes?" She leaned into him.

He gazed at her for a long moment, his eyes going darker, and then he placed his lips over hers. His lips were soft and warm and made her want to stay home to make love with him all night long.

All too quickly he pulled away from her. He shoved an errant strand of her hair away from her cheek. "Have fun and be safe," he said.

She smiled. "With my mother and sister by my side, nothing and nobody would dare try to get to me. I'll be fine and I'll see you later. Casey promised me it would be an early night."

Despite all the bad things that had happened since her accident, her heart was light as she left the porch. Everything with Nick felt so easy, so good. Although they hadn't talked about their engagement and plans for a wedding since her car wreck, she knew those things were definitely in her future.

She frowned as she reached the car and realized her mother wasn't inside. She opened the door and slid into the passenger seat. "Where's Mom?"

Casey put the car in Reverse. "She and Dad went out to some farmhouse close to Smithville to look at some antiques. We're supposed to pick her up there."

Julie laughed. "Which means we're riding to her rescue. You know how long Dad can take when he's negotiating for more stuff."

"Forever," Casey replied. She shot a quick look at Julie. "How are you doing after last night? I heard about you being attacked."

Julie had tried all day long not to think about what had happened the night before. Even now in the safety of Casey's car an icy chill threatened to overwhelm her. The back of her throat tightened as she remembered the man's hands wrapped around her neck. She'd used makeup to dust across the faint bruises that had appeared.

"I'm fine," she replied. "I really don't want to talk about it. I don't even want to think about it."

"And you really don't know why somebody is after you?"

"I really don't, although my memories are coming back and I think it won't be long before I'll know exactly what's going on."

"That's great. Maybe then you'll remember that you borrowed my cute pink blouse with the white cuffs and you'll return it to me."

Julie laughed. "Okay, I'll get that back to you as soon as you return my favorite winter boots."

Once again Casey glanced at Julie and then returned her attention to the narrow highway. "I borrowed those boots in ninth grade," she protested.

"And I've never forgiven you for not returning them to me," Julie replied with a grin. Casey laughed and a surge of love for her sister welled up inside Julie.

Sure, Casey was flighty and irresponsible. She was spoiled and could be petulant, but she could also be such fun to be around.

Julie cast her gaze out the front car window. A plethora of trees stood tall and thick some distance away on either side of the road. That was one of the things

Julie loved about Kansas City. Within a fifteen-minute drive from the northern suburbs you could be out in the middle of nowhere.

Even though the highway was just a two-lane, there was plenty of traffic since it led to a lake where many families enjoyed boating and other summer fun.

"I'd ask how you and Nick are getting along, but from the slobbery kiss I saw you two share before you left the house, I would guess that everything must be going great," Casey said.

Julie laughed once again. "It wasn't slobbery and everything is better than great. I just wish I could remember all the time I've lost with him."

"Too bad there isn't a drug you could take that would instantly restore all the rest of those memories," Casey replied.

Every muscle in Julie's body tensed. *Drugs. A large box of prescription bottles.* She closed her eyes as the memories suddenly assaulted her.

She'd been in the office to retrieve her cell phone...

THE BACK DOOR opened and male laughter echoed up the small hallway. She peeked her head out of the office and saw a large, young man with bulky, tattooed arms carrying a large box. His bald head gleamed in the light overhead and his eyes widened in surprise when he saw her.

JULIE'S EYES FLEW OPEN, but still the memories came.

Casey stepping up behind the man with a box of pill bottles in her arms...

Julie looking at the bottles in the box... OxyContin. Oxycodone. Xanax. And others, probably even street drugs. They'd been selling them outside the back of the shop at night...

Julie'd had a rough idea what those kind of drugs would fetch on the street and remembered thinking that Casey and her boyfriend Ace had to be raking in big bucks.

"Don't tell!" Casey had screamed at her. "Just get the hell out of here now and forget what you saw."

Julie had left, but there'd been no way she wasn't going to tell. Casey and her boyfriend were not only doing something illegal, they were also jeopardizing everything her family had all worked for. If those two were caught selling dope out of the pawn shop, then it was possible the whole place could be shut down.

When Julie left the pawn shop on that terrible night, Casey had followed her. Julie had never seen her sister so out of control, so enraged, as she'd confronted Julie in Julie's living room. That night Casey's eyes had shone with lethal intent. When Casey had physically attacked her, Julie had thrown the candle at her and then run outside and jumped in her car.

Danger.

It rang in the air inside the car. It screamed inside Julie's head.

Keep your cool, a small voice whispered inside her.

"Dad sure dragged Mom a long way from town," Julie said, glad her voice didn't give away any of her inner turmoil. There was no way Julie now believed

Casey was taking her to pick up their mother for a lovely dinner together.

Was she taking her to meet up with her boyfriend? The man Julie now was certain had been the one who had tried to kill her the night before.

She needed to get out of the car. She couldn't trust Casey. Last night had been a failed attempt to silence her forever. So, now where were they really going?

With terror crawling up the back of her throat, she considered her options. She only had one. She had to get out of the car.

She drew in a deep breath for courage, knowing she was taking a huge chance. She prayed she wouldn't wind up dead as she reached over and grabbed the steering wheel.

"What in the hell are you doing?" Casey screamed.

Julie fought for control and yanked the wheel as hard as she could toward her. The car careered off the road, dove down and then up the ditch, and finally rolled to a halt.

Julie didn't waste any time. She tore off her seat belt and shoved her door open. She took off running for the woods. It was only when a deep male voice yelled from someplace behind her that she slowed and threw a glance over her shoulder.

Her blood ran cold and she nearly stumbled in shocked surprise. Casey stood next to her car. The trunk was now open and running toward Julie was the bulky man who had tried to kill her the night before.

Oh, God…had she just played into their hands? Had

this been their plan all along? To get her out in the middle of nowhere and kill her?

The only choice she had now was to run like the wind and hope like hell she could find someplace to hide until somehow, someway, help would come. She desperately prayed that somebody else found her before her sister and her boyfriend did.

THERE WAS NO sense of homecoming when Nick walked through the front door of his house. He walked around, touching things he and Debbie had bought together and remembering the plans they'd once made for their future together.

The anger, the self-destructive rage, he'd dwelled in after her murder was gone, replaced by the normal sadness of loss. He would always remember his first wife, but right now he had another woman on his mind.

Julie. He'd nearly lost her last night to dark forces that remained buried in her mind. What had she seen? What did she know that now had her life at risk?

He walked into the master bedroom, turned on the television on the dresser and sank down onto the foot of the bed. Julie needed to get all her memories back.

The only times he didn't want her to remember anything was when he held her in his arms and when her eyes lit up with such love for him. Whenever they shared a kiss or made love, he didn't want her to remember that she had never met him before the night of the accident.

She needed to remember that she'd never loved him.

He saw no happy ending for them. But he desperately wanted a happy ending for her. He wanted the danger gone and Julie free to live her life…to find love and move forward with her dreams.

Again a sadness gripped his soul, especially as he thought of her with another man. Maybe this was his penance for entering into an agreement that would celebrate six men's murders.

There was no way he believed Julie would forgive him when she learned the truth. He'd not only pretended to be her fiancé, he'd made up a whole history that was nothing but a fantasy to serve his own needs.

She wouldn't remember that he'd held her when she'd been frightened during a thunderstorm. She wouldn't care that he'd been there for her through her laughter and her tears.

He'd built a past with her based on lies. He'd also made love to her under those false pretenses. Who in the hell would want to build a future with a man like him?

When she'd opened her beautiful eyes after the accident, she'd taken all that he'd told her at face value. She had openly and trustingly given him everything… her body, her heart and her soul.

He loved her. He loved that she had little self-edit when it came to what thoughts she expressed out loud. He adored her sense of humor and how often they laughed together about the silliest thing.

Yes, he loved her with every fiber of his being. He wanted his future to be with her, but his feelings didn't matter. He could love her to the moon and back, but he knew she was going to hate him when the truth came out.

He got up from the bed and walked over to his closet. If he couldn't be with her forever, he could at least keep her safe until her memories returned.

He reached up on the closet's top shelf and pulled down the hoodie wrapped around the weapon.

Once again, the gun felt cold and alien in his grip. It wasn't that he didn't know how to handle one. He and a couple of the other coaches occasionally went to a gun range to shoot. Yes, he knew his way around the weapon, but it was how and why he'd gotten this particular gun that made it feel like it didn't belong in his hand.

He grabbed a small duffel from the bottom of the closet. He placed the gun in the bottom and then folded several T-shirts and placed them on top.

Glancing at the clock, he noted that it was time for the evening news. He figured he still had a couple of hours before Julie would be back home, so he placed the duffel on the bed and once again sat down.

He'd been trying to catch the news every evening to see if there had been any follow-up to Brian McDowell's murder. However, each day the news was filled with other murders and crimes, making it impossible for him to follow the investigation. He also watched the news to see if any of the other men on their hit list had been killed.

How he wished he could rewrite the history of the past year. How he wished he would have really met

Julie in a coffee shop and everything he'd told her about their relationship was real.

His attention was captured by a picture on the television. He grabbed the remote and turned up the volume.

"Police have been called to the scene of an accident along 169 Highway. Eyewitnesses say a car spun out of control and a woman jumped out and ran into the wooded area. Two other car occupants also abandoned the car and ran. This video was shot by a bystander."

The blond newscaster disappeared and a shaky video came on showing a car on the side of the road and a woman in a red dress jumping out of the passenger seat.

It was a brief clip but Nick's blood stopped flowing through his veins. A tight pressure filled his chest. That was Casey's car and it had been Julie who had run away. He didn't know exactly what was happening, but he knew with certainty she needed him... now!

He grabbed the duffel bag and raced out of the house.

Once he was on the road, questions began swirling through his head. What was going on? Why would Julie get out of the car and run away from the scene? From her sister and her mother? It didn't make sense.

She would only do that if she believed she was in immediate danger. Casey? Their mother? He couldn't imagine one of them being the source of the threat, but he knew in his gut Julie was in a wealth of trouble.

He thought of the gun he carried with him. He

would have no problem putting a bullet into some-body who was trying to hurt Julie. He didn't give a damn who they were.

All he had to do was to get to her in time.

Chapter Thirteen

Julie's heart nearly beat out of her chest as she ran through the thick woods. A thrashing came from someplace behind her, letting her know her sister and Ace were coming after her.

The sweltering late-evening heat made it even more difficult for her to catch her breath as she frantically looked around for someplace to hide.

Brush and thickets tried to trip her up, grabbing at her legs and catching on her dress. Damn her choice of a red dress. It was like a vivid target in the green depths of the woods.

She had no idea where she was going. All that was important at the moment was that Ace not catch her. There was no question in her mind that if he caught her, he'd kill her. He'd already tried once and, if he had his way, she wouldn't make it out of these woods.

Gasping for air, she ducked behind a tree to catch her breath.

"Julie…come out," Casey called from someplace in the distance. "We don't want to hurt you. We just want to talk to you. Come out so we can have an adult conversation about things."

Julie squeezed her eyes tightly closed against the tears that threatened to fall. She didn't believe Casey. Her sister had probably been in the pawn shop when Ace had tried to strangle her. It had probably been Casey who had turned out the lights. Nobody who wanted to have a conversation with you hid their killer boyfriend in the car trunk.

She stuffed down the sense of betrayal, shoved the utter devastation away. She couldn't deal with that right now. She had more important things on her mind, like trying to stay alive.

"Come on, Julie. I promise everything is going to be okay. Just talk to us for a few minutes and then we can all go out to eat and we'll take you back home," Casey said in a smooth, reassuring voice.

Julie wasn't reassured. The woman attempting to get Julie out of her hiding place had nothing to do with the sister Julie had grown up with. She had no idea what had changed Casey, and right now she didn't care.

"Julie…" The deep male whisper seemed to come from right behind her.

Too close. He was far too close. With a gasp, she took off running again. She ran as fast as she could, blinded by tears and terror. She cried out as she stumbled over a tree root and fell to the ground.

She jumped up and cast a quick glance behind her.

Ace was visible and as he saw her he raised an arm. Was that a gun in his hand?

Drawing in a deep gulp of air, she dove to her right

and rolled until she came to another big tree. She crawled on her hands and knees to get behind it.

A siren sounded from the direction of where she'd run from the car. Thank goodness, help was arriving. Still, she couldn't exactly dash out into the open to get to the police. The siren wailed for another minute and then went silent.

She remained plastered against the tree trunk, holding her breath and praying Ace hadn't seen where she'd rolled when she'd hit the ground. Still, no police officer would know where she was unless she let them know.

A rustle sounded far too close to her. Drawing in another deep breath, she released a scream that sent birds flying from the tops of the trees. And then she ran again.

Once again she darted ahead blindly, just wanting to keep one step ahead of Ace. She tried to weave a path that would take her back toward the highway where hopefully police had arrived and could save her.

However, she'd become disoriented and, without the sound of the siren, wasn't sure in which direction to run. Again she leaned her back against a tree trunk, her gaze shooting frantically all around.

How long had it been since she'd run from the car? Minutes? An hour? It felt like forever. Nick. Her heart cried out his name.

How she wished his strong, loving arms were around her right now. She needed him. She frowned, her mind racing for more memories…any memories of him.

A strong hand grabbed her wrist and she screamed

as she was pulled away from the tree and the tight hold released. "Hands up."

She stared into the barrel of a gun, a police officer's gun. "Oh, thank God," she exclaimed to the middle-aged man clad in a khaki uniform. "They were going to kill me. They didn't want me to tell what I knew. At first I didn't remember what I saw, but my memories all came back and they want to kill me…"

She knew she was babbling, but she couldn't stop herself. "He was hiding in the trunk. Ace…my sister's boyfriend…he was in the trunk of her car. My sister told me we were going out to dinner, but they were taking me someplace to kill me." A deep sob escaped her.

"We'll get everything sorted out, ma'am," the officer said as he holstered his gun. "Right now, I need you to keep your hands up over your head and walk that way." He gestured for her to walk to her left.

She walked in front of him for some distance and finally they broke out of the woods.

She froze as she saw Casey and Ace standing next to Casey's car with two other officers.

"Why aren't they in handcuffs?" she asked. "They wanted to kill me. They need to be arrested."

"Julie, come on, honey. Everything is going to be okay," Casey called.

"Jules, we were just going for a nice drive," Ace said as if they were the best friends in the world.

Jules? What in the hell were they playing at? A hundred knots twisted in her stomach as the officer moved her forward.

Casey leaned toward the officer standing next to

her and spoke, but Julie was too far away to hear the conversation.

Still, the look the officer gave her was full of speculation.

Casey, who could charm the bark off a tree. What had she been telling the officers about Julie? What lies had she told them to save her and her boyfriend's asses?

"Julie, everything is going to be okay," Casey said when Julie reached the car. "You're safe now." Her voice was filled with such caring, but her eyes held a hard edge Julie had never seen before.

"I understand you were recently in a car accident, Ms. Peterson." The officer next to Casey was a big man and he wore a name tag that identified him as Deputy Ben Rodman.

"What does that have to do with anything?" she asked defensively.

"Julie, you know you haven't been yourself since the accident," Casey replied. She looked at all the policemen. "We've all been so very worried about her."

"We thought she might enjoy a nice drive, but she freaked out and grabbed the wheel and then bailed from the car," Ace said.

"Shut up." Julie snapped at him. "You were hiding in the trunk for a reason. I don't even know you and you tried to kill me last night in the pawn shop."

The big, bald man shook his head with a sad smile. "Now, Julie, you know that isn't true." He looked at the deputy who had brought Julie back. "She's been paranoid since her car wreck and thinks her family members are out to kill her."

They were trying to make her look crazy and, by the expressions on the officers' faces, it was working.

"He's lying and what I told you is the truth," she replied frantically. "Check it out with the police department in Kansas City. I was attacked last night and it was because they don't want me telling anyone they've been selling drugs out of the back of the family business."

"Julie." Casey shook her head in obvious pity.

"You've got to believe me," Julie exclaimed. Tears burned at her eyes. "They were taking me someplace to kill me so I couldn't tell anyone about what they've been doing."

"She needs mental help," Casey said. "My family has been talking about having her committed for a little while so she can get the help she needs."

Julie gasped. This was all going so horribly wrong. "He had a gun," she said and pointed to Ace. "I saw it. He pointed it at me and was going to shoot me."

"Julie, honey, the deputies patted down Ace. There's no gun," Casey replied as if she were speaking to a three-year-old.

Julie looked at each of the deputies' faces. Oh, God, they believed Casey and Ace's story. She was in big trouble. It was possible she'd wind up in some mental hospital and nobody would ever believe her about what Casey and Ace had been doing…what they had already done.

At that moment a familiar car screeched to a halt behind one of the police cars and Nick got out. She'd never been so happy to see somebody before in her entire life.

"Nick!" Before anyone could stop her, she ran to him. His arms awaited her and enfolded her tight. His heart beat against hers in the same frantic rhythm.

"Are you all right?" He pulled slightly away from her as his gaze bore into hers.

"They're trying to make it look like I'm crazy. They were taking me someplace to kill me, Nick." Before she could say anything more, Deputy Rodman joined them. "This is my fiancé, Nick Simon. He can tell you what's going on. He'll tell you I'm not crazy."

Rodman held up his hand. "We're taking you all in to the station to sort this out."

Nick released her. "I'll follow you there."

Minutes later Julie was in the back of a police cruiser and her sister and Ace were passengers in another vehicle. Fear still tightened her muscles and dried her mouth.

Were they going to let Casey and Ace go? She wanted them locked up. Her heart not only ached for the little sister she'd loved, but also for her parents, who would be devastated by Casey's crimes.

IT WAS HOURS later when Nick and Julie finally walked out of the police station. Ace was being held for pending charges and two outstanding warrants. Casey was also under arrest. A search of her car had uncovered a box of prescription pills not prescribed to her.

Julie slid into the passenger seat of Nick's car and

leaned her head back as Nick got in behind the wheel and started the engine.

"Tired?" he asked.

"Mentally and physically exhausted," she replied. She looked down at her dress. Pulls and tears in the material evidenced her mad dash through the woods. Thank God, her dress's was the only death that had occurred today.

She pulled her cell phone from her purse and stared down at her parents' number. "I need to call Mom and Dad and tell them what's happened. This is going to absolutely break their hearts."

"It would have broken their hearts if Casey and Ace had succeeded in killing you," Nick replied. His voice deepened as he continued. "It definitely would have broken mine."

She flashed him a grateful glance and then hit the button on her phone that would connect her with her parents. It was the most difficult conversation she'd ever had.

She cried. Her mother cried and her father cursed. They were in shock, but ultimately they proclaimed their love for Julie and the fact that Casey would now have to face the consequences of her actions.

"Are you sure you're all right?" her mother asked.

"I'm fine," she replied. "I'm with Nick and I'm okay. I'm just tired and ready for my life to get back to normal."

By the time the call had ended, she was utterly drained. Once again she leaned her head back and closed her eyes. The memories she'd been missing again flashed through her mind.

Difficult customers in the shop… Joel's new dog… Casey and Ace coming in the back door with drugs… Casey attacking her in her living room, breaking the lamp while Julie threw the candle, hitting the glass on the painting and, finally, her jumping into her car to escape.

She opened her eyes and sat straighter as Nick came to a stop in her driveway. Her heart started a new quickened pace, one of disquiet…of uncertainty mingling with a faint touch of fear.

She looked at Nick in the purple shadows of twilight that had descended. He had been by her side through everything. She was desperately in love with him, but at the moment that didn't matter.

"I've been desperately searching my memory to find you and I realize now that my memories of you aren't missing. They were never there to begin with. You aren't my fiancé, so who in the hell are you?"

NICK HAD WAITED for this moment to happen. Initially he'd anticipated it and then he had dreaded it. Now it was upon him and a swell of desperation filled his chest.

"Can we go inside and talk?" he asked.

Her eyes were dark and filled with mistrust. She gave a curt nod of her head and then, together, they exited the car and walked to the front door. At least she wasn't locking him out before she could hear his side of the story.

Her shoulders were stiff, her beautiful face emotionless as they went inside and sat on opposite sides of the sofa. Only able to imagine the trauma she'd been through as she'd run for her life through the woods, the only thing he really wanted to do was to hold her close and assure himself she was really okay. However, everything about her posture let him know she wouldn't welcome any kind of touch from him.

"Who are you and why are you in my life?" she asked.

"I'm the man who is in love with you," he replied.

She raised a trembling hand. "Don't. I know you weren't in the car with me on the night of the accident. I also know you and I didn't have a fight in my living room.

"Casey and I fought that night and I got into my car alone. Why are you here and where did you come from?" Her gaze searched his features as if she'd never seen him before this moment.

Where did he begin? How did he even start to try to make her understand what he had done? He was desperate to get her to believe that none of that mattered, that he was in love with her now and that he believed she'd fallen in love with him.

"I was on the street when you wrecked your car. I'm the one who called for help," he said.

She stared at him without blinking, obviously waiting for him to make sense of things.

What had made sense to him on the night of her accident now seemed completely insane.

"So, how did you go from Good Samaritan to my fiancé?" she asked.

His chest ached with regret. He averted his gaze, unable to look at her and tell her about all of his elaborate lies.

"I was at the wrong place at the wrong time that night."

As he thought about his intentions and the reason he'd been on the street, it felt as if it had all happened in a nightmare or to somebody else.

"You were unconscious in the car and I made an impromptu decision to pretend to be your fiancé. I only intended to pretend until you got medical help, but then the responding officer took me to the hospital and I couldn't tell him I'd lied to him about our relationship. Then you regained consciousness and believed I was your fiancé, and I only intended to continue the pretense until you came home."

"You use the word 'pretense.' Call it what it was, you lied." Her harsh tone made him look at her again.

Her arms were folded tight across her chest and looking at her caused a new pressure to build inside him. Her eyes were bright with anger, but her lips trembled with a vulnerability that spoke of pain.

He nodded. "My initial impromptu lie spun way out of control. When I brought you here and saw the damage in the room, I knew you might be in some kind of trouble. I didn't want to tell you the truth then. You got that threatening phone call and I didn't want to bow out of your life."

He leaned forward. "Julie, our relationship started

with my lie, but it became real to me. I'm in love with you. I don't just want you to be my pretend fiancée, I want you to be my wife."

A laugh escaped her. A bitter sound that shot a sharp arrow into his heart. "I don't know you. I don't know what all you lied about. I don't even know if your name is really Nick Simon or not."

"That really is my name and I really am a high school physical ed teacher and coach. I didn't lie about who I am, and the feelings I have for you are very real."

He couldn't stand it any longer. He had to touch her. He scooted closer to her and tried to ignore how she stiffened at his nearness. He reached out a hand toward her, but she jumped up off the sofa before he could make any contact.

"You allowed me to make love with you without telling me you were a stranger in my life." For the first time, tears glinted in her eyes. "You let me fall in love with you, knowing all of it was a lie."

"But that part wasn't a lie," he protested. "What I feel for you is real and, if you look deep in your heart, I know you'll realize the love you feel for me is just as real."

She swiped at a tear that trekked down her cheek then raised her fingers to her temple and rubbed. "I need you to leave."

He stood. "Julie, don't throw this all away. I'm sorry. I'm so damned sorry about everything." A simmering desperation filled him. He had a feeling that if he left here tonight it would be the end of any hope he had to have her in his future. "I love you, Julie, and I need you in my life."

"And I need you to go," she replied. She dropped her hand to her side and didn't meet his gaze. "I thought Casey's betrayal of me was the worst I'd ever know. But this…? You…have utterly gutted me."

He remained in place, willing her to look at him again, but she kept her gaze averted as tears slowly oozed from her eyes. She looked broken and the fact that he was responsible for that ached in him.

"Please go," she said softly. "You can come back and get your things tomorrow or the next day. And leave my house key on the table."

Dammit, he didn't want to leave. He wanted to pull her into his arms, somehow make her see that they were meant to be together forever.

He hesitated for what felt like a lifetime, a wealth of pain stabbing his heart. Then, with deep resignation, he pulled his key ring from his pocket. The silence between them was deafening as he took her house key off and laid it on the coffee table.

"It would have been so much easier if we'd really met in a coffee shop a year ago," she said softly. She finally met his gaze and in the depths of her eyes was the darkness of pain, of betrayal so great it stole his breath away.

He thought about her words and released a heavy sigh. "Julie, I wasn't a good enough man for you a year ago."

He hoped she'd stop him as he walked toward the front door, but she didn't. He held on to a modicum of hope until he stepped out the door and heard it slam and lock behind him.

Would he get an opportunity to talk to her tomorrow? Or would she pack his things and place them on the front porch? At least he was leaving with the knowledge that she was safe now, although there would certainly be emotional fallout from Casey's actions.

Fighting against the wave of heartache that threatened to consume him, he got into his car. He'd been a fool to think she would be able to easily forgive him. He'd been completely delusional to ever believe there would be a happy ending in this.

Now he was left with a fiery love for a woman he'd probably never have in his life and a gun he didn't want in his glove box. At least he could do something about the gun.

It was representative of the man he had been, an angry animal who had lost all of his humanity and dignity to grief. He wasn't that person anymore and he couldn't ever imagine becoming that person again, no matter what happened in his future.

He headed north, his headlights cutting through the darkness of night. He couldn't go home before getting rid of the gun. It was the last piece that tied him to a dark past.

As he drove, his head replayed each and every moment he'd shared with Julie. She'd helped him not only get his sense of humor back, but also his passion.

He'd looked forward each morning to getting up and spending time with her. He'd wanted to be there with her for all the good times and the bad.

A hollow wind blew through him as the landscape in front of him washed out like a watercolor painting. He wiped the sudden, unexpected tears from his eyes.

He passed the spot on the highway where Casey's car had been parked and the woods where Julie had run for her life. Thank God, at least the danger to her would be no more.

She'd been so closed off from him. He clenched his hands more tightly around the steering wheel. Could he really blame her?

He was guilty of wanting her enough to take her to bed, to make love to her. He was guilty of lying to her over and over again about the little things that made up a real life, only in this case it had been a false life that he'd invented.

He turned onto a narrow road with thick trees on either side. This road would take him to an old dock on the big lake north of the city.

Although he deeply regretted hurting Julie, it was difficult for him to regret the forces that had brought them together. He wouldn't take back a minute of his time with her. He would cherish the memories of loving her forever.

He reached a small parking area and pulled his car to a halt. He turned off his lights, then reached into the glove box and retrieved the gun and a small cleaning towel he kept there to occasionally wipe off his windshield.

As he got out of his car the hot, sultry night air quickly embraced him. He walked out onto the dock and sat at the edge. His father used to bring him fishing here when he was a young boy. Nick hadn't been back to this dock since his father and mother's death.

For a moment his head filled with happy memories of those times with his dad. If he'd had his parents' support when Debbie had been murdered, would he have walked the same path of rage and revenge? Probably not. But when that murder had occurred, he'd been all alone and ripe to fall in with the other men who were in the same mental hell.

Wiping down the weapon, his thoughts turned to the five men in the pact. He assumed their plans would go forward and more deaths would occur. He wished he could make them understand that the way to ease pain and heartache wasn't murder but was, instead, love.

It sounded like a damn cliché, but maintaining that kind of rage for any length of time only ate up your insides and made it impossible to move on. No amount of vengeance would bring back their loved ones.

In any case, the pact no longer mattered. He was out. He would never see those men again unless it was a chance meeting at the grocery store or on the street.

With the gun carefully wiped down, he stood. This was the last thing that tied him to a killing rage, to a darkness he knew he'd never plunge into again.

Drawing a deep breath, he threw the gun into the water. He knew from those days of fishing with his father that this particular area was filled with crappie beds. He hoped the gun would tangle so tightly in them that it would never be found again.

The moon overhead was big and bright, reflecting on the water that occasionally rippled with fish or insects. For the first time since arriving, he became aware of the cacophony of sound that surrounded him. Insects clicked and whirred and the deep bass croaking of a bullfrog filled the air.

As his thoughts returned to Julie, burning tears blurred his vision. He'd never wanted anything as badly as he wanted her. He sank back down to sit on the dock and allowed his tears to run free. The ball was now in her court and he had the terrible feeling that she'd never be able to forgive him.

Chapter Fourteen

Nick.

Julie woke with his name on her lips and tears in her eyes. The heartache that rocked through her was definitely more painful than the bruises and scratches she'd sustained from her ordeal the day before.

Minutes later she stood beneath a hot shower and tried to halt the seemingly endless supply of tears she had. She told herself she was weeping because her knees and elbows were bruised by her tumble over the tree root.

Every muscle in her body ached from her exertions the night before. Her own sister had wanted her dead. She had plenty to cry about, but she couldn't fool herself. This morning her tears were solely for the loss of Nick.

Last night after he'd left she'd cried for hours, not knowing if she was crying because of Nick's betrayal or Casey's. She'd never felt so alone.

He loves you, a little voice whispered inside her as she dressed for the day. But did he really? How could she accept words of love from a man who had lied to her so many times about so many things?

It was funny…she'd believed herself madly in love with him the minute she'd been told that her fiancé was in the waiting room at the hospital. She hadn't questioned that love the entire time they'd been together. Even though she couldn't remember him, she'd fallen in love with him all over again.

He'd stood by her side through the worst things that would ever happen in her life. He'd done his best to protect her from danger when he could have just walked away.

She was so confused. But the one thing she wasn't confused about was the fact that she was madly and deeply in love with Nick.

She'd just sat to have a cup of coffee when a knock fell on her door. Her heartbeat accelerated. Was Nick here to get his things already? She wasn't ready to face him yet. She was still sorting out her emotions where he was concerned.

When a second knock sounded, this one louder than the last, she reluctantly got out of her chair and hurried to answer. She didn't know if she was glad or disappointed that it was her mother.

"Mom," she said in surprise. Her surprise went to shock when her mother pulled her into a tight embrace. It had been years since Julie had been really hugged by Lynetta.

She finally released Julie and cleared her throat. "I smell fresh coffee."

"I was just sitting down for a cup," Julie replied.

A few moments later they were both seated at the table. "I had to come by and check on you," Lynetta said. "I'm so sorry for what you went through last night. Your father and I feel partially responsible."

Julie looked at her in surprise. "It isn't your fault."

"We've always been too easy on Casey. We didn't discipline her like we did everyone else and she chose the wrong paths and the wrong people."

Lynetta appeared older today than Julie had ever seen her.

"We spoiled her rotten and when we tried to cut the financial ties, she chose the easy path." Lynetta shook her head. "I still can't believe they were selling drugs out of the pawn shop."

"I'm sorry, Mom."

Lynetta quickly covered Julie's hand with hers. "There is absolutely no reason for you to apologize for anything. What Casey did was beyond inexcusable, first by selling drugs out of the shop and then in driving you someplace where that man could kill you." Her face paled. "I don't know what we would have done if they'd been successful and we'd lost you."

"You would have been able to hire somebody to work at the shop and take care of the books," Julie replied.

Her mother stared at her for a long moment and then anger flashed from her eyes. "Is that what you believe about us? That we only care about you because you're a good worker?"

Lynetta's eyes filled with tears and she squeezed Julie's hand. "Oh, honey, if that's what you believe, then your father and I have really messed up. I couldn't give a damn what you do or don't do in that shop. You're my daughter and all I've ever wanted was for you to be healthy and happy."

Julie burst into tears. Her mother's words soothed a part of her that had been wounded for a very long time. She finally pulled her hand from her mother's to wipe at the tears. "You have no idea how much I needed to hear that," she finally said when she regained control.

"Then I wish I would have told you that every single day of your life," Lynetta replied. "You're my firstborn daughter, Julie. I couldn't wait for you to be born. You filled a space in my heart that had been empty and you've made me very proud to be your mother every day of your life."

"I want to quit working at the shop." The words tumbled from Julie's mouth before she'd known she was going to say them. She held her breath to see how her mother would react.

Lynetta sat back in her chair, her features registering surprise.

Julie had been through a man chasing her around in the woods in an attempt to kill her. She'd also survived the man she loved telling her that love was built on lies. She suddenly felt strong enough to go after what she really wanted.

"I want to go back to school and get a nursing license," she said.

"A noble profession. Your father and I would support you a hundred percent if that's what you want to do."

It was Julie's turn to be surprised. "I expected you to freak out and try to talk me out of quitting the shop."

"I told you, I want you happy, and if being a nurse is what makes you happy, then go for it. What does your fellow think about it?" Lynetta frowned. "As a matter of fact, where is Nick? I figured he'd be here with you today."

A renewed sense of pain speared through Julie. "We had a fight and he left last night."

"So, it was a serious fight?" Lynetta asked, and Julie nodded. "I hope you two work it out. I've never seen a man look at you with such love as Nick has when he looks at you."

"Really?" Julie stared at her mother intently.

"Really. That boy is head-over-heels in love with you. Trust me, your father sometimes still looks at me that way. That's the kind of love that will last a life-time."

Julie couldn't help the way her heart swelled at her mother's words.

AN HOUR LATER she was still thinking about her conversation with her mother. She'd been both surprised and relieved by her mom's response to Julie telling her she wanted to quit working at the shop. She had definitely underestimated the love and support her parents had for her.

Was she also underestimating Nick's love for her? Was it possible she could get past all the lies he'd told her? Could she really believe his love was real when so many things had been pretend? She really didn't know.

There were questions she still needed to have answered. What had he been doing out on the street at midnight on the night of her accident? What, exactly, was true and what was false?

She didn't know where he lived. Did he really have a murdered wife? What about his parents? Had he lied about them being killed in a car accident?

Despite how angry she'd been with him, there was no question she couldn't imagine how she would have gotten through her ordeal without him.

He'd been there for her on the night of the horrible phone call and when the doll had been left for her to find. His arms had been the ones she'd wanted around her both on the night she'd been attacked in the pawn shop and yesterday when he'd pulled up behind the police car.

Why hadn't her heart told her immediately that he was a stranger? Even if her brain had malfunctioned with the amnesia, why hadn't her heart or instincts told her that their love wasn't real the moment he'd come into her hospital room?

The problem was…it didn't matter that she had no memories of him before her accident. Since that time she'd fallen helplessly in love with him.

She jumped as the phone rang. For just a brief moment she gazed at it in fear.

It's okay, a small voice whispered in her head. *The danger has passed.*

She answered.

"Julie?"

She squeezed her eyes tightly closed at the sound of his deep voice. "Yes?"

"Uh… I was wondering if now would be a good time for me to come over and get my things."

Her heartache deepened. He hadn't called to say he loved her. He hadn't called to tell her he couldn't live without her. He'd called to get his things.

"How about in an hour," she replied.

"That's good with me as long as it's good for you," he said.

"Then I'll see you in an hour." She quickly hung up the receiver and sank down on the sofa. She didn't know why she hadn't told him to come over right now.

But if she looked deeply into her heart, she knew the answer. As long as his items were in her house, she could pretend they were still a couple. When he picked up his clothing, the end of them would be final.

She got up from the sofa and walked upstairs. Instead of going down the hallway to her own bedroom, she veered into the guest room where he'd been staying.

One of his T-shirts lay on the bed. She picked it up and held it to her nose, breathing in the familiar scent of home and security.

The sight of a pair of his socks on the floor almost made her laugh as she remembered their conversation about his penchant for not picking up his socks. Instead, tears leaped into her eyes.

She threw the shirt back on the bed and angrily wiped at her tears. She was through crying over Nick Simon. It was time for her to start getting over him.

However, an hour later when the doorbell rang, her

heart leaped with the anticipation of seeing him again. Her hands trembled with nervous energy as she opened the door to him.

For a brief moment she couldn't speak. Oh, why did he have to look so wonderful in his jeans and a camo-green T-shirt that complemented the color of his eyes? Why did the mere sight of him threaten to break her heart all over again?

"Come in," she said quickly after an initial awkward pause. She opened the door further for him to enter. As he swept by her, his familiar scent wrapped around her broken heart. "Feel free to go upstairs to get your things," she said.

"Can we talk first?"

Once again she hesitated.

"Please, Julie," he said softly...pleadingly.

She gestured him toward the living room, although she wasn't sure they had anything to discuss. He'd used her until he didn't need her anymore and now he was here to take the last pieces of him away.

He walked into the living room and sank down on the sofa. She sat opposite him in a chair. There was no way she wanted to sit close to him. She didn't want to smell his familiar scent, feel the warmth of his body heat as he told her goodbye.

"Julie, I can't let this end like this," he said. He leaned forward, his eyes glittering bright and intent. "There's no question that initially I did you wrong. I made selfish choices that served only myself."

"Do you really have a wife who was murdered?"

"Absolutely. Why do you think I would lie about such a terrible thing?"

"The problem is I don't know what you lied about and what you didn't. What were you doing out on the street on the night of my accident?"

For the first time since they'd come into the living room, his gaze shifted away from her and to some point over her left shoulder.

He released a deep sigh. "If I tell you everything about that night then I'll be betraying the trust of five other men." His gaze met hers again. "I can promise you that I did nothing wrong and I can't regret what happened that night because it brought you to me."

Although he'd piqued her curiosity about the other men, she realized it didn't really matter what he'd been doing that night. What mattered were the lies that had fallen so effortlessly out of his mouth during the weeks they'd been together.

"You're a terrific liar," she said, unable to help the bitterness that crept into her tone.

"You might think so, but you don't realize how difficult it was for me. I hated each and every lie I told you. There's no question that initially I used you to my advantage. But, Julie, it didn't take me long to realize I was falling in love with you. I don't want to take my things and go home. My home is here with you and I will spend the rest of my life trying to make up for all the hurt I've done to you."

Was it possible for him to manufacture the love that shone from his beautiful eyes? Everything was out in the open now; what possible reason would he have to lie about loving her?

Her heart began to beat at a quickened pace. He was who she wanted in her life. Despite their crazy path so far, she believed he loved her. And she loved him.

She might never fully understand why he'd made the choices he had on that night. He was a good man. He could have run right past her car and left her unconscious. It might have been hours before anyone had found her.

He could have dumped her off at her home and exited her life immediately, but he'd seen the remnants of the physical fight she'd had with Casey and had stayed because he'd thought Julie might be in trouble.

Most men would have walked away, unwilling to become embroiled in a stranger's drama, but Nick had stayed. To her surprise, the light of forgiveness filled her heart.

"You'll make it up to me for the rest of your life?" she finally said.

"Just give me the chance, Julie. Give us a chance." He gazed at her intently, as if holding his breath for her reply.

"When are you going to put a ring on my finger?"

A burst of excited laughter escaped him and he jumped up off the sofa. "Today...tomorrow...right now!" he exclaimed as he walked over and pulled her up from the chair and into his arms. "And I'm intending a very short engagement," he said before his lips captured hers in a kiss that nearly took her breath away.

When the kiss finally ended, he placed his hands

on either side of her face and stared deeply into her eyes. "Julie, I swear to you I'm the man you dreamed of when you thought of love and marriage. I'm going to be the best husband any woman would ever want."

"And I'm going to be the best wife," she replied. Her heart expanded with happiness. "I think maybe it was fate that brought us together. I was so lonely and ready for love in my life."

He nodded. "And now there's going to be two less lonely people in the world."

"If you start singing that song, I'll never forgive you. Nobody does Air Supply better than Air Supply," she replied.

He laughed and then lowered his head to kiss her once again. This one tasted of his love, of his sweet longing for her. It tasted of the promise of forever.

He raised his head and smiled at her. "I love you, Julie Peterson."

"And I love you, Nick Simon," she replied.

"I can't wait to make you Julie Simon. Maybe we should just elope."

It was her turn to laugh. "My mother would hate you forever if you took away her opportunity to be mother of the bride at a traditional wedding."

"I certainly don't want to start out with the wrath of George and Lynetta focused on me," he said.

"There's no reason why we can't plan a fairly quick wedding."

"Can we enjoy a little honeymoon in your bedroom before the wedding?" His gaze was light and teasing, but with a fiery hunger that instantly lit one in her.

She twirled out of his embrace and ran for the stairs. "Last one up has to cook dinner," she cried over her shoulder.

His laughter chased her up the stairs where they would make love and plan a wedding and plan a future together filled with children and laughter and love.

Epilogue

"Hold them," Nick yelled to the defense. Thank goodness this was a practice and not a real game. The defense still left a lot to be desired. As the play ended, he motioned the teenagers in.

While he waited for them all to gather around, he shot a glance at the bleachers where Julie sat with several of the kids' parents.

As he gave the boys his usual pep talk, his mind drifted over the events of the past two weeks. They had definitely been eventful.

He'd put his house up for sale as he and Julie had decided to live in her place. They'd also been busy making wedding plans. She now sported a pretty diamond engagement ring, pleasing not only her but Lynetta, as well.

He still checked the news every day, hoping not to see any of the names that had been on a hit list of sorts. But that time of his life seemed distant and alien to him now.

As the sweaty boys headed in to the locker rooms,

he waved to Julie and followed them. He was thrilled that she was taking an interest in the team and had sworn she would be at all the games.

She'd told her parents she would continue to work part-time at the store until classes began at the community college where she was enrolled. She was taking action on achieving the dream of becoming a nurse.

Casey had been held over for trial and while Julie and the rest of Casey's family were sad at the choices Casey had made, they'd also agreed that she had to face whatever consequences the court handed down.

Once he saw that all the boys were gone from the locker room, he headed toward the bleachers where she was the last one remaining. He couldn't help the way his heart lifted as he approached Julie.

With each day that passed, he only loved her more. She was his heart, his soul, and each day with her was a gift. And the amazing part was that he knew she felt the same way about him.

"Hey, Coach," she said as she stood from the bleacher seat.

"Hey, gorgeous," he replied. "You know what I've always wanted to do?"

"What's that?" Her eyes sparkled with happiness.

"I've always wanted to kiss the woman I'm going to marry on the fifty-yard line."

Her grin was infectious. "Then what are you waiting for?"

He grabbed her hand and together they ran across the neatly manicured grass of the field.

Together…forever…the warmth of love embraced him. It was the way they would run to their future… together and with love.

HE'D SUSPECTED ALL along that when the time to act came, Nick Simon would falter. That was why he had done Brian McDowell. That scumbag had deserved a painful death. A bullet to the head had been too easy.

He'd wanted Brian's death to be slow and painful, which was why he'd brought the large knife with him. It had been so easy. The large flower pot had been a handy tool to throw at the sliding-glass door.

Knowing the noise would rouse Brian out of bed, he'd simply waited in the shadows. When Brian had stumbled toward the shattered glass, he'd attacked.

Brian had squealed like a pig as he'd driven his knife in him over and over again. God, what a high it had been. His adrenaline had pumped hotter, faster, through his body than he could ever remember. It had been such a rush, like having sex, only better.

He didn't even mind the thick, coppery scent of blood or the ultimate odor of death that wafted in the air when he'd finished. He'd remained seated on the floor next to the body for several long moments.

He'd liked it. He'd liked it so much he was going to do it again. There were a lot of bad people in the world that the justice system had allowed to walk scot-free. He even had a list of the next five men to start with. He'd be patient and he could be careful.

It was time somebody cleaned up the trash on the streets. He wondered how long, how many bodies, it would take before the cops realized the *V* carved into he dead men's foreheads stood for vengeance.

Oh, yes, he couldn't wait to strike again.

* * * * *

TRIBAL BLOOD

JENNA KERNAN

Chapter One

Kacey Doka felt the warm gush of liquid surge down her thighs as her water broke. She knew what it meant, knew she must alert the guards. After eight months of captivity, she would be the first to see what happened next.

She didn't know what frightened her more, the prospect of giving birth or what they would do to her when she was finished.

"Don't tell them," said her friend Marta, her eyes wide with terror. Marta Garcia was also nineteen and had been taken before Kacey. She was bigger around the middle, so all the girls trapped with Kacey in this dusty basement thought that Marta would go first.

"They are going to notice a baby," said Brenda Espinoza, who was two years younger, was well into her second trimester and no longer able to deny the child that moved within her.

Brenda was the third to arrive. In May, according to their floor calendar, three months after Kacey.

"And that you're no longer pregnant," Brenda added. "How do you expect to hide that?"

She didn't. Kacey knew that she had no alternative but to alert the guards. She glanced to Maggie Kesselman, the newest arrival here, just over a week ago. Kacey felt so sorry for her. Maggie was the youngest at only fourteen and still grappling through tears and disbelief at what had happened to her.

"Call them," said Kacey.

Marta walked laboriously up the wooden steps from the basement to the metal door that opened exactly twice a day. Marta glanced back with wide, troubled eyes and Kacey nodded. Marta knocked and then retreated down the stairs. All the windows were covered from the outside and barred from within, so the only light was the single overhead bulb that never went out and that now cast Marta's shadow before her as she descended. Marta hurried along with a heavy, rocking tread, gripping the banister for support, anxious to be back on the cold concrete floor before that door swung open because they didn't like them hanging by the door when it opened.

Kacey did not know where they were being kept. But she did know that screaming for help brought only the guards. Vicious, heartless guards who spoke in a thick foreign accent.

"They'll find us soon," said Kacey to the other three. "They'll come and rescue us."

She kept saying it, believing it until the others

believed it, too. Their families, their tribe, the authorities were all searching. They'd come for them.

"If I don't come back, I'll send help. I promise."

Marta hugged her. Maggie started to cry again. Brenda stared at the floor with an unfocused gaze, her hands laced, locked and pressed to her mouth.

Kacey knew the guards did not like being disturbed between feedings. Whatever they were doing, interruptions resulted in blows.

The door banged open and two men descended the stairs with clubs. The girls screamed and fled to the corners of the large empty basement area. Only Kacey remained at the bottom of the stairs.

Their captors had provided them each with a blanket and mattress. They also had a sink and toilet behind a partition. The toilet smelled of bleach and soap, both provided, but the basement held the musty scent of wool, dirt and decay. An appearance of a new mattress always signaled the imminent arrival of a new girl. Yesterday, the fifth mattress had appeared. To date, four had entered through that metal door and none had left. Kacey was about to leave their prison.

Would they bring her to a hospital to deliver her baby? No, of course they couldn't do that because she could speak to any of the medical staff and alert them that she was a prisoner.

"What is dis? Why you are knocking?" The one they called Oleg spoke to the group. His English was best but still difficult for them to understand.

The girls looked from one to the other, none willing to speak to Oleg because although his English was the best, his temper was the worst. Kacey's insides seemed to have a will of their own and began squeezing so hard that she cried out.

"Her water broke," said Marta, pointing to the wet spot on the concrete floor.

Oleg turned his pale blue eyes on Kacey. Then he glanced to the large pool of water darkening the concrete. He motioned his head toward Kacey, and the second man, Anton, stepped forward and captured Kacey by the arm, hurrying her toward the stairs.

She glanced over her shoulder to see the girls coming together in the center of the room, huddling tight as they stared after her. Oleg grasped her opposite arm and she was thrust up the stairs before them and through the prison door.

On the floor above the basement, she saw an office with tight dark carpeting and three desks with computers and phones under harsh fluorescent lighting. A television had been mounted on the wall, and a mini fridge sat beneath it with a half-full coffeepot resting on the top. The shape of the room and the two doorways made Kacey think she was in a large house. The normalcy of the layout clashed with the terror below her feet where the others huddled in near darkness.

The windows furnished views of a busy road where cars buzzed past trying to make the light. Beyond that squatted a strip mall, housing a Chinese restaurant, nail salon and pet grooming. The sunlight seemed especially bright and she used her hand as a visor.

"Call the boss," said Oleg.

Anton released her to move to the phone. The third guard, whom she had never seen, watched her intently as her eyes moved from Anton to the door and then to his face to see the wicked smile challenging her to go for it.

Kacey wrapped her arms around her squeezing stomach and clenched her teeth. Anton lowered the phone.

"The boss said he'll call the doc."

Oleg thrust her into one of the office chairs. Kacey's eyes went from the computer to the phone as she calculated her chances of using either. The big unfamiliar guard stalked forward and sat on the edge of the desk. Then he folded his arms across his wide chest. He looked so smug and superior that instead of feeling defeat, Kacey felt rage.

"Not there," said Anton. "She'll bleed all over everything. Take her to the exam room."

She was lifted by the upper arms with such force she momentarily left the floor. Kacey soon found herself in a small windowless room dominated by a short black examination table with two metal gizmos that reminded her of small riding stirrups. Her flesh began to crawl.

The pain ripped across her back and she doubled over.

"It hurt?" asked Oleg.

She nodded, blowing out a breath as sweat beaded on her forehead.

"Good. That mean baby is coming."

The door closed but not before she heard Anton ask Oleg, "What about her?"

Oleg's answer was not in English, but Anton's reply was.

"Dump her or sell her?" asked Anton.

She could not understand the reply but did not need to. She had her answer. After the baby was born, she would be sold or killed.

Kacey held her throbbing middle. She knew the child she carried was not hers. But somehow it did not matter. She loved it and would protect it. That meant staying alive.

She pounded on the door. "I need to use the toilet."

"Use the sink in there."

"I can't climb up on that sink!"

The door opened and Anton entered. He took her arm and hauled her up another flight of stairs to a very nice, clean bathroom with a claw-foot tub, white shower curtain, shampoo, conditioner, soap and clean towels. She scowled at the bounty as the anger built inside like lava. She and her friends had one bar of soap among all of them, worked down to a thin wafer. Meanwhile the guards had this. She glanced from the toilet to the small window.

"So go," said Anton.

He wanted to watch? Fine. She drew up the sheath

dress they had provided and sat. After several minutes, he urged her to hurry.

"I'm not done."

"You better not have that kid in that toilet."

She had her weapon. Kacey closed her eyes and pushed, crying out. She peered at her captor. He was glancing back toward the hall.

Kacey cried louder.

"Oleg! Get up here." He stepped out of the door and vanished.

Kacey had the door shut and the bolt thrown in a moment. Anton pounded on the door as Kacey opened the window and scrambled out onto a flat roof overhanging the first floor. She ran to the edge and glanced to the lawn. It seemed a long way down. Then she turned back toward the house. How long did she have?

She threw one of her princess slippers off the roof. Then she threw the other one. The roof coating was so hot, it burned her feet. Kacey ran along the roof to the other side of the house, where she found a half-open window. She could see Oleg and the third man rush down the hall toward the bathroom.

Kacey was sliding the window open the rest of the way when she heard a crash. The bathroom door, she thought. Kacey slipped inside the house and down the stairs to the first floor as the men shouted from the bathroom. She hurried through the office and to the entrance hall. There on the stand beside a hat rack were three sets of car keys. She grabbed all three and was turning toward the basement door to release her friends when she saw Oleg through the dining room window as he passed by on the outside of the house. How had he got off the roof so fast?

They made eye contact and he shouted to the others, breaking into a run. She glanced to the locked basement door. If she went that way, he'd have her.

Kacey made her decision and charged out the front door. She descended the porch stairs, hitting the unlock button on one of the car fobs. A car beeped. But that one was trapped behind the others. She tried again, reaching the drive as Oleg made it to the walkway.

The next car was the one she wanted. It looked new and fast. More important, it was closest to the road. She dived into the car as Oleg pounded both open hands on the hood, denting the metal.

She pressed the lock on the fob as his hand slipped onto the latch and tugged. Kacey looked for a key, but there was none. Just a button beside the steering wheel that said START. She pushed it and the engine turned over. There was no gearshift, just a knob. She rotated it to R as Oleg shattered the driver's-side window with his fist.

"I rip dat baby from your belly!" he bellowed.

His hand extended toward her, his fingers forming a claw. Kacey screamed and threw herself sideways across the console. Then she jammed her foot down on the gas. The car sailed backward down the drive, over the curb, hitting something that flew over the roof before she righted herself. She could barely reach the pedals because the seat was so far back, but she managed to get the car into Drive and turn the wheel so the tires were back on pavement as she raced away. She saw Anton running after her in the street. She thrust her arm out the open space where the window had been and extended her middle finger, giving him a gesture of farewell.

She had all their keys and she knew where they were keeping her friends. All she had to do was get to the police and tell them what had happened.

But Marta told her that she had heard Oleg say the police were on their payroll and that they knew about the house and did nothing. Not the police, then. Her tribe—tribal police. She had to get home to Turquoise Canyon.

Where was she? Sweat beaded on her forehead and her stomach muscles cramped. She slowed as she made a turn onto a strange road. The landscape was familiar. She looked around and then into the rearview at the way she had come. She knew they hadn't taken her far from home because of the amount of time she had ridden in the back of the van. Soon she had herself oriented.

She was in Darabee, Arizona. And everyone in her tribe knew that Darabee was the police force who had set the stage for the Lilac Shooter to be assassinated right in the station. The investigations were ongoing. The police chief had been replaced, but she believed what Marta had told her. This police force could be on the Russians' payroll, so she was not going there under any circumstances. Kacey was halfway to her home in Turquoise Canyon when she realized that this would be the first place they would look.

Her mother couldn't protect her, assuming she was even there. And going there would only put her brothers and sisters in danger. Her best friend, Marta, was still a captive. Kacey needed to get the girls out of there before they did something terrible to them all.

The tribal police, she trusted them. They could find the house. She drove to Piñon Forks, past the activity at the river, construction mostly, with dump trucks, bulldozers and backhoes. She ignored them as she drove to tribal headquarters. The parking lot was eerily empty. There were no police cars and no tribal vehicles. She drew up to the fire lane in front of the station, peering at the dark empty building.

Something was very wrong.

She craned her neck. Why were there no pickup trucks on the road? She had passed no one and seen not one soul since arriving on the rez. The town looked deserted. Where was everyone?

A car appeared in her rearview and she jumped. Was it Oleg?

The man who stepped out of the vehicle was white and wearing some sort of uniform. Her heart hammered as she considered fleeing before he reached her. But she needed information.

He approached from the driver's side. Kacey prepared to shift her foot from brake to gas. He stood before her window. She meant to lower it only a crack, but the window was gone, leaving her vulnerable. Her heart pounded in her throat.

"You looking for tribal headquarters?" he asked.

"Yes." Her voice sounded strange to her ears. Barely a squeak.

"They moved," he said.

What? Why? That didn't make any sense at all. "Where?" Her voice was all air and very little sound.

He cocked his head and gave her an odd stare as if she should know this.

"Up to Turquoise Ridge." He glanced at her distended belly. "Oh! Clinic is up there, too. They're in trailers, one beside the other. Can't miss it. You need me to drive you?"

"No. Thanks." She did not wait for a reply before accelerating away.

They'd moved? Why would tribal government ever leave their main community for the rough mining settlement of Turquoise Ridge?

The women's health clinic was right next to the police station, looking just as deserted. But she couldn't go to the clinic, even if it were open, because the Russians would probably look for her there, because someone there had done this to her. She and the other girls had compared memories. They had all been to the tribal health-care facility shortly before capture. But what had happened there was a yawning blank, for her visits and theirs. Why couldn't they remember?

She had to get word to tribal police.

It was several minutes before Kacey became aware of her surroundings again. She was already in the tribal community of Koun'nde and heading for Turquoise Ridge. She should turn around.

And go where?

Where could she go where she would be safe and where they could not find her? Somewhere she could find help for her friends but not endanger her sisters and brothers?

And then she knew. She would go to him, the boy who had promised to go away with her and instead left her behind. Kacey knew he was scheduled to come home from Afghanistan. His brother Ty had told her so and that he was changed. He had been discharged after something that had happened over there. Ty said that Colt had been captured with comrades in an insurgent attack and then recovered.

Afterward Colt had spoken to Ty from Maryland and said he wasn't ready to come home. Ty talked him into coming back anyway. Colt agreed but only if he could live up in the family's claim off Dead Horse Road beyond the community of Turquoise Ridge.

Ty had told her Colt wanted to see her after he got his act together. But she'd been taken before he came home. She knew Colt's plan had been to make over an old cabin. Colt had shown it to her once. She knew where it was. It was a good place to hide, and if Colt was there, he could help her rescue her friends.

What she didn't know was if she had the physical strength to reach it. Her middle began to squeeze again and she bucked back in the seat, swerving dangerously. She had to reach him before her body forced her to stop, before the men pursuing her captured her again.

I rip dat baby from your belly.

She shivered at the memory of Oleg's words. The tears she had held for months now poured down her cheeks, blurring her vision. But she ignored the tears and pain in her middle and the ache in her heart as she pressed down on the gas.

Time had become the enemy.

COLT REDHORSE HEARD the screeching of brakes and the slide of tires on gravel as someone made the turn leading to his cabin way too fast. His brother Ty was known to drive like that in his youth, trying out the various cars he was improving. But lately he always approached Colt's retreat slowly and with proper notice. Often he sent his dog, Hemi, in first as envoy.

So it wasn't Ty.

Colt collected his rifle. The pistol was always on his hip or beside his head on those few occasions when he slept. He didn't sleep much. Too many ways for his enemies to reach him in dreams.

He moved between the trunks of the trees quickly and without much sound. Whoever it was would not hear him coming. He was like death itself—silent and without mercy.

Since he'd returned from Afghanistan, Colt's emotions boiled down to only two—fear and fury. Right now, it was just fury. No one came up here un-invited. His brother Jake had tried more than once. Colt hadn't shot at him, but it had been hard hiding while Jake violated his personal space. The mining cabin belonged to all of them, as did the claim. But the way he figured it, it was his by occupation and because he just couldn't stand to be around anyone yet. His skin itched like that of a junkie coming down from a high. He checked to see if a bug was crawl-ing up his arm and saw only smooth brown skin.

He wasn't back in Afghanistan anymore, he told himself. He was home. This was Apache land. Safe land. This settlement lay tight against the turquoise-bearing ridge from which the town got its name.

Turquoise Ridge, the most remote of the three settlements on the Turquoise Canyon Reserva-tion. Most folks here were miners. Living up on the ridge required a person to tote water and live with-out electricity or plumbing. Other than the miners, there were a few recluses, like him, he supposed. His closest neighbor was a Vietnam vet, former army, who went off the rez hoping to be a code talker like the Navajo and came home as crazy as Colt felt he himself was rapidly becoming. Randy Hooee hung tinfoil around his cabin to keep the CIA from listening to the thoughts in his head. As far as Colt could tell, it seemed to be working.

Colt's breathing slowed and his skin now only buzzed with adrenaline, not the flesh-crawling fear that threatened daily to have him hanging out bits of tinfoil, as well.

He had a purpose. Find the identity of the intruder.

He resumed his operation, moving close enough to see the road. The car was black and unfamiliar. A sedan, dust-covered with a dented hood. Parked at an odd angle and stationary now as the dust continued to settle back to earth. The tinted windshield showed him nothing. His eyes narrowed.

Why didn't they all just leave him alone?

The door opened and a hand appeared on the top of the driver's-side window. Small, slim and gripping hard as if the driver had to haul himself out of the car. Colt lifted the rifle, using the scope to aim at where he knew the center of the driver's torso would be in just a moment. Should he kill the bastard or just shoot out the windshield beside his head? He shifted between his two targets. This or that? That or this? A smile twisted his lips. He'd learned a lot from the US Marines but even more from the insurgents who had held him for three days.

And then the target's head popped up above the door frame like a fox leaving its den. Colt's hands went numb and he dropped his rifle.

It had been eighteen months, but he knew he would never forget that face. That was his former girlfriend, Kacey Doka. She'd tried to convince him not to join up after he graduated. Not to leave her behind. He had explained that if she wanted to get off the rez, this was their way. He hadn't wanted to go because he loved it here, couldn't imagine living anywhere else. But Kacey could and he loved her enough to try to give her what she wanted. It had cost him, deeply.

He had planned to give the signing bonus and his pay to her, but she wouldn't take it. She wanted them to go together, but he had committed himself. How had he messed that up so badly? She had not answered his letters. When he'd finally made it back home on a psych discharge, her home was the only place he'd stopped before coming here. Kacey had left, her mother said, months ago. She hadn't been back, wasn't expected back. But she sure was back now.

Kacey glanced up the hill toward his position, the sunlight highlighting her black hair blue. Colt flinched. Had she heard him drop his rifle? He watched her glance back the way she had come. From here, he could not see much of the road because of the trees. But she would have a clear view.

What was she doing here after all this time? He'd been home for months. Had Ty called her? That thought made his stomach flip. The only thing worse than being a walking basket case was having Kacey Doka know about it.

"Colt?" she called to him.

He pressed his back to the flaking bark of the ponderosa pine and squeezed his eyes shut.

Go away, Kacey. Please.

"Colt, it's Kacey!" She was shouting now. Judging from the sound, she was cupping her hands to her mouth to amplify her voice. "I need to see you."

No, you don't. Not like this.

Ty had sent her. Damn his meddling older brother. Colt had told him he didn't want to see anyone. That he wasn't ready. Had Ty given up hope that he was improving? But he was. He made it through more than one day without a panic attack. But the nights were very long. He knew his lack of sleep wasn't helping. But he wouldn't take anything that Ty had offered.

"I'm in trouble, Colt. Please, please answer me."

Trouble?

Colt's eyes opened as he pushed himself off the tree. What kind of trouble could she be in?

Was this a trick?

Despite her mother's neglect, Kacey had done well in school, missing only when her mom took off, leaving Kacey to take care of her siblings. Ty told him that Kacey had been accepted at Phoenix University and planned to use her Big Money for as long as it lasted. Big Money was what they called the allotment of the tribe's revenue distributed annually, but kept in trust for members under eighteen. The distributions often went for vehicles, something big and flashy. Colt noticed that there never was another new truck after that first one. He knew thirty-year-olds still driving that Big Money truck. So he had not spent his on a vehicle. Instead he kept his for them, him and Kacey. He figured his pay, his bonus and Big Money could get them a house right here on the rez.

He was certain that if he could get them their own place and provide her a real home, she would change her mind about leaving. To do that, he'd enlisted in the Marines. That was when she'd ended it between them. When Ty told him she'd gone, Colt had been expecting it.

Had she used her Big Money to run away?

She'd loved him once. He knew that. And he had loved her, which was why he wasn't going to let her see him now. It would kill those feelings she'd held as surely as a snake crushes a baby bunny.

But he could see her. He'd give himself that at least. Just for a minute and then he'd go.

"I'm coming up there. Don't you shoot me, Colt Redhorse, or so help me, I will tell your mother."

His mother liked Kacey and she was worried about him. Ty had said so. And his mother wasn't well. Why didn't Ty tell him that Kacey was back? He could have used a little warning to prepare.

He heard the crunch of her footsteps as she crossed the gravel on the road. Her tread was slow and heavy. And she gave a cry as if she was in pain. Colt popped his head around the trunk of the tree. What he saw made his jaw drop.

Was Kacey pregnant?

She was! Very, very pregnant and she was holding her swollen belly as her face twisted into a mask of pain. His eyes widened. He'd seen that same expression on his mother's face when she went into labor with his little sister, Abbie. He'd only been six, but the fear made the memory stick.

Was Kacey in labor?

That was impossible. You'd have to be crazy to come up here to deliver a baby. He craned his neck to see her as she momentarily disappeared from view behind the trees. She was heading for the trail they had used to climb up to his family's cabin. She knew the way.

Kacey had been a part of his family, had spent more time living in his house than in hers. Not that he blamed her. But she'd go home when her sister Jackie or Winnie would come and tell her that their mom was gone again. Running drugs for the Wolf Posse, Ty said, taking her cut in either money or product.

Colt moved parallel to Kacey as she walked along the road toward the trail, catching flashes of Kacey between the tree trunks. She looked thin, despite her swollen belly, and pale as if she had not been in the sun in months. Her gait was a scurry that combined the side-to-side rocking motion of a woman far along in her pregnancy with a girl in a hurry. She held both hands under her belly. Why did she keep looking behind her?

Kacey stopped, hunched and turned toward the road. What could she see that made her eyes round and her mouth swing open like a gate? Kacey ran now. She ran to the woods and rock outcropping with a speed he would not have believed possible.

"They're here! Colt, do you hear me? They're going to take me again."

Again?

Oh no, they are not.

Colt didn't know who *they* were or why they were after Kacey. What he did know was that they wouldn't succeed in reaching her. He had the high ground, a rifle with extra rounds and the will to kill anyone who threatened Kacey. He might be a mental mess, but he remembered what it felt like to be in love with her. But now that memory only made his chest ache and his breathing hitch. Whatever part of him that understood how to love a woman had died back there in Afghanistan. But that didn't mean he wouldn't protect her. He would, with his life.

Colt moved to a position that gave him a good vantage of her car and waited as the second vehicle approached. Colt lifted the rifle, pressing the familiar stock to his cheek and closing his left eye. The crosshairs fixed on the gray sedan.

He felt centered, calm, relaxed.

The first shot sent a bullet at the driver's side of the windshield. The glass should have shattered into tiny cubes but instead remained intact. The second shot went to the passenger's side. If there was a passenger behind the windshield, he should now have a bullet in his head, but instead the glass showed only a tiny nick. Colt was using .38 long-range ammunition. That windshield should be compromised. But it wasn't and he knew why. The glass was reinforced.

"Bulletproof," he muttered.

He had not seen that since Afghanistan. This was a very expensive vehicle. From within the luxury auto, someone shifted the sedan's gears and the car reversed direction with a spray of gravel.

Colt marched down the hill. When he reached the road, the car was turning around. He got two shots into the side of the vehicle with nothing but damage to the paint. He missed the shot at the rear tire. The next shot pinged off the rear window of the retreating sedan. Who the heck was after her?

Whoever it was, they had money—lots of money.

He put a hole in the license for no reason except as a final farewell and a good riddance. If they came back, he'd use a hand grenade on their asses.

Colt turned to the woods, where Kacey now stood beside the outcropping of rock she had used for cover. She bent forward at the hips, clutching her belly with one hand and the boulder with the other, eyes pinched shut. Colt had a sickening feeling that while he had been up here brooding over Kacey's departure and collecting the bits and pieces of his mind, Kacey had been in real trouble. He was equally afraid she was going to have that baby right here and right now.

Chapter Two

"They're gone," Colt said, his voice slightly deeper than she remembered. He was at her side in an instant, rifle slung over his shoulder. His long black hair hung straight and loose past his shoulders. She met his stare, seeing the familiar espresso color of his irises, just slightly lighter than his pupils. His skin was bronze from the sun and his brows were thicker than she recalled, balancing the rich brown of his eyes and the symmetrical nose that seemed small by contrast to his wide mouth and full lips. The cleft in his chin looked deeper and his face leaner. He'd lost weight but gained muscle, she realized, making his body look harder and more dangerous.

She was safe. For the first time in months and months, she was safe and she was home. The joy bubbled up inside. She threw her arms around his neck, kissing him full on the lips. The warm familiar scent of pine and warm male skin enveloped her. He stiffened as their bodies met, his hands coming up to her shoulders, and for a moment she thought he would push her away. For another heartbeat, he hesitated and then he gathered her up and held her as his mouth took hers, deepening the kiss. She was home in his arms and everything would be—

He gripped her shoulders, increasing the tension as he pushed her to arm's length. He stared at her, panting and feral, like a mad dog. Then he pressed his hand over his mouth and wiped away her kiss. The pain in her stomach morphed from sorrow at his rejection to another contraction. She grimaced and groped behind her for the solid security of the rock, seating herself as the contraction gripped her.

He was not the boy she recalled, the one who kissed her and told her that he'd come back for her. That boy had been joyful and optimistic. But the man before her was taller, leaner and harder than Colt Redhorse. There was a wildness around the whites of his eyes that reminded her of a mustang the instant he feels the rope cinch around his neck. Colt's nostrils flared and he stepped back, his gaze sweeping down to her bare feet and then back up to her face.

She imagined what he must think, and the shame sent a guilty flush into her face, making it burn with heat. Kacey placed a hand on her distended belly and the other on the hollow below her cheekbone. Somehow in just over a year, everything had changed between them and they were strangers.

Beneath the skin, her muscles were contracting, sending pressure all the way around to her back. This one was worse. She hunched and groaned, squeezing her eyes shut.

"You shouldn't do that. I'm not… I can't."

She heard the blast of air as he forcefully exhaled.

"They'll come back for the baby."

Colt glanced down the road in the direction of their retreat.

"Should I bring you to the clinic?" he asked.

Her reply was a shout. "No!"

Colt flinched. "All right. Where, then? Your mom's?"

"They'll look for me there. My sisters and brothers, I don't want anything to happen to them." Finally the pressure in her back eased and she could straighten. That was when she noted that Colt had one arm around her. The other she gripped, squeezing with a force that matched the contraction. She released his arm and saw the white print of her hand disappear as the blood returned to his forearm.

How long would this go on? It had been over an hour already.

"How did you know where to find me?"

"Ty said you agreed to come home after your discharge if you could come here." She didn't mention the reason for his discharge. Had Ty told her that his kid brother had been a POW, rescued and returned stateside?

"So you came here looking for me?" Colt asked.

She lowered her gaze. "I didn't know what else to do."

He made a sound in his throat and then said, "I'm honored."

Kacey's mouth dropped open and her gaze flashed to him. Colt smiled down at her and for a moment everything was good again. He was here with her and she knew he would protect her.

She looked up at him, noting the unfamiliar breadth of his shoulders. His hair gleamed with good health. She reached up and fingered a strand, placing it on his chest and pressing it into place.

"They didn't make you cut it," she said. His hair still reached to his chest and she was so glad.

"Nope. Just made me wear it tied back and under my shirt or in a bun."

"A bun?" Imagining that made her smile. He smiled, too.

His wide mouth drew back to reveal white, even teeth. He'd had the chip in the front repaired and now she could not even remember which tooth he had damaged. His jaw was more prominent, as were his cheekbones.

"You're too skinny," she said.

He pressed his mouth closed, still smiling as he nodded. "That's what Ty says, too."

"You see him? How is he?"

Colt shook his head. "I don't talk to him."

Her brow wrinkled. "But you said—"

"He comes sometimes. He talks to me. I let him see me. But I don't speak to him. I don't speak to anyone."

Her frown deepened.

"But me?" she asked.

He blew out a breath through his nose. "I guess so."

"How long have you lived like this?"

"Since they released me."

"Released?"

Didn't she know? But she didn't. He could see it in the wide earnest expression that showed nothing but confusion. Well, he sure wasn't going to tell her.

His lips went tight. He led her down to the car. "Let's get you out of here."

She took a few steps and then stopped. "I can't go to one of the settlements or the police."

"Why?"

"They're looking for me. They'll take me again."

His eyes shifted and one hand went to the strap of his rifle. "Who?"

"Those two and I don't know who else. I heard more of them. But I've only ever seen Oleg and Anton. Oh, and one other guy. I don't know his name."

"Oleg?"

"Russians."

He looked back toward the road. "They have an armored car." He swung the rifle before him, lifting it to his shoulder. "Plug your ears," he said.

She did and he took a shot. The bullet punched a hole in the rear door of the car she had stolen.

"That one isn't armored." He swung the rifle so the strap held it behind his back. "Okay. Let's go farther up into the ridge. There's a second cabin."

"Anyone know that?"

"Ty."

"Let's go." She allowed him to help her to the car and flushed as he pulled the safety belt over her distended belly and clipped it in place. She sank into the seat, closing her eyes.

"How long did they have you?" he asked.

She turned to him, opening her eyes. "Since February."

"February!" He straightened, his brow sweeping down over his dark eyes. That was eight months.

"Yeah."

"Everyone said you ran away."

"I didn't." She reached and gripped his hand. "Colt, there are more of us. More like me and they're all from Turquoise Canyon."

Now he was staring down the road where they had gone. "I could call Jake. Maybe he could pick them up."

"You have a phone?" she asked.

He shook his head.

"They'll kill Jake." The next contraction built across her middle.

He gripped her door frame and glanced down the empty road. "But you said there were others."

Her eyes widened. "Yes. Three others. They have Marta Garcia. She was in my class in high school. They took her before me. And Brenda Espinoza. She's five months pregnant. And Maggie Kesselman. They're all like me." She motioned to her belly. "Marta's due any day."

"What will happen to them now that you escaped?"

A cold shot of terror ripped through her. "I don't know." But the possibilities terrified her.

"We have to tell Jake," said Colt.

His brother was the newest hire on the tribal police force and she knew he could be trusted.

"I think so."

Her back cramped. "Oof!" she said and clutched her middle.

"We're getting you somewhere safe. But I need to find a woman to help you."

"No. Anyone who sees this baby is in danger. Colt, I wish I could have thought of a way by myself. But I'm scared. I need your help."

"But I've never—"

"Neither have I."

He shook his head and she saw something she had not seen before in him: fear.

"Colt Redhorse, you left me once. Don't you dare do that again."

She'd told him not to go. She'd felt something terrible would happen to him. As it turned out, something terrible had happened to both of them.

"I promised to come back."

"You didn't."

"I did. But you were gone."

She glowered at him.

"I'll get you somewhere safe, Kacey. I promise."

Kacey sighed. The air here was so sweet and clean. She thought of the musty basement where she'd been kept for months and shuddered.

"So, call Jake. All right?" he asked.

She nodded.

He rounded the hood at a run. A moment later, they were in motion on the rough road, heading back toward the center of Turquoise Ridge.

COLT HEADED FOR David SaVala's claim. It was close and David could be trusted to deliver a message to Ty. Ty could get to Jake. Then Colt was going to take Kacey to his cabin and help her bring this baby into the world. Colt planned on keeping this car hidden but close in case he needed to get Kacey to a hospital. With luck, Ty would be here soon.

Colt had three older brothers and his younger sister. The oldest brother was Kee, newly board certified as a doctor. Colt wished he could bring Kacey to him, but she would not go near the clinic. He planned to find out why. His next oldest brother was Ty, who, unlike Colt, had made it through his service in the US Marines to be honorably discharged. His tales of the service had convinced Colt to join.

But Ty had not chosen to enlist. He had signed to avoid federal prosecution after he and their father were arrested for armed robbery. Ty had already been in the Wolf Posse, the tribe's gang. The tribal leadership felt he needed discipline, so a deal was struck. Charges dropped if Ty enlisted. His father had previous arrests, so the tribe allowed federal prosecution. Now Ty lived between the gang who had claimed him and the family that couldn't keep him from choosing that life. Ty had often said it was easier to leave the military than a gang.

Finally there was Jake, the newest member of the Turquoise Tribal Police and six years Colt's senior. Jake had looked after him when their father went to prison. Colt had been lucky. He'd sort of had three fathers.

"Ty lives in Koun'nde. He has a phone. If I can get SaVala to lend me his phone, we can take it far enough to get service and call Ty and Jake. Then I can call Kee and ask him to come deliver this baby."

She had her eyes closed again and was blowing through pursed lips. Sweat beaded on his brow.

"Kacey?" he whispered.

She turned her head to look at him, her cheeks puffing out and in as she blew.

"They won't get you," he promised.

Her head dropped to the headrest. He knew she was already nineteen, but she still looked like the girl he'd first loved, still loved. Why had he left her? She'd been right about everything. Something terrible had happened to him and to her. He'd been so sure that the Marines would be a shortcut to what she wanted, with money to provide the life away from her mother and the shadow of his father. He'd been trying to prove he was strong like his brother Ty and smart like Kee and good like Jake. But he wasn't any of those things. He was a fragile wreckage of a man who couldn't even talk to people since…well, since everything that had happened over there.

He hadn't had the chance to be a hero. He'd just been taken like a sheep from a pasture to the butcher truck. Fate had made him the last lamb in line.

He pressed the web of his hand between his thumb and index finger to his forehead, trying to ease the pounding. He was in a car again and there was not enough air. He released his head to grip the wheel, bracing for the blast, waiting for it.

This time he'd be ready.

Colt was not going back there now. Kacey needed him. He was here on Turquoise Canyon and he had to stay focused. But he knew he wasn't keeping the panic attack away. He was only postponing it. The doc at Walter Reed in Maryland said he needed counseling and put him on the list. With luck, it would be decades before they would get to his name, because he wasn't talking about that with anyone ever. No one who wasn't held by insurgents could possibly understand.

His gaze flicked to Kacey, who sat with her head dropped back on the headrest but turned toward him. She smiled at him, her face relaxed and her hands laced over her belly. Her dark hair was gathered in a loose braid that lay on her shoulder. Her once soft, round face had changed. Her deep brown eyes were still bright, but there were dark smudges beneath them. Her lips were full and pink, but her jaw and pointed chin seemed too prominent in her thin face. How much weight had she lost? Kacey had always been slender, but now she was skinny, way too skinny. How much had they given them to eat?

Not enough—clearly.

The rations that he'd been given during his captivity rose in his mind and he pushed the memory of that down. One sure way to be of no help to her was to think about that.

No one understood that the captivity wasn't as hard as the memories that just would not go away. It wasn't getting better with time. It was worse. Colt gripped the wheel. He hated cars, trucks, anything that rolled. No one in his family understood. They were worried, but they didn't get it. He could not think about it, but he was stuck somehow. Afraid all the time.

Kacey was now looking in the side mirror, watching for trouble. Perhaps she could understand, he realized. Because she'd been a captive, too. But then she'd also understand that he was the very last person capable of helping her. That was why he was leaving her with his brother. Any one of his brothers was a better choice than him.

The corner of his mouth twitched.

"Almost there," he said to himself as much as to her.

Chapter Three

Kacey's body relaxed. The contractions were not as strong now, fading as if taking a pause. How long did labor last? Hours? Days? She didn't know. Her mother just went to the clinic and came home the next day with a brother or sister. Kacey assumed that by tomorrow at this time, she would have a baby. But exactly what happened in the meantime was vague.

She'd learned about childbirth in high-school health class. At the time, the lesson seemed theoretical. The abstract phases of birth just one more thing to be memorized and spit back on a quiz. Stage I—Early Labor. Stage II—Active Labor. Stage III—hand the baby to a nurse and take a nap.

Colt pulled off the road and up a short turnoff that was composed of two ruts in the yellow grass. A cabin came into view against the ridge, sitting up on concrete blocks. The step before the front door was clearly slag rock from a turquoise vein. She was Turquoise Canyon Apache, so she recognized what base rock surrounded a vein of the precious blue stone.

Colt barely had the car in Park before throwing himself against the driver's-side door in his hurry to be out of the cab. He scrambled out onto all fours. It took him a moment to right himself before he straightened and returned to the car.

"Colt?"

He was sweating as if he'd run from his claim to this one. He peered in at her through the open door.

"Call him," he whispered.

Kacey opened her door and swung her legs out, bare feet touching the long yellow grass as she inched forward on the seat. Colt retrieved his rifle and then rounded the car to stand beside her door.

She called a greeting. They were met first by a skinny white dog. The muck on his shoulder showed he'd been rolling in something, and the stench said it was something dead.

The claim holder arrived shortly afterward, dressed in coveralls coated with a fine white layer of rock dust. All claims belonged to the tribe, but families worked them and passed them along. Her family's claim was worked by others, leased for a period of five years at a time.

David SaVala tried to shake Colt's hand, but Colt chose to place his hand on the shoulder strap of his rifle. David greeted her instead, peering at her from beside Colt, but his smile was gone.

"Good to see you two back together."

She smiled and nodded. That seemed easier than explaining.

David took another step toward her, moving beyond the open car door, and his step faltered.

"Oh." He glanced from her swollen belly to Colt. "Oh, I see. Congratulations, you two."

Kacey used the door and the frame to heave herself up. Colt rubbed his neck but said nothing. He backed toward the woods, but Kacey gripped his arm to prevent his escape.

She told David what they needed and he retreated to his cabin with his dog for the phone and handed it off to her with the pass code and instructions on where she would first find a signal. The distance and her condition required another car ride. They headed out with the dog trotting with them as far as the road. Colt was shaking by the time they reached the high point of Dead Elk Dip and the place that allowed a weak cell phone signal.

"What's wrong?" she asked.

"Don't drive anymore."

"Claustrophobic?" she asked. This was new. Ty had told her of Colt's capture but had been short on details. She just now understood what helping her was costing him. Was it leaving his claim that upset him or the driving?

His skin was pale. He retrieved David's phone. Colt placed the call and gripped his hair in one fist as he waited for the phone to connect.

Kacey heard a male voice issue a greeting.

Colt squeezed his eyes shut. His fist tightened in his hair.

"Who's this?" came the voice on the other end of the line.

His jaw clamped shut and he thrust the phone at her.

"Hello?" she replied.

"This is Redhorse." She recognized the voice of Officer Jake Redhorse, one of Colt's older brothers. Kacey identified herself and relayed the high points. Escape. The stolen car. The gun battle. Her condition and the location of the missing girls.

"You're with Colt?" Disbelief resonated in his voice.

"Yes. He's the one who called you."

There was a moment's pause.

"Where are the girls?"

"I don't know exactly. I just drove until I figured out where I was."

"I need the exact address," said Jake. "And if it's in Darabee, I need to notify their police department."

"No. They might be connected. Like they were with that assassination in their station. Karl Hooke and the Lilac Mine Mass Shooter," said Kacey.

"How do you know that?"

"Marta Garcia overheard our captors say so before I got there." Kacey knew that the Darabee police were being investigated by the federal and state government for corruption. Several of the force had been suspended and charges filed.

"Can I speak to Colt?" Jake asked.

She relayed the request and was met with a firm shake of his head.

"He says no."

"I'm calling my chief for instructions and en route to you. Head toward Turquoise Ridge. Okay?"

"Yes. I understand."

"I'll need you to identify the house, Kacey. Can you do that?"

That meant going back. She gripped her free hand to her throat. "I'm in labor and those killers are still out there."

"So are your friends," Redhorse reminded her.

That hit her harder than the contractions. Colt shook his head. Clearly he did not want her to go back.

She had promised them that she'd send help. "Yes. I'll go."

Jake told her to tell Colt what to expect and ended the call.

Now Kacey's heart was pounding. "He said the FBI is coming for that car."

Colt scowled.

She imagined they could find something in there, fingerprints at least. A clear image of Oleg smashing his hands on the hood of the car came to her. She glanced at the twin dents there as a shot of panic made her ears ring.

"Where? From Phoenix?"

"No. Your brother said that they have FBI in Piñon

Forks since the explosion. Colt, what happened? What explosion? What is he talking about?"

"You must have passed through Piñon Forks on the way here. Didn't you see it?"

"I saw construction vehicles. The station was abandoned. Some man in a uniform told me that tribal headquarters had moved to Turquoise Ridge. But I took off before he told me why."

"Everyone has moved to Turquoise Ridge. They're in FEMA trailers or reclaiming their mining cabins."

"Why?"

"Come on. Let's get David's phone back to him."

En route, he told her everything, and the happenings were tragic. Some eco-extremists organization had blown up Skeleton Cliff Dam in hopes of compromising the Phoenix electrical grid. The dam was upriver from their reservation. Destroying the dam meant flooding their biggest community, Piñon Forks.

Apparently, an explosives expert from the FBI had managed to make a temporary barrier on their river by demolishing a huge section of the canyon ridge. Her actions had saved everyone there. But the rubble dam was failing. Evacuations were necessary.

She thought back to her wild race through town early this morning.

"I didn't even look at the canyon rim," she admitted. Her focus had been internal, on her own body, and external to the men she knew would come for her. "Have you seen it?"

He shook his head. "Haven't been off this claim since I got home. Until today. Heard about it from Ty. Only happened a couple weeks ago. Let's see. Third week in September, so nearly three weeks ago now."

He put his hand on the door latch and froze. He wiped a hand across his upper lip.

"I'll drive," she said.

"You're in labor."

"I know. Let me." She held her hand out for the fob.

He hesitated, then gave it to her and stepped aside.

"I'm sorry," he whispered.

She jostled herself awkwardly down into the seat and waited as he rounded the hood and then paused at the passenger side. She lowered the window. "Get in."

"I can't."

"Colt, please."

"I'll run to David's place. Through the woods. Be there before you get there."

"What if they're waiting on the road?"

Colt climbed in, his expression grim. He folded his arms over his chest as if he were freezing. She didn't even suggest the seat belt as she put them in motion. She headed back to David SaVala's claim. On arrival, she tooted the horn, afraid if she got out, Colt would run. David's dog was still covered in something, and David appeared shortly afterward. He approached her window and she returned the phone. The dog jumped up and placed her front paws on

the door, giving Kacey a stomach-turning whiff of
dead animal.

"Get down," he said, pushing the dog off. "Sorry.
She found a dead deer and keeps getting after it."

Kacey smiled and exhaled, trying to rid her nostrils of the stench.

The miner leaned down to look through the cab
to Colt.

"Good to see you out, Colt," said David. "Been
worried."

Colt nodded but said nothing. Why wouldn't he
speak to anyone?

David glanced at Kacey, who gave him a shrug.

"My dad was in Vietnam," said David. "Still
jumps at every truck that backfires. It changes you,
I guess." He pushed himself off the car, straightened
and forced a tight smile.

"Thank you for the use of the phone," she said.

"Sure." He scraped his knuckles over the stubble
on his jaw. "Well, stop by anytime. Love company.
Don't get much, though."

They were off a moment later with David waving
after them despite the dust they kicked up. The rainy
season had come and gone. They were back to hot,
dry days and cold, clear nights.

Jake met them en route with three other vehicles.
Colt drew his pistol and flicked the safety off.

Kacey was suffering from the end of another contraction, so she spoke through gritted teeth as she
clutched the wheel. "Don't shoot your brother."

He nodded and holstered his weapon before leaving the vehicle. Kacey watched as he greeted Jake with a nod. Kacey knew the two men who exited the next vehicle. The first was Detective Jack Bear Den. No mistaking him because he was the biggest man she knew. From the opposite side of the SUV came tribal police chief Wallace Tinnin. He was limping, as if he'd injured his foot. The chief had come to speak to her high-school class her senior year. It had been the January awards assembly and he had shaken her hand when she made the honor roll. Had that only been ten months ago? Yes, she realized. Just months before she had been taken.

The next two cars were black sedans with tinted windows. FBI, she guessed. She didn't recognize the man or woman who exited the first vehicle but was surprised to see they both appeared to be Native American.

From the next sedan came two white men with short military-style haircuts and dark glasses. They had the same stony expressions as the Secret Service men who guarded the president.

Jake approached her door and she leaned out the broken window.

"We're going to transfer you to Detective Bear Den's unit, Kacey. That be all right?"

She nodded and he opened the door.

Colt was already speeding away from the vehicle.

Jake helped Kacey rise and then looked across the hood to Colt.

"Good to see you, brother," he said.

Colt looked away.

Jake glanced to her and she shook her head. She did not understand any better than he did why Colt would not speak.

"Did he talk to you?" Jake said, his voice low.

She nodded.

Jake released a sigh and escorted her toward the SUV. On her way, they paused for introductions. The man was FBI field agent Lieutenant Luke Forrest of the Black Mountain Apache tribe. The woman was FBI explosives expert Sophia Rivas, also of the Black Mountain Apache people.

"Are you the one who saved our town?" asked Kacey.

"Well, I had some help." She glanced at Bear Den, and Kacey sensed their relationship might be more than professional. "But I set the charges."

"Colt says you stopped the river from destroying Piñon Forks."

"That's true. Why don't you sit with me? I have a few questions."

Kacey cast a look at Colt. She was not leaving him.

"We're riding with Bear Den and Colt's brother," she said.

"All right. I'll just come along. That be okay?"

Kacey glanced to Colt, who inclined his chin.

"All right."

The contractions were now just an irregular flurry of spasms across her belly and back.

She walked past the last two men, who scanned her from head to toe.

Once past them, she asked Sophia Rivas who they were.

"Our guys. They're taking possession of your vehicle."

"Evidence?" asked Kacey.

Rivas smiled and nodded. "We sure hope so."

Bear Den held the rear door of his SUV open for Kacey. She struggled to climb inside. She wished she had something better to wear than the ugly sheath of a dress they'd given her. But what was important was getting to her friends before something happened to them. Those men, Oleg and Anton, they couldn't fight against all these law-enforcement officers.

Could they?

Colt slipped in beside her and she gripped his hand, fingers laced. He gave her comfort and she hoped she did the same for him. Jake took the front seat. Rivas climbed into the opposite side, so Colt slid to the middle of the broad back seat, separating her from the FBI agent.

Jake Redhorse told them that the FBI had opted not to notify the Darabee police of their presence based on the information she had given Officer Redhorse. So they sailed through town and back toward the house she had fled only four hours earlier.

Her contractions were no longer increasing in strength or frequency and they interfered little on the ride back from the rez to Darabee. What was going on? she wondered.

Still, her body concerned her less than the tic Colt displayed beneath his eye and the way he repeatedly flexed and stretched his free hand like a beating heart. His breathing was irregular, as if he were in pain.

She answered all Rivas's questions as they rode back down the mountain and through the settlement of Turquoise Ridge. Bear Den asked a few questions as they covered the road between Turquoise Ridge and Koun'nde. Then Jake told them some things that she hadn't known.

A classmate of hers and Colt's, Zella Colelay, had delivered a baby girl on September 23, the Saturday before last. She'd left the infant in Jake Redhorse's truck and he was being granted temporary custody of the baby by the tribe.

"You're getting custody?" asked Kacey. She did not quite keep the disbelief from her voice. A single man wanting custody of a baby was unusual.

"Lori Morgan and I are back together now. She's agreed to be my wife."

Kacey blinked at this news. She knew that Jake and Lori had once been a couple. Rumors were that Lori had got into trouble and the teens had been encouraged to marry before the baby came. Colt had confirmed it and told her that the miscarriage had wrecked the relationship. Now it seemed a new baby had brought them back together again.

"Congratulations," said Kacey.

Jake grinned. "Thanks. Just got married." He lifted his left hand, showing the gleaming gold band. Jake looked to Colt. "I wanted you there, brother. Have you stand up with me."

Colt lifted his shoulders and shuddered.

"What about Zella?" asked Kacey. "What will happen to her?"

Bear Den took that one. "She's been relocated, faces charges for abandonment of the infant. But she's young, and with the circumstances, I doubt she'll receive more than community service."

"One more thing," said Jake. "The baby. It's white."

Kacey frowned and rested her hands on her belly. How could Zella deliver a white baby? Did he mean the baby was a mix of Apache and Caucasian or what some here called a mix-up? Was Zella like her and the rest of the captives? Had this happened to her but somehow she had evaded capture? "Does Zella have a boyfriend?"

"No. She told us she has never been with a boy."

Kacey gasped. Just like her, Marta and Maggie. She needed to speak to Zella. Kacey turned to Colt to tell him that Zella might be one of them and she noticed he was trembling.

Colt's eyes were darting about and his leg was bouncing like that of a junkie coming off a high. She pressed a hand to his knee.

"You okay?" she whispered.

He jumped at her touch and then clutched her

hand so hard she winced. Colt had not even visited his family since his return from Afghanistan. Now he was surrounded by people.

"I need to get out of this car," he said. "We're trapped back here."

"Pull over," said Kacey.

Bear Den glanced back at them in his rearview mirror.

"What?" said Bear Den.

"We can't stop," said FBI agent Rivas.

Colt's gaze flashed to the closed door.

"The baby. Pull over," said Kacey.

He did and the line of cars behind them stopped, as well. The lead car drove a few yards on and then noticed the delay and also pulled over.

Kacey tried the handle and found it locked.

Bear Den was quick for a big man. He had her door open an instant later and Kacey slid sideways, legs out of the SUV. Colt bolted past her and ran a few feet. Then he stopped, facing them, panting. His complexion was gray and his eyes were wild.

"Colt?" said Jake, hands raised.

Colt had his hand on his pistol.

"Take your hand off the weapon. No one is going to hurt you."

"I have to go back," he said. His eyes were wild as he searched for escape.

"Colt. Kacey needs you," said Rivas.

Colt stared at her, his expression tortured. "I'm sorry. I thought I could…"

"It's all right, Colt. You don't have to go," Kacey assured him.

"Don't get in that Humvee, Kacey," he said, pointing at the SUV. "Don't go. They'll take you."

Kacey's blood iced. It was her greatest fear, to be taken again, by the Russians, the feds, the Darabee police. Her throat went so dry she couldn't even swallow and she wanted to go with him.

"Not a Humvee," said Bear Den, his words an aside to Tinnin.

"Colt," said Rivas. "You're scaring Kacey."

Kacey headed toward Colt. She needed to touch him. Bring him back and save herself from the terror now crawling over her skin like scorpions.

"Don't," said Bear Den, clasping her arm and holding her back.

Colt made a feral sound between a snarl and a roar as his eyes were pinned on the place Bear Den touched Kacey.

"Let go," said Kacey.

Bear Den's hand dropped away. Kacey continued forward to Colt as he drew his pistol, holding it down and at his side. Behind her, she heard handguns leaving their plastic holsters. When she reached Colt, she took his face in her hands and pressed her forehead to his.

"I'm here, Colt. You're safe. You're home."

His body relaxed and his breathing slowed. "Stay with me," he said.

"It'll be all right."

"Don't go with them."

"I have to. I promised them, my friends, that I would send help. I have to go. Can Jake take you home?"

He nodded. The pistol slid from his fingers, thudding to the ground.

"All right. Wait for me. I'll be right back."

It was what he had said to her before he shipped out for boot camp. *I'll be right back.* That had been nearly two years ago.

He shuddered and turned to Jake, who was already holding his brother's abandoned handgun. The two brothers walked back along the line of cars to Jake's police unit, which had been driven by Chief Wallace Tinnin. Jake helped Colt into the rear seat and then shut him in. Colt's eyes darted about the closed compartment. What had happened to him? Kacey wondered. Jake hurried behind the wheel as Colt locked his fingers together behind his head and ducked like an airline passenger preparing for impact. The vehicle made a U-turn and sped away.

When Kacey returned to the vehicle, it was to find FBI field agent Luke Forrest in the passenger's seat, Jack Bear Den driving and Sophia Rivas holding open the rear door for her. Kacey felt alone and afraid. Her heart beat so hard that it hurt. But she thought of Marta's pretty thin face and her own promise.

She hoisted herself back into the rear seat. "Let's go."

Chapter Four

Colt felt so dizzy he thought he would pass out. When he finally lifted his head from his hands, it was to discover he no longer had a pistol in his holster and he was sitting belted into the rear seat of Jake's police unit like a criminal.

Call Ty, he wanted to say to Jake. But he couldn't manage to say the words aloud.

Ty had been to the cabin, and unlike with Jake, Colt had let Ty see him. He never spoke to Ty when he came, but it was good to hear Ty's voice and his words—until it wasn't and Colt had to step away into the forest again.

Jake didn't move to retrieve his phone as he drove away from Koun'nde. Colt released the restraining belt and slid to the far side of the rear seat so he could see more than the back of Jake's head.

"Let me out," said Colt. He'd said that aloud, he realized. Or he thought he had. Jake did not reply.

His brother did glance at him in the rearview mirror, brows lifted in surprise. Colt felt a cold trickle of dread shiver down his spine. "Will they bring Kacey back to me?"

Jake adjusted his grip on the wheel. His expression was stony as he clenched his jaw.

The grim look on Colt's brother's face made him feel sick. He needed to get out of this car.

"She's in labor. They'll bring her to a hospital or call in a midwife, like Lori."

He was talking about the woman Jake had dated in high school. Now his wife, Colt remembered. He looked back in the direction they had taken Kacey. This was better. She was with people who didn't collapse into the past every time they heard an engine. People who weren't afraid to go out in the world.

"You got her to safety, Colt. You did a good job."

Until he'd freaked out again. It was why he couldn't come off the ridge. Why he was such a bad choice to look out for Kacey. He knew it. Everyone knew it. Why didn't Kacey?

"It's good to see you, brother, and to hear your voice. We've been..." Jake's words trickled off.

Colt continued to look back at the empty road behind them. What if they were waiting back there for Kacey? He spun in the rear seat and stared back the way they had come.

"They've got her. She has three units," said Jake, interpreting his movements.

Colt recalled the semiautomatic weapons Kacey said the Russians had used.

"Turn around," said Colt.

"What?"

"Go after them."

"Colt, we need to get you home to Turquoise Ridge. I called Kenshaw Little Falcon."

That was the tribe's shaman. He was also a licensed therapist and had two degrees. Psychology and philosophy, Colt recalled. Ty had been trying to get Colt to see him for months.

"No. I need to get Kacey."

"Maybe tomorrow."

Colt laced his fingers through the cage that divided the front and back seats and shook the metal barrier. "Now."

Jake glanced at him in the rearview. "You drew your gun, Colt. On me and on federal agents. Do you even remember that?"

He didn't.

"You're lucky you're not in federal custody right now or dead. Now I owe Tinnin for the rest of my life for letting me take you home. We had to use the sovereignty of our tribe to get Agent Forrest to release custody. But you can't see Kacey and you can't leave the reservation. Got it?"

Colt stared at the back of Jake's head. Kacey had come to him for protection. Not to her family. Not to the feds. Not even to tribal police. To him, and he was going to get to her with or without help. But first he had to get out of this car.

KACEY WAS SURPRISED that she had no trouble finding the house. Once there, they waited for FBI to swarm the property. It looked like some scene from a movie with grenade launchers throwing tear gas and men and women in navy blue windbreakers approaching the quiet house with guns drawn. The mailbox lay broken on the curb and she realized it must have been what she had crashed into. The eerie stillness of the house disconcerted her. Shouldn't her friends have been screaming when the gas poured into the basement?

Her contractions had started up again, building now and making her want to push. Word came back that the house was empty.

"Empty? That's impossible."

"Are you sure this is the right house?" asked Rivas.

Kacey glanced out the side window, recalling running along that roof. "Yes, I'm sure. This is the house."

"All right. We're checking it out. Meanwhile, let's get you to the hospital to have this baby."

"The hospital. No. They'll find us there."

"You'll have protection twenty-four seven. FBI agents stationed outside your house."

"No. I want to go back to Colt."

Rivas gave her a sympathetic look. "Sweetie, he's mentally unstable. That's why he was discharged early. You know that, right?"

Kacey was shaking her head. "What happened to him?"

"He was captured by insurgents and held for three days with six of his unit. Record shows he was held under torture and was the only survivor. Afterward he couldn't adjust. He's seen mental health professionals there and here. He's received a psychiatric discharge and referral to seek help. But he has not done so. In fact, according to his brother, Colt has been home for four months but lives like a hermit and won't talk to his family. He's only been seen by the brother with the record..." Rivas rolled her eyes up as she tried to recall the name.

"Ty."

"Yes. Right. Ty Redhorse. Charged with armed robbery at eighteen. The tribe did not permit federal prosecution and charges were dropped in lieu of service in the US Marines. Known gang affiliations. No recent convictions or arrests." She smiled, as if pleased with her recall.

"If the tribe's gang is tied up in this, then you don't want to see or be seen by Ty," said Lieutenant Forrest from the front seat.

But Colt had called him, hadn't he?

"Do you know why you were impregnated?"

She shook her head. "Do you?"

"We have a theory based on the Caucasian infant born to Zella Colelay. Possible sale of fetal tissue."

"Tissue?" She clutched her stomach.

"That or human trafficking for surrogacy. We have a lot of questions for you. But we'll get you to the hospital first."

"In Darabee?" she asked, horrified.

"That's the closest medical facility."

"No. Not Darabee."

Rivas gave her a tight smile. "You need to relax, Kacey. We got you."

Her words did not reassure Kacey. She sank back in the seat as she realized she had traded one prison for another.

"SHE'S IN DARABEE hospital," Jake told Colt.

"We have to get her out."

"Bear Den says she delivered in the ER. They just got her there in time."

"How do I get to her?"

"You don't. She's got FBI security."

"Kee works there," said Colt, referring to their oldest brother and the family's only MD. "He could get to her."

"Maybe, but he can't get her out of custody."

Colt pressed one fist into his opposite hand and brought them to his mouth, thinking.

"And why do you believe that she'll be safer with you than with the Bureau?" asked Jake.

"I don't. But she does."

"She might feel differently now…" Jake's words fell off.

"Now that she's seen me, you mean."

Jake shifted as if his clothing were suddenly uncomfortable. "Or she sees that the FBI can keep her safe."

"She's a captive again."

"Well, if there are people after her, she can't just go tramping around in the woods with you. She has a baby, Colt. Babies need somewhere warm and dry with a microwave to heat formula."

"Our ancestors raised us without all that."

"I know our history, brother," said Jake.

"I need to see Kacey."

"You need to see a psychiatrist."

Colt threw himself back against the rear seat, folding his arms before him. The ceiling of the car seemed lower than before and the buzzing in his ears escalated, making it harder and harder for him to think.

Finally, he said, "They have psychiatrists in Darabee."

Jake's eyes flashed to the rearview, meeting Colt's. "You'll see someone there?"

Colt nodded.

"This a trick to get to Kacey?"

"You said I have to see someone. So I'll see someone."

"Because of her."

"Everything I do from this second onward will be because of her." But the voice in his head whispered that he was not safe to be around a baby. What if he freaked out and hurt it during a panic attack?

"It's possible they will let you see her. But I wouldn't get my hopes up."

"Is Kee working there today?"

Jake shrugged. "Don't know his schedule." Jake passed Colt his mobile through the slot in the wire cage that separated the front from the rear seat of his police unit. "He's in my favorites." Jake gave Colt the pass code and Colt took the phone, staring at it for a moment. Then he cleared his throat several times. Finally, he lifted his chin, locked his teeth and made the call.

Kee only hesitated a moment before responding to Colt's request. Kee was at the tribe's health-care clinic today but said he'd see what he could find out. Jake accepted his phone back and used it to call his chief. He wanted assurances that if he brought Colt off their tribal lands, Colt would not be arrested. He listened and then disconnected.

"He's looking into it," Jake said.

Jake pulled over before leaving their lands, waiting for the call back. Colt asked to step out of the vehicle and hoped that Jake would refuse. He needed out but also knew if he was allowed to set foot on the ground, Jake would never get him back inside his police unit again.

Jake refused, thank God. The ceiling dropped another two inches and Colt had to hunch down below the seat to keep it from crushing him.

His brother pivoted in his seat and peered at him through the wire mesh. "What are you doing?" Colt was saved from answering by Jake's phone. "It's Kee."

Jake put the call on speaker.

"She's in Maternity," said Kee. "Mother and baby in good condition. Vaginal delivery. It's a boy."

"Hers?" asked Jake.

"Not sure," said Kee. "My colleague can't find anything out about the baby."

Jake scowled. "What colleague?"

"Dr. Hauser. He's in Darabee today."

Jake swore. Now Colt was scowling. Why did Jake have a problem with Hector Hauser? Hauser had been Kee's mentor and the one who had got him to the specialist who corrected Kee's leg-length discrepancy. He was also the head physician at the tribe's health-care clinic.

"Jake? Take me off speaker a minute."

Jake complied and held the phone to his ear.

"Yes. I know that." He paused to listen. "Seems so." Another pause. "Well, he's talking. I'd call that progress." Jake's gaze flicked to the rearview mirror and met Colt's eyes as he listened. "Maybe." Then another pause. "All right. See you there."

"See me where?" asked Colt.

"He wants us to stop by the urgent-care trailer."

"Trailer?"

"Everything is in Turquoise Ridge now. Temporary FEMA housing. You know about the dam, right?"

Colt nodded. Ty had told him.

"What's your problem with Hauser?" asked Colt.

Jake's gaze flicked away as he shook his head. "Can't say."

Police business, Colt knew. Active investigation was his best guess. What did this have to do with the clinic?

Colt sat back, thinking. He knew he had panic attacks. He knew they made him sweat and shake, but he always knew where he was. He never flashed back to that time. No breaks with reality. His reality was hard enough without jumping back to Afghanistan. Oh, he thought about it and dreamed about it. He knew he had issues and maybe he was a little paranoid. But one thing he was certain of was that visiting a woman in the maternity ward in Darabee did not require a stop in the tribe's urgent-care center in Turquoise Ridge.

Jake and Kee were about to throw a butterfly net over him. He knew that for sure. He had been getting better. The shakes were nearly gone. It was just driving in a damn car. He hated feeling trapped as he waited for something bad to happen.

And talking. His voice vibrating through his body reminded him of the screaming of his fellows. Their cries vibrated the same damn way as if it were him screaming. Maybe it was.

He shouldn't have left her.

"Almost there," said Jake.

Chapter Five

Three hours later, Kacey was resting in the delivery room after bringing her baby into the world. They had placed the pink, wiggling infant on her chest and she examined the tiny fingers, counting each one. She cradled the wet head, misshapen by the process of birth.

He was very pink, had large dark blue eyes and damp fine black hair. In other words, he did not look like any of Kacey's brothers and sisters when they came home from the hospital.

"Does he look Apache to you?" she asked the nurse who had talked her through much of the delivery.

Kacey's body ached down there because she had come in too late for the pain medication. How long had she been in here? It couldn't have been more than an hour since they brought her in. They said she was fully dilated when she arrived, whatever that was.

The nurse peered down at the newborn and hesitated. "Well, I can't really say."

Couldn't say or wouldn't say.

"He's beautiful. I know that much." The nurse gave her a smile.

Kacey held her baby. So the speculation among the girls was true. None of them were carrying their own child. She glanced down at the infant, who stared steadily up at her.

So whose child was this that she had delivered? Hers, she decided. Every cell but two had come from the nourishment of her flesh. And this baby was hers.

The contractions began again. Then a nurse whisked him away to be cleaned up. Kacey reached after him.

"I want him in the room with me," she said.

The nurse cast Kacey a smile that seemed patronizing before she lifted the naked boy. "We'll bring him to you when he's hungry."

No. That was not good enough. She knew they wanted this baby. She still didn't know why. But they'd get him if she wasn't watching. "They'll take him."

Another nurse stepped before her. "Honey, we have tight security. No one gets near our babies except the mommy and daddy."

They would. She knew it. "It's not safe."

"Listen, nothing like what happened at your health clinic will happen here."

The fear moved from her stomach to her heart. "What happened at our health clinic?"

The doctor's brow furrowed. She was an older

woman with a close-cut cap of dark curling hair and thin penciled brows. She had been very good at explaining things. "The two shooters who came in and tried to steal a baby. The one that police officer found in his truck."

Zella's baby? Her skin went cold. It proved her point. These people—the ones who had captured her, impregnated her and then held her against her will—were not going to let some little hospital keep them from getting that baby.

"Let me up," she said, taking her feet from the metal stirrups.

"You're delivering the afterbirth. You can't get up."

Kacey watched them care for her baby as the contractions gripped her again. The afterbirth came quickly and intact, according to the doctor. They massaged her stomach then. The doctor said that was to stop the bleeding.

Kacey endured the pain of this and then sat up.

"You should rest a bit. We'll be moving you to a room soon and you can clean up."

"With Charlie," she said.

"Is that what you're calling him?"

"Yes. I can name him, right?"

"Of course. If you plan on keeping him," said the doctor, her voice full of mirth. "Lie back down. They'll get you a bed and wheel you right to your room."

They wanted to take the baby to get shots and some other things while they took her to her room, but she refused to go. When they tried to cajole, she resisted, and when they ordered her to lie down, she pitched a fit that would have made any middle-school girl proud. She yelled so loud that an unfamiliar FBI agent, the female FBI agent Rivas and Jack Bear Den all came into the delivery room to check on them. And there she was, half-dressed, bloody and screaming like a wild woman.

The agent suggested they give her something, and that scared her into silence.

"We can't give her anything. Whatever you give her goes into her blood and right into her breast milk."

The agent made a face. Bear Den suggested they give her back her baby.

"We told her about the abduction attempt at your clinic," said one of the nurses.

"Brilliant," said Rivas.

Bear Den turned to Kacey. "We arrested and captured those two. They won't be coming for you or your baby."

"But someone will," she said.

"That's why we're here," Bear Den said.

Kacey demanded her baby and they finally turned him over.

In the end, they let her watch the processing of her child, including a heel prick for a blood sample that made him cry and the inking of his feet for a print. Shots, a sponge bath, a tiny bracelet on his ankle. She got a larger model. The nurse explained that the security bracelet kept anyone from taking the baby on the elevators, near the laundry chute or near the stairs.

"It locks them?" she asked.

"Elevators, yes."

So not the stairs.

"Can someone cut off the band?"

"The alarm sounds if it's not touching skin or if it's cut."

"Who has the key?"

"So many questions." The nurse's smile seemed fixed and her eyes tired.

The nurse showed her the key while another gave Charlie his first diaper and swaddling. At last, they put Charlie in her arms.

"He's not Apache. Is he?" she asked the doctor.

The woman peeled back the flannel blanket to peer at Charlie's face.

"I don't know. He sure could be."

She glanced to Jack Bear Den, who met her gaze and gave his head a slow shake, confirming Kacey's suspicions. She wasn't a mother. She was a surrogate.

"Will blood tests show if I'm his real mother?" she asked.

"They might," said the doctor.

"How long will that take?"

"Not long. We sent them up to the lab. Should hear back soon. Now you need to rest. We'll put Charlie in a bassinet right next to you in your room. How will that be?"

She nodded and allowed them to transfer her to a gurney. She held Charlie as they transported her to a single room with the agents that walked with her and stopped outside her private room. A glance at the window showed the tops of trees and the strip mall across the parking lot and street. She was on the third or fourth floor.

The attendant showed her how to use the button to call the nurse. He offered to put Charlie in the bassinet beside her bed, but she rejected the suggestion. She was keeping him with her until they let her out—if they let her out.

COLT REFUSED TO go to the urgent-care center in Turquoise Ridge. It was the wrong direction, for a start. Kacey was in Darabee. But Jake would not let him out of his police unit. By the time he got to the Turquoise Ridge urgent-care center, he was throwing himself against the cage between the front and rear seat like a feral animal. He told himself to stop, but the screaming in his head had taken him. He was on his back on the back seat, preparing to kick out the rear window, when Jake pulled over.

"Okay. You can get out."

Colt righted himself. They were in a wide field filled with trailers. They sprang up in the yellow grass of the open field like white mushrooms on a rotting log. Jake opened the rear door and Colt dived through the opening and ran. Jake shouted after him, but he ran and kept running until he was far enough away from the gas tank and the vehicle to be safe from explosions.

There he stopped, hands on knees. He panted. Sweated. His sides ached. But he could breathe again. Dry air, but cool. Not like Afghanistan.

"Colt," called Jake from his position halfway between his police cruiser and his younger brother. He motioned with one arm. "Come back."

Kee jogged out and stopped beside Jake, watching him. Behind him, coming at a walk, was a woman Colt did not know. Colt retraced his steps, giving the cruiser a wide berth. His throat was so dry.

They wanted him to go inside one of the trailers. He walked the perimeter first. No engine. But there was a generator outside that ran on gas.

"You'll have to see me here." Colt sat in the grass.

All three of them stared at him. They then shared a silent exchange that involved long glances and head gestures.

In the end, they did as he asked and gave him what the marine doctors had given him. A prescription for antidepressants, sleeping pills and an appointment to see a shrink. He sagged with relief. Now he had to get to Kacey.

Colt thanked them. But then he had to face Jake's car again. He started sweating. He hated himself as he considered asking for the shot. The one they'd used to transport him back home and to get him safely to Phoenix. He'd walked from there to Turquoise Canyon. It had taken eight days.

But if he took that medicine, he'd be good for no one, especially not Kacey. Still, walking to her would take hours. So he asked them for a phone and he called his brother Ty.

Ty listened and agreed to help, as he always did. Colt wanted to go to Kacey, but Kenshaw was right. First he needed to help himself. The FBI was guarding her. They were better able to keep her safe. He knew that. It was reasonable. Rational. So why did he feel so uneasy? Because, just like last time, she had come to him for help and he had let her down, again.

He heard the familiar roar of a Harley long before he saw his brother Ty. Colt's older brother ignored the curb and rolled right up beside him where he sat on the grass surrounded by medical professionals, tribal police and his brothers Jake and Kee.

Ty ignored them all and spoke only to Colt. "You driving or should I?"

Colt stood.

"I think we should admit him," said Kee to Ty.

"Yeah? What does he think?" asked Ty, looking at Colt.

Colt shook his head.

"We only need two family members to sign the papers," said Jake, siding with Kee as usual.

"Screw that," said Ty, straddling the bike with one booted foot planted firmly on each side. He dismounted, holding the bike with one hand as he looked to Colt.

"You drive," he said.

"At least let Kenshaw speak to him," said Kee.

"You know where to find him," said Ty.

Colt straddled the bike and turned the key. The motor roared to life.

"Go on," said Ty.

Chapter Six

Colt drove to Darabee on the 1990 Harley-David-son Heritage Softail in the early afternoon. The bike was cream and coffee with a maroon pinstripe and enough chrome to resurface the top of the Chrysler Building. This was Ty's pride and joy and had been refurbished with love. More important, Colt felt none of the anxiety and claustrophobia when riding in the open air on the chopper.

Why hadn't he tried this sooner?

Because he had no reason to leave the ridge. That was the answer. Kacey had given him a reason to leave, to fight and to come back to the world.

He sailed into Darabee and parked in the hospi-tal lot but got as far as the lobby, where FBI agents waited and were disinclined to let him pass. He used the hospital phone to call her room but got no answer. He didn't leave a message. He was still waiting in the lobby when the world outside the lobby windows faded with the daylight. The first of the outside lights had just flickered on when Kenshaw Little Falcon arrived with Colt's brother Jake. Kenshaw was the tribe's shaman, a licensed therapist and a longtime friend of the family.

"They won't let me see her," he said.

Jake's mouth was a slashing grim line. "Because they think you're a threat."

"Threat's out there," said Colt.

"Are you armed?" asked Jake.

Colt shook his head. "You got my pistol, and my rifle was in my truck."

"Knives?"

"No." It was a fair question because both he and Jake knew that Colt threw a knife with the accuracy that some shot arrows.

"They'll come for her," Colt told Jake.

"Don't you worry about that," said Jake. "The FBI is guarding her."

"She's Turquoise Canyon. *We* should be guarding her."

Colt had done more talking today than the sum total since he'd been released from the hospital in Bethesda, Maryland.

"How long will she be here?" he asked.

Jake rubbed his neck, tipping his Stetson down over his eyes. "Don't know. I do know that she's in the delivery room."

"You think they'll try to keep her?"

"Not your worry. Besides, that's up to her. She agreed to protection."

What other choice had she had? Him? He must

have seemed a lunatic in her eyes. Colt stared at the polished tile floor and swallowed at the lump in his throat. "She came to me for help."

"After she tried the old tribal headquarters. No one was there. This is not your fight, Colt."

Kenshaw motioned to the chair beside the end table, perpendicular to the one Colt had vacated. "Mind if I wait with you?"

Colt had always liked and respected their shaman. He radiated calm and strength.

"I'd like that," said Colt and resumed his seat.

Jake's brows lifted.

"Why don't you see if you can get an update on Kacey? See how she's doing and if she needs anything from us," said their shaman to Jake.

Dismissed, Jake spun away and headed for the elevators. The two agents posted by them delayed Jake briefly before allowing him to pass.

Kenshaw rested his hands on the armrests of the chair and said nothing. The shaman had a way of blending with his surroundings instead of taking them over until it was almost as if he was not even there.

Colt looked out the window to the darkness broken by streetlights in the parking lot while he tried to imagine he sat in his place in the woods.

Colt's father had made the mining cabin with his brother using planed pine obtained from the tribe's lumber mill. Colt never asked how they got the lumber but recalled helping them load it well past dark.

Building the mining cabins was as close to honest work, as far as Colt was aware, as his father had ever done. His father now resided in federal prison in Phoenix on a final robbery charge that tipped the scales from misdemeanor to felony and serious jail time. It had taken his mom three years after that to decide to divorce him.

Colt wished he could divorce himself from the name they'd given him. Colton Redhorse, Jr., a chip off the old block. He'd spent a lot of his teen years tipping between proving folks right or wrong. If not for Ty riding him and Kee encouraging him, he never would have finished high school.

Colt glanced at his silent companion.

Kenshaw Little Falcon had not aged a day since Colt had last seen him. He still had long hair streaked with gray and a face that showed hard lines around his mouth and forehead. Gravity tugged at his jowls and made rings around his neck. His body was trim and strong, and he dressed like a rancher rather than the holy man that he was.

Colt found he did not mind the older man's presence in his space. But Colt's mind was with Kacey and his plans to get to her. He suspected she was in a lock-in floor. What was the best way to get her out?

"Sometimes the only way out is through," said Kenshaw, replying to the question that Colt had not voiced.

Colt's brow wrinkled as he stared at the holy man. Had that been a lucky guess?

"To see her, you will have to prove you are not a danger to her or yourself. And it will have to be her wish. Not just yours."

His shaman decided to speak in Tonto Apache then. It had been Kenshaw who had taught them all the language of their birth, and he spoke to Colt now, telling him of the dam disaster and how Colt's brother Jake had saved the FBI explosives agent, Sophia Rivas, from the police boat after the explosion she and Detective Bear Den had initiated to save them from the flood.

He talked a long time, and Colt did not feel anxious or have to resist the urge to walk off in the woods to get away from him. Instead, he had to resist the urge to start walking toward Piñon Forks and the tribe's fight to reinforce the rubble dam.

Finally, they got back to Colt's troubles. Colt told him some of it, nothing that everyone didn't already know.

When he finished, Kenshaw nodded. "I can see why you stay up there. You have a lot to work through. I'd like to help. I am a therapist, but I know a good man, a veteran who also suffered some losses."

"All right." Colt needed to quiet the screaming in his head. He needed to get to Kacey and be there when she needed him.

Colt told Kenshaw what Kacey had told him about her capture and imprisonment.

"She's not on our land," said Colt. "She's out here

and she's a captive again. I believe what she said. They won't let her go or let her keep her baby."

"She want to keep it?" Kenshaw asked.

"She should have that choice."

"And why are you better suited to protect her than our tribal police?"

"They follow the law, while I will do whatever it takes to defend her."

"You would break the law," he said.

Colt inclined his head. No question. No hesitation.

Kenshaw gave him a long contemplative gaze. Finally, he nodded and sat back in his chair. Then he laced his gnarled thick fingers over his flat stomach. "To care for others, you first must be capable of caring for yourself."

"I know that. It's why I agreed to see your therapist."

"Then I'll help you," said their shaman.

Kenshaw made no move to depart. Eventually the elevator doors opened and Jake emerged from within. Colt was on his feet as Jake approached.

"How is she?" Colt asked.

"She's still in the delivery room."

"Who's watching her?"

"Detective Bear Den."

Her pursuers would be checking maternity wards. Colt resumed his seat.

"You going to sit there all night?" asked Jake.

Colt planned to do just that.

Three hours later, Detective Bear Den strode from

the elevators, holding his hat like a football against his side. Kenshaw had gone a little after midnight and Colt was alone except for the FBI agents at the elevator, the receptionist and security guard.

Colt rose to his feet, staring at the detective as he tried to ascertain at a glance if Kacey was all right. "How is she?"

"She had the baby."

"She okay?"

"Fine. Normal delivery. The baby is healthy."

Colt squinted. He'd said that twice now—*the baby*. Not *her baby* or *Kacey's baby*. "Hers?"

Bear Den didn't answer. Colt put a hand on his arm, and the detective looked at it and then at Colt.

Bear Den's scowl deepened. "Blood work shows it's not Kacey's."

"She delivered it."

"She's a surrogate, just like Zella Colelay."

That was the girl who had left the newborn in his brother's truck. Kacey said Zella knew her from school, but Colt didn't remember her.

"FBI is expediting DNA testing."

"Can I see her?" asked Colt.

"She's sleeping."

"Not what I asked."

Bear Den scraped his knuckles over the stubble on his jaw. "Not my call. Forrest says you stay off the maternity ward."

"What do you say?"

"Let her rest."

Colt remained standing. "Anything on her friends?"

"We got zip." Bear Den shifted and glanced to the door. "You should go home and get some rest."

"I'm staying."

"See you in the morning." Bear Den replaced his hat on his head, pressed it down with one giant hand and strode through the exit.

Colt resumed his seat.

Colt saw the shift change at six in the morning when two new FBI field agents replaced the old. He was sitting on a stool at the hospital cafeteria lunch counter nursing some weak coffee when Detective Bear Den and his brother Jake arrived. Jake was in his tribal police uniform, his name tag on the left breast pocket, handgun on his hip and his hair drawn neatly back in a single braid. Unlike Ty, Jake radiated his emotions, so Colt knew there was trouble before Bear Den spoke. The muscles between Colt's shoulders hitched as he braced in preparation.

He took the seat one away from Colt.

"You still talking this morning?" Jake asked.

Colt said nothing. Jake swiped his hand over his mouth and ordered black coffee from the server behind the counter. She brought it promptly and set it before him with a napkin.

He took a swallow of the coffee and winced. "I told Ma you're down off the ridge. She wants to come see you, but you know Burt has the truck and she can't drive because, you know, her medical issues."

Colt said nothing, but he knew his mother's vision

was not good because of the diabetes and that she'd had two toes amputated because of the same illness.

"Any chance you could stop up to the house?"

Colt spun his stool back to face the counter and his cold cup of coffee. "You going up to see her?"

Jake stood. "Yeah. Kenshaw signed off that you're no threat to Kacey. I'm the delivery boy." Jake patted the papers protruding from his rear pocket.

Colt had not even known that he was being evaluated.

He followed Jake as far as the elevator, where he waited for the doors to open and close and take his brother to Kacey. If they didn't let him up there soon, he was going to blow Kenshaw's faith in him by doing something stupid.

AFTER THE NIGHT in the hospital, Kacey woke up with a new heaviness in her breasts and some soreness down there. She was surprised to see daylight outside her window. How long had she been asleep?

Where was Charlie?

They'd taken her baby twice so far for changing, but they'd always brought Charlie right back.

She tried to sit up, but the soreness made her gasp. On her second try, she rolled to her side and swung her legs gingerly off the bed. The agents posted at her door looked surprised at her appearance but only shadowed her as she shuffled down the hall. She tracked Charlie down to the nursery and found a nurse feeding him from a bottle. Her eyes narrowed.

Kacey crashed her open hand against the glass viewing window and shouted, making both nurses inside the room jump.

The one who was not holding Charlie came to speak to her. "We didn't want to wake you."

"If he's hungry, you bring him to me," she said.

The nurse looked confused. "But you told us you don't want to breastfeed."

A tingle of alarm trickled down her spine. "When did I say that?"

Chapter Seven

The nurse gave Kacey a look of bafflement at her question. She had not told anyone that she did not want to breastfeed her baby.

"It's in your chart."

"It's a lie. Give him to me."

Kacey tried to push past the nurse to get to Charlie, but the nurse blocked her way to the door.

"You can't go in there."

Kacey rounded on the nurse, preparing to fight. The nurse must have seen the crazy in Kacey's eyes because she lifted her hands in instant surrender.

"Clean environment," she said, hurrying her words. "You have to wear a mask and…let me just… I'll bring him out."

Kacey lowered her chin and glared. "Do it."

The tightness in her chest eased as they slipped Charlie back into her arms. He fussed at having his meal interrupted and Kacey felt the flow of milk in her breasts.

She turned to the agents. "I want to see Colt Redhorse."

"No visitors, ma'am."

"You get me your supervisor or I walk out of here right now."

The men exchanged a look. Perhaps the idea of tackling a mother holding an infant gave them pause. They eyed her warily but did not reply to her demand.

"Fine," she said and marched past them. She only got two steps before one of the matched pair stepped before her and the other spoke.

"I'll call our supervisor."

"Now," she said.

Kacey took Charlie back to her room and fed him. Was it just a mistake or did someone want to replace her with a bottle? Was it the FBI or the Russians? She examined the security bracelet on Charlie's ankle. There was no way to get it off without cutting it and then the alarm would alert them all.

Charlie yawned and Kacey adjusted the cotton cap on his head. A few minutes later, FBI field agent Lieutenant Luke Forrest appeared. He said he was against letting her see Colt. He offered a visit from her mother or sisters. Tempting, but endangering her sisters was not on the list. And seeing her mother would bring more drama than she could handle right now. Did the FBI know about her drug use? She didn't think so. There would be nothing to see in a background search, as her mom had never been arrested, though it had been close.

What Kacey needed was someone she trusted. That was a short list. Marta Garcia, still with her captors, and Colt Redhorse.

"Colt," she said.

He gave her a long assessing stare. "We can protect you, Kacey."

"You're Apache," she said. "You understand my reluctance to surrender to federal authorities. And as a member of the Turquoise Canyon Apache people, I have certain rights." She played the only card she had and then stopped talking.

"You sure he's the guy? He's been less than stable."

"He's the guy."

BEFORE THEY BROUGHT her lunch tray, there was a commotion outside her room.

"One at a time," said the new guard who stood in the hall before her door.

"We're tribal police," said a familiar voice. That was Colt's brother Jake.

"One."

A moment later, in stepped Colt Redhorse. Suddenly she wasn't afraid anymore. Colt was here. She reached for him, her stomach aching in protest. He clasped her hand and then lifted it to his mouth, dropping a warm kiss there. Her skin tingled at the contact. She squeezed his fingers and tugged, drawing him closer, and he sat on the bed beside her hip.

"You all right?" he asked.

She shook her head. "They want to take him."

His dark brows descended. "Who?"

Again she shook her head. "Something is happening," she said. Then she told him about the bottle-feeding.

He did not dismiss her concerns. Instead he said, "We need to get you home."

Home was exactly where they would look for her. She shook her head. "They'll find me there."

Colt drew his hand away and rubbed it on his thigh. "Jake said you were considering relocation with the Justice Department."

Cold panic surged. "They said that? I haven't made up my mind yet. All I said was that I would help them find my friends. But I need to protect Charlie, too."

He blinked at this. "Charlie. Is that his name?"

She nodded, waiting for his reaction. He looked away, staring off at nothing she could determine. Then his gaze swept back to hers. "I like it."

"Would you like to hold him?"

Colt straightened, his warm smile replaced by an expression of alarm.

"Put out your arms," she said.

He did, looking as if she were going to load them with firewood. She shifted forward so that her shoulder grazed his as she set her baby in his arms. His gaze dropped to the boy's tiny face. Charlie gazed up in wonder at this new person.

"Hi," breathed Colt.

There was a tug in her chest as she watched them together. Colt stared a long time and Charlie stared right back. Colt used one finger to connect with Charlie's tiny hand. Her son grasped the offered finger and Colt laughed.

"He's strong!" He flicked his gaze to hers, giving her that lopsided smile she had loved. "He's perfect, Kacey."

She stroked her baby's soft cheek with one finger. "They told me that he's not mine by blood."

His smile faltered.

"But he's mine by birth and I am not giving him to the Russians."

He nodded and brought Charlie closer to him. "I'll help you protect him, Kacey."

"We have to get Charlie out of here."

"They can't keep you if you want to go home."

"I think they can. I heard one of the agents say I'm a material witness to a surrogacy ring."

Colt glanced toward the door. "I'll get you out."

Suddenly the world seemed a little brighter, like he had poked pinholes in the blackness that shrouded her and sunlight poured in. "You will?"

"Yes. You and Charlie."

"How?"

LATE MONDAY AFTERNOON, Colt had not left Kacey's room except to speak to Kenshaw right outside her door. Their shaman had agreed with Colt's suggestion on freeing Kacey from custody. The matter was complicated by her currently being off their tribal lands, but Kenshaw believed they might still gain her transfer to Turquoise Canyon.

Charlie stayed in the room with them, and when the nurses took him, Colt went with them. When they objected, Kacey insisted and he was permitted to shadow Charlie.

By midday, Jake appeared in the doorway. He motioned to Colt with his head. In the hall, Colt discovered Detective Bear Den waiting. The three men walked far enough from the guarding agents to avoid being overheard but within sight of Kacey's room. To ensure their privacy, they spoke in Apache.

"Can we get her out?" asked Colt.

"Working on it," said Jake.

"There's a problem," said Bear Den.

Colt's body braced and he glanced toward Kacey's room.

"We just got a call from Eddie SaVala," said Bear Den.

Eddie was the brother of his neighbor, David.

"He said he found his brother dead in his cabin. Someone shot him twice in the head."

A cold chill slithered down Colt's spine.

"FBI know yet?" asked Colt.

Bear Den shook his head.

"They're looking for Kacey," said Colt.

"Who is?" asked Jake.

"Her captors."

"That makes sense," said Bear Den. "From what we can see, they beat David first."

To get information, Colt thought. His mind provided a perfect memory of the sounds of his comrades screaming under torture. He pushed it aside. No time for the past right now. "Were they at my place?"

"No."

He closed his eyes and thanked David SaVala for his sacrifice.

"Any idea why they'd think Kacey was at Sa-Vala's?"

"We borrowed his phone to call Jake."

"Why didn't you use your phone?" asked Jake.

"I don't have one," said Colt.

Bear Den scowled. "It's not easy to track the location of a mobile phone or figure out who owns it."

The implication was clear. Someone who could do that was very dangerous.

Colt suppressed the urge to run back to Kacey. "She's been here too long."

"She might be better off with the FBI," said Bear Den.

"She might be or with Justice," said Jake. "They can put her in witness protection, safeguard her identity."

"Make her disappear," added Bear Den.

Colt recalled that Bear Den's twin, Carter, and Carter's wife, Amber, had been in that program. Ty had told him about it. Everyone thought that they'd never see them again.

He didn't want Kacey to disappear. She'd only just returned and her arrival gave him a reason to try again. If she left, he'd just go back to that cabin and mining turquoise. There was satisfaction in striking those rocks. But nothing compared to holding Charlie or seeing Kacey's smile again.

"She's Turquoise Canyon Apache," said Colt, as if that were a reason to stay where there was danger. His heart was tripping along as if engaged in a long run. Had Kacey found her way off the rez? She'd always wanted to leave their mountains and had begged him to take her away, but he wanted to stay on their lands.

Turquoise Canyon was his home, and coming back to it was all that had kept him from losing his mind during those three terrible days.

Now he found himself in the same place again, convincing Kacey to come home when that might not be what was best for her and her son.

"We have to make a decision," said Jake. "Taking her out of federal custody might be a bad move."

"If her captors don't know she's here, they will soon," said Bear Den.

"They'd have to be crazy to come here. They've got four agents guarding her," said Jake. "She should stay here."

"Back home, the gang can get to her," said Bear

Den. "We know that two known members, Earle Glass and Minnie Cobb, are involved."

Colt knew from Kenshaw that these two had tried to snatch Jake's new baby, the one Zella had given birth to, and were now in federal custody.

"They won't know she's there."

Jake scoffed. "You borrowing your brother's bike was a bad move. Might as well have sent the gang a telegram."

Colt's jaw tightened. Everyone knew Ty had been a member of the tribe's gang. He wasn't now.

"He doesn't roll with them anymore," said Colt.

"Not according to the feds," said Bear Den.

Jake had told him that Bear Den was now formally engaged to the FBI explosives expert, Sophia Rivas. Had she told him something? Colt pressed down the doubt. He didn't know if Ty was tangled up with the Wolf Posse again. He did know that Ty had his back. Hadn't he turned over his bike to help Colt get to Darabee?

But had he then gone to Pike and reported Colt and Kacey's location? Faras Pike was the tribal gang's leader and once the best friend of his brother Ty, back when they were both new recruits of the Wolf Posse. Once Ty had said they were his family. Were they still?

"This means they were on our land," said Bear Den. "I've got to notify the FBI about the death of David SaVala. They might want to move Kacey to a safe house."

"Kee told me she should have been released by now," said Jake. "You know any reason they haven't moved her already?"

"We have to get her out of here," said Colt.

"That's impossible," said Bear Den.

"She thinks the FBI will take her into custody and separate her from her child."

Jake gaped at him. His eyes flicked to Bear Den's and held.

Bear Den dismissed the idea. "That's crazy."

Colt told them about the chart and how they seemed to be weaning Charlie away from Kacey. The men scowled.

"You have any reason to doubt her?" Colt asked.

"Test results indicate the child's genetic lineage is Asian and Caucasian," said Bear Den.

Colt's gaze flashed to Jake, who looked just as off balance at this announcement.

"In other words, it's not her child," said Bear Den.

Colt dug in his heels. "She carried it. She delivered it. If she says the baby is hers, that's all I need to know."

Bear Den made a face. "You're borrowing trouble."

"Bring it."

"Fine. *If* she wants out. But you'll need help."

"My brothers," said Colt.

"The tribe," said Bear Den. "You need the backing of the tribal council. That's the only way I know to get her past security or away from the FBI."

"This means we lose FBI protection," said Jake. He turned to Colt. "You sure about this?"

He wasn't. She had told him often before he joined the Marines that she wanted to be away from their tribe and her mother and everyone who thought she was nothing and no one. Did that list now include him?

Chapter Eight

Colt had given Kacey the options of staying with the FBI or coming home to Turquoise Canyon. He said that Kenshaw would invoke the protection of Tribal Thunder. She knew that name. It was the warrior sect of the tribe's medicine society. The men and women of this group had taken a vow to protect their people. Was her tribe's warrior sect strong enough to protect her from what Luke Forrest had identified as the Russian mob? Agent Forrest had assured her that his agency had not changed those orders regarding the birth mother's wishes about the infant's feeding. But someone had.

He was arranging discharge from the hospital and removal to a safe house. Unlike Colt, Forrest did not offer her a choice, which made her decision easier.

By noon on Tuesday, Kacey was dressed and ready as she waited for the delegation from her tribe to arrive to demand custody of both mother and child. Unfortunately, either the FBI got wind of their plans or their timing just stank, because she was informed by the hospital staff that she was being moved. Colt had contacted the tribal council, but when the FBI came for her, it was just her and Colt. It took three agents to hold Colt down.

Kacey held her baby and screamed for them to release Colt, but it did no good. One of the nurses appeared and Kacey braced to fight her off until she saw the key and realized the nurse was here to unlock the security bracelets on mother and child. Once free, Kacey's instinct was to protect the baby and that kept her from going to Colt's aid. In her moment of indecision, two agents took hold of her arms. They were taking her.

She held Charlie and called to Colt as she was marched out past Jake Redhorse, who was arguing and talking on his radio simultaneously.

"Jake, stop them. Don't let them take me."

They hustled her down the corridor and to the elevators. Her heart hammered in her chest. What was happening? The agents accompanying her would not answer her questions, and their grips on her arms made it clear they thought she'd run.

They rushed her down a long corridor and out a side door. There she found a single black sedan waiting with an agent standing beside the open rear door.

She knew if she got in that car she wouldn't see Colt or her people again and she feared that they might take Charlie from her. She dug in her heels. This slowed them not at all.

Three familiar tribal police units arrived. From

one SUV came Detective Bear Den and tribal police chief Wallace Tinnin, who leaned on a single
crutch. Two uniformed tribal officers emerged from
the police unit behind that one. From the next came
a third tribal police officer who opened the door for
the tribe's executive director, Zach Gill. The FBI
was now outnumbered.

A side door banged open and out rushed Colt, a
handcuff dangling from one wrist. He didn't slow as
he covered the ten yards that separated them with
astonishing speed.

One of the agents turned when Colt made his
tackle. The man holding her opposite arm released
her to help his companion, drawing his pistol.

Kacey took a step toward Colt, remembered she
held Charlie and froze. Bear Den called a warning to
the agent to holster his weapon, his hand on his own.

"He's unarmed," called Tinnin.

Colt now had the agent on his back and was straddling his waist, holding both arms pinned. He'd been
a wrestler in high school, she recalled, a very good
one.

Tinnin and Jake Redhorse were at Kacey's side.
They hustled her and Charlie into the tribal SUV.
Bear Den waited until she was in the back seat be-
fore calling Colt off.

Colt released the agent, who scrambled to his feet
as Colt charged toward Kacey. Tinnin used his crutch
as a barricade between the agent and Colt, who hurried into the SUV with her.

"He's under arrest," said the agent.

"Come and get him," said Bear Den.

The agent pointed at Kacey. "She's a material witness. We have custody."

Tinnin shook his head. "You might think twice before you touch anyone in that vehicle. That car constitutes sovereign land, an extension of our reservation."

Colt's breathing wasn't slowing down.

"You saved us," she whispered.

Colt was sweating and hugging himself now. The closed vehicle, she realized, was affecting him again. She wrapped her free arm around him and he rested his head on her.

Bear Den slipped behind the wheel and set them in motion.

She spun to look back at the three agents facing off against Gill, Tinnin and Colt's brother Jake.

Had she made a mistake, choosing her tribe? After all, they'd done little to protect her during her childhood and she had needed protecting often.

"Is that true about the sovereignty of this vehicle?"

"Not that I'm aware," Bear Den said.

The agents had a choice between drawing their weapons or their phones. One lifted his phone as they made the turn from the hospital to the street.

"They'll come after us," said Kacey.

"Then we best get to Turquoise Canyon," said Bear Den.

She sat in the back holding her baby boy. No one was taking Charlie from her again. Not the nurses or doctors or the Russians who had held her captive.

Colt's eyes rounded and the rocking turned to a steady banging of his shoulder against the side door as if he was trying to batter it open while holding himself back.

"Colt," she said.

He turned, the whites around his dark irises making him look like a frightened horse.

"Hold Charlie for me?"

He looked at the newborn and shook his head.

She laid her baby in his lap. He hesitated only a moment and then cradled him close but not tight.

Charlie was awake and fussing. Colt stroked his cheek, and her baby opened his eyes, staring up at Colt in wonder. Colt smiled. His rocking now was forward and back and completely appropriate. Kacey breathed away a sigh of relief.

A smile curled Colt's lips. If not for the sweat beading on his forehead, he would look the picture of peace. Even his breathing was changing, slowing back to normal.

She glanced up to see the detective's reflection in the rearview mirror. He nodded at her and then returned his attention to the road.

This time, when they traveled through Piñon Forks, she took note of the huge section of rock missing from the canyon wall across the river. How had she missed that? She tried to imagine seeing that collapse under explosives set by the FBI agent. The rubble dam was visible from the road, leaking water, but holding back a lake from the river town. Men worked with heavy equipment, scrambling like ants to shore up the temporary structure.

En route to Koun'nde, Bear Den told her about the murder of Colt's neighbor, David SaVala. She remembered borrowing his phone.

"We killed him," she whispered.

"No. The people who are after you did that," Bear Den said. "It's not safe at Colt's cabin."

It wasn't safe anywhere. Not as long as they were hunting her.

"Where will we go?" She couldn't go to her mother's house. That would put all her brothers and sisters in danger. And truly, she didn't completely trust her mother.

"We meet at the tribal gathering place. They've invoked the protection of Tribal Thunder."

If anyone needed protection now, it was she and Charlie.

THEY REACHED THE river and Kacey breathed a sigh of relief. She was home again, but the feeling of security was an illusion. The Russians were hunting her.

Still, she was glad to arrive at the familiar gathering grounds. This was where she had danced all night for her Sunrise Ceremony, the Apache girls' coming-of-age celebration. She still had her white buckskin dress and the fan of eagle feathers she had carried as she transformed to Changing Woman to bring blessings to her people.

She had made the dress herself, as her mother had been gone again. Her favorite teacher had helped her and had come with the gifts that Changing Woman was expected to distribute to her tribe during the ceremony. Mrs. Trans had kept her from embarrassment, and her mother, who did make the ceremony, had pretended all the while, as Kacey carried the basket full of treats, that she was responsible for the bounty. Her mother's actions might have embarrassed Kacey more than having nothing to offer.

Bear Den pulled in and Colt slipped Charlie back into her arms.

"Thank you," he said. "I didn't think I could make that ride again."

Bear Den opened Colt's door first, as if anxious to be rid of him. Colt stepped out, glanced back at her and then made for the woods.

"Wait!" Kacey called.

He didn't and he didn't look back. Members of her tribe stepped forward, surrounding the SUV and blocking her view of him. The detective opened her door and she stepped onto tribal lands once more.

She was first formally greeted by their shaman, Kenshaw Little Falcon. Her mother was there and her young brothers, Jeffrey, who was eight, and Hewitt, who had turned five without her there. Her sisters, Jackie, Winnie and Shirley, each hugged her in turn. It struck her then, looking at them, that they had all changed. Jackie, now sixteen, had cut her hair short as if in mourning, and Shirley, now eleven, was very thin. Winnie, just past thirteen, had grown several inches. Kacey realized suddenly that she had missed Winnie's Sunrise Ceremony. Had Mrs. Trans been there to help her?

Her throat constricted at the loss of those precious months of her captivity and at the joy of seeing them again. Her next thought was for her friends, still in captivity.

As she hugged her mother, her resolve hardened to flint. She must help the FBI find her friends and bring them home.

Her sisters fussed over Charlie. Hewitt nudged between them, standing on his toes to look. Kacey's proud smile dropped when she saw her mother staring at Charlie. Her expression made it seem as if she smelled something bad and she refused when Kacey asked if she wished to hold Charlie.

"Held enough babies in my time," she said.

That rejection hurt as much as any her mother had ever given her. But she bit down, clenching her jaw as she held Charlie out for them to see. She hadn't needed her mother's approval to get her first job or apply for college. She certainly didn't need it now.

"Is that my baby brother?" Hewitt asked, peering at the baby.

"Well, no." Kacey glanced to her mother, who looked away.

"That is your nephew," said her sister Shirley, with

no hint of shame or hesitation. "You are an uncle, Hewitt."

"I am?" He glanced back at their mother.

"If she says so," said her mother.

Hewitt beamed, then leaned down to kiss the baby.

And just like that, she and Charlie were accepted by her brother. Kacey offered her mother a smile of thanks and she nodded in return. Her mother had not always been there for them and she had her problems. Kacey hoped that accepting her baby into the family would not be one of them.

The October sun filtered down through the trees and glowed golden on the tribe's open gathering ground. She was escorted by her two youngest sisters, Shirley and Winnie, to the center of the dance circle. There she was formally welcomed home by Hazel Trans, now a new member of the tribal council, who spoke in place of Zach Grill, their executive director, who had aided in Kacey's escape. It occurred to Kacey that Mrs. Trans had been in her last year of teaching and was now retired. A loss, thought Kacey. It was Hazel Trans who had encouraged her to take the SATs after Colt left for the US Marines. It was because of Mrs. Trans that Kacey had been accepted into the university. Her head dropped an inch in regret as she realized she had missed the start of her freshman year.

Kacey held Charlie as she pictured what had been stolen from her. It had been all she wanted in the world, to go off the rez and earn her degree and be able to support herself. She wanted to create the stable home her mother never provided and then help her sisters make their own way. Now her aspirations were changing. Now all she wanted was to keep Charlie safe and out of the hands of the men who hunted her.

She glanced around for Colt. He had left the car with her, but now he had vanished. Was he watching from somewhere away from the crowd?

Hazel Trans finished her welcome and stepped aside to allow Kenshaw Little Falcon to speak. He told the gathering that this baby had not been Kacey's choice but that he was here now in this world with them and he was Turquoise Canyon Apache by birth. Because he was one of them, they would protect him. It was a sacred duty shared by all, to keep their young safe and teach them well. Kacey looked down at the subject of their speeches. Charlie yawned and squinted against the sunlight.

After Kenshaw completed his short speech, he offered a formal blessing using a fan of eagle feathers. His voice turned to a song rising to the blue sky.

When he finished, Kenshaw told them all that the men who had taken Kacey were outsiders with Russian accents. If they saw such men on their land, they were to call the police.

By the time all the well-wishers had spoken to Kacey and offered their advice on the baby, she was past exhausted. When Charlie fussed, Kacey's mother offered her a blanket to provide her some privacy as she nursed.

She released her baby only to allow her sisters Jackie and Winnie to change him with her overseeing the proceedings. They both had changed Hewitt and Jeffrey in the past. Jackie, the next oldest to Kacey, was the same age and class as Brenda Espinoza, still in captivity. Kacey prayed their captors had not harmed any of them because of her.

When Zach Gill arrived at last, he and Kenshaw got all but the most stubborn visitors back into their trucks and off the gathering grounds just in time to keep them from setting up a drum circle and camping there for the night. Kacey said goodbye to her family and was shown to a cabin. She paused to glance back at the lodge where the council conducted business.

There on the wide porch gathered some of her tribe members who had remained behind. A few of the faces were familiar. She recognized three of them because they were members of their nationally known hotshot team. This was her tribe's elite wildfire squad distinguished nationwide. She had met Carter Bear Den, Ray Strong and Dylan Tehauno. She also knew the woman beside Jake, Lori Redhorse, who was a nurse at the tribe's health-care clinic, where Kacey suspected this had all begun. Kacey remembered then that Jake had told Colt that he had made Lori his wife.

The chief of tribal police, Wallace Tinnin, nodded

at her from his place between Carter and Jack Bear Den. Amber Bear Den, Carter's wife, held her husband's arm, and Ray's wife, Morgan Strong, stood to her right with her eyes on the river. There were others Kacey did not know, but they all looked toward her. And then she realized exactly who they were.

Tribal Thunder.

This was the warrior sect of the Turquoise Guardians, the protectors, drawn into service to keep her safe. She had been told they would watch over her, but she had never seen them before today. These were the best of their numbers, hand-selected for their bravery and dedication to their tribe. She scanned the faces for Colt and did not find him or his brother Ty or Kee. Only Jake Redhorse stood among the warrior sect of her people.

Kacey raised her free hand in salute and then carried her son into the cabin where they would stay until their safety could be assured. She wanted to trust them, but her experience was that the tribe had not been there to help her or her siblings when her mother had left them for days and days. Protective services had come and gone, taking them from and returning them to their mother as if they were sheep changing pastures. It had got worse until finally her only option was to leave this place.

She'd hoped to convince Colt to come with her. But he'd had his own plans for them that included her staying put for two more years. Kacey blew out her regret in a long stream of air and gathered Charlie tighter to her chest. Things did not always go as planned. That much she knew for certain.

The cabin's interior held the warm glow of a kerosene lantern, just like the ones at her home. Unlike those lanterns, this one had fuel. The interior was familiar and just as she recalled from her Sunrise Ceremony. Each of the cabins had nearly the same style. The inside was all knotty pine with wide plank floors. She remembered that there was a bedroom behind one door and a bathroom behind another. The main room had a table and chairs and a small living area that included a stone fireplace. Someone had lit a fire to chase off the chill.

Upon the opposite wall, a cast-iron stove sat on a brick pad. The table was laden with so much food there was no open place to eat it. The long sideboard held boxes of diapers, baby toys, blankets, baby clothing and even a small bassinet. Beneath the sideboard sat a stroller and car seat. Gifts from her people, she realized.

If she had known about the food, she would have sent some home with her sisters, for she suspected there was little food there for them. How long until her mother vanished again?

The bedroom door opened and Kacey jumped. Then recognized Colt standing there. The cry that escaped her morphed from fear to joy. She was safe and he was here with her. Kacey began to sob. Colt gathered her up in his arms and she realized the handcuff was no longer clasped to his wrist. He led her to the bedroom.

She had not felt safe in the hospital. Some part of her had feared for Charlie's safety there and she hadn't been able to rest.

Now in the cabin's bedroom, Colt rubbed her back as the tears washed down her cheeks and into the absorbent fabric of his white T-shirt. Her throat ached and she felt bone weary but somehow cleansed when she drew back.

Charlie's forehead wrinkled and he began to cry, as well.

"Let me take him," said Colt.

She passed her baby carefully to him.

Colt took Charlie and rocked him as he had just rocked her. Kacey's arms and back ached from holding the baby since her escape from the hospital. She sank to her seat on the bed. Charlie blinked in a way that foretold of imminent napping. Colt continued to sway, dancing without moving his feet, with her baby in his arms.

Her heart gave a catch at the picture they made. Man and infant, one so strong and one so helpless. She breathed a sigh of contentment mingled with longing. This was what she wanted. But how?

All throughout her captivity, every day and every night, she had been certain that at least one person was searching for her. When she had told the other girls that *they* would come, she had meant Colt. But she'd been wrong. No one had come because no one had searched. They were runaways, lost to their tribe by their own choice. The sorrow grew sharp in her throat like the point of a spear. Their disappearance had been like a rock dropped in the water. Once the ripples ceased, there was no sign of the stone's passing.

Colt carried the sleeping infant to the outer room and returned with him in the bassinet.

"He's had a busy day," said Colt. Then he turned to look at her. "So have you."

She nodded. "Do the police know you are here?"

"Yes. I spoke with Jake. He gave me this." Colt held up a mobile phone for her to see, then set it on the table beside the bassinet. "Even charged it for me."

"What about the FBI? You tackled one of their men."

"I can't leave the reservation."

Her chest tightened. He couldn't leave and she did not want to stay.

"How did you get away from them?"

"They couldn't hold me because they weren't prepared to kill me."

"You've been in here all along?"

"Most of it." Colt sat beside her on the bed.

"Why didn't you come out for the welcoming?"

"I just can't stand so many people. It makes my skin crawl."

"But you'll stay with us?"

"Right here beside you and Charlie."

Kacey swiped at the tears and smiled. "I was so afraid they would take him."

Colt rocked back, bringing her to the mattress with him. Her body throbbed with fatigue and ached from giving birth. But her heart sang and her mind floated as she lay in the warmth and security of his arms.

"Rest now, Kacey. You're safe."

She nodded and nestled closer, dozing, drifting as he stroked her hair. She woke to Charlie's cry. Colt left her to retrieve her newborn. She roused to watch him carry Charlie out of the bedroom and return a moment later with the changing pad. He set this on the dresser and proceeded to change Charlie's diaper and then dress him in a onesie. He moved with more expertise than she did, but Charlie continued to fuss and cry. Her brow wrinkled.

"Where did you learn to do that?" she asked.

"YouTube," he said. "They have Wi-Fi here now. Installed it after the flood. I was in the lodge during your welcome, watching videos on newborn care, and if the information was right, he's still crying because he's hungry."

She held out her arms and accepted her boy. Her breasts ached and milk already flowed before his little mouth latched on to her breast. Charlie was a hungry baby, but after his meal, he was sleepy again.

"He really sleeps a lot," she said, brow knit.

"That's what they do. Eat, sleep and go through diapers." He grinned and her anxiety melted away.

This was the old Colt, the sweet boy who was always there with a ready smile and a kind word.

"What about you?" he asked. "You hungry?"

"Starving."

He carried the empty bassinet out to the living area. She followed as soon as Charlie had finished his meal, placing him in the padded carrier. He yawned and closed his eyes.

"Looks comfortable," Colt said.

"They brought me everything I need and more."

They dug into the food provided by their tribe. Kacey was drawn to the sliced roast beef and the hash. She grinned at Colt, who was eating chicken salad. It was almost as she had hoped it would be, before he'd shipped out and she'd been taken.

She cast him a smile. "I'm so glad to be back."

He grinned and it was easy to imagine that he had never changed. But he was different inside now. She sensed it. Were they both so altered that they could not go back?

"Me, too," he said.

"Will you stay here with me?"

He lowered his sandwich. "Yes. But, Kacey, I'm not your best choice. Ty is smarter about this kind of thing and he has Hemi. That canine is the best tracker and guard dog I've ever seen. Jake is a police officer, so he's got a gun and badge and all. Any of the members of Tribal Thunder would stay with you."

"Colt, when my mother took off and we had nothing to eat, the tribe didn't show up. You did. Not your brothers. Not Tribal Thunder. Not protective services. You." She rested a hand on his as the gratitude welled up with the sorrow. Her mouth pressed to a tight line as she forced down the lump in her throat. "You have had my back since second grade when you stepped up for me on the bus. So you are the one I'll trust now."

Colt turned his hand to clasp hers. "I've changed, Kacey."

Her laugh held no mirth and she looked at Charlie sleeping in his bassinet. "We both have. I trust you, Colt. Nothing can change that."

Chapter Nine

Colt dropped his chin to his chest and shook his head as if he could not understand her choice. "Then I'll stay."

She offered him a smile. "Thank you."

Colt reached across the table and took her hand, and the zing of contact darted up her arm toward her chest. "I missed you. When they released me and I made it back, I went to your house."

Her eyes widened. Kacey withdrew her hand from his. "I didn't know that."

He nodded, his gaze drifting to his hands laced before him and rocking restlessly on the tabletop. "First thing. I spoke to your mother. She said you had run off months ago and hadn't bothered to call. She seemed…"

Kacey could imagine her mother in various states. Needing a fix, after a fix or all business, preparing to leave them again for another long stretch. She swallowed but he said nothing more.

"She thought I'd run," said Kacey. "I'd threatened to more than once."

"No one would have blamed you," he said.

But he knew now that she had not run. Her jaw worked back and forth as if she chewed something tough.

"I didn't understand it. Should have known. You were so excited to start college. I'm ashamed that I believed her. I thought you just couldn't stand to be in that house a minute longer."

She didn't know what to say. Perhaps that she thought he knew her better. "You thought I'd leave my sisters to take care of everything."

"You took care of it alone."

"I had your help, your mother's and Mrs. Trans's."

"You should have had more."

Her gaze drifted away to things unseen. "I've missed the fall semester," she said.

"You'll start in the spring. You can still go."

"With a baby?"

"Why not?"

She realized that he believed she could do it, and that made her think that maybe she could. He'd always given her confidence. She cast him a smile and he returned it. Then she remembered the men who hunted her. Her stomach squeezed and her eyes shifted, glancing toward the locked door. Her smile died as her jaw tightened, bracing herself. There would be no school, no return to normal life, because they were out there. She felt it.

"Well, not for a while, anyway," she said. They shared an uneasy silence. She rubbed the bridge of her nose, thinking of a time he did not want her to go to school.

She'd told him that she'd finally decided the only way to really help her siblings long-term was to get an education. Instead of supporting her choice, he'd joined the Marines and come to her with money to buy them a house. On that day, she had told him she wouldn't be marrying a man who didn't hear her words.

Colt's mom was in failing health, and with his brothers gone, Colt was left to care for May alone. The man she'd found and married, Burt Rope, was loving but not able to cover May's medical bills. The medication costs alone were staggering. So Colt had used his bonus to buy his mom a motorized scooter and banked the rest for her care.

"I wish you had never gone over there," she said.

Colt's expression clouded and his gaze slipped from hers. The tension returned to his shoulders.

"I'm sorry," she said. "I just wish we could both go back to senior year and… I don't know, run away together."

He nodded, but his chin dipped and his gaze became unfocused. "I'd go this time. But now I wish a lot of things."

"What, Colt?"

"That I could sleep through the night. That I didn't break out in a sweat when I have to get into a car.

That I could be around my brothers without wanting to press my hands to my ears and run in the opposite direction. And most of all, I wish I could have been here to protect you."

"I wish I could have been there to protect you, too, Colt."

They stared at each other across the vast expanse of the few feet that separated them. She still wanted to leave. He still wanted to stay. And neither of them would ever be the same again.

"Will you tell me what happened, Kacey?"

Now *her* gaze slid away. "It's hard to talk about."

"I appreciate that."

"Have you spoken to anyone about what happened to you?" she asked.

"Recently. I spoke with Kenshaw. He's getting me a counselor, a man from our tribe who saw action in Afghanistan. We both agreed that living up on the ridge was not making me better. Up until a few days ago, I didn't care. I just wanted to be left alone." He met her gaze. "Then you showed up."

"And now?"

"I want to be there for you, Kacey. That means I have to face what happened and get better."

"Do you think Kenshaw could find me someone to speak to, as well?"

Colt nodded and a smile played at the edges of his full lips. "I'll ask him."

"I didn't talk about it to anyone but the FBI, Colt. I only talked to them because it might help find my friends." She scrubbed her palms over her face, her fingers sliding down her cheeks and away. "They asked me so many questions. I told them all I know. But I never told them how this all made me feel and they never asked. I'm so angry at those men for taking us and so afraid for the girls that they still have. What if they kill them all because of me?" She remembered too late that Colt's entire team was killed. All except him. Her eyes widened and she covered her mouth with one hand. "I'm sorry, Colt."

He swallowed, his Adam's apple bobbing, and he took a moment. "It's hard to live with."

Then he told her about the IED that had destroyed the first Humvee, killing everyone within and disabling his vehicle, wounding two of the five men on his team.

"They had us for three days. They killed the men in my company, one by one." He glanced up at her. "I don't know how you lasted months, Kacey."

She wanted to hear the rest of it, so she did not allow him to draw her away from his story. "How did you survive?"

He laced his hands on his lap and then beat them rhythmically against his thigh. He cleared his throat more than once, but no words came.

She stood and moved her chair to sit beside him and rested a hand over his. He stilled, took a deep breath, then let it go. His voice sounded small now and tight as if he had to force it up from somewhere a long way away.

"They said they were saving me for last. That I was worse than the other infidels because I was brown-skinned like them. They wanted to know what I was."

"Oh, Colt, I'm so sorry."

Colt grimaced. "They'd bring their bodies back one by one and leave them with me. Finally, I was alone with the bodies."

"Jake told me that a SEAL team rescued you."

"They did. But they were too late for my team."

She rubbed his back and then left her arm draped over the tight muscles of his shoulders.

"Too late," she said. "You were the last one out and I was the first. You know what happened to your men and it was awful. I imagine horrible things. I still have hope, but it lives with the terror of not knowing. I might never know. The hope chases dread like a mockingbird chasing a crow from her nest."

Colt's chin dropped, but he peered up at her from beneath his dark brows and spiky lashes. "It's hard to be the only survivor. I see their faces. In dreams, I hear their voices. I hope they find your friends, Kacey. I don't want you to have to go through this."

"Marta and I had the same due dates. She could have delivered already. What will they do to her then?"

He met her troubled gaze. Neither of them had the answers. Only questions.

Kacey looked in his eyes; saw the pain and the loss. She needed to change the mirror that reflected back to her all that she might suffer. So she kissed him. A light pressing of lips. Colt's eyes closed and his hands slid up her arms to her shoulders. His breathing changed and a hum came from his throat. He deepened the kiss and then she did not think of her friends or his lost comrades because the need took her.

The heat built and her blood pounded. She wanted this, wanted Colt. Kacey pressed herself to him, sitting half across his lap. He dragged her closer until her breasts pushed tight to the firm warm muscles of his torso. The contact was delicious, drawing a moan of pleasure from her.

There was a light tapping on their door. Kacey drew back as Colt released her. She blinked up at him, trying to make sense of the sound. He cursed under his breath and then rose, answering the door. Morgan Strong stood on the porch.

"Kenshaw would like to see you both, if that's possible."

Kenshaw was not only their shaman. He was the head of the medicine society and leader of their warrior sect.

Colt looked to Kacey and she nodded, rising wearily to her feet. She gathered up the carrier where Charlie slept and carried him to the front porch, surprised to see Jack Bear Den standing watch over them. He nodded to her as she passed across the open ground that separated her cabin from the main lodge. There were others watching over them as well, out in the night. Instead of feeling happy at the realization, she thought of all there was to do with the relocation. Surely the detective had other things to do, other cases to solve. The whole thing made her feel guilty to be another drain on their overtaxed resources.

Colt paused outside the lodge, looking at the lights glowing from the windows. She stood with him beneath the stars, holding the plastic handle of the baby carrier. The tension in his body and the change in his breathing drew her attention. She cast him a concerned glance.

"You coming in there with me?" she asked. Kacey didn't know if she could face them alone, but she didn't want to force Colt into a situation where he became anxious.

Colt clenched his teeth, making the muscles in his jaw bulge. Then he nodded. "Yes."

But he didn't move.

"We can leave whenever you say."

He cleared his throat. "Let's get it over with."

She didn't know if it was the gathering or the building that troubled Colt. It didn't matter. He was going for her and she was grateful.

At the lodge, they were greeted by not just Kenshaw and Chief Tinnin, but also FBI field agent Luke Forrest. She hesitated, unsettled to see the FBI here with her protectors.

She stepped back and Kenshaw rose.

"He's not going to take you, Kacey. You're on sovereign land and under the protection of our tribe."

Kacey nodded but did not move forward until Colt placed a hand on her back and gave a little nudge. It surprised her that he was the one to set them in motion. His jaw still clenched, but his eyes were clear and focused as they took the offered seats at the circular council table. Kacey had never been inside the lodge and she looked around at the polished blond logs that supported the high ceiling. The massive fieldstone fireplace sat below the tribal seal, which showed the river, turquoise canyon and a single eagle flying in the blue sky above. The messenger to the great creator, she knew, because this raptor flew higher than all others.

She set Charlie's carrier on the seat beside hers and then took her place, resting her hands on the smooth cool surface of wood. A channel of inlaid turquoise cut through the center of the circular council table and she thought it was intended to resemble the river that gave them life. The wood seemed to radiate a power, and she felt her heartbeat slowing. These men and women were here to help her and protect her baby.

Kacey lifted her head, meeting Kenshaw's gaze. He nodded and gave her an encouraging smile.

"Agent Forrest has told us that you do not remember how you became with child but that you were only seen at our tribe's health clinic. We are therefore initiating an investigation of our clinic. We have hired a new detective. Detective Hood, of the Yavapai Nation, is expected next week and will head this investigation. We thought an outsider might be able to work undercover at the clinic. Also, Detective Hood taking this case will allow Chief Tinnin and Detective Bear Den to continue with their investigation of the eco-extremist group and the supervision of the relocation of our people following the dam breach."

Kenshaw told Kacey that two members of the Wolf Posse had attacked Jake and Lori Redhorse while the couple were protecting the baby they had adopted. Kenshaw set out three photos.

Kacey felt a cold shiver lift the hairs on her body. Her chest went tight, making it difficult to breathe. She knew them. The men were the same pair who had captured her from the high-school athletic fields shortly after her second appointment with the tribe's health clinic. The woman had been in the car holding a gun.

She pushed the photos away and confirmed what they already knew.

"Trey Fields is in federal prison and Minnie Cobb and Earle Glass are on their way there."

He told her that Trey was convicted for endangering a federal officer, Agent Sophia Rivas. Both Minnie Cobb and Earle Glass were in federal custody awaiting trial after twice attempting to snatch Zella's baby.

"I heard about that," said Kacey. "Zella's baby." She didn't know how to say that the baby in question was white.

"Yes," said Agent Forrest. "Similar situation, only Ms. Colelay is giving up parental rights."

"According to Zella, these two were stalking her for months but avoided capture," said Kenshaw.

Kacey knew who had warned Zella. It was her friend Marta. She knew this because Marta had told her during their captivity that she had told Zella that two bangers were following her. Kacey could only imagine what Zella thought when Marta disappeared and then the two gang members came after her. They'd all been at the clinic the same day. Marta had seen Zella there. But unlike Marta, Kacey did not remember the visit or meeting Zella or anything until the following day. It was like a big black hole.

Before her capture, when she'd told her mother about her memory trouble, her mother said that she wasn't bringing her back to the clinic unless she was bleeding or on fire. Her mother always said that. She'd only taken Kacey in the first place because she needed her college admissions physical. Marta had been there for a high-school sports physical and Kacey had no idea why Zella was there.

"And is her baby safe?" Kacey asked Agent Forrest. She imagined the Russians would want Zella's baby.

"Neither Minnie nor Earle has implicated the gang, but we feel that neither of them would do something like that without permission at the least. It's more likely that they were under orders. Since their arrest, there have been no further attempts against the infant."

"What about Charlie?" she asked.

"We don't know. That's why we're taking precautions. We have a perimeter and guards posted."

"They killed David SaVala," said Colt, his voice quiet but clear.

"And Bear Den is investigating that death," said Tinnin. "We do think it is related."

"His mobile phone," said Colt. "How did they track that?"

Kacey felt sick to her stomach.

"They'd have to run records for everyone in this area and they'd need the names of the residents up here," said Tinnin.

"That's the kind of information the Wolf Posse could provide," said Agent Forrest.

The Wolf Posse's involvement made the threat greater and more terrible because it now came from within their tribe. The local gang could easily supply the names of everyone who lived up on Turquoise Ridge, including David SaVala.

Another terrible thought came to her. "How did they pick the girls they were going to take?"

Tinnin met her gaze with a look that seemed pitying. "We don't know that yet."

But he had a theory. She'd put money on it. She thought about the others, comparing them to herself. They were all from large families. Those families all had either single parents, like hers, or neglectful parents. Probably both. Most of their folks had occasional run-ins with either the tribal police or child protective services.

Tribal police had been to Kacey's house more than once during those times when her mother left them for days or weeks. She never knew where her mother went, but she always came home with money or drugs or both. Kacey thought of the other girls. She knew from Marta Garcia that protective services had been to the school to speak to her. Brenda Espinoza said that her dad was taken away for hitting her mom. Kacey knew Zella had at least one older sister who had got into trouble very young and Kacey knew that Zella's mom drank.

She made the comparisons and connection. Large troubled families, girls of a certain age. Kacey had considered running away more than once, but to where and what? She was stopped because her sisters and brothers needed her. And she'd had Colt, her rock, until he'd left her to join the service.

She met Tinnin's gaze.

"Did the gang pick us because we wouldn't be missed?" she asked.

Tinnin scrubbed his palm across the stubble on his cheek. "Maybe. You each fit the profile for a runaway."

All the days they had waited for rescue. No one was even looking for them.

Kacey straightened in her seat. Her muscles still ached, but she was determined. It was important that they keep Charlie safe. But it was just as important that they find the missing.

"They think you're looking for them, Chief Tinnin," said Kacey. "They believe that their families and their relatives and their tribe have noticed their disappearance and are searching. They believed me when I said I'd send help. You're telling me that up until I showed up, you had us all listed as runaways."

Tinnin dropped his gaze.

Kacey rose to her feet and rested her palms flat on the table. "You listed us in some database and hoped we got picked up on the streets of Phoenix or wandered on home. Right? No way. They're captives. Taken. And each one of them is pregnant. So we are finding them *now*, before they have their babies and something even worse happens to them."

"FBI is looking for leads at the house you gave us."

"That's not good enough."

"What do you suggest?"

"The clinic. Something happened there," she said. "Something I can't remember."

"Detective Hood will be looking into that connection."

"Next week!" she shouted. "We need to get to the clinic now!"

"What doctor did she see?" asked Colt.

Tinnin looked away.

"I don't remember," said Kacey.

Agent Forrest answered, "Her appointment was with Dr. Kee Redhorse."

Kacey gasped and turned to Colt, who had gone pale. Could Colt's oldest brother have done this to her?

Chapter Ten

Colt looked as if Agent Forrest had punched him. His face went gray and he seemed momentarily stunned. Gradually, he lifted his chin and met Tinnin's stare.

"No," he said. "No way. Not Kee."

"He has taken on substantial debt," said Tinnin. Both his tone and his eyes reflected sympathy. His words, however, cut again.

"Lots of people have debt," Kacey said, coming to Kee's defense. She knew that Colt's oldest brother was both an example and a father to him. She also knew that when Kee left for college, Colt missed him terribly.

"What about Ty?" she asked. "He's a member of the Wolf Posse. Isn't he more likely to be involved?" Only after the words were spoken did she realize what she had done. Implicating his other older brother did not make things better. She gasped and pressed a hand to her mouth.

Colt's jaw muscles bunched and he flinched, telling her without words how much her comment hurt him.

"We are aware," Tinnin said, "and are exploring his possible involvement."

So they were looking at Ty and Kee.

Kacey slipped her hand from her mouth and whispered an apology to Colt. He cast her a cutting glance and then looked away.

"We request that you two stay here on this property so Tribal Thunder can keep you safe. We also ask that you limit your interaction with both Kee and Ty," said Tinnin.

"Limit it to what?" asked Colt.

"Zero," said Agent Forrest.

Colt looked from one man to the other.

For how long? she wanted to ask. She had escaped her captors and found safety, but for Colt, this was a different type of prison. He did not like being confined and she suspected the size of the property made little difference.

As for herself, she was relieved that Charlie was safe. But it sat badly that she was free when her friends were still captives. What if their captors had done something worse than move them? What if they had been killed because of her? Or had their babies taken?

The theory of growing fetal tissue rose in her mind like a waking nightmare, and her gaze cut to her sleeping baby.

She couldn't live with that. They had to find them.

"Any progress on locating Brenda, Marta and Maggie?" she asked.

Tinnin sighed and pushed his gum to his cheek

before answering. "FBI is still processing evidence, but there is nothing new." His jaw worked the gum between his molars. "Listen, you've had a long day. We'll check back in the morning." His gaze flicked to Colt. "If you plan to stay, we've got you in the cabin beside Kacey's."

But the implication was clear. Tinnin didn't expect Colt to remain or perhaps he did not want him to stay. In fact, with the investigation now centering on both Kee and Ty Redhorse, it was very possible that the chief would prefer that Colt leave.

Colt glanced to her. She reached out and clasped his hand.

"Stay," she said on a release of breath.

His nod was tight. Then he turned to Tinnin. "I come and go as I like." It wasn't a request.

Tinnin lifted his dark brows, turning the skin on his forehead into a road map of horizontal furrows.

"You need to stay on-site," said Tinnin.

Colt said nothing to this. Forrest and Tinnin exchanged a side glance. Forrest arched a brow. One more Redhorse to add to their list of suspects, she thought. Or just a loose cannon? Colt's mutiny meant more work for a police force already stretched past its limits. But she knew that neither of these men nor Tribal Thunder could keep Colt here if he did not wish to stay. Colt was like a shadow in the woods.

He stepped around the table to face off against Agent Forrest, and his hands squeezed into fists.

Nothing good had ever come from two men posturing like that, she knew.

She lifted Charlie from his bassinet and stepped up beside Colt, pressing her shoulder to his. He tore his gaze away from the field agent and glanced first at her and then at Charlie, who slept with his mouth open. Kacey didn't ask; she just placed Charlie in Colt's arms.

Forrest stepped back as if she'd handed Colt a live grenade. It seemed she had found the men's weakness. Babies made many men uncomfortable. But not Colt. He cradled Charlie's head as her baby nestled against his shoulder.

"We need to get him to bed," she said. Of course, Charlie didn't care if he slept in a bassinet, his mother's arms or in a cradleboard. But Colt needed to be free of these two men.

He cast the two tribal police officers one last look, his mouth going tight. Then he turned away, still cradling Charlie.

Kacey lifted the empty bassinet and faced Tinnin, Forrest and Little Falcon.

"Good night, gentlemen," she said to them. "I thank you for providing us a safe place. I wish my friends had the same."

Kacey followed Colt out across the wide-open ground that separated the main lodge from the row of cabins along the river. The trees that lined the shore provided glimpses of the silver ribbon of water moving swiftly along. Too swiftly, she realized now that the dam no longer controlled the flow of water.

She gazed up at the deep dark skies alive with bright sparks of light. The wind brushed over her skin and she closed her eyes to savor the beauty and the peace as she gave thanks to the One Who Lives Above.

She was free. Just days ago, she had fled for her life and now she was here on her tribe's lands. It seemed impossible. She opened her eyes to look at the heavens and found the star that does not walk around, the North Star. It was there as it had been every night of her life. It had not changed in her absence. Stars were constant. Would any of her friends ever see the night sky again? The tears came then, streaking down her cheeks.

When she lowered her gaze from the night sky, it was to find Colt staring back at her. He used the warm pad of his thumb to wipe her cheeks dry.

"It's so beautiful here." She swallowed against the lump that rose suddenly in her throat.

"Yes." He took her elbow and gave a squeeze.

"I wish… I wish my friends could see this."

His hand stroked up and down her arm and then rubbed across her back.

"I'm afraid what they'll do to them because of me."

His face was serious and he offered no false hope. He had friends as well, comrades who would never see the night sky or anything else again. He understood and did not minimize her fears with words. Instead, he gave comfort a different way by wrapping his free arm around her shoulders and ushering her forward to the cabin.

"I'm sorry for what I said about Ty," she whispered.

He didn't answer as they crossed the open ground and she thought he did not hear her. When they reached the porch, he turned to face her.

"It was a natural conclusion," he said. "He was in the gang. But he's not in it anymore."

"My mother says no one ever leaves the Posse." What she had actually said was that the only way out was dying. But Kacey wouldn't say that aloud.

"Maybe so," he said. "Let's get Charlie inside. Cold out here."

Every evening was cold in the fall. With no cloud cover, the earth cooled rapidly.

Colt held open the door and she stepped inside.

Charlie roused when Colt handed him back to her. Colt used a match to light the lantern and set about rousing the fire in the cast-iron stove to chase off the evening chill.

As he continued to feed the growing fire with sticks of kindling and then logs, she fed Charlie. She tried not to feel guilty that she sat in the comfortable cabin or wonder where her friends were right now. The skin of her naked breast puckered at exposure to the cool air, but gradually the fire's heat reached her. By the time she switched Charlie to her opposite breast, she was humming.

She did not forget her pain or her promise, but her baby needed her. Could she risk something else happening to her? What would happen to Charlie then? Her mother was incapable of caring for him. Kacey had been in the tribe's foster-care system at various times. Sometimes she stayed with Colt's mother and helped look after Colt's sister, Abbie.

Many foster families here were good, but many were little better than the family from which she had been taken. She didn't want that for Charlie.

She looked down at the sweet face of her child. He stared up at her from deep blue eyes. The irises hinted that his eyes would be dark one day. His skin was lighter than her little brothers' had been, and the fuzz on his head was a soft brown. She stroked his perfect head.

Not hers, but still hers.

"I don't care about DNA and genetics," she said to Charlie. "They took my freedom, so I'll take you. Fair exchange. You're mine."

She felt Colt staring at her. She lifted her gaze from her baby to him and smiled.

"Do you think they will let me keep him?" she asked.

"The tribe, yes. The FBI, I don't know."

"He's not evidence. He's a baby. My baby."

"As long as you stay here, they have no power to take Charlie."

"Are you staying here tonight?" she asked.

"Maybe not in the cabin. I like to sleep outside."

"I could open the windows."

"Won't it be too cold for Charlie?"

"No. We have blankets and someone left a wolf pelt."

"You want me to stay?" he asked.

She nodded. "I feel safe when you are here."

He stood and used one finger to rub at the corner of his eye. "You heard them, right? About Kee and Ty."

"But your brother Jake is a member of the police force and he's a member of Tribal Thunder."

"Do you think it's possible, what they suspect?" he asked.

She lifted one shoulder and then let it drop.

"Do you remember who saw you at the clinic?" he asked.

"Which time?"

"The first."

"January sometime. I know that much." Kacey shook her head. "I told you. I don't even remember going to the clinic or much of the following day. It's like I just jumped over them."

"I wish I could forget, sometimes."

She could understand that.

"Do you think you can't remember because of the trauma?" he asked.

"No. None of us could remember." Kacey didn't think she was blocking out her experience. The other explanation she refused to say aloud.

"Could you have been drugged?" he asked.

She shrugged. "I don't know." But she suspected.

"They might have used that date-rape drug," said Colt.

She lifted her brows and prepared to agree and instead shook her head. "I don't think so."

"You don't remember," he said. "What about your mother?"

At the mention of her mother an instant knot gripped the muscles between her shoulder blades. "What about her?"

"She might remember who saw you."

Kacey snorted. "She only drove me because she needed the car. She told me that she didn't go in for the physical with me, just dropped me off at the door." Like a stray cat outside an animal shelter, Kacey thought. But that was better than the alternative. "Then they called for a follow-up in February. Mom was annoyed. The woman who called said there was a problem with my blood sample and they had to redo it."

"They found something?" he asked.

"Lost it, was what my mother said."

"Who did she speak to?" he asked.

"I don't know. I found the note on the counter telling me to drop in. No appointment necessary. I did and they took blood and urine. I have no trouble remembering that appointment. That was February 20th. They took me on February 22nd."

"You remember that?"

"Every detail."

Chapter Eleven

Colt listened as Kacey described being snatched off the road after leaving the late school bus after volleyball practice during the half-mile walk to her home. It had been dark, even though it was well before six in the evening and she had been alone. Her brothers, still in elementary school, took an earlier bus, and her sisters, Jackie, Winnie and Shirley, did not play sports. No one else used that stop.

It had been Kacey and two male attackers. She knew their names or at least the names that they called each other. Earle and Trey. She had seen them around. Minnie had been there, too, in the car. Kenshaw had shown her their photos and said they were all members of the Wolf Posse. Trey was in prison and Minnie and Earle were in custody.

She could not find it in her heart to be sorry. From each girl's description, Marta had been taken by Minnie and Trey, Brenda by Earle alone and Maggie by someone else. Kacey hoped to God it had not been Ty.

Kacey knew her abductors were all gang members because they wore yellow and black, the Posse's colors. They had simply lifted her off the ground and thrown her into the van. She had lost one of her sneakers; evidence, she had thought at the time. A clue to lead someone to her. Now she knew better.

Once they were inside the van, Minnie pointed the pistol at her. Earle and Trey used duct tape on her wrists, ankles and mouth. They threw her backpack in the back with her. They carried her from the van and into the house. All the while, she had been wiggling like a fly wrapped in a spider's web with just as much chance of escape.

In the house, she saw the Russians for the first time. They paid Trey in cash. When the Russians had taken her to the basement, she was certain she would never again come back up those dusty wooden stairs. She shivered, the terror fresh as raw meat.

"You told Tribal this?" Colt asked.

She nodded. "Took them to the house, too. You know, every episode of that FBI show flashed in my mind. The body, the evidence, but not what the victim suffered," she said. "Not the days and weeks locked in a basement."

Colt took her hand. She wondered if his own capture was roaring through his mind, because his forehead glistened with perspiration.

"After they left me there, still taped up like a carpet, Marta appeared."

Marta had been taken at the beginning of February and had been alone in that basement for nineteen days. She had released Kacey, told her what little she knew.

"We thought they were crazy, telling us to eat and take care of the baby. But then Marta started throwing up."

She told him of living in the basement for months. And how they kept a calendar on the floor, scratching in the days. That was how she knew that Brenda Espinoza came in May and Maggie Kesselman arrived in late September.

"Do you think they moved them?" he asked. The implication was clear. If they were not moved, then they were dead.

"I hope so. None of them cared about us. But they sure cared about the babies. Kept us fed. Gave us vitamins. Let us wash and gave us each a mattress and a wool blanket. They were scratchy but warm. This was about the babies."

He thought of Charlie and wondered where he would be now if Kacey had not escaped. "Do you know anything about the people who are the genetic parents? Do they know?"

She rubbed her brow with the heel of her hand, then let it drop. "I don't know anything about them. I have spent a lot of time thinking about them. All I know is what Agent Forrest told me during our first interview. The FBI lab report said that Charlie is Caucasian and Asian."

"No. He's Turquoise Canyon Apache," Colt said.

She smiled at that. Her heart twisted in her chest at the sweetness of his smile and the sorrow in his eyes.

"Well, you're safe now with Tribal Thunder protecting you."

"They still want Charlie," she said.

"Too bad. Because they won't get him," said Colt.

She smiled and glanced back to where her baby slept. In the lamplight, she could see his mouth working as if he sucked, even in slumber, with his hands raised beside his head, perfect fingers curled into tiny palms.

Colt stepped up behind her, his arms slipping around her waist and his mouth descending to her neck. They had told her at the hospital that she should not sleep with a man for two weeks or more. That her body needed time to heal. But her body did not know or care about rules. And her heart did not know caution, for her heart sped, galloping along in anticipation. She lifted her hand to stroke his head, drawing his sweet mouth closer to the juncture of her neck and shoulder.

She turned in his arms and he lifted his head, meeting her gaze. Her brows rose as she pressed their hips together.

Colt stiffened as her stomach met the hard ridge of male flesh.

"It's too soon," he said.

"For that," she said. "Do you remember all the times we went to the river?"

His eyes rounded. Kacey had kept her virginity. She and Colt had never had sex. But they had learned how to reach their pleasure without intercourse.

Colt's smile was slow and languid. She stroked his arousal.

"I remember," he said. "Everything."

They moved into the bedroom, Colt carrying the lantern and Kacey carrying Charlie. He left the door open to let the heat from the stove follow them.

She wrapped Charlie in the wolf pelt and laid him back in the crib beside the bed. He did not even wake as she moved him.

Colt waited for her on the bed. He'd drawn back the covers so that only half of the bright red, green and black of the Navajo-patterned blanket was visible under the white sheets. The lantern now sat on a shelf above the bed, made for that purpose.

She sat on the opposite side and turned to look past the two pillows and the wide expanse of linen at Colt. He offered her a wicked smile.

Kacey removed her shoes and socks, but nothing else, before lying on the bed. She rolled to her back as he settled to his side. They met in the middle.

His kisses moved from her neck to her ear, sending delight shivering over her skin. Kacey caressed his head, gliding her fingers through the loose satin of his long hair before entwining her fingers behind his neck and pulling him down until his body pressed tight to hers. All the while, he continued to score the flesh at her neck with his sharp teeth. His fingers danced feather light across her hip and stomach until she could not stand having their clothing separating them.

He helped draw away her blouse, kissing the skin he revealed as he stripped her out of her jeans. When he finally climbed back up to lie beside her, Kacey was breathless and dressed only in a bra and panties. Her body hummed with anticipation as he turned away, stood and shucked out of his jeans, flannel shirt and undershirt.

When he returned to her, she reached for him, using her hand to do what her body was not ready for as he slipped a hand beneath her panties and caressed the wet wanting flesh at the junction of her thighs. His fingers moved expertly, parting her and finding the bud of needy flesh. He stroked as he rocked against her hip.

"I missed this," he said.

"I missed us," she said.

His gaze locked to hers and she saw the tension build. But he continued with long, even strokes as he teased and rubbed her toward her release. Her head dropped back and her breathing changed. He moved faster, his hot breath blasting against her throat. She arched up to meet her release, her body stiffening a moment before the wave of pleasure broke within her. She gasped and then gave a hum of pleasure. He kissed her then, pressing her back to the pillows as he cried out, his release pulsing in her hand.

His body went slack and he dropped to her side.

His heavy arm fell across her middle. She clasped hold with both hands and rolled toward him until their foreheads touched.

"All you all right?" he asked.

The muscles that had responded to her need now ached. But she smiled. "I'm fine."

He rolled away and returned with a small damp towel for her and one for him. When she felt clean again, the exhaustion returned. She changed Charlie's diaper and saw him settled before crawling into the nightie someone had provided for her and then returning to the bed. Colt appeared a moment later dressed in low-slung sweatpants that gave her a view of his chest and abdomen that she would never forget.

"You're staying?"

He smiled. "I don't feel trapped when I'm with you. It seems natural to be here." He rubbed the back of his neck. "I haven't talked so much since I came home."

"I missed talking to you," she said. "Sometimes, while I was in that basement, I would imagine what you would say to me."

His hand dropped to his side and he looked bereft. "What did you imagine I'd say?"

She smiled. "'Be brave.'" She looked away, fluffing the pillows. She did not tell him the rest. *Be brave. I'll find you.* Even though he'd not been looking for her. Knowing that hurt her down in the place below her heart.

He slipped in beside her and stroked her hair away from her face.

"We never did this before," he said.

"Yes, we have."

"No, not this. I never had a chance to sleep beside you afterward, Kaccy. I always had you home before it got too late."

As if the time of day had anything to do with what teens wanted to do when they were alone.

"That's true." She glanced toward the window. "They'll all know you slept here."

"I'll leave if that is what you'd like."

She gripped his hand. "No. I need you here."

"I don't sleep much," Colt admitted.

She cast him a smile. "Maybe tonight will be different."

Colt reached up and snuffed the lantern. It glowed a familiar eerie orange ghost light before fading so slowly she was not sure she saw the moment it went out.

Colt moved close and gathered her up against the welcome heat of his body. He pressed a kiss to her temple and then laid his head down on the pillow beside hers. She rested as his breathing fanned her forehead, feeling his body relax as he drifted to sleep.

She closed her eyes and gnawed at her lower lip. She was safe here. Kacey knew it. And that was exactly the problem.

The food and the warmth and the comfort of the

bed all offended her. Why were they not all out looking for Maggie and Marta and Brenda?

They were all out there waiting, huddled together, watching their bellies grow bigger day by day. At least she hoped they were still captives, because the alternative was too terrible to consider.

Kacey had promised them that she'd send help, and just like everyone else, she had failed them.

Kacey did not sleep well. Between her dreams of the various horrors that might be befalling her friends and the needs of a newborn, she spent as much time in the bedroom as she did in the outer living space. When she finally did fall deeply asleep in the hours between night and dawn, it was to visions of rescue. Only this time when she dreamed of her friends' release, Kacey was with them.

All this time, she had been waiting for someone to find her, to rescue them. She woke with a start, her eyes flashing open. Kacey blinked in the gray predawn light that made it possible for her to see nothing and everything all at once. She held the dream in her mind, trapping it in her conscious thoughts.

She knew what she must do. The idea was simple and terrible and dangerous. But it might work.

Chapter Twelve

Colt's eyes opened and he took in his surroundings. The cabin was familiar but not his own. He knew where he was, but the light from the window told him this was morning.

And that was impossible.

It would mean that he had slept through the entire night. He had not done that since before his capture. In a moment, he knew the reason. The weight of the body next to him on the mattress was the answer. Kacey slept at his side. She was safe, so he was safe. Nothing would touch them here. He let his eyes drift closed and then he realized what had woken him. Kacey's breathing was wrong. He turned to look at her as she stared straight up to the ceiling.

Had she been dreaming—rushing sloth-like from the grip of some unseen terror? Colt knew nightmares intimately. All types. He had the ghosts of his comrades to dog him. She had the ghosts of her friends haunting her.

He took her in his arms and dragged her close.

He lifted his head to look at her. She lay rigid as a corpse with eyes wide open. Whatever frightened Kacey, it was no nightmare.

"Kacey?"

She didn't answer or even seem to hear him. Now his heart was pounding.

KACEY LIFTED HER hand over her mouth because the idea scared her so much. Her eyes went wide as the pieces tumbled against each other like river rocks rolling in floodwaters. None of the law-enforcement personnel could find the missing women because none of them were willing to use the one thing that might bring her captors out of the shadows.

Was she willing?

Someone had wanted Zella's baby badly enough to send Minnie Cobb and Earle Glass after her. That gave Kacey the lure, something the Russians wanted and the gang wanted. The FBI and tribal police had both given her the place, the clinic. Somehow someone there had notified the gang when Zella's baby arrived. Would they do so again?

She had the who and the where. All that was left was when and how.

Kacey would never use her child as bait. But she would use herself. She knew the risks. Knew them precisely. But that would not stop her.

She had promised her friends that she would send help and she had failed. Now she saw a way to keep her promise.

"Kacey?" Colt's voice held a mix of concern and uncertainty.

She turned to meet his dark eyes to find him watching her with knit brow.

"Didn't you hear me?"

She shook her head. Had he spoken to her?

"What's wrong?" he asked.

It was hard to say it aloud. Somehow she did. "I have to let my captors catch me."

His nostrils flared and he pushed himself up to one elbow, so that he loomed over her. "No."

It wasn't up to him. Perhaps he knew that, which was why he looked so fierce.

She sat up in bed and tucked a leg up underneath herself as she turned to face him. "Tribal police can't find them without me."

"They'll have to."

"It's taking too long."

"Be patient. Give the force time to work."

"Time?" She made a strangled sound that combined the gnashing of teeth and the growl of a beast. "How can you say that to me?"

"The FBI is working leads. Agent Forrest said so. It's only been a few days."

"You were only captive a few days."

His face contorted as if she had struck him and she knew her verbal blow had hit its mark.

Colt opened his mouth to argue and then shut it again.

"Marta is due any day," said Kacey. "She might

already have had her baby. What happens to her then? I'll tell you what will happen. I'll repeat what I heard them say about me. 'Sell her or dump her.' You understand? Once the baby comes, the Russians either sell her into slavery or kill her. That's what is happening right now."

Colt's brow descended and his dark eyes turned to flint. "I don't care what happens to her. I care what happens to you."

"Well, if you knew that any day, any hour those evil men would kill me or sell me, what then? Would you still not care?"

He stared belligerently at her, unrelenting. She slipped from her side of the bed. The pine planks chilled her bare feet as she gathered one of his clenched fists in her two hands.

"Colt, what if your comrades were still in captivity? What would you be prepared to do to free them?"

His eyes shifted, darting away as he looked at something far off.

"Anything," he whispered.

She smiled. He understood.

He flicked his gaze back to her. "But you are not a soldier, Kacey. You are a mother with a child. What happens to Charlie if you don't come back? Will you leave him for your mother to raise?"

Colt was fighting back, hitting her in her most vulnerable place.

Kacey swallowed at the lump that rose in her

throat, but it remained lodged like a shard of glass. She dropped his hand and stepped back. He followed her, sliding across the empty bed and coming to stand before her.

She turned her back. Colt knew exactly how bad her home life had been, because he'd seen it and because she'd told him. It was one of many reasons that everyone assumed she had run. Why would anyone stay in such a home a minute longer than necessary?

Colt took her in his arms, drawing her back against the strength and heat of his body. His arms wrapped her in a warm embrace, and his breath fanned her neck. She gave in to the perfect fit and the compelling heat of him.

His breath whispered over her skin, bringing a delicious shiver.

"I came home for you, Kacey. I only just found you again and now you're asking me to risk losing you, too? I won't."

Somehow she mustered the courage to step away. She faced him, meeting his angry stare. He was going to protect her with or without her permission. She narrowed her eyes, astonished at how quickly they had gone from lovers to opponents. Well, for her friends, she would fight even him.

He seemed to know her mind, because his brows fell low and menacing over his dark eyes. "I'll lock you up myself."

She exhaled, centering herself and finding her strength, knowing she would need both. Then she turned away, separating from him, but he clasped her arm, tethering her with a firm grip.

"Don't leave me, Kacey. Don't do this."

"Let me go, Colt."

"I can't."

She met his gaze with a defiant stare. If she had to hurt him to save her friends, so be it.

"You did once," she said.

His hand slipped away as his eyes widened. His jaw dropped and then snapped shut as he whirled, heading toward the outer room.

She somehow resisted the urge to go after him by picturing Marta giving birth in the room with silver stirrups. She saw to Charlie's needs as Colt stomped around between the woodpile and the stove.

She retreated to the bathroom to clean up. It was Wednesday, and with each day, each hour, as Marta, Brenda and Maggie grew heavier, their chances of rescue grew slimmer.

After showering, she dressed in clothing provided by her tribe. They were nicer than anything she had ever had in her closet.

She stepped out to the bedroom and gathered Charlie in her arms and fed her baby.

Colt returned as she was snapping the onesie onto Charlie's kicking legs.

"I brought breakfast," he said and retreated.

She followed him to the outer room. The stove warmed the room, and the air held the aroma of bacon. She set Charlie in his carrier in the seat beside her and then seated herself. Colt set a plate before her with crisp bacon, fried eggs flecked with black pepper, charred toast and browned potatoes mixed with onions and bits of red bell peppers.

"So what's your plan?" he asked.

"Do you think Ty could get word to the Wolf Posse about where I am?"

Colt stopped eating. "He's managing to keep those bangers at arm's length. Why would you drag him into this?"

"I need the Russians to know where I am."

"You think the Wolf Posse doesn't know exactly where you are? They know, so the Russians know."

She realized that was true, and with that recognition came another. "I'm too well guarded for them to reach me."

"Exactly. Isn't that why we're here?" He motioned to the cabin, safe in the tribal headquarters and surrounded by the guardians of her people.

"I have to leave."

"With Charlie?"

The cold flash of terror of that possibility caused a physical pain to tear across her middle. Her denial was quick. "No. He stays here, where he is safe."

"They don't want you. They want him."

"I know that."

"Do you think the tribe will protect this child if you leave?"

"'This child'? What are you saying?"

"He's your baby if you say so. Your say-so also makes him Apache. But without you here—"

"He's Apache," she insisted.

"Without you to claim him, he would need to be adopted by another member of our tribe. These men and women are risking their lives to protect you, Kacey. But who would adopt a child who endangers their lives?"

This part made Kacey's insides hurt. But she pressed on, crossing her arms over her middle and hunching as if expecting a kick. "Your brother Jake and his new wife, Lori, are both Tribal Thunder and they have a newborn. Zella's baby."

"Yes."

"Well, how is it that their baby is safe?"

"Zella Colelay was not a captive."

"But her baby came to her in the same way. The FBI told us that members of the Wolf Posse tried to capture the baby Jake and Lori are adopting. So why doesn't the Wolf Posse want her anymore?"

Colt shook his head. "I have no answer."

Kacey needed to protect Charlie and she needed to help her friends. She was torn. "Would Ty know?"

His gaze cast down and he did not answer for a long stretch. Finally he spit one word. "Probably."

"Would Lori take Charlie?" she asked.

He was scowling. "Lot to ask."

"She swore an oath to protect," she said.

He grimaced. But he did not say that they protected members of the tribe. She counted Charlie

as one of them and she believed Colt did, as well.
But many might think otherwise. Charlie had no
tribal blood and everyone knew it. Adopted children
were accepted by her people. But if no one would
adopt Charlie, what would happen to him? And who
would be brave enough to adopt him, especially if
he brought danger to their tribe?

"Taking Charlie would jeopardize their little girl,"
he said.

The Turquoise Canyon people were only just rising after the attack by the eco-extremists. People
had to evacuate from their homes and move to temporary housing. Now she returned with the Russian
mob on her tail. It was terrible timing.

"I'll call Jake and ask him to stop by."

He made the call and reached his brother. He told
Jake that he was putting the call on speaker.

"I was just going to call you," said Jake. "I have
some bad news."

Kacey braced for word that her friends had been
killed.

"We're missing another girl."

"What? Who?" asked Colt.

"Louisa Tah."

Colt glanced at her and she shook her head. She
did not know Louisa.

"School reported Louisa missing on Monday, October 2nd," said Jake.

Six days before Kacey had escaped, another girl
had been taken.

"Missing. Ran or taken?" asked Colt.

"We don't know."

"You just finding out now?"

"No. We've been investigating," said Jake. "We got word on Monday from the school of Louisa's absence because they could not reach the mother. We made contact and her mom thought that Louisa would turn up. She hasn't. Her mother is hazy on when she last saw her daughter, so exactly when Louisa disappeared is unknown. Louisa was in school Friday and missing on Monday."

Louisa had been gone for days before her absence had been reported. Kacey's heart squeezed. She already knew Louisa without knowing her. All she needed to do was look in a mirror. No one had missed her.

"Yeah. She's sixteen. Lives in Koun'nde. Ran with the gang but never made it to initiation."

Colt set down the phone on the table and gripped the arms of his chair. Kacey found she'd made a fist of her right hand and was pressing it to her mouth.

"After the school reported her truant, one of our guys tracked down her grandmother, because Louisa stays there sometimes, but she wasn't there. I did the interview with mom. Mrs. Tah was intoxicated when I got there Monday afternoon. I called protective services and waited for them to arrive. Mrs. Tah has three other children all under the age of six."

Kacey closed her eyes against the dread.

"Anyway. Both mom and grandmom thought Louisa was staying with the other one."

"That's terrible," said Colt, his eyes on Kacey now.

She shivered as if the temperature in the room had dropped.

"Was she seen at the clinic?" asked Kacey.

"Checking," said Jake. "Listen, it's an active investigation. I just called to ask if Kacey saw her."

"Saw her when?"

"During her captivity."

"No," she said.

"Okay, Lori and I are on our way over to the tribal grounds now. We'll be there in a few minutes," said Jake.

"Good. We have something else to discuss with you and Lori. See you soon," said Colt.

"'Bye for now." Jake disconnected.

The silence stretched.

"They didn't bring a mattress," she said.

"What?"

"The day before they arrive they bring a mattress. They didn't bring one."

"Kacey, this isn't your fault. No one expects you to go out there like the Lone Ranger."

"Call Ty."

He met her stare with a look of frustration. He pushed the phone at her. "You call him."

She lifted the phone in a trembling hand. Her hands shook so hard it was difficult to even bring the screen to life.

"What if you don't come back?" he asked.

She had once asked him the same thing after she learned that he had enlisted.

"I have to do this." It was what he had said to her.

"Call Forrest. At least tell him what you're planning."

"They'll stop me. I need your help, Colt."

"I'm not helping you get Ty arrested or yourself killed."

"Will you take Charlie?"

"What?"

"You're a member of the tribe. Full blood. You can adopt him."

"They won't let me adopt a baby. Psych discharge, remember? They think I'm loco, baying at the moon."

"You could do it."

He frowned, his lips pressed thin. His answer ground between clenched teeth. "No."

Was that the truth or was it just a way to keep her here?

"I have to help them. I promised."

He rose to his feet, his face red and his breathing ragged. "How will getting killed help them?"

She reached for him and he backed away, arms raised as if to say he would have no part in this. "You are not going," he stated.

She lowered her chin. He held her gaze and saw no wavering in her conviction.

He lifted his hands in surrender. "All right. I'll

talk to Ty. I can't talk about this on the phone. I have to go to him."

"Thank you."

He stormed out of the cabin without his phone. She scooped up the baby carrier and the phone, but by the time she reached the porch, Colt was already on his brother's motorcycle, pulling out.

She watched him go, disappearing from sight in the tunnel of pines that led in and out of the tribe's gathering place. She slipped his phone into her pocket and then paused. The sound of an engine kept her there on the porch, listening. It idled and she thought that he might have changed his mind and turned around. But a few minutes later, two vehicles pulled in.

The first was a silver F-150 pickup. She recognized the driver. It was Jake Redhorse, she realized. He must have passed Colt on his way in. What had Colt told his brother, the newest member of the tribal police force?

As the truck turned toward the lodge, she more clearly saw the second vehicle, a dust-covered black Ford Escort, and the driver, Jake's new wife, Lori.

Kacey watched Jake pull up before the lodge. The Escort parked beside his truck. He emerged first.

Colt's next oldest brother resembled his mother much more than Colt did, with a heavier brow and fuller mouth. He was out of uniform today, wearing jeans and a long-sleeved shirt. He spotted her and waved as he rounded the truck, opening the door of the dusty compact car.

Lori emerged from the car dressed in blue scrubs and a top covered with pastel graphics of children's toys. Her hair was tied in a bun and she wore her hospital identification tag around her neck. Lori had a regal look about her and clear light brown skin with coral undertones. Jake's new wife paused to open her window, likely to prevent the car's interior from heating up.

The implications of the two vehicles and Lori's attire struck Kacey, and her breath caught. Jake was coming to work with Tribal Thunder, and Lori was headed to work…at the clinic.

Kacey lifted Charlie from his carrier and crossed to them. What had Colt told his brother?

"We just saw Colt," said Lori. "He's finally going to see his mama."

Kacey blinked at the lie. He had told her he was going to see Ty. Should she tell Jake where Colt was really heading?

Jake regarded her and she tried to keep from squirming.

"How did you manage that?" he asked.

Colt had lied to someone. He was going to see either Ty or his mother, but not both.

"Not sure," she said. Colt was on a mission. She just didn't know which one. "Any word on Louisa?" she asked.

Jake shook his head.

"My friends?" she asked.

"Not that I've heard."

Lori stepped up on the porch and asked to see Charlie. Kacey hesitated only a moment before turning him over. Lori was a member of Tribal Thunder and a prenatal nurse. But she worked at the clinic. And that was where this all had started.

"You heading to work?" asked Kacey.

"Yes, in a few minutes. I just need to check my schedule here first."

Kacey recognized that this output of time and effort could not go on indefinitely. If they did not catch the men responsible, these men and women would eventually need to return to their lives.

The trunk of Lori's Escort was covered with bumper stickers urging you to donate blood, kiss a nurse and have Native Pride. Kacey stared at the vehicle and then her gaze flicked to the open front window.

She lifted her gaze to find Lori fussing over Charlie. The neonatal nurse held her baby with confidence. Her newborn must have sensed it, for he did not fuss as he relaxed against Lori's chest and shoulder.

"How are you feeling?" asked Lori.

Kacey answered that and several other medical questions before Lori was satisfied. Kacey turned to Jake.

"How is it that no one is after your baby girl?" asked Kacey.

Jake glanced at Lori, who nodded.

"Tell her."

"I made a deal with Faras Pike."

That was the leader of the tribe's gang, Kacey knew.

"Told him that we're expecting a new detective who could be assigned to gang violence or the eco-extremists case based on what Faras decided to do about my little girl."

"A threat? And that stopped it?" Kacey asked. It seemed too convenient. Surely the threat Faras received over *not* delivering the infant was worse. Something didn't seem quite right about his story.

"I also spoke to Ty."

Now, that she believed. It was not threats that convinced Faras to withdraw but something Ty had said or offered. What? she wondered. A deal? A favor? Then the other shoe dropped.

Kacey could not prevent the gasp. If Ty worked a deal with Faras, then he owed Faras.

What was that favor? Was it Charlie? She resisted the urge to snatch Charlie back. She'd sent Colt to Ty, and Ty might very well be working for Faras. Suddenly all the warmth left the day and she shivered.

Jake had been leaning a hip against the rear fender of his wife's compact car. But now he came upright and his arms dropped to his sides.

"Kacey? What's wrong?"

"I asked Colt to speak to Ty about Charlie."

Now Jake seemed alarmed, judging from the way

he swung his gaze about in the direction Colt had disappeared. "Is that where Colt went?"

"He said so, yes. But I don't know."

Jake pinched the bridge of his nose with his thumb and index finger. "I already spoke to Ty. He said there was nothing he could do."

She wondered if the grief showed on her face. The possibility that Colt might persuade Ty to help protect Charlie had kept her hope alive. It died now with the silence of a snuffed candle as her convictions hardened to flint.

"Can he help find Marta and Brenda, Louisa and Maggie?"

Jake's hand moved to the back of his neck. "He's not in the gang, Kacey. They don't tell him things like that. He fixes their cars and trucks. He looks the other way on things he shouldn't and tries to walk a very fine line between them and us. I'm not asking him to do something that I know can get him killed."

She thought that he might already have done that. "I understand." She opened her arms for Charlie, and Lori handed him back.

"I've got to call Colt," said Jake.

Kacey slipped her hand into her pocket and flipped Colt's phone to mute just a moment before it began to vibrate with Jake's call.

"I'll see you two later," said Jake, his phone to his ear as he marched off. Lori looked after her husband as Kacey retreated a step toward her cabin.

Kacey directed her next comments to Charlie. "Nap time for you, mister."

Somehow she held her smile until after she was walking away.

placed her hand on the bed and then turned after the two well-lit figures.

Chapter Thirteen

Kacey turned at the porch and watched Jake and Lori make their way to the main lodge. Jake still pressed his phone to his ear. When they disappeared inside, Kacey's knees gave way and she sat hard on the porch of the little cabin. The weight of her decision pressed down on her and she could not rise. She thought of all the ways her idea could fail, and the list was long. Then she thought of the seconds she had to make her decision ticking away. Finally, she imagined what might happen, the release of her friends and her promise fulfilled.

I'll send help.

No one was coming for them. The FBI didn't know where her friends had gone. Her captors had moved them, and the possibilities were endless. Kacey knew that the Russians could vanish in plain sight. It was a game of days, days that her friends did not have.

Kacey lifted her sleepy baby and carried him inside on shaking legs. There, she tucked him into his bassinet and kissed him on the forehead. Then she turned to the job of collecting all she needed.

With all the toys and stuffed animals her tribe had left in the cabin, it was easy for Kacey to create a bundle that was the approximate size and shape of a newborn. One of the baby dolls seemed convincing when partially draped with a baby blanket, and an extra baby blanket filled out the doppelgänger's shape nicely. She left a hastily scrawled note under Charlie, whose full belly and fresh diaper ensured that he would sleep for a time. Kacey pressed her lips to the soft place on the top of his head as she prayed for his safety. Then she straightened and shook herself.

Colt had no means to rescue his comrades and he carried the burden of that truth each day. But she had a chance, a slim, dangerous chance, and she was as much a warrior as any here.

She had promised to send help. But she never expected the help would be her.

They wanted Charlie. So let them come and take him from her. If she failed, she would be satisfied that she had done all she could to save Marta, Brenda, Maggie and now Louisa. The knife in her boot ensured that, this time, she was not defenseless.

Kacey checked Colt's mobile phone and saw two missed calls, both from Jake. She didn't play the message as she opened the door of the cabin, carrying the swaddled doll.

Her plan would depend on several things: that the

FBI and tribal police were correct in their beliefs that the clinic was indeed involved in the disappearances and that the clinic would quickly inform her captors of her arrival. After that, either the Russians or the Wolf Posse needed to attempt to capture Charlie and not kill her. Finally, she needed to contact help and lead them to her friends.

Even if the Russians didn't take her or did not take her to the same place as her friends, the FBI would at least have her captors.

Kacey thought about the possibility of having to surrender her life to save her friends. She did not wish to die, but she did not wish to go on knowing that she hadn't done all she could to find them. It would kill her bit by bit, wondering and waiting for the lost that never came back.

She hoped Colt could forgive her.

Kacey cast one look back at Charlie and choked on the lump that rose in her throat. Would she ever see him again? The ache grew, spreading outward from her heart. Colt would protect him. She was certain. She had to be.

She stepped out on the porch and waved to the sentry. He nodded and turned back to watching the road. After all, any abduction threat would come from outside their lines. She walked beside Lori's car, seeing Lori's purse, tote and nylon lunch bag on the passenger seat. Kacey opened the door and popped the latch for the trunk. Then she eased the door closed. A glance about showed that the sentry on the road still stared off toward the entrance and the one before the lodge watched the river.

It took only an instant for Kacey to roll into the trunk and close the door.

COLT RODE THE chopper Ty had loaned him. The Harley had been waiting before one of the cabins, delivered by Ty or Jake, Colt did not know. Somehow driving the motorcycle did not make him feel trapped. Rather he felt free. He made it to Ty's place, arriving in his driveway around eleven in the morning. Ty knew things that went on here on the rez, things the tribal leadership and tribal members never knew. Mostly, Ty kept this information to himself. Colt hoped Ty might make an exception for his kid brother.

Since his discharge from the US Marines, Ty fixed cars, detailed cars, rebuilt cars and, occasionally, sold cars. But he preferred working on the beautiful, old classics.

Colt spotted his truck parked before the open bay door. He parked and left the bike, finding Ty in the garage, beyond the bay door with his head under the hood of a Pontiac GTO with a dented side door. The tires were flat and the trunk showed more rust than blue paint.

"That's a beauty," he said.

Ty straightened but did not turn. There was a tension in his shoulders. Was he surprised to hear Colt's voice?

After all, though Ty had been to his place many

times since his return to Turquoise Canyon, Colt rarely let Ty see him and they had spoken only when Colt asked to borrow Ty's bike.

Finally, Ty glanced over his shoulder at Colt, dark eyes narrowing against the bright morning light. After a moment, the crooked mischievous smile appeared. If he guessed at Colt's mission, his open expression gave no clue.

"Original matching numbers and only 39,000 miles," said Ty.

"She's fine. 1970?" Colt guessed.

"1967."

Ty's hair was cut at his jawline and was perpetually dropping before his eyes, yet he never drew it back. His smile always seemed more challenge than mirth, and his bright dark eyes swept over his baby brother. Colt was certain he didn't miss a single detail.

He didn't ask why Colt was here or exclaim on his decision to travel and speak.

"I got her at auction," he said, motioning to his current work in progress. "When I'm finished with her, I should make out pretty good unless I keep her. I'm tempted." Ty wiped his hands on a greasy rag and leaned back on the grille, waiting. Ty had a way of looking completely at ease in any situation.

Colt's second oldest brother had given him his first ride, a 1957 Chevy, mint green with pinstripes and an elaborate airbrush painting of a running mustang—a colt—on the front fender. It was waiting for him on his discharge. Now it sat before Ty's garage.

Colt thumbed at the truck. "You brought it here?"

"Jake did. He also brought my bike to the compound. See, you found it. Would have told you but, you know. You don't answer your phone."

Colt pressed a hand to his empty front pocket. He'd forgotten his phone.

"You just missed Abbie," said Ty.

Colt felt an instant stab of guilt. He hadn't even seen their kid sister since his return to the rez. "Yeah?"

"She pedals over here on her bike sometimes."

"How is she?" Colt asked.

"Tall. Nearly as tall as me."

Abbie was fourteen and growing by the minute.

"She asks about you."

Colt said nothing to this.

"You should go see them."

Colt nodded. He should. But he wouldn't. Not yet.

Ty lifted a wrench and motioned in the direction Colt had come from. "Kinda far from the tribal gathering grounds, aren't you?"

"Kacey wants me to ask you to ask them to call it off."

Ty looked down at the spotless wrench, polishing it with the rag. "Can't."

"You did it for Jake and Lori."

"Different situation. The Russians had a backup."

"Backup?"

"Another girl with the same baby. Same parents, I mean. Boy, I think."

Colt felt sick. His mouth twisted in disgust. How

could Ty be mixed up in this? "What do they do with the backups if...?"

Ty pressed his mouth tight and shook his head. "Don't know. Don't want to know. Didn't know anything until Jake dragged me back in. Faras did me a favor and reported to the Russians that Zella miscarried. So no baby girl to look for."

Colt's eyes rounded. What had Ty done for Faras in return? "You pay back the debt?"

"Not yet." Ty's brow lifted. Was he surprised that Colt understood exactly what Jake's favor had cost?

Then another possibility crept into his consciousness like a slug on a piece of ripe fruit.

Was that favor Kacey? Kacey and Charlie? Colt looked back the way he had come, wishing he had never left her. The hitch in his breathing and the pain in his heart told him what he should have seen before. He wasn't protecting Kacey because she asked him. He was protecting her because he still loved her. Now that love might bring him to have to fight his brother Ty.

Colt knew that, because of the favor he had done for Jake, Ty couldn't refuse Faras Pike. If Faras demanded Ty turn over his kid brother, his brother's girl and the baby, then Ty would do it or suffer the consequences.

He looked back at Ty and saw the resignation there. Ty recognized that Colt had worked it out.

"You know where they are keeping her friends?"

Ty set the wrench aside on the pink cloth draped

over the open hood but maintained control of the greasy rag. He didn't answer.

"Do you?"

Ty twisted the rag. "Colt, listen—"

"Can you find out?"

"Not without joining the gang again. Faras would like that. Cut me out as a middleman."

Colt did not know exactly what Ty did for the Wolf Posse besides the obvious, supplying them with fast cars, cars that were much faster than, say, a state trooper's cruiser.

He wished Ty had never joined the Wolf Posse in the first place. Their home life had been hell when he joined, or that was what Jake had told him. They had all been afraid of their father, with good reason. But he'd only ever hit Ty.

"Is it Kacey?" asked Colt.

Ty didn't patronize him by pretending not to understand the question. "He hasn't asked. Yet. But I heard where she is, so they know." He draped the rag over the shoulder of his T-shirt. "You heading home, Colt?"

"To the compound?"

Ty shook his head. "To your cabin."

This was a warning and advice, all in one. Ty didn't want him to go back to Kacey and Charlie. He didn't want to have to do anything that would hurt his brother. Colt felt the same way, but some situations could not be avoided.

"I'm going back to her. She's determined to find her friends."

"Only way she sees them again is if they catch her." Ty's stare was cold as ice water. "And then *you* won't find her."

Colt's heart frosted over. That was what Kacey had been planning. "FBI offered her relocation."

Ty nodded. "She should take it."

"I'm in love with her."

Ty's hard expression dropped and Colt saw the sorrow. The tough big brother who was always there for him now had eyes filling with tears.

"Then you should go, too. Soon."

Colt hugged Ty, and Ty squeezed him so tight it took his breath. When had he grown to the same height as his big brother?

Ty broke away first.

Colt wiped his eyes. "Jake is looking at you."

Ty blew out a breath. "Figures. No good deed… Maybe I can get a cell near Pop."

It had only been because of Kenshaw Little Falcon that Ty had been allowed to join the Marines instead of facing prosecution like their father after the armed robbery.

Colt studied the dust clinging to his boots.

The cell phone in Ty's back pocket vibrated. He drew it out and stared at the screen. "It's the favorite son." He turned the phone so Colt could see Jake's name. Then he answered the call.

Colt could hear Jake's voice because it was loud and held a note of alarm.

"Have you seen Colt?"

"Why?"

"Because Kacey is missing. Have you seen them?"

Colt's body stiffened as the downpour of panic washed over him.

OLEG PICKED UP the phone and grunted into the receiver. Their contact at the clinic was now refusing to provide new girls, the chickenshit.

"She's here," said his contact. "Kacey Doka. She just walked into Urgent Care."

"It's a trap," said Oleg.

"I think so, too. But you said to call if—"

"She alone?"

"Yes."

"Trap," Oleg repeated. Why else would she show up alone at the clinic?

"She has the baby."

Oleg thought it stank. And that was why he would pass it off on the bangers on the rez. Let them eat their own, and if they did manage to snatch the girl, so much the better. "I'll send someone."

"I don't know how long she'll be here—"

Oleg hung up. Then he called Faras Pike.

KACEY DID NOT know whom she had expected but certainly not Colt's older brother Ty. But there he was, striding toward her.

By way of a greeting, he said, "Jake called Colt and told us you were missing. He sent me and he's pissed."

Kacey frowned. She tried to act as if she believed him, but she could not control the trembling. Neither tribal police nor the FBI had yet arrived. So, what Ty said might be true, but it was just as likely that the Wolf Posse had sent Ty Redhorse for her.

She held the bundle of blankets and baby doll close as she walked with Ty out of the urgent-care center. Why, of all the possibilities, did it have to be him? Colt's big brother, the one he looked up to and loved. Maybe he'd never have to know.

Ty led the way and she followed him, climbing into his muscle car, some kind of Pontiac from the seventies that looked as if it had just come off the line instead of out of a field somewhere.

"Is that purple?"

"Violet metallic with black interior. Seventy-three Plymouth Hemi Barracuda."

"It's…" *Garish*, she thought.

"Fast," he said, finishing her sentence.

He held open the door for her. She spotted a huge, familiar dog sitting on a blanket on the back seat.

She offered her hand, and Hemi licked her. "Good to see you, girl," she said.

Kacey slipped inside and Ty closed the door. She glanced around as the tingle of fear lifted the hairs on her arms.

Ty slid behind the wheel and set them in motion.

She wondered how long she had to pretend she didn't suspect that he was not taking her to Colt.

He blew out a blast of air. His expression was no longer calm. Instead his jaw clamped and his brow arched as he cast her an angry stare.

"What did you drag me into, Kacey?" asked Ty.

And then she knew. It was Ty, the one they had sent. Not Oleg or Anton or the one whose name she did not even know. Not a banger in a yellow Mustang wearing gang colors. They sent someone she trusted to take her.

She sat back and stared out at the road ahead. "Where are you taking me?"

"Damned if I know."

Chapter Fourteen

Kacey eyed Ty with a mixture of disappointment and dread. "I should have guessed."

"You should have. And you should have listened to Colt and stayed put. What'd you think, you could bust this thing up all by your lonesome?"

She had only thought that her sacrifice might provide a lead. It hadn't.

"He doesn't think you're in the Wolf Posse, you know," she said.

"Best he never finds out."

"I saw this in a movie once. They sent the man's best friend to kill him."

"This isn't a movie. And I'm not here to kill you, but you're killing me."

"Does this repay the favor you owe Faras Pike?"

"How do you know about that?"

"Officer Redhorse has a baby that the Russians want or would want if they knew about her. Surely Pike knows. You're the only one I can think of who could make him go deaf and blind."

"You got it all worked out, huh?"

She gave him a satisfied smile.

"You call the FBI?" he asked.

"No," she said.

He cast her a long look. "You wearing a wire, Kacey?"

She shook her head. "Where would I get one of those?"

"At the compound before you stowed away in Lori Redhorse's car."

"You think the FBI would let me do this?"

"Well, you must have some plan. Either that or you have a death wish. So now might be a good time to fill me in."

"Why should I tell you anything?"

"Because I'm the guy Colt sent for you."

A bubble of hope rose inside her.

"Lucky, because I'm also the guy who talked Faras into sending me instead of your mother."

"My...my mother? What are you saying?" She swiveled in her seat to face him, holding the bundle to her body as if it were a real baby.

"Kacey, she's a mule. Been working for the Posse for years. You have to have known that."

Kacey knew what a mule was. It was someone who carried drugs from one place to another. She knew her mother used drugs and that she disappeared for long stretches, but she had never put together the pieces that had been given to her until Ty threw them in her lap all tied up with a bow.

She couldn't stop shaking her head in disbelief, even though she believed him. "I didn't know."

Ty snorted. "Then you didn't want to know."

The knot in her stomach spread to her chest, constricting her breathing. What did he mean, her mother? "They wouldn't send my mother."

Ty's reply was a snort of disgust.

"How can I believe anything you say?"

"I don't know. Most folks don't."

But Colt trusted him and Kacey trusted Colt.

Ty headed back through Koun'nde toward Piñon Forks.

"My opinion," he said, "you should have turned your mother over to tribal police years ago. What I would have done."

Kacey thought of his father, Colton, now serving time in federal prison for a job in which he had enlisted Ty as his getaway driver. If anyone knew about terrible parenting, it was Ty.

"Lucky for you, you didn't have to. Tribal arrested him for you," she said. She readjusted the mannequin and checked it as if it were really Charlie.

"Who were you talking to on the phone outside the clinic?"

So she'd been spotted before she'd even entered the FEMA trailer. She'd called Jake Redhorse, asked him to phone Agent Forrest and given him her location.

"Who is it?" she asked.

"Who is who?" asked Ty.

"At the clinic. Is it Kee?"

"All I know is what I'm told. So here I am like a good little lapdog." He glowered at her. "Chances are high they will kill you and take him."

"And you?"

"Survivor, same as always."

"Where are we going?"

"To the Russians."

"Darabee? Is Colt there?"

"I sure hope so," said Ty. "He should be, unless they caught him already. Tribal police are behind us somewhere. I called Jake. First time we've had a conversation lasting more than a minute in years. Please tell me that the FBI can track you."

"They should. I have Colt's mobile phone."

"Where is it?"

She hesitated.

He eyed the baby doll. "Inside the blankets?" he guessed.

She lifted the swaddled doll protectively and said nothing.

Ty motioned a thumb toward the bundle. "That's not Charlie."

"How do you know that?" she asked.

"Hasn't moved." He thumbed to the rear seat and his sleeping dog. "And Hemi showed no interest. She'd definitely notice a baby in the car and give it a thorough sniffing. So that doesn't smell like a baby. Plus, you would never bring a baby where you are going."

She laid the toy across her lap, surrendering the ruse

"When they figure that out, you are out of time."

She tried not to let the panic block her throat, but her words held a certain strain. "I promised them I'd bring help."

He gave a slow shake of his head as if she was not to be believed. "Getting yourself killed won't help."

"Neither will hiding," she said.

He pressed his mouth into a hard line and said nothing.

"What do you know about the exchange?" she asked.

"Where, when and who. Ten minutes, Antelope Lake Overlook and you are expected by two Russians." He made the turn away from the river road, away from Piñon Forks. This way led past Turquoise Lake to Red Rock Dam to the west. Beyond that was a steep winding road along the cliff face that led down the mountain to Antelope Lake. Between the dam and the lake was a spectacular overlook that included a picnic table and a trail down to the bottom of the dam.

"Do you know where they're keeping my friends?" she asked.

Ty snorted. "I don't know anything except what Colt told me and what Faras told me. If I hang around after the drop, the FBI will arrest me. If I don't hang around, Colt might get himself killed. If you don't survive, Colt will blame me. If you do survive this ridiculousness, you can turn me in and I still go to jail. In other words, I'm having a really, really bad day."

Kacey held the hand grip as they entered the last switchback before the overlook. Signs warned of falling rock, and the shoulder of the road was punctuated with great hunks of stone that had rolled onto the road.

In the rear seat, Hemi rose to sit, trying vainly to maintain her balance as they hugged the final curve, making her rock into the car door. Ty liked fast cars and he knew how to drive them.

"Do you think they'll bring me to my friends?"

He gave her a pitying look. "They want the baby. Not you. You are a liability because you've seen them and you can be replaced, have been already if what Colt said is true. Louisa Tah," he said, mentioning the newest missing girl. "Right? And if they don't get that baby you carried, they'll just feed the waiting parents some story about the fetus not being viable and call a do-over."

"But if we can capture one of the men who held me…?"

"Then what? They'll give up and lead you to your friends?" He gave a strangled sound that fell between laughter and a growl. "They'll die first. Kacey, you're young and inexperienced, so I'll give you a pass on this. But your plan sucks." He eased on the brakes. "We're here. Now take out that phone and dial Luke Forrest's number. Then mute the call and put it on speaker."

She did as she was told and finished as they rolled into the dirt lot. The parking area was empty except for an eighteen-foot RV before which sat two lawn chairs beneath an awning. Between the seats sat a large forest green cooler with cup holders molded into the lid.

"They aren't here yet," she said.

Ty glanced at the ceiling and blew out a breath. Then he cast her a sidelong glance. "Look again."

She scanned the empty stretch of sand and then came back to the RV. It looked so completely normal…just like the house in which she had been held. Kacey shivered.

"Exactly."

"Where's Colt?" She had a sinking feeling Ty had only dangled that hope before her to keep her from doing something stupid. Or perhaps more stupid.

Ty leaned forward, his chest nearly pressed to the wheel as he glanced around. "Don't know. High ground, I hope. He's a hell of a good shot. But so are they." He thumbed toward the RV.

He smoothly turned the muscle car in a half circle so that her door faced the trailer at a distance of about twenty feet.

"Get out," he ordered. "If you hear shots, get down and stay down. And do *not* get in that trailer."

Kacey hesitated.

"Out," he said.

She lifted the doll to her chest, feeling the squarish lump of Colt's cell phone tucked inside the baby blanket. Then she opened the door. She had barely gained her feet when Ty peeled out, his passenger door slamming shut as he performed a perfect doughnut, raising a cloud of dust.

Anton stepped from inside the camper first, holding a black semiautomatic weapon at his hip. He motioned to her with his opposite hand and she remained where she was, coughing and fanning at the stinging dust. Behind Anton, Oleg appeared in the open door.

Ty continued to perform his show of motor muscle, making one more circle before fishtailing out of the parking area. His tires sent another wave of dust back at them.

Anton glanced around the empty overlook parking area and came toward her, his outline obscured by the fine swirling cloud of red dust.

"Nowhere to run, Kacey," said Anton.

Kacey remembered Ty's warning. If she got in that RV, she was dead. She turned tail and ran toward the worst of the swirling dust, following the course Ty had taken and running as fast as her legs would carry her.

COLT WATCHED HIS brother Ty turn his '73 'Cuda in circles in the dirt, covering his previously spotless hood with grime and giving Kacey the cover she needed to run away from her pursuers. From his vantage point, the Russians should have made easy targets, but the dust also prevented him from getting a bead on them.

But he heard them. They were shouting at Kacey as she ran. He hadn't counted on the nerve-jolting fear that seeing Kacey in jeopardy would bring. His mouth was as dry as the dirt beneath him and he couldn't muster the spit to swallow.

Colt feared they would reach her before he could take them both down. That forced him to leave cover and charge out in the open toward her.

He made his move, streaking across the lot with the rifle raised. He debated calling to her because she was running at an angle that would take her away from him but closer to the cover of the rocks positioned to prevent inattentive sightseeing drivers from plunging into the canyon.

But if he called to her, he would reveal his presence before he had a shot off and possibly bring her between him and his targets. He could see them more clearly now and noticed that one held a semiautomatic weapon pointing at Kacey. The shoulder strap across the chest of the other man meant he might also have a similar weapon.

Kacey spotted him now and her stride faltered. She turned toward him and managed three more steps before her pursuer caught her, stretching out a hand and capturing her arm at the same time he noticed Colt.

The Russian bellowed and swung his semiautomatic toward Colt as Colt squeezed off a round, sending a bullet into the Russian's chest. Bullets sprayed the ground before Colt, forcing him to dive clear and then roll to his feet. Kacey dropped to a crouch, protecting the bundle he knew was not Charlie. Her pursuer grasped her loose hair and tugged Kacey up before him. He released his weapon, which swung on its strap to his side, and used his free hand to cover the bullet wound on his right side. Then he used Kacey as a shield as he retreated. His partner fired at Colt.

Colt scrambled for cover, reaching one of the large boulders that edged the lot. When he peeked from cover, it was to see Kacey's captor still dragging her backward toward the RV. The second man kept Colt pinned in position with a barrage of lead as the first pulled Kacey toward the steps.

There was a struggle as she dropped the baby doll and slashed at the arm of her captor with a boot knife. His boot knife, he realized.

Her captor howled in pain as he released her. Kacey dropped to the ground and rolled beneath the camper, knocking over one of the lawn chairs. The second man retrieved the bundle, lifted it and then gave a roar of rage as he threw the dummy over the precipice. Then he sank to his knees and sent a spray of bullets after Kacey.

Something inside Colt snapped. He stood, aimed and squeezed off three well-placed rounds, dropping both men. He was sure he hit each in the upper thorax, but they were both still able to crawl after Kacey and away from him.

"Should have taken head shots," he muttered and

followed his moving targets. Were they wearing body armor? His cartridge rounds still should have defeated Kevlar.

Kacey appeared at the back of the trailer at the same moment that two dusty black sedans skidded into the entrance of the overlook lot. The FBI had finally arrived.

The second gunman charged the cars with his semiautomatic, spraying bullets across the reinforced glass of the windshield. The first vehicle did not slow as it hit the gunman, carrying him along on the fender before pinning him to the side of the RV where he slumped across the hood.

Colt saw Kacey scramble down the embankment followed by her remaining pursuer. The man let his weapon dangle from the arm strap over his shoulder as he hurried after Kacey. He gripped his right hand over his forearm and the wound Kacey had given him as blood seeped through his fingers. The right side of his back was crimson with blood from Colt's first shot. Lung shot, Colt decided, but even with only one lung, the Russian continued after Kacey.

Colt knew the signs. The man was trapped, shot and desperate. But he had not given up on his objective and he still had enough time and enough blood in him to kill Kacey. Colt took aim. No mistakes this time.

He aimed for the man's head and squeezed the trigger just as the man dropped to his seat and slid down the embankment after Kacey. Colt's bullet sped out into the empty space where his target's head had been.

KACEY GLANCED BACK at the sound of metal striking metal. Part of the RV now jutted past the embankment. What had hit it? She prayed it was the FBI. A second glance showed her that Anton was sliding down the trail behind her on his backside. He released his bloody arm to grip his weapon, giving Kacey just enough time to scramble off the trail.

Unfortunately this switchback was a steep grade that offered nothing but cactus and loose rock to stop her as she clawed at the sliding rock that fell along with her. She landed hard on her back on the flat spot that was the trail. Kacey stared up at the blue cloudless sky as her lungs refused to obey her command to breathe. Colt's knife lay in her open palm, and her other arm dangled over the precipice that marked the next switchback in the trail.

She caught movement and saw Anton on the trail above, taking aim at her. The air rushed back into her lungs, dry and hot. Anton lifted his weapon in a bloody hand and Kacey closed her fist on the knife. She would not risk another slide down the cliff face. She knew the trail well enough to remember that this next section included stairs and a sheer drop. So she would have to face Anton or die trying. She sat up, drawing her arm back and throwing the knife as Colt had taught her.

COLT PURSUED THE Russian chasing Kacey. Colt was fast and agile from years spent climbing up and down such cliffs and he closed the distance. The Russian moved slowly, gripping the rock some ten feet below Colt. Below him, his target directed his weapon at Kacey.

She threw her knife. Her pursuer ducked as the blade spun and then flashed past his head, striking the cliff face beside him, falling to the trail at his feet. Then he straightened and aimed his weapon at Kacey. Colt knew that this time he would kill her.

"Hey!" yelled Colt at the same time he targeted the man in his sights. Kacey's pursuer glanced back in time to hear the click that signaled Colt's rifle jamming. Colt tried again with the same result.

The Russian turned back to face Kacey.

Colt released his rifle so it swung on its shoulder strap and then he dived off the trail toward the Russian. The weight of his body took them both over the lip of the trail and out into space.

The Russian screamed. Colt had a perfect view of the trail below the switchback, just a little too far away for them to land safely. Beyond was nothing but the air between him and the lake that lay far, far below. In that moment, he saw each rock and the gaping shock on Kacey's face as he and her attacker sailed past.

Chapter Fifteen

Kacey scrambled to her feet when Colt tackled Anton from the switchback above her. She had only a moment, a lifetime, to judge the distance and recognized that neither of the men locked together would land on the path. Colt was leaving her behind again. Her reaction was swift. She dived as well with only the single thought to stop him. Catch him. Hold him. Keep him.

She could not keep him from joining the US Marines. She could not keep him from choosing to live like a hermit in the woods. She could not keep him with her when she left the reservation. But she could keep him from sailing over the cliff and out of her life forever.

Her hands clamped on his leg and she latched on with all her might. Some part of her brain screamed a shrieking siren of distress, like a tripped fire alarm, as her instincts fought against her will for survival. Her added weight only changed the direction of Colt's descent. But not enough. If she didn't let go, they'd carry her over, as well.

She didn't let go.

Instead, she drew her body forward and clung to his leg as Colt released Anton. The Russian was now as free as the wind, a flightless bird sailing out into the blue sky above the river.

She hit the rough rock and gravel beside the trail first. Kacey's stomach landed on Colt's leg and foot, driving the wind from her lungs again. Her shirt and jeans shredded beneath her. She saw stars as they slid along the rock and sand. Colt's hips and chest bounced on the ground and then slid over the edge. Kacey cried out, a strangled sound, and closed her eyes, bracing for the inevitable fall.

Some long-buried instinct caused her to spread her legs wide and hook her feet, making a sort of anchor. She felt the vibrations of the earth dragging beneath her toes all the way up to her jaw.

It took a moment to realize that they were no longer moving. Kacey blinked open her eyes. Her fingers locked tighter around the loose fabric of Colt's jeans. Her cheek was resting in the crook behind his knee. Her elbows and legs stung as if she had scraped away all the skin there.

She could see Colt's hind end but not his upper body.

"Colt," she shouted.

"Don't let go, Kacey."

Oh, she wouldn't. She wasn't letting him go ever again because she loved him. It was the only explanation for her actions. She let the truth settle over her with the dust. It didn't solve anything. He still wanted to remain on the rez and she still wanted to leave it behind, take her baby and go somewhere safe where girls were not taken like spring lambs. But her love had saved his life, just as he had saved hers.

She felt him twisting. One of his arms appeared, reaching back, clawing at the ground. Gradually, he hauled his chest back onto the trail. Only when he was entirely on solid ground did she ease up on her hold. Colt rolled to his back and she crawled on her bleeding hands and knees to reach him.

"I got you," she said.

He wrapped an arm around her. "He can't hurt you again," he said and let his head drop back to the solid ground beneath them.

For the next few moments, she just breathed in the familiar earthy scent of him, her eyes closed at the sweetness of their survival. The difference between life and death, at times, came into sharp contrast.

"That was dangerous," he said.

She chuckled. Everything hurt, which meant she was alive. "Not as dangerous as diving headfirst off a cliff."

Now he chuckled. His arm around her tightened. "True."

"Is he…?"

Colt laid his free hand across his eyes, his breathing labored. "Not sure." His body shuddered. "I thought he'd kill you."

She lifted her arm to examine her elbow. Blood

oozed from several gravel-filled wounds. He sat up and cradled one of her hands, turning it gently.

"We have to clean these up."

Kacey looked toward the cliff a mere three inches from Colt's hip. In her mind, she saw him sailing over her and thought of what might have been. Kacey's throat burned and her vision went blurry as the tears came in great choking sobs.

He gathered her up in his arms and she clung to him, reveling in the warm, solid comfort of his body. He was still here with her and she thanked God for it.

Kacey pushed past the fear, finding her voice.

"I—I almost l-lost you," she said between sobs.

Colt stroked her head and dropped kisses there as he murmured assurances. She was safe. Charlie was safe. He'd bring her home to him.

She wanted to tell him that she had been afraid for him. Afraid of losing him. But then another fear rose in her heart. What if, now that she was safe, he would let her go?

"You found them. The men who took you," he said. "Maybe now the FBI will find your friends."

She nodded. Unable to speak past the aching lump in her throat.

"If I could have," he said, "I would have done the same for my friends."

She closed her eyes and a tear squeezed between her lids, trailing down her dusty cheek. He understood.

A moan came from the trail below them.

Colt looked over the edge. Kacey moved to her stomach, sprawling in order to safely peer down. The trail ran forty feet below them at an incline that consisted of a series of steps followed by open stretches.

Anton lay on one of the series of steps. There was blood trickling from his nose and mouth. His shirt was soaked with blood from the bullet wound. He stared up at them and spoke in Russian. His eyes had a vacant expression and his mouth gaped open when he finished.

"Anton?" called Kacey.

"Can't move my legs," he said.

Colt spoke to her. "Look at his body. The angle. I think he broke his back."

She replied in a tone just above a whisper. "Look at the blood."

"I don't know how he survived."

Anton lifted a hand. "Give me a gun."

Colt snorted. "Yeah, right," he said.

"A knife, then."

"He wants to kill himself," said Kacey to Colt, certain she was right.

"And rob the FBI of a witness," said Colt. "No way. He knows where your friends are or he knows who knows. He's not checking out."

Kacey agreed. They needed him to find Marta and the others. He was their best chance at that.

"Please," said Anton.

"You live," said Colt, his words a decree.

Anton moaned, his blood bubbling up from his mouth.

"He won't live long if we don't get help," she said.

Colt pressed to his feet and offered her his hand. "Can you walk?"

In answer, she took his hand and allowed him to draw her up beside him.

A familiar voice came from above them. "You two all right?"

They turned simultaneously and saw Lieutenant Luke Forrest standing above them on the trail.

"About time," said Colt.

"Had trouble with your position. Signal kept going in and out."

"Mountains," said Colt.

"Where's the other one?" asked Forrest.

Colt thumbed over his shoulder. Forrest lifted his radio.

"He run?"

Kacey shook her head. "Fell."

"Can't move or so he says," added Colt. "Bleeding to death."

A moment later, four FBI agents in navy blazers jogged down the trail, paused briefly at Forrest for instructions and then hurried past Colt and Kacey, disappearing around the turn. Kacey watched them reappear below them.

"Let's get you two out of here."

Kacey let Colt guide her up the trail. Normally steady when facing climbing or heights, she found her legs unstable and her body jolting and shivering as if determined to ignore all her instructions.

"Kacey?" Colt said. "You are really pale."

Her knees gave way then. He caught her in his arms and lifted her.

"I don't know what's wrong with me."

"Shock," he said. Then he called to Forrest, "Ambulance en route?"

"Yes. Fire and rescue."

Colt met Forrest on the hairpin, but Colt wouldn't let him take Kacey and he made the rest of the upward climb in record time.

"The other one?" asked Kacey. "Oleg?"

"Pinned against the RV. Shot himself in the head. He's dead."

Her heart sank as the chances of finding her friends flickered. Was it all for nothing?

The sound of sirens reached them, coming from below them, down the mountain.

Kacey remembered reaching the overlook, still safe in Colt's arms. She caught a glimpse of Oleg's body sprawled over the hood of the truck that pinned him in place to the RV. Something was wrong with the top of his head. Kacey realized what she was seeing, the aftereffects of a bullet through his skull, and looked away too late.

Colt muttered, "He got off easy."

He set her in the shade, in the lawn chair beneath the canopy. She watched with a frightening disinterest while the rescue trucks rolled in. They had to shout at her to make her understand. Cleaning her wounds brought her back, the sting and the abrasions of the gravel embedded in the long scrapes that ran down her thighs and over her elbows. She looked at the bright blood and wondered how she had ever held on to Colt. Because she had to, she decided. And now they were safe and she would be a protected witness and Colt would go back home to Turquoise Canyon.

They carried Anton past her on a spine board. He turned to fix her with a steady stare, cursing at her in the language that she had begun to understand over her months of captivity.

"Did he say where they are?" she asked the EMT before her.

"Where who are, honey?" she asked.

Where was Colt? She had not noticed him leaving her. She wanted to say goodbye and tell him that she loved him. It wouldn't be enough to get him to come with her. She knew that. But she also knew that she could not stay on Turquoise Canyon Reservation. The men and women of Tribal Thunder had important work, and her presence there was keeping them from protecting others. It was time to go.

They took her to the hospital in Darabee. She rode in the ambulance with one of the FBI agents. He said Colt had to stay at the overlook.

Kacey's breasts ached, her body ached and she missed Charlie. She asked for him. But all they gave her was intravenous fluids.

"Will they find my friends?" asked Kacey.

"We are looking. That RV will help us, and apprehending one of the two suspects will help us. You did well, Ms. Doka. But now you need to rest and let us do our jobs."

"They kept me for eight months," she told the agent.

He nodded. The EMT checked her blood pressure, so she had to stretch her neck to see the agent. "I think being paralyzed will be worse."

The agent nodded again.

At the hospital, they checked her through the ER and later moved her upstairs, rolling her to the elevator and down one corridor after another. She managed the transfer from gurney to bed with only a little help. Her room smelled of floor wax and chicken broth. She had a view of the clear blue sky and an AC unit that whistled like the wind down the canyons.

She was so tired. But she kept asking for Charlie. Finally, Agent Luke Forrest arrived and told her that Lori Redhorse had Charlie and said that he would remain on Turquoise Canyon rez until Kacey could come and get him herself.

Kacey smiled. Charlie was safe. Jake and Lori Redhorse would protect her baby until she could get back to him.

Agent Forrest drew a chair up beside her bed. "It was a dangerous thing you did," said Forrest. "Foolish."

"I wanted to find my friends. I promised."

"You might have died out there."

"I didn't find them," said Kacey. "You didn't. Did you?"

The slow shake of his head crushed the tiny flutter of hope.

"We are getting closer," said Forrest.

"It was for nothing?"

"No. We now know which mob is involved. This organization is, well, extensive. So we're expanding our search, checking other Native tribes and their lists of runaways. We're afraid there may be more of you."

Kacey swallowed. "How many more?"

"We don't know. There are a lot of missing women. But thanks to you, they are starting a special task force."

Kacey turned away. *A task force.* She felt like crying again.

"It's important, Kacey. What you did."

"I failed. I didn't find them." And she knew now that she might never find them. They might be among the forever lost. And she would have to learn to live with that, just like Colt was trying to do.

Everyone in her tribe knew someone, a sister, a daughter or a friend, who had disappeared. It was all too common and not just in her tribe. All over the country. Native American women went missing and were never found. She was lucky. Marta was not. Kacey closed her eyes and said farewell to the friends that she could not rescue. And cursed herself for the promise she could not keep. "I promised I would send help."

"Kacey, there was a GPS in the RV," said Forrest. "We reversed the directions and backtracked. We found a camp out in the desert near San Carlos Reservation. There were girls there. Twenty-three, all like you and your friends. We found them because of you, Kacey. You did send help. Those captives are free because of you."

Tears spilled from her eyes and rolled down her temples to soak into her hair. It had not been for nothing. They had found some of them. Kacey covered her eyes with her hands and wept. As the sobs continued, she crooked her arm over her eyes.

Agent Forrest rubbed her shoulder, and when she lowered her bandaged arm from across her eyes, he sat back.

"We'll keep looking for your friends, Kacey. We won't stop. But you need to stop now."

She met his gaze and saw the determination there. He wouldn't give up and there was nothing more she could do in the hunt.

"Yes," she said.

"I have talked to the Justice Department about you, Kacey. We believe that Anton's survival will ensure that someone else will be coming after you and Charlie."

She wasn't safe here. Her gaze darted to the door and then back to Forrest.

"We would like to relocate you."

She nearly forgot to breathe. She wanted that, too. But she still had ties to the rez.

"What about my sisters and brothers?" She was afraid to leave them with her mom and she was afraid to tell Forrest what Ty had revealed about her mother's work with the gang. As much as Kacey longed to get away, she would not do so at the expense of her siblings.

Forrest looked away. "They have already been placed within your tribe."

She'd been removed to foster care a time or two. They always sent them back to their mom.

"For how long?"

"It's permanent this time. Your mother has given up custody."

Kacey's brow sank. "She would never do that."

"Kacey, I have really hard news. Your mother was involved in your disappearance."

Her words were a whisper. "That's not true."

"She's admitted to accepting payment for you, Kacey."

Kacey's ears began to buzz and she thought she might be sick. She clamped a hand over her mouth, breathing through her nose.

"She's addicted to heroin," said Forrest. "We got a tip, so we've been watching her since your return. She's been moving drugs. We caught her and she's facing felony charges."

A tip? Was that Ty? No, he'd never rat out a member of the gang. But Ty had been right. Her mother had been a gang member all along.

And her mother was going to prison. Just like Colt's father. Kacey's hand dropped from her mouth as the shock was replaced with a dull numbness. She felt anesthetized and did not know if she should be happy or sad about the news regarding her mother. Both, she decided, all tied up in a hard knot in her stomach.

Agent Forrest kept on talking. "She made a deal with the DA. Reduced sentence in exchange for all she knows about this case. She helped the Wolf Posse pick girls, Kacey. That's why your friends were taken. You and Marta were classmates. And Brenda was a teammate on your high-school volleyball team. Right?"

She had one hand pressed tight to her forehead at this new shock but managed to nod. Her mother knew Brenda and Marta. Of course she did. The contents of Kacey's stomach heaved, threatening to come up. She swallowed hard. She squeezed her eyes shut to concentrate on breathing as saliva filled her mouth.

"I'm going to be sick," she promised.

Forrest had a pail before her in time. Afterward, he offered a damp washcloth. He would have made a good father, she thought, but Colt said that he was unmarried.

"You okay?" he asked.

"No."

He nodded his understanding.

"Your sisters are going with Jake Redhorse's mom and her husband, Burt Rope. You lived there awhile in high school, right?"

Mrs. Redhorse had some health issues, but she was a good woman and a good mother. Several times, she had given Kacey the kind of home she had always dreamed about during her difficult teen years.

"My brothers?" she asked and set aside the cloth. The heaving in her belly ceased, replaced by a squeezing tension.

"One of your tribal leaders has asked to foster them."

"Who?"

"Her name is Hazel Trans."

Mrs. Trans had been Kacey's absolute favorite teacher. She had recently retired and Kacey thought her brothers would be lucky indeed to have Mrs. Trans as a foster mother.

She nodded her approval and offered a smile. "Thank you."

"Sure," said Forrest. "Tomorrow you'll be discharged and we'll bring you back up to Turquoise Canyon to collect Charlie. If you like, we can arrange for you to see your siblings, too."

He didn't say *for the last time*, but that was the case. She was going and would not be coming back.

"In Darabee, someone tried to take Charlie," she said. "They changed the orders about feeding."

"We're looking into that. Creating a list of everyone who had access to those orders. We'll find whoever did that, Kacey. But it was not the FBI. We have no intention of separating you from Charlie."

Forrest gave her a warm smile and rose to go. He made it to the end of her bed and then snapped his fingers as if just remembering something. "I almost forgot. One loose end. Who drove you from the clinic to the meeting at the overlook, Kacey?"

It was Ty. She glanced away.

"Colt came on a motorcycle," said Forrest. "We found the tracks and the bike, which belongs to his brother Ty. But how did you get there?"

"I—I don't remember." She met his gaze and saw the smile beneath the sharp hawkish eyes. He didn't believe her.

"Is that so? Any other gaps in your memory?"

"Just the clinic visits."

One dark brow arched over an eye. "I see."

Kacey forced herself to hold his gaze and not fidget. Her nose itched and her lips tingled. She did not like to lie, but she knew Ty was tied up in this somehow.

"Your deal with justice will depend on your complete honesty."

She held her silence. Ty had been ordered by the gang to transport her. But they had not ordered him to raise that dust or call Colt and be sure he knew where she was being taken. If she had to jeopardize her deal to protect him, she would.

Forrest looked away and then back. "Well, it should be easy to figure out. We have tire tracks and they're nearly nine-and-a-half inches wide. Classic muscle-car tire like for a Corvette or a Barracuda." He paused, watching her intently.

Her forehead felt damp with sweat.

"Nothing? Well, we'll find the car and then the driver. Have a few suspects."

It would probably be easier to find the car if the man who owned it did not also own a body shop. Kacey wondered if Ty's precious Barracuda was already in pieces.

She held the agent's gaze, determined not to implicate Ty, no matter what the consequence. Ty had helped them and she would not repay his kindness by turning him over to the FBI.

"My memory won't improve," she said. "If that jeopardizes my eligibility with the Justice Department, then so be it."

He rested a hand on his belt, his long fingers drumming on the black leather. "Did it occur to you that the Wolf Posse were the ones who delivered your friends over to the Russian mob? I wouldn't be protecting gang members, Kacey."

She said nothing.

"Care to tell me how you got to the meet?"

"I don't remember."

He snorted. "Well, we'll talk again soon. Maybe your recall will improve."

"Can I see Colt before I go with the Justice Department?"

"I don't see why not."

She wanted to ask why Colt had not come to see her here, in Darabee, but she did not because she was afraid of the answer. Would it be harder to leave without telling him her feelings or harder to admit that she loved him?

Chapter Sixteen

Colt finished with the FBI. He had done as Ty had asked and told them the truth. Ty had picked up Kacey because the Wolf Posse trusted him and knew that Kacey would come with him. He'd then called Colt and told him where they were heading. Colt had then called the FBI.

Ty was now safely back on tribal lands and Colt would do everything in his power to help keep him there until he had assurances that the FBI would not go after him for his part in recapturing Kacey. Until then, Ty would be a virtual prisoner on tribal land and would be lucky if the tribal leadership did not arrest him. The only good news regarding Ty was that Kenshaw Little Falcon had offered to represent Ty to the tribal council, which Colt found encouraging.

Colt contended that it was important that both the Russians and the Wolf Posse believed that Ty had done as he was ordered. If they didn't believe it, Ty would not keep breathing for long.

Forrest drove Colt back to Turquoise Canyon.

"No trouble driving in cars now?" he asked.

"Some," Colt admitted. "But I'm getting better." He did not admit that he continued to pretend that Charlie was in the car with him. Picturing Charlie here did two things at once. It grounded him in the reality that he was here on the rez and it also helped him believe that he was safe. Colt had talked about it with the therapist Kenshaw recommended, who assured him that such a simple trick was well worth using.

"We'll be bringing Kacey back to the rez tomorrow."

Just the sound of her name made his heartbeat increase.

"She wants to collect some of her things."

Colt's head snapped toward Forrest. "Collect?"

"She isn't staying, Colt. She wants to keep the child that she carried. We have no objections to that, but all evidence indicates that chances are high that both she and Charlie will continue to be targets if they stay."

She was going with the Justice Department. She had no other choice. She was leaving as she always wanted. And he was going back to his cabin in the woods.

Colt clamped down hard, locking his teeth together until the muscle at his jaw ached. Once all he had wanted was to get back to Turquoise Canyon and never leave again. Now he wanted Kacey and Charlie there with him.

His perfect picture of Kacey and Charlie coming home to him evaporated like the sweat on his forehead. He had to let them go, for her sake and for Charlie's.

KACEY RETURNED TO the compound along the river. Hazel Trans was there with her brothers. Her sisters arrived soon after with Burt Rope and Colt's mother and his kid sister, Abbie. The reunion was brief. She did not tell her brothers that this would be the last time she saw them. They were too young to understand.

It was a monumental relief that her sisters and brothers would be safe and well taken care of. She trusted Mrs. Trans and Colt's mother, May. Abbie was all smiles and laughter at the news that she would be gaining three new sisters. At fourteen, Abbie had given up hope that her mother would produce a sister. She asked Kacey where she would live. Colt told her they were still working that out.

Kacey took comfort in the certainty that May and Hazel would be there for her siblings. Kacey had called protective services on her mother the last time her mother left, and she'd caught hell for it. Now she wondered if that was what triggered her mother's decision to offer Kacey to the gang. Kacey was a threat to her, a growing threat.

Perhaps it was best that she would never know. She was not planning to see her mother before her trial or after.

"What if she wants them back?" she asked Mrs. Trans.

"I don't think she really does, Kacey. I've spoken to her. She isn't in a good place right now and she recognizes that."

Mrs. Trans hugged Kacey and then slid behind the wheel.

Hewitt spun in the rear seat, waving with enthusiasm as they drove away. It was her undoing. Shirley asked her what was wrong and she told them in a rush of tears and sobs that she had to go away.

Soon they were all crying and hugging. They asked her if it would ever be safe for them to return, and she had no answer. She knew only what the Justice Department had told her and what she now repeated to them. Her relocation was permanent and she would be safe only if she made no contact with the ones she left behind.

She knew she was lucky. She had escaped and would have a new life. She would attend college somewhere as she had always hoped and the Justice Department would arrange for all her needs. She expected to not require their support forever, but only until she was able to provide for herself and her son.

Her sisters left next. She hugged them each in turn, and the tears that ran down her cheeks mingled with theirs as they embraced for a final time.

"I'll never forget you," said Winnie.

Shirley would not even talk. When they were all in

Burt Rope's car, Jackie broke away and ran back to her, giving her one more hug. And then they were gone.

Tomorrow she would see Colt for the last time and that was one parting that she did not think she could bear. She had lost her friends, her family, her home and her tribe. It seemed too much that she would lose Colt now after just finding him again.

But that was tomorrow's trouble, she thought. And then she heard the truck engine.

A familiar mint-green pickup truck rolled up to the lodge, and there behind the wheel was Colt Redhorse.

COLT FOUND KACEY standing still as one of the posts that supported the roof of the porch before the tribe's lodge. Only her eyes moved. In her arms, Charlie lay wrapped in a fuzzy baby blue blanket that trailed over Kacey's arm. She was wearing a button-up orange shirtdress tied at the waist. The short sleeves revealed the white gauze that circled both her forearms. The knee-length cotton hid the wounds on her knees and made her look older somehow. Perhaps that was because of her sad expression and the circles beneath her eyes.

Kacey was the oldest nineteen-year-old Colt knew. She was leaving them. But she was not leaving him. Not if he could help it.

He jumped down from the truck and reached her.

"They said you were coming tomorrow," she said.

"Couldn't wait." He reached for her, clasping her

upper arm above the bandages and coming in for a brief kiss. Or he had meant it to be brief, but the contact was like a match dropped on dry paper, igniting into a scorching openmouthed kiss that left them both panting. He drew back and looked into her eyes, wanting to kiss her again, but he needed to settle things first.

He noticed the guards watching from the other end of the porch, both armed with rifles. Jack Bear Den stood beside Ray Strong. They nodded at Colt, Jack scowling and Ray smiling. It was hard to believe that the pair were such good friends, because they were different in almost every way.

Kacey's breath was returning to normal. "Would you like to go sit by the river?"

She was trying to gain them some privacy, or what little they could find and still be under the watchful eye of Tribal Thunder, the FBI and soon the Justice Department.

He offered to carry Charlie and she turned him over. He had missed the baby boy more than he cared to consider. If Kacey would not allow him along, he might lose them both. The thought tore him up like a cat clawing through cardboard.

She sat on the split log bench and he returned Charlie to her.

"He's bigger, isn't he?" Colt asked.

Kacey's smile was sunshine on a cloudy day. "I thought so, too. Lori took great care of him."

"How did things go with the FBI?" he asked.

"I didn't tell them who drove me. I said I didn't remember."

Colt snorted. "How did that go?"

Her stare was glassy. "They didn't believe me."

"Ty told me that they know anyway. They have the recording from my phone. It caught some of your conversation with Ty."

Kacey's head sank.

"You don't need to protect him," said Colt.

"Well, someone should," she said.

"What do you mean?"

"He takes care of things, really dangerous things, and he seems to always end up holding the bag. Why is that?"

Colt had never thought of it that way. He just needed help and Ty always gave it to him.

He had no answer, so he watched the river flow. It marked the time passing along between them. How could he convince her?

"They didn't find my friends," said Kacey.

"They still might," he said.

She looked down at Charlie, using her knuckle to stroke his cheek.

"I'm sorry I dragged you back into this," she said. "And for nothing."

"Kacey, you did all you could."

She blew away a breath. "I'm sure Marta has delivered by now. I'm so afraid that they'll find her body dumped somewhere, or worse, that they won't find it."

"Don't give up. They're all looking. Our tribe. The FBI. Someone will uncover something."

She met his gaze, searching. "Do you believe that?"

"I do."

Kacey nodded, her mouth tight. "All right, then."

"So you are going into witness relocation?" He tried to sound casual, but his voice cracked. She noticed, giving him an odd stare. He saw a flicker of something, as if she were trying to puzzle something out.

"They don't think I have much of an option. They believe the Russians won't give up."

Colt understood that. Letting her live was bad for their reputation and their business. And there was no telling what else she might know about them. Details she might still recall.

"Permanent?" he asked.

Her gaze skittered from his and lifted up to the canyon beyond the river. Her swallow was audible and finally she nodded, a short rapid bobbing.

"Will they take me, too?" he asked.

Her gaze snapped to his. "What do you mean?"

"I want to go with you, Kacey."

"With me?" She was shaking her head now, reluctant, it seemed, to even consider the possibility.

His heart dropped down into the cavity below his chest and began banging around, like an animal suddenly falling into a pit.

"You can't. This is your home. Your brothers are

here, your mother. My sisters are all living with her now, too. You should help her, be there for her."

"I want to be there for you."

"Colt, the only thing we ever argued over was my wish to leave the rez and your need to stay."

"I love you, Kacey," he said, thinking that explained everything.

She gave a long moan and was on her feet, swaying as if wanting to run but having nowhere to go.

"No, no, no," she whispered, lifting Charlie's head to her cheek and whispering the words. Tears overflowed her lower lids and dropped to the ground, coming faster as he watched.

He took hold of her shoulders, turning her to face him.

"Kacey, did you hear me? I love you."

"I heard," she said. "But you won't. You'll long for this place. It's a part of you, like your skin or your heart. You can't live without it."

"I want to go with you."

"You won't be able to come back."

"I understand that."

"It costs too much."

"That is my decision. All you need to tell me is if you love me, Kacey. If you love me, then we should be together."

The tears kept coming. Rolling along, one after another in a waterfall down her cheeks.

"You'll blame me," she whispered.

"Blame you? For what?"

"For what you have lost. For who you have lost." She looked at the ground. "You'll miss them. Your brothers. Your sister. Your mom."

"Of course I will."

"They'll hate me, too."

"It's not their decision. It's ours."

She wept into her hands.

"Kacey?" He used two fingers to lift her chin until their eyes met. "The only thing I cannot live without is you."

She broke into a sob and he pulled her tight, holding her in one arm and her baby in the other.

"Let me come with you, Kacey," he whispered, stroking her head. "Let me love you and marry you and be a father to Charlie. Let us build a life together away from the men who are hunting you. I'll be there to protect you and you will be my tribe and my people."

"Oh, Colt, it's so hard."

He rocked her, pressing his lips to her temple. "Not as hard as losing you."

He felt the moment of surrender, when her body sagged against his. He closed his eyes to offer a prayer of thanks.

"Will we be a family?" he asked.

"Oh, Colt, I wish you wouldn't do this."

"Because you love me?"

"Yes."

He drew back and smiled. Then he brushed his thumbs over her cheeks, wiping away the tears.

"Wonder where we'll go?" he asked, already looking forward.

"They are giving me a choice of several places."

"We should be married before we leave the rez," he said. "I'd like to have my family there for that."

"And mine. But I'm leaving tomorrow."

"We're leaving."

She nodded. "Yes, we."

Colt draped an arm around her shoulders and started them back toward the lodge. "Hope it's not Hawaii."

"Why is that?"

Colt nodded toward Jack Bear Den. "The detective is bringing his fiancée there to meet his father's people."

"I heard that. His dad was Hawaiian, right?"

"That's what they say. Explains a lot."

"Well, I doubt they'll send us there."

"Can you picture him on a surfboard?"

Kacey tried to imagine the massive man balancing on moving water and giggled. "Or with a ukulele?"

Now Colt was laughing. "I'd pay good money to see him in a grass skirt spinning a fire stick."

They reached the porch, side by side.

"Can you call Agent Forrest? There has been a change of plans," said Colt.

"What change?" asked Ray.

"We're getting married," said Colt.

Both Ray Strong and Jack Bear Den stared in dumb silence.

"They won't like that," said Ray at last.

"Call him," said Colt and walked Kacey inside to meet with Kenshaw. It was their shaman's opinion that they should be married before they told the Justice Department. Unlike out there, here on the rez they did not need a waiting period or blood tests or anything but a witness to their marriage.

They were married that evening before the fieldstone fireplace under the great seal of their people. Their shaman performed the ceremony before Colt's family and Kacey's sisters. Colt asked Ty to sign the certificate, and Kacey chose Hazel Trans. They presented the paperwork to the Justice Department the following morning. There was some pushback, but the marriage was valid, so accommodations were made.

"I wish you didn't have to leave Turquoise Canyon," said Kacey to Colt. "I know you love living here."

"I wasn't living, Kacey. Before you appeared, I was existing. You brought me back to my family. I'm whole again because of you. And I plan to spend every day of my life showing you what you mean to me."

They were transported to Phoenix. Colt thought he saw a familiar motorcycle following them down the mountain. He didn't mention this to anyone, but he did see a familiar face in the airport as they boarded their flight with their new identities six days later.

He did not know how Ty would figure out their connecting flights, but when Ty again appeared in the Seattle airport, disembarking from the same plane, Colt smiled. Colt had done nothing to jeopardize their new identity or their relocation. It was not his fault if his brother Ty was a better tracker than the Justice Department could have anticipated.

When they reached their final destination in Anchorage, Alaska, Colt glanced back to look for Ty. He did not see him, but somehow he believed he was still there.

"I'm already registered at the university," Kacey said, pointing out the campus on the map. "Spring semester. It's only a few miles from the house."

"Perfect," he said.

"You won't start work until the breakup," she said, meaning the time the river ice finally came crashing downriver and the fishing season could begin. "Will you be bored?"

They had arranged for Colt to work as a fishing and hunting guide with a local outfit. He had the skill set and would only need to get acclimatized to fishing for salmon rather than trout, bass and pike.

"I've got the little guy to take care of until then," he said. "When Mommy is in class."

"You mean Taylor," she said, trying on the new name they had assigned Charlie.

"That's right, Kalyn," he said and grinned at her.

"Almost there, Cash," she said.

Her husband held the door to the Jeep under

the watchful eye of their escort in Anchorage. She
stepped into the vehicle that would bring them to
their new home.

"Seat belt, Mrs. Tsosie," said Colt.

Kacey complied as Colt strapped Charlie's car
seat into the seat beside her. They had made a game
of using their new names, to become used to them.
Cash and Kalyn Tsosie and their newborn son, Tay-
or, headed for their new home and new life.

It was just one of many adjustments they would
be making over the next few weeks. Their escort
had told them that Tsosie was a somewhat common
name among the native peoples here. That and their
brown skin and black hair would help them blend,
and if their features did not quite match those of the
indigenous men and women of Alaska, it would be
obvious only to the most observant.

Colt and Kacey traveled up a mountain road with
sweeping views of the valley below in Anchorage.
Finally the car slowed.

As she moved forward, Kacey thought back. She
would not forget those they had left behind, but she
would move forward into this new life with gratitude.
Somehow through all the pain and loss, life had led
her to what she had always desired.

Colt stared out at the window at the large A-frame
home sitting off the road and up against the hillside.

"That can't be it," said Colt.

"It is," said the Justice Department agent in the
front passenger seat.

Kacey smiled in delight. With Colt and Charlie she would find what she had always wanted.

"Look at that," Colt said, his voice full of wonder.

"Yes," she said. "We're home."

* * * * *

LET'S TALK
Romance

For exclusive extracts, competitions
and special offers, find us online:

🄵 facebook.com/millsandboon

🄾 @millsandboonuk

🄱 @millsandboon

Or get in touch on 0844 844 1351*

For all the latest titles coming soon, visit
millsandboon.co.uk/nextmonth